The

ICE MEADOWS

EDMUND BURWELL

PAGE PUBLISHING, INC.
New York, NY

First originally published by Page Publishing, Inc. 2019

ISBN 978-1-68456-267-1 (Paperback)
ISBN 978-1-68456-266-4 (Digital)

Printed in the United States of America

Introduction

This book is a work of fiction. Names, characters, places and incidents either are products of the author's imagination or are used fictitiously. Any resemblance to actual events, locales, or persons, living or dead, is coincidental.

Chapter One

The headmaster stepped gingerly over the brittle grass like a cautious crow, his black suit and white dog collar dramatic against the bright athletic colors. He was just over forty, but strangers mistook him for a much older man. He came forward nodding to parents and students, pausing here and there to dispense a bit of advice or receive somebody's praise. The faculty and some of the parents turned to him with smiles and moved forward to shake his flaccid hand. His students hung back, stiffening only when his eyes fell upon them. He processed through the crowd, and people in his wake returned quickly to whatever they had been doing.

Stephenson watched this performance with amusement. The headmaster drew near, bowed his head slightly, and uttered "Father?" in his direction. Moving past Stephenson immediately to the wealthy parents of a first former, he resumed the duties for which he had been born. Stephenson tugged a moment at his own clerical collar, which, unlike the easy fit of the headmaster's, often felt tight and uncomfortable.

"Father?" said a voice behind him, mimicking the headmaster's tone with accuracy.

"Coach?" replied Stephenson in the same tone. "Why aren't we winning?"

"Patience is a virtue, Reverend," replied the assistant soccer coach, an unfortunately ugly young man who compensated with an enviable wit.

"Just beat the hell out of them and worry about patience later!" said Stephenson. "I see how they play. What can you expect from downtown D. C.? Common street fighters."

"They'll all grow up to be lawyers," said the assistant coach.

"Or preachers. Go ahead. Say it."

"Father!" exclaimed the assistant coach, with a look of pained dismay. "Shame!" And shaking his head, he moved off toward his players.

Stephenson liked the assistant coach and the other young teachers. Some of them worked too hard at fitting in, but they were a decent lot. A few, like the assistant coach, had some vision and were destined for a life beyond the rarified atmosphere of rural boarding schools. They would teach here for a year or two and then return to the real world.

Where would they go in life, he wondered, these appealing, clever students and their young teachers? He loved to watch as they moved about the playing field, energetic in the cool November air. Seeing them made him hopeful. They drifted on currents of privilege of which they had little understanding. *Undertows of entitlement,* he thought, an intriguing phrase. They took their gifts for granted, most of them. Was the next Charles Dickens here, rooting about in his gym bag like Dr. Mannette fumbling with his tools, or barging through the crowd like the pushy lawyer? Was a Barbara McClintock on the hillside? A William Temple out there on the field? Ella Fitzgerald? Terry Fox? It was possible.

Joe walked up the hill to where Kate was seated in a lawn chair with other spectators. He liked to walk the sidelines during Ted's games, keeping pace with the play or standing nearby if Ted was on the bench. He was careful never to stand too close so as not to embarrass him, but near enough to see his face and hear his voice. Joe liked moving about in the cool fall sunlight and watching his son with his friends. Kate preferred to sit. Leaving her made him feel guilty, as though he were absent from his post without permission. He knew she expected him to remain beside her and that she could see no reason why anyone would want to walk or stand when it was possible to sit.

Sitting with Kate meant attending a familiar lecture. He knew the subject well enough to pass a test, but with Kate's tests, Joe always failed. Like the fractured images in a kaleidoscope, the discourse kept within variations on a theme. The details were constantly changing, however, and he could never quite keep up.

Kate and some other women, wrapped in fall coats and seated in lawn chairs, were observing the game from the top of the hill. He wondered at what point he would arrive in class and take his seat, a totally unfair apprehension he could not dispel. His wife's eternal discourse was one part academic scheduling minutia, one part general school gossip, and one part complaints about her colleagues and students. As a faculty member as well as the parent of a student, she felt qualified to comment on anything, and this she proceeded to do.

"So tell me how I'm supposed to grade papers, answer calls from parents, and plan for the science fair all at the same time," Kate was saying. Her voice, animated exasperation, was rising. "I mean, come on! And on top of all that, Father expects me to supervise a table at mealtime too. You should see the manners of some of these kids. And they've cut down our lunch period from thirty-four to twenty-eight minutes. And part of *that* is taken up with announcements! I mean, give me a break!"

Stephenson winced at the comment about student manners expressed to women who were their mothers or who knew them. He stood beside Kate's chair but did not interrupt as he had done sometimes in their early days of marriage. Attempting to redirect a conversation had never worked and had always left him as the bad guy. He had learned to accept the things he could not change. He knew Kate knew he was there, but she did not acknowledge him. She talked on while the other women shifted their attention politely from the game to Kate and back again. They looked at him and smiled, and he smiled back. He recognized one whose name he thought was Anne or Annie. A pretty petite ash blonde who looked no older than some of Ted's girlfriends, she was the mother of a huge boy on Ted's team. Joe marveled at how good-looking some women became as they grew older, lovelier than they had been, he guessed, at twenty or twenty-five. She raised her small hand in a quick wave, well aware that she was interrupting Kate.

Kate turned to him quickly as though just realizing he was there. He bent down and kissed her temple and straightened up and said hello to the other women. He did not know their names, and he knew it would not occur to his wife to introduce him. She looked up at him quickly with an instant grin and half-closed eyes and immediately resumed her talk to the other women. Their attention had already turned to the game. Kate was beginning to explain the increasing length of faculty meetings when the halftime horn brought everyone to attention. The crowd applauded the players as they loped briskly off the field and began raising the lids of big ice chests behind their benches.

"Our boys are playing well," said Stephenson.

"This whole game is a pain," said Kate as she stood to stretch her legs.

"Ted is playing well."

"They could all play better than this. They need to try harder. The Washington team is good, but they could beat them if they tried. Have you been to the store? Did you get the things I wanted?"

"I think I got them all. You had 'pineapple' on your list, and I didn't know whether you wanted crushed or fresh or what. I bought a can each of rings, chunks, and crushed."

Kate laughed and looked away. "I'm making a congealed salad, Joe. That means crushed. Nobody uses rings except to bake a ham. But I'll use them sometime, probably."

For a second or two Stephenson recalled the pineapple upside down cakes his mother made in a big iron skillet when he was young, and he caught a glimpse of the golden flat round being turned out onto a platter with glistening pineapple rings surrounding their ruby cherries. He searched the crowd for a glimpse of Ted. "Sorry," he said. "I did not know what you were planning."

"Remember?" said Kate immediately. "I told you I was going to the nurse's shower for the history teacher, the one having the baby?" There was a quiver of admonishment in her voice.

"Ah, no. I don't think we've talked about that."

"We did, Joe!" she shot back. "Remember? We were standing outside on the driveway? We were saying goodbye to the Wilsons?"

A sense of fatigue began to spread through Stephenson like a stain, accompanied by an ache in his side, and he recognized a test he could not pass. *But, Kate,* he started thinking, *we haven't seen the Wilsons for six weeks. How am I supposed to connect something you said six weeks ago to food you're preparing now? And why did you talk about it anyway while we were saying goodbye to...* Suddenly he felt very tired, and he knew it was evident.

"Just forget it, Joe. It doesn't matter. But it would help if you would just listen to me sometimes when I talk. I explained all this to you this morning." She was beginning to raise her voice. People would soon be looking.

That morning Kate had left home earlier than usual, saying she had to organize materials for a laboratory test. They had barely had time to speak at all, and Stephenson was absolutely certain that their brief conversation had not touched upon congealed salads and the history teacher's shower. For a moment it occurred to him to speak up, but he knew it would only intensify an argument he would not win.

"Well, well," said Kate loudly in a changed, animated tone. "If it isn't my favorite headmaster. To what do we owe this honor, Father Hervey?"

Joe's discouragement deepened. He turned from watching the crowd, hoping to catch sight of Ted, and turned to the headmaster and smiled. To those who knew them both, it had been clear from the beginning that Hervey despised him. From their first meeting, when he had accompanied Kate to her second job interview, the young headmaster had been cool and excessively formal.

In the whole church of God, there were not two more dissimilar people than Andrew Philip Arthur Hervey and Joe Stephenson. With a veteran's instinct for self-preservation, the headmaster had discerned the differences between them in all their subtleties the first time they met. Although he had watched for it for years, Stephenson had detected no moderation in Hervey's carefully controlled distain. For the benefit of Kate and Ted, Stephenson had pretended to take no notice. He realized this made him appear to Hervey as even more unsophisticated, but he knew of no better way to handle it.

"Father?" said Hervey, with no emotion. "I hope you are enjoying the game. Ted has played well. We are all proud of him for scoring his goal."

"I always enjoy the games and especially on a day like this," said Stephenson. They shook hands.

"Oh, Father! Ted was in, but he didn't score. Wallace Wong scored our goal. You must have missed it. It was Wong, not Ted," said Kate with intensity, looking rapidly from Hervey to Joe and back again like a child seeking approval for discovering something everyone else had overlooked.

Stephenson wished she had just let it pass. His eyes moved over the crowd, searching for Ted, as Kate and Hervey began to discuss the fall examination schedule. He saw Ted walking between two girls, his arms around their shoulders, their heads touching like conspirators. Suddenly they all began to laugh, and one of the girls looked up and covered her eyes with a slender white hand. Joe excused himself and walked down the hill toward them.

Ted was a miracle and a mystery in his father's eyes. His sense of humor, his growing interest in writing, his many friends, athletics, everything about his son was a source of joy in his life. At his most difficult moments, when frustration raged, the bishop was snubbing him, when Kate would neither listen nor respond, the sight of his lanky, good-natured son was like a transfusion. Ted had been a loving and compatible child to raise. If, since beginning high school at St. John's, he had become a bit sullen, well, he was a teenager, after all.

He watched his son's lively conversation with the girls. From the edge of the field, a student, one of Joe's parishioners, called "Hey, Joe!" and Stephenson waved. At the sound of his father's name, Ted looked around, caught sight of Joe, and looked away. *Teenagers,* thought Stephenson. *What a time of life! I wouldn't be young again for anything. It was hard enough the first time.*

His son's slight frown made Stephenson hesitant to go to him. Young men deep in talk with their girlfriends do not appreciate Dad's interruption. So he stood at a distance and watched and spoke to friends, many of them his parishioners, as everyone milled about during halftime. *Degas at the races*, he thought. *The colors, the autumn trees, brilliant sky, uniforms like racing silks. It gladdens the heart.*

"You should have stayed and talked to Father and me," said Kate, coming up behind him. "It was rude of you to walk away like that. He'll probably ask me tomorrow what's wrong with you." Then, raising her voice, she shouted, "Ted! Ted! Ted! Ted! Ted! Coach is talking to the team. Get over there!" Leaving Stephenson, she walked in Ted's direction. Ted jogged away with the two happy girls keeping pace with him until he crossed the sideline and ran onto the field where the team was huddled around the coach and the froglike assistant.

Stephenson caught up with Kate and placed his hand on her shoulder. They walked up the hill to the chairs where people were beginning to sit down for the second half. A big Irish setter was roaming mindlessly through the crowd, his leash trailing behind him over the grass. An inquisitive Jack Russell terrier ran up suddenly with a bark, and the perplexed setter shifted uncertainly and turned in circles to face him. They examined each other's rear ends for a moment and then proceeded to explore the crowd happily together like old friends.

Stephenson stood beside Kate's chair for the second half of the game, while Kate talked about teachers—never a name, always a function, "the English teacher…the chemistry teacher…the social studies teacher"—and students, examinations, grading papers, and recent disciplinary problems. Some piece of office equipment had broken down that morning, forcing her to wait hours to copy a test she had planned for the coming week. While waiting in the office for the repairman, she had noticed for the first time how antiquated the office equipment had become, and she intended to bring it up at the next faculty meeting. She was certain the athletic director would object to buying anything new before he got the new wrestling mats he had talked about all fall. If the coaches could only see her own long list of biology supplies, especially the new filing cabinets she really needed, maybe they would understand that other teachers needed things too.

The game ended with a 4–2 loss for Ted's team. The parents and other spectators applauded warmly as the expressionless St. John's players formed a line to congratulate the winning team. The boys filed past each other, swatting hands without making eye contact and muttering "Good game" to each delighted enemy player. The St. John's boys straggled up the hill as people congratulated them on every side.

"Mom, I'm hitting the showers. I'll see you at dinner," called Ted, and he disappeared into the crowd.

Stephenson reached for Kate's folding chair, but she grabbed it first, oblivious of him as she folded it and rammed it into its green canvas case. Without a word, she strode off across the hillside in the direction of the cars, scanning the crowd and carrying the chair in one hand and her purse in the other. She marched past students, parents, and teachers without speaking as Joe hurried to catch up.

He had long ago concluded that such complete focus on herself was not a conscious act of rudeness or neglect. Twenty years ago he had found it amusing, one of the many things that had endeared her to him in the beginning. Within a few years, he had found himself noticing the mild offense it aroused in others, and he had winked and smiled at anyone watching. At such moments, interpreting her to the world in the most agreeable light had seemed his spousal duty. He had figured that in time, she would become aware of how others perceived her. She was his wife, and he loved her.

Chapter Two

H e drove home through the twilight thinking, as was his habit. On each side of the road, the mustard fields of autumn sloped gently up to the ridges where the big oaks and maples trembled in the dusk. Their blowing tops, golden and tomato red in the fading light, beamed against the coming blue night. Here and there white sycamores loomed from their low places, and the crimson foliage of dogwood ranged up and down the fencerows. At the crest of a rise, Stephenson pulled his vintage Honda to the side and watched for a few minutes as the sunlight faded over the western hills. Great shadows were filling the low places and staining the hillside furrows. A hundred feet away, a thicket of tall sassafras shook their rose and purple mittens in the chill. A big hickory tree glowed a rich yellow on a distant hill, lovely and assertive against a line of black cedars. The sky was a cloudless blue that diverged into lilac above the distant hills. He loved to admire the intoxicating palette of the land, taking in its hints and subtleties and moods. Winslow Homer, Monet, Samuel Morse, and George Caleb Bingham entered his mind in succession as his eyes scanned the alluring distance. The land had kept its glorious, park-like appearance for centuries, a legacy of the Indians' custom of burning the great forests to increase the herds of deer and buffalo. Behind him, the eastern sky glowed with the blue of a robin's egg—contemplative, peaceful, and calming. Mary's color, he said to the empty car and drove on.

Clothed in the luminous dying day, suffused with its elusive nostalgia, the countryside brought to mind the landscapes of Claude

Lorraine with their beckoning, expanding space. The rolling land, filled with echoes of antiquity, merged in these parts into a long valley that ran for almost a hundred miles between the mountains, interrupted on this end only by the river and little hills. He tried to imagine the autumn ochers and reds through the eyes of Marion Wachtel and Granville Redmond, and he wondered how they would render this lovely land of the East, so unlike their molded trees and saffron hills of the California coast. "Our own 'mists and mellow fruitfulness,'" he said aloud. His thoughts raced across the canvas of his mind, spilling color onto nourishing white as the evening gathered around. He turned on the headlights, and his longings raced with them into the darkness, toward home.

How does a man stay devoted in indifference? How can a person cultivate denial, keep pretending that everything is "fine, just fine"? He knew the answers. Accepting them, however, called for a certain detachment. His experience had brought him that far, at least. But detachment, regardless of every way he tried to figure it, implied somehow a lack or loss of love, a betrayal, an abandonment. He knew it was a false analysis, but he couldn't help it. Thinking about it depressed him. He longed for home.

He could hear Kate's voice responding over the years with her unchanging refrain, reflexive and dismissive.

"Hello, Kate. How are you?"

"Fine."

"How's the family?"

"Fine."

"I heard your mother has been sick."

"Oh, she's fine now."

"I heard Joe had an accident in the car!"

"Oh." (Laughing.) "He's fine."

"I understand his head was cut off..."

"Oh, he's fine now, though. I have to work this Saturday. Take up tickets at the basketball game. And they want us there early, so I guess I'll have to stay over the night before. I don't know when I'm going to have time to grade papers."

In the face of denial, one can only change himself. After twenty years of changing, what do you do about the fatigue? If you have a conscience—at least he could say *that* for himself. He was a person of conscience. At times, he wished he were not. When you've changed and changed again as much of yourself as you can, how does a man manage the fatigue?

The trouble with you is you think too much. He could hear his father's brooding voice as though he were in the passenger seat. *You think too damn much. You ought to just go on with everything and not worry so much. Your problem is you worry too much. Who gives a damn? You're lucky to have everything you got. Let her alone. What the hell! You're not perfect. Ain't nobody perfect. Accept it and get on with life. What the hell do you have to complain about? You got Kate. You got Ted. You got a job. You could have had a different one, but you got a job. You got friends. You're smart as hell, smarter than I ever was. Stop complaining. If I'd had what you've got...*

Stephenson turned on the radio and lowered his window. The whiney voice of an NPR commentator swelled into the small car, finding fault with America over something or other, and he turned it off. The cool air felt clean. He crossed the wide river, glittering in the last light, and slowed down to look west. On the water's surface, the stones of an ancient fish weir were just visible, pointing downstream in a great V, its ragged line dark against the river's silver surge. It had been there for centuries, before the earliest English explorers, a relic of the ancient native people who had been the first ones next to God to love this stunning land.

On the south side of the river, the traffic vanished, and there were fewer distracting lights in all directions. He turned right off the main highway and drove slowly along the winding country road that crossed into the big bend to the north where the Yankees and Confederates had fought each other to a standstill over a series of rickety dams. The light was off the fields now, and windows had begun to glow in small houses at the ends of lanes. He loved the smoky indigo hush of the early evening. He also loved to be outdoors in the hour before sunrise when the world was tinted an expectant blue, the day's Advent, its own Blue Period.

Joe Stephenson's usual mood was one of gratitude for life and the world, *for everything you got,* as his father used to say. At other times he wondered at how difficult it was to do what others took for granted. His mind raced through shadowed corners of the past like someone searching the abandoned rooms of an empty house, opening doors, letting in light here and shadows there. The hollow spaces echoed with words said and unsaid, things done and left undone, and the resonance was saddening. In all the doors he opened, he stood as an intruder, conscious of his own awkwardness. In the darkness, wondrous images emerged and receded, filling him with longing and tenderness: Kate's face as they stood beside a waterfall in Linville Gorge; Ted playing in the surf; Kate reading in a rocking chair in the early morning, her favorite time of day; his parents cooking together and talking in the kitchen at home, smiling at his graduation, wedding, ordination; Ted as a baby, smiling all the time; the kindly face of Bishop Spencer; the soft down on Ted's cheek as a child; Kate emerging from the shower, glowing, like Renoir's *Bather Arranging Her Hair.*

A buck and three does looked suddenly out of the darkness ahead of him, and Stephenson slowed down, turning the car slowly into the opposite lane and coasting past them quietly as they watched in stillness. It seemed half the people he knew had hit a deer.

When he needed to rest his mind, which seemed like all the time these days, he thought of Ted. He would be leaving the gym about now and walking with his friends to the cavernous cellar that served the St. John's students as a dining hall. He could see him descending the stairs in a crowd, laughing, complaining about the food before they had even tasted it, discussing the coming weekend.

Kate would be taking her seat, "supervising a table," as she liked to say.

"What would you do," he had asked her once, "as supervisor if the table went berserk and ran out of the room, scattering dishes and chairs all over the place? And do you think any of the students would notice?" She had laughed loudly and squeezed his arm. He loved it when she was happy.

Kate would be listening now with selective, critical attention to the teenage gossip around her on which she doted and that shaped so much of her thinking. He could be there listening too, he knew. It was his choice, and he had chosen to go home. The day had been difficult and demanding. He needed peace and quiet and the comfort of familiar surroundings. But he felt guilty leaving her, and it was useless to try to deny it. Kate, and to some extent Ted too, had not the slightest idea or interest in what he did all day. It was not connected to Kate's teaching at St. John's, and therefore it generated little or no interest.

Where the road met the river again, he turned west and drove along the narrow byway that ran above the gorge toward the mountains. There had been a trail along this bluff since prehistoric times where humans and animals moved back and forth along the great river. Buffalo, Seneca, Mohawk and Delaware, English settlers, French spies, Germans from Pennsylvania, George Washington, Confederates, Yankees all moving along the river or above it on one side or the other. Now here he was where they had been, thinking his piddling thoughts. The lane to his house was bordered by colossal white pines that loomed in the headlights like great startled marine creatures, the shifting shadows under their bows opening like mouths of coral caves. They made him think of South Sea tales and stories by Jack London.

Life was so different now. Children didn't play in the streets or explore the roads on their bicycles as he had as a child. Scouting was going, the young couldn't hitchhike anymore, and they didn't play outside unless there was a pool or the first snow had fallen. Fathers and fatherhood as an honorable estate, going or gone. The mysteries of nature, replaced by gadgets.

The headlights created shadows in the overhanging boughs. Big evergreens made him think of snow. He liked to walk on snowy nights when the sky glowed mother of pearl and stand still and listen as the falling flakes twirled and drifted in the muffled light of the streetlamps. Snow falling for miles around had a soft hush of a sound. Few people he knew had ever thought about listening to the falling snow. The crunch of it underfoot, unlike any other sound, and the generous look of it at morning calmed and thrilled him at the same time, like the land in Monet's *Snow at Lavacourt.*

Among his greatest pleasures was being snowed in at home with Kate and Ted. School and work canceled, unable to go anywhere; there was a security about it that inspired him. There had been several such blessed days while Ted was still in the local middle school, before he began attending St. John's. It was especially good if they knew before bedtime that school was canceled for the following day. They could get up late, and she would cook pancakes. He would make coffee. When the snow ceased, a neighbor would usually drive around on a tractor and clear the driveways. Ted would come out, and together they would clean the cars and dig a path from Kate's van to the back door. During one memorable snow, the three of them had spent the day shoveling out the entire drive. In the cold air, the sounds of children drifted occasionally over the wide lawns as they roamed about with sleds. He could read for a while in the afternoon or watch a movie with Ted. With these happy thoughts, he stopped beside the mailbox. A bird, startled in a nearby bush, flew away into the darkness with an indignant screech. In the stillness that followed, he heard Cory barking up at the house.

He put down his briefcase and newspaper and went upstairs immediately and changed into old clothes. He put on water for tea, carried food and fresh water out to Cory, and listened to the calls on the answering machine. Five parishioners wanted to see him the following day. The sheriff wanted him to open a meeting with a prayer. A newspaper reporter, an inquisitive girl whose articles he admired, wanted his comments on the closing of a halfway house because the neighbors had complained. An old friend from Raleigh had called just to talk. Two callers hung up without leaving messages. Two telemarketers wanted to sell him magazines. A local girl whom Ted had known in middle school had misplaced his dormitory phone number and was trying to reach him about going to a dance at the public high school. A representative from their long-distance provider had called to ask why they were moving to a competitor. This one puzzled him because he had made no such change. The last was an old friend near

Richmond wanting to talk about a fishing trip. He wrote down a brief note about each message.

He brewed a pot of green tea and left it to steep while he went round the house emptying the wastebaskets. The following day was trash day. He had a poor sense of smell, but even he noticed the reek in the refrigerator from several plastic containers in the back. Before tying the bag, he rummaged through the refrigerator and disposed of whatever else seemed spoiled, and the half-empty bottles of flat soft drinks, tossing the food into the bag and rinsing the bottles and carrying them out to the recycling can in the garage.

Careful to control his tremor, he carried his tea upstairs with both hands and sipped it as he straightened the bedrooms. He changed the beds, folding hospital corners into the sheets and knocking the quilts in under the pillows and smoothing the covers. He folded Kate's comforter carefully on her side of their bed. He put out fresh towels in the bathrooms and set out new boxes of tissues. He spent a few minutes picking up clothes in Ted's room, putting shoes in the closet and under the bed, and hanging up jackets and a few school neckties. He returned to their big bedroom and cleared away a pile of magazines on the floor on his side of the bed. He liked to read at night and had a bad habit of accumulating a bedside pyramid of magazines. They were folded open to half-read articles or marked with scraps of tissue or notepaper. He set a stack of books outside the bedroom door to return them to the cellar, being careful not to include any of Kate's books. He wiped down the bathroom sinks and faucets with Comet and a sponge. He gathered the used sheets and clothes in a laundry basket, piled on the stack of books, and descended two floors to the cellar.

Stephenson had organized one of the cellar rooms into a family library. It was shabby but clean and organized. He had done his best. An assortment of old bookcases, bought at secondhand stores and yard sales, lined the walls and were filled with hundreds of books. They were arranged according to broad subjects: theology, painting and sculpture, history, short stories, novels, wildlife, fishing, hunting, poetry, the law. There were reference books of all kinds. A filing cabinet held family papers, bills, deeds, wills, taxes, and in one drawer the meager sum of his literary ambitions. One drawer was filled with Ted's report cards, writing assignments, drawings, and school projects. A large file contained cards and letters written to him by Kate during her summers at the beach. Another held postcards from Ted, sent to him from summer camp and several school trips.

In one corner stood a cabinet overflowing with Kate's sewing materials. It was no longer possible to close the doors and one of the shelves inside had collapsed under the weight of rolls and bolts of cloth and bags and boxes. The contents, jammed in over the years and forgotten, spilled onto the floor in a pile.

In another corner stood a long collapsible worktable that forever stirred in him profound memories and regrets. He had bought it years before together with a used typewriter in his first week of practice before he could afford a secretary and a real office. It was on this folding utility table that his career as a lawyer had begun. A dated computer, an old electric adding machine, some framed photographs, and several old lamps completed the appointments of this room, a place full of good intentions.

Ted came down at times to use the computer while he was living at home during middle school. Kate never came down to the cellar unless called upon to help husband or son with the computer (usually husband; son had known all there was to know about a computer before the age of twelve). Like his mother, in the field of technology, Ted learned quickly.

This "library" was a basement room without windows. Kate found it dark and uninteresting. Since their marriage, she had always kept her own books separate from Joe's, always resisting the idea of combining her things with his. Her books reposed in a second-floor guestroom where there was no danger of commingling. He was used to it by now, but for the first ten years of marriage, her insistence on keeping her possessions separate had been confusing and hurtful. At first he had seen it only as a habit acquired over years of living alone before marriage, one of many peculiarities that married life would soften and modify in each of them. When after years she was still secreting away anything personal, he began to accept it. Her books in an upstairs bedroom, the title to her car and other papers in a drawer in the dining room, her videos at the back of the hall closet, her bills in her handbag until it was time for him to pay them—it had disturbed him for a long time. It had made it difficult to keep family finances in order.

In the adjoining laundry room, he sorted the clothes into piles of whites and colors, and a third heap of sheets and towels. He washed Ted's soccer uniforms and socks first so he would have them for the weekend. He checked all the pockets, removing from Kate's shirts and jeans the tissues that were always there and rolling down the cuffs of her long-sleeve shirts. He placed her bras and panties in a net bag. A load of whites was in the dryer from the night before, and these he removed and folded on top of the quivering washing machine. This was another room Kate avoided. With the exception of summers spent at her second home, she was not interested in washing, ironing, or cleaning the house.

He had learned long ago that dark, closed places made her sullen and argumentative. She became depressed unless a vacation or some other special occasion waited in the near future. She grew despondent immediately after any school holiday. Every January began the most difficult time of year in family life. It would last until April, when she would brighten considerably for a week or two when flowers bloomed. Then an impatient agitation would consume her until exams ended and summer vacation began. As Kate approached this special moment, toward which she had struggled and complained since New Year's Day, her disposition improved a bit each week. Within hours of her final duties at school, or a day at most, she had departed to spend the summer in her family's vacation home, leaving the mess created by her packing and departure for Joe to deal with.

Ted would go with her. It was a lovely place called Wicomico Island, a rustic coastal region where her family had owned land and conducted business since the War Between the States. Standing in his basement now in November, the thought of their summer departure made him clear his throat and shake his head as though warding off a wasp.

He had spoken to Kate many times about the possibility of seasonal affective disorder. She had considered it herself and had taken a mild interest in some literature he brought her from a seminar. When she learned that it had been a mental health seminar, the brochures disappeared, and Kate avoided any further discussion of the subject. She would not agree to consult a doctor, not even her gynecologist, in whom she had always had trust. When Joe brought up the subject in the previous spring, she became angry and complained that he did not understand her or appreciate all she had to deal with. He had let the subject drop for the final time. He had long ago learned to bring up any sensitive issues after Ted had gone to bed.

He carried the folded laundry up to the kitchen and sat down at the table and drank another cup of tea. Several paper sacks filled with bulbs, huge amaryllis as heavy as coconuts, sat on the table. Their severed onion tops revealed narrow chartreuse streaks, evidence of great blooms awaiting light and water. In the other bags were narcissus and hyacinth bulbs for forcing. He would see to them all on Friday, his day off. If his timing was right, they could be in bloom for Christmas.

Everywhere he turned, there were sights that filled him with contentment and emotion. This was the home, these were the rooms, where they lived together. Around this kitchen table they had eaten, talked, worked, and cried. For years Ted had sat here at night with his homework, Kate had prepared tests, and they had talked while she cooked. They had wrapped Christmas gifts, talked on the telephone with his family (whom Kate loved), and celebrated birthdays.

He remembered years of arguments to judges and juries trying to make them understand. Every American who watched television or read newspapers was familiar with a thousand burglaries every year. Breaking and entering was no longer news in the sophisticated world of terrorists, scientific evidence, and drug cartels. Burglaries were as common as cold sores. The light penalties were no longer a deterrence.

"Think of it, ladies and gentlemen. Consider, Your Honor, the nature of what was done here. The defendant invaded the victim's most sacred, intimate space. He violated the rooms where this family nursed their children, celebrated birthdays, decorated their Christmas tree, dressed for Easter services. The defendant pawed around in drawers where

the victim kept her grandmother's jewelry, her children's baby clothes, and her own underwear. The accused crept around where this man's children played, where he made love to his wife. This was their sacred space, their home, the place where they felt secure. His very presence there was a violation of that precious intimacy. It is not unlike rape in that—"

"Your Honor, I object to that. It's calculated to prejudice the ju—"

"Sustained. We're dealing with burglary here, Mr. Stephenson. That characterization could be considered inflammatory."

Through the living room door, he could see Ted's video games scattered on the floor near the television. On a chair near the door was a collection of Kate's pocketbooks, book bags, and coats. A plastic grocery bag on the coffee table was filled with shells, stones, and beach glass he had collected a year before and was now separating into glass jars. There was nowhere like home.

Chapter Three

Of the old buildings in Catoctin Springs, the red-brick Church of the Redeemer is the best known and most venerable. Older than the courthouse, clerk's office, or jail, it has stood at the crossing of George and Duke Streets since 1803. It was then that the original Redeemer, a square stone structure with a log roof built about 1765, was declared to be unsafe by the new minister. He was a cautious cleric lately arrived from faraway Norfolk, and he insisted that a new building was absolutely necessary. The town notables respectfully pointed out that the old church had suited the former parson just fine and commenced a great deal of what the New Testament calls grumbling. Word went round that the new rector would leave if he could not have his new building. It had taken some three years to get him, while the congregation endured the monthly ministrations of an ascendancy cleric from Pennsylvania with an unintelligible County Monahan accent. The vestry met at the Brunswick Tavern and, after some animated discussion, agreed to build a new church. It was erected in haste a few blocks from the old one on a lot donated by a former Continental Army officer, a dreary Calvinist whose persuasive wife had been a loyal established church member since birth. Determined that this one should be permanent, the congregation built their new church of bricks kilned on the site and dignified it with one of the first slate roofs in town. The beams and floors were constructed of chestnut and oak from surrounding farms.

Dozens of the faithful contributed to the purchase of silver communion vessels made in London and brought over in time for the consecration in 1806. Some fifty years later, Colonel Smythe, the warden in 1862, buried them in his garden, and there they remained for three years until the surrender at a distant place called Appomattox Courthouse. The set was stolen by burglars in 1972 and recovered from thieves in Maryland about a year later, before it could be melted down. The old silver chalices, paten and flagon, long regarded as community treasures, now repose in a bank vault up the street from the church. They are used at Christmas, Easter, and whenever a bishop visits.

The original Holy Table, several enclosed pews, a primitive stone font, and a rickety walnut lectern were moved over from the old church when it was razed, rattling through the muddy streets of Catoctin Springs in wagons pulled by mules. The font is said to have been carved by Hessian prisoners on the orders of General Wayne. It has long been a subject of curiosity among historians and is mentioned in scholarly journals from time to time. Conscientious vestries and devoted altar guilds have preserved all these venerable pieces for two hundred years.

The Redeemer congregation grew with the community and by 1850 numbered 143 souls. Some of them traveled miles into town for worship on Sunday afternoons, tying their horses to trees and rails outside the church and along George Street while they prayed devoutly in their brick church. As the years passed, the small church-yard filled up with gravestones and a few simple monuments, and the congregation had to purchase an additional burial lot on what was then the edge of town. In time this too filled up with the parish's dead. The "old" and "new" cemeteries remain today a few blocks apart, venerable leafy oases in the town's run-down business district. Beneath the huge copper beeches and some sagging catalpas, the old stones tilt in all directions, their weathered inscriptions recording the lives of the region's pioneer forebears. A few times each year, teenagers climb over the fences in the middle of the night and topple the old gravestones for fun. No arrests are ever made. As an act of community service, a local Boy Scout troop sets them back up again. Older members of the Redeemer flock come around to pull weeds each year before the Daughters of the American Revolution spring observance and again just before Confederate Memorial Day.

To pay for the new Redeemer, the vestry had pulled down the unsound stone church and sold the lot and fieldstones to a banker from Baltimore. He built a square two-story brick house on the site in 1816 and erected a handsome dry stone wall to separate his lawn from the muddy public street. Sections of his wall still stood until the early 1960s along what is still called Church Street. After the War Between the States, the banker's great-grandson, a Confederate major who had lost a leg at Cold Harbor, sold the place and moved to Virginia to live with his wife's relatives. A row of frame houses was soon constructed on what had been his lawn, and big gaps were knocked in the stone wall in front of each one so occupants could get through to Church Street. After years of service as a "colored" school, the old brick house was demolished too, during World War I.

The railroad, advancing through the Potomac Highlands like a determined snake, had arrived at Catoctin Springs in the summer of 1852. Mill hands, laborers, shopkeepers, and two more blacksmiths came with the rails. Small businesses flourished with connections to the distant ports of Baltimore and Alexandria. Catoctin Springs, long a village on the colonial outskirts, was becoming an energetic small mercantile center in a vast region of farms and orchards. The frontier, now far, far in the west, had become a memory.

When hostilities ceased in 1865 and adjustments to a new era got underway, small industry replaced the livery stables, blacksmith shops, and some of the older homes in the center of town. Apples, corn, and grain that had sustained the economy were joined now by trade. Many of the former landowners, ruined by the war, moved out and went south with their families. In many ways what had once been known as the south left with them, a transition that would continue gradually into the next century. People came from the north and bought the old farms from the departing ancestors of the original settlers. Greeks and Italians passed through on their way to jobs in the developing distant coalfields. Some of them settled in Catoctin Springs and established small businesses almost overnight, contributing a momentum of spirit and energy that would enrich the area for generations. Most of the former slave descendants drifted away to the big cities on the coast, leaving behind a small core of hardworking black families to carry on.

During these changes, the Church of the Redeemer and her clergy provided a certain stability for old-timers and newcomers alike. Newer and far less liturgical denominations appeared and appealed to a wider range of the faithful but did little to diminish Redeemer's historic community role. Her name appeared in every issue of *The Catoctin Gazette.* Whatever else they might come to blows over, many a northerner and southerner, rich and poor, farmer and trades-man, had managed to kneel down together to worship God within Redeemer's walls. Politicians, landowners, leaders of business and society, farmhands and laborers and their spouses and children, white and black, and a few swarthy souls claiming to descend from the last few Indians over in West Creek Valley had all referred to Redeemer as "the Church." Here they had prayed, argued, and rejoiced. They had dozed through interminable sermons, though none quite so long as were routinely committed in other, newer churches, and puzzled over the mysteries of Holy Scripture. They had been baptized, married, and buried and endured all the pain and transitory satisfaction of life in between.

By the Depression, agriculture was beginning its long, slow decline. A generation later, the great orchards began to follow. The peach trees and venerable old varieties of apple were cut down and never replanted. A few seasons passed, and fewer of the standing groves were harvested. The old trees that remained, glorious in bloom even untended, were neglected except for people who climbed over the collapsing fences to pick enough fruit for use at home. The names of growers famous for a hundred years were disappearing from mar-kets all along the Atlantic coast. Old varieties of apples, peaches, and cherries were replaced by the glossy, tasteless fruit of far-off places. With the going of the orchards, as with the change in farming, a way of life was passing away.

Unlike the old church itself, the Redeemer congregation was becoming less and less distinguishable from those of other churches. A small commercial upswing, accompanied by some general optimism, followed World War II. However, by the 1960s, the long decline had resumed. The inept state government discovered innumerable ways to foster division and defeat. Openly dismissive of the needs and opportunities with which the Catoctin region was rife, it consistently siphoned away tax revenues to shore up poorer and less skilled populations elsewhere in the state. Outside developers were tempted by the region's cheap land and low cost of living, but regional poverty and substandard services drove them to build their dreams in other states. Families attracted by low taxes worried about the poorly funded schools. The Greek merchants departed for more prosperous towns, leaving their painted names behind to fade for generations on the facades of their former stores. The young went away to college and invariably sought out careers in happier places.

Prosperity flourished in adjacent states, however, and people who crowded there to work needed housing and wanted low taxes. In spite of the Catoctin area's captivity to a bungling state government, overcrowded schools, and cumbersome water districts, the lure of cheap housing continued to swell the population. The new people agitated for unheard of luxuries such as zoning, recreation facilities, and a consolidation of overlapping public utilities, needs not recognized or valued in the rest of the state.

By the late 1980s, another farmer went out of business every month. Land worked by the same families since the Revolution was sold and partitioned into subdivisions with names like Happy Creek Acres and General Braddock Downs. They were built in haste by developers untroubled by where the children would go to school or whether public utilities and law enforcement could meet the needs of the new occupants; like zoning and setback restrictions, these were problems the state legislature had never been efficient enough to address. Catoctin Spring's largest employers, a hosiery mill, and shoe factory closed their doors. Men and women, whose forebears had worked in them for generations or on the surrounding farms, began to commute by train to Washington for jobs and higher wages. In states to the north and south factories and distribution centers were constructed, a few of them close enough that some local residents could find jobs in them. People who had lived in the same homes for decades were selling to outsiders, new residents who seemed to move in and out again overnight, making way for yet another new, transient family. On shady streets where children once played and residents had sat on porches in the evenings, rocking and chatting as their friends ambled by, many people no longer knew their neighbors. It seemed that half the people were Latino or Middle Eastern in the aisles of Lowes and Walmart. The public schools struggled to keep up.

A variety of domestic and commercial structures rose and fell where the colonial stone church once stood. A series of convenience stores has occupied the site since the early 1980s. The latest franchise tore up the parking lot and installed vast gasoline storage tanks and floodlights that would illuminate a football stadium. It is open all night. Over the years, the stores have been the scene of robberies and other violence perpetrated by migrant workers and drunk rednecks and people passing through, gaining the site a significant local reputation. The road is still called Church Street, although only a few amateur historians remember why. Several blocks away in the dreary business district stands the "new" Redeemer, almost two hundred years old now, a reminder of more genteel times. Surrounded by banks, the dilapidated courthouse, shuttered stores, and a municipal parking lot, Redeemer retains an antique charm that draws long second looks from passersby.

Most of the other early buildings were razed long ago. Following the Depression, anyone with a little cash could buy what remained of a historic heritage. In the elegant fieldstone Smythe mansion, Stonewall Jackson had spent a few rare, restful nights. The Mooring, built by Admiral Dandridge following his triumph in 1812, where his nieces had entertained governors and senators, had the first spiral staircase west of the mountains. The lovely row of mellow brick townhouses that had stood on Queen Street since the 1840s, the Potomac Hotel with its late Tiffany skylight, the old Brunswick Tavern, Judge Pitt's big Federal house where Teddy Roosevelt had been a guest, the Greek revival Farmer's Bank, the handsome stone house on the west end of town called Bewley Hall—all demolished, victims of regional poverty and a powerless Historic Review Committee, whose reluctant members for generations had felt constrained to err on the side of commerce. It was the loss of a heritage scarcely noticed in the community, but it would drive historians to grief in later years.

In the surrounding countryside a number of historic structures had survived the years of decline. The old farm families struggled on because for many of them, there had been nothing else to do. No profit came of it, only a form of maintenance that over the past seventy years had left the buildings and fields in decline. Most of the landowners got through from year to year earning just enough to pay taxes and living expenses and little more. When it was no longer possible to put off replacing a tractor for another season, or when a son or daughter wanted to go to college, families sold land. As the years passed, the boundaries of the old farms began to resemble the rims of doilies with edges scalloped away by quarter and half acres, sometimes more. The meandering rural roads had once provided views of stunning beauty, and where the orchardists struggled on, the land in spring and early fall could still inspire awe. But now the country roads were lined with miles of small dwellings, sometimes two or three deep. Trailers and doublewides and four-room bungalows stood in treeless plots with an occasional storage shed or small aboveground swimming pool in the front yards. Due to a want of zoning and municipal planning, small businesses, repair shops, and garages emerged almost overnight in residential areas. The once lovely landscape, part of the nation's oldest settled region, was becoming a terrain of irregular lots and inconsistent uses. In places the land resembled a third world country.

Those who remained of the area's founding families usually could be found on the Redeemer roles. As the generations passed, there were fewer of them to list, and some had not been observed at worship in years. Some of the oldest names had addresses in distant managed-care facilities or nursing homes or lived with relatives far away. They faithfully sent in yearly pledges, usually very small, and mailed money once each year when their turn came to provide altar flowers for Sunday worship. They read the monthly newsletter with great interest, remarking to companions on all the new names and wondering about friends whose forgotten funerals had taken place years before. The clergy and women's group at Redeemer were kind to these ancient members, visiting those who lived reasonably close and sending cards throughout the year to those far away. In time, most of these aged members returned for their final service to the place where they had fidgeted as acolytes or appeared as lambs and angels in Christmas pageants of long ago.

Less than half of Redeemer's families had been members since birth. Most came into the parish from other denominations. Some had never had a church affiliation before. Whether raised at Redeemer or in another church, many had ceased attending about the age of thirteen, or as soon as they became tall and heavy enough to defy parental demands. Many reappeared over the years to be married in their "family" church. After another year or two, they would begin to have children of their own, and they returned to have them baptized. When the children could walk, parents who hadn't thought about the church for years began to discuss Sunday school. Eventually, they appeared to enroll their little ones. Some of the parents then resumed regular attendance for the first time in their adult lives.

There were many older members, retirees mostly, who devoted much time to parish life. They would be a blessing in any church, industriously organizing activities, leading committees, raising money for outreach, and remembering the birthdays and anniversaries of members older than themselves. They joined their clergy in visiting nursing homes and hospitals, prepared luncheons and dinners for meetings and other parish occasions, saw to the care of the building, and assisted the clergy in countless valuable ways. They were people mostly easygoing, living lives of responsibility and decency without much notice, and desiring none, and glad to be able to be a part of things.

Like all worshiping communities, Redeemer had its mean and self-centered contingent. The blessing was that it was so small, but they shared a big desire for control. As they had been around for a while, their true motives were recognized, and the congregation quietly made allowances, acquiescing in their efforts to get into leadership roles on the diocesan level. This way, at least, they were not involved in the day-to-day ministry of the parish.

Chapter Four

The Stephenson family moved to Catoctin Springs when Ted was eleven. For Ted's welfare, Joe argued, they needed a place where he could grow through middle school and high school in one community with the same friends. Joe had known many of his own friends since the first grade, a source of astonishment to people everywhere. The young of mobile America seemed to count relationships in months or a few years, not decades. To a child of the South like Joe, having routine contact with childhood friends was not at all unusual. He wanted his son to have the blessings that would develop in long-term friendships. He did not want Ted to be uprooted before going away to college.

The Stephensons had made a good start in Dorchester, their first assignment after Joe's ordination. They liked the community, and Kate enjoyed her work at the community college. She had begun to make friends. St. Andrew's, Joe's first assignment as a priest, was a kind and reasonable congregation.

For the many frustrated faithful in the world, churches have always provided safe places to get rid of anger. There were a few angry members at St. Andrew's who routinely took out their frustration with life's disappointments—spouses, jobs, unfulfilled dreams—upon Joe. He was a new and convenient target. It happened in every denomination, a hazard nobody had bothered to explain in seminary. Unfortunately the grumblers of St. Andrew's included the rector's irritable wife, who developed an immediate dislike for all his assistants. It was an occupational peril no one had mentioned in Joe's job interviews. And a few others, although not exactly angry, felt displaced by Joe in his new capacity as assistant, and they took some time to become friendly. He told himself that God was giving him these challenges to develop his patience and conciliation. The sour ones were only a few in the larger, welcoming congregation. Still, it wouldn't hurt God, Joe confided to Kate, to cultivate these good qualities in him in less trying ways, without the rector's wife as an enemy agent, say. In any case, it was all more than made up for by the kind rector, the compassionate veteran parish secretary, and the great good-natured majority of parishioners.

The kind rector had been at St. Andrew's for twenty years, had a daughter preparing to enter college, and a mortgage whose rates had been determined in far less costly times. Although following his three-year commitment the congregation wanted Joe to stay, it was clear the rector intended to finish his own career at St. Andrew's. Besides, even if the rector should retire, Joe knew that Bishop Spencer would not approve this large congregation calling him so soon after seminary. St. Andrew's had come through one financial crisis in his second year with them, where even those who felt closest to him had been forced to admit that eliminating his position might be the only way out. They found another way, but his close call had given Joe much to ponder. To stay on as assistant, subject to the vagaries of the economy and uncertainty of pledges, was like living atop a geologic fault. Sooner or later unseen forces would displace his family. For Ted's well-being, and for Kate's, although it hurt to do so in the short run, Joe believed God was telling them that the time to move had come. Following a conversation with Joe and much of what Joe hoped was private reflection, Kate had reluctantly agreed.

As distant parishes began to show interest in Joe, Kate signified her agreement with weeks of sullen evenings and petulant responses to anything Joe said. She found fault with everything. She closed herself off to him. As always during such times, he got very little sleep. Kate would snap shut her book, turn out her bedside light without comment, and in seconds be sleeping soundly. Joe lay beside her, staring into the dark. He listened to her deep breathing and marveled at her ability to sleep soundly when she was so obviously unsettled.

It was clear now she did not want to move from Dorchester. All three of them liked the town. Joe wanted to stay too, but in another year, Ted would enter middle school, a critical time in his life. Joe still thought it better for all three of them to be settled somewhere before then. He was sure that Kate had thought so as well. Perhaps she still did. If only she would talk to him, explain her feelings, open up. Reading between the lines was wearing him out. As between his wife's labile emotions and his child's long-term welfare, was there really a choice? What would any husband or father do? Having to choose, being forced to sort it all out, especially when he thought they were in agreement, preyed on his mind. No matter how clearly he rationalized the need to find a more permanent position, Kate's attitude still made him feel guilty, as though he was hurting her. But what could he do now? Ted needed a long-term community. He had given notice at St. Andrew's and the people had finally, reluctantly, accepted his decision. He was already exchanging letters and telephone calls with parishes that might want him. The bishop knew. He prayed for guidance.

With his flashlight, he checked on Ted two or three times in the night. More than anything, he wanted to shield him from Kate's anxiety. So far Ted had anticipated their move with curiosity and a sense of adventure. Joe saw it as a healthy attitude, an important step on the way to self-esteem and trust. He sat in the quiet kitchen at night and drank milk and conducted mental rehearsals of conversations with Kate, searching for words or actions to unlock the secrets of her inexplicable resistance to routine responsibilities of marriage and life.

Because she would not discuss with him her moods and thinking, Joe spent hours, sometimes whole evenings, trying to imagine the coming move from her perspective. She liked her work at the community college, and she had gradually come to enjoy Dorchester. She had made a few friends, something he knew was difficult for her. They had lived in Dorchester for three years, the same number of years they lived at the seminary, where Kate drove courageously for miles to work through relentless traffic. Here, her drive to work took five minutes. Moving meant facing the unknown, which would make most people feel insecure. He knew that transitions, even to better things, always included stress. With his family counselor, whom Kate refused to see, he explored transition anxiety, his own and everyone else's, and how it affected mood, temperament, and compassion. He wanted to help Kate. He wanted to protect Ted from falling into the seductive snare of her skeptical, negative cynicism. He thanked God that his son was a happy, gregarious child wholly involved in the liveliness of being young.

* * *

Of the three parishes that considered Joe as a priest, Redeemer had been the first to extend a call. Joe had liked all three congregations and believed that his family could be happy in any one of their communities. Had he been a single man, he would have gone to the place with the greatest apparent need. But he had made his vows to Kate before making them to the church, and the two of them had been blessed with a son. Joe believed that God had positively charged him with making decisions with their welfare, as well as the church's, in mind.

St. Anne's, Shackelford Harbor, was a new diverse parish at the southern end of a rapidly developing coastal vacationland. The area was known for its excellent beaches and increasingly expensive real estate. Trinity, Carrollsville, was a colonial church in a quaint small town of flower gardens and remodeled antique homes. In recent years, photographs of Trinity and its fashionable surroundings had appeared in national magazines a half-dozen times and on a calendar of East Coast historic sites, to the immense satisfaction of the young professionals who had been busily purchasing the splendid old houses in the neighborhood. The third parish was Redeemer, a fine historic church in a rather blue-collar town that had seen better times.

Joe believed that God's call to him, as a married man, included certain expectations. His relationship with Christ meant being a good husband and father. Parish ministry began around his own family table. Doing right by his own was the beginning of pastoral wisdom in the world. Years before, at a conference for people considering studying for the ministry, Joe had heard a seminary dean say, "If you are considering life as an ordained person, and your spouse does not believe 100 percent that it is right for your whole family, you should prayerfully consider whether or not your spouse's position is a message that God is not calling you to an ordained ministry." Kate was sitting with Joe a few feet from the dean when this was said and facing the dean when he said it. When Joe brought it up in later years, she always claimed the dean had said no such thing. The apparent importance to her of denying what Joe considered a pivotal statement, which seemed after all to be wholly in her favor, mystified Joe. In time, he accepted it as yet another facet of her inmost reasoning, which she would neither discuss nor explain.

The dean's advice nurtured in Joe a seed planted well before he ever met Kate. He believed that God spoke to him through the words and actions of other people—not all the time, not always distinctly, and most of the time not at all. But he had no doubt that from time to time God used other human beings as messengers, channels of guidance in his life and in the world. Once in a great while, in listening to someone—a stranger passing by, an old friend in conversation, someone quoted in a book or newspaper—he found himself moved by the clarity and simplicity of the truth that came through to him. He always accepted it with amazement and gratitude, often writing down what he heard and meditating on it for days. He did not hear such messages often. It intrigued him to think of how many of them he had missed in the pace of life's busyness. He knew he was not the best or brightest, by any definition. He needed all the help God would give him. Out of all this, he had become a good listener. The least of all the resulting benefits had to do with his success as a trial lawyer; he had learned to listen with all five senses and could sometimes tell what a person was thinking by the way she walked or held her hands. He had never bothered trying to explain it to anyone. But he felt in his heart that God spoke to him, and mostly through other people. He believed it was only logical that God should speak to him through those closest to him, and the closest was his wife. Kate was the most important person in his life. After her came Ted and his bishop and parents and friends. But Kate was always first. When the dean spoke about spouses as God's messengers, Joe recognized he was in familiar territory.

Kate's obvious irritation at taking part in family discussions, never even so much as hinted at before she said "I do," created in Joe an ongoing anguish. Her negative attitude was equaled only by her anger at Joe's ever daring to decide anything of consequence without consulting her first. She initiated discussions herself only about Ted, her job, her mother, her summer house, or something she wanted to buy or do. Apart from these issues, she confined herself to light banter about traffic, weather, television, or general complaints about people she encountered during the day. When Joe was able to pin her down on a time and place to talk about something important (it was not unlike setting an appointment with a busy executive), she sat, silent and betraying no apparent emotion, as though her presence alone satisfied any need for involvement. Often the "talk" would conclude with Joe believing they had reached a decision on something, only to discover later how wrong he was.

Kate never grew used to Joe trying to talk things over. She resented it as an unwanted intrusion on her routine. Over the years she developed a repertoire of avoidance and denial tactics, which Joe, in the early years of their marriage, had failed to recognize for what they were. Very much aware to her annoyance, he was never sure whether her resentment was toward him or the issues he wanted to talk about. They were subjects that figured in all marriages: sex, time, and money, in all their multitudinous variations. In the bygone days of his domestic relations practice, he had witnessed countless issues considered only on the back end of marriage. By then it was often too late. As a clergyman providing marriage counseling, approaching it all from the front end, he found that the variations changed, but the themes played on like an eternal performance of *Pomp and Circumstance*, or the *Bolero*. Kate's resistance made him feel foolish, inadequate, and increasingly a failure as a husband. This too he struggled to hide from Ted and everybody else.

* * *

His parents talked with each other and argued vigorously once in a while the whole time Joe was growing up. His mother's understanding voice had spoken in his heart since he entered the first grade, following him into life with a tender persistence and devotion that he would fully comprehend only when he became a parent himself.

"Now you listen to me, Joey Stephenson. When your teacher speaks to you, I don't care what she's talking about, you listen to her. And look her in the eye when you do. She's in this work because she loves to teach, and she cares about every one of you in that class. I'd better not ever hear of you talking back to her again. Think of all the good things she's taught you. Your daddy and I raised you to have good manners, and we expect you to be a perfect gentleman when you leave this house to go to school or anywhere else. Mrs. Claiborne is a very nice lady. She has taught hundreds of children, and she knows what she's talking about. So you be nice to her and to every other teacher you have. Do you hear me, young man?"

In his small southern town school was an extension of home. The neighborhood, his Boy Scout Troop, summer camp, parties, church, his parents expected him, as his father said, to *behave like a gentleman, goddammit. You use good manners, you tell the truth, say "Yes, sir" and "No, ma'am," and thank people when they do something for you. And don't ever be a tattletale. Nobody can stand a tattletale. It's as bad as not telling the truth!* His father had also said at some point that *telling the truth, no matter what, shows what a person is made of on the inside. Not telling the truth is like wearing dirty underwear. After a while untruthful people begin to smell bad. And everybody knows it.*

Few tragedies in life were more crippling, more profoundly humiliating, than being known as untrustworthy. All his friends accepted as he did the uncomplicated principle that truth and honesty were outward signs of being real on the inside. None of them could have defined character any more than they could have explained integrity, or any other complexity of adult life. But in the classroom, playing basketball in the neighborhood, visiting the homes of friends, doing what came naturally, they knew a lie when they heard it. None could imagine themselves ever having to wear that badge. Like body odor or bad breath, it marked a person as unclean.

"And, honey, don't ever call anyone a fool," said his mother. "It's in the Bible."

"*Liar* is a bad word, a terrible thing to call somebody," said his father.

The very word itself was taboo, and what it stood for was evil. Every adult he knew believed this—all his teachers, his scoutmaster, his parents' friends, the people at church, Mr. Robinson the minister, his friends' parents, his neighbors. None of them spent much time talking about it. No one brought up the subject of honesty without fitting provocation. But the cultural conviction surrounded them all like the mountain air they breathed, and it entered their worldview just as unconsciously. Honesty was a quality necessary for a person to have in life, as integral to a human being as lungs, heart, or brain. It was a necessary component of becoming a man or woman and conducive to the welfare of family and society as a whole. Where he was raised, it was how a decent person behaved. As a child, when he told a lie, he felt he had soiled himself like a baby, and it was hard to look at his parents, even though he knew they didn't know. Lies and any other dishonesty stained the transgressor and his family as well. As a boy he and his friends had played with walnuts, throwing them at one another and at squirrels, and their hands had become stained with brown sap that nothing could wash away. A lie was like that, a tarnish that had to wear off.

At his college, he had found this attitude clarified and given additional emphasis. People spoke about "honor," and high value was placed on it. Honor and reason were inseparable. Honor, logic, and reason were sure ways of coming to truth. God was up there somewhere, and God had put it all in place and set it going. Once in a thousand years or so, God stepped in to work a minor readjustment perhaps, but it was altogether up to men and women to improve themselves and live decently with other human beings. Integrity was the essential attribute of a healthy, balanced personality. Moral qualities and ethical standards, whether coming from the inside or learned from wiser people, tied certain personalities together. They had in common a search for conformance to a higher, greater good. At his university, faculty and students all accepted it and expected each other to abide by it. If this was not precisely what Joe had learned in church over the years, it was close enough to satisfy his conscience.

Although he did not know it during his years at the university, Joe would never again live in a place of such standards. He could leave a dozen books, his overcoat, gym uniform, and billfold in a pile on a table somewhere, and put a ten dollar bill on top if he ever had one, and leave it all there for a week. When he returned, it would be just as he had left it, unless someone had moved it aside a few inches to dust or study.

Years later, as a teacher, Joe had observed the keen regard for fairness with which his young students evaluated their troubled lives. Not necessarily fair to each other, they nevertheless expected life to treat them, personally, with a generous fairness. After a few years in the classroom, he would come to view this expectation as a type of desperate self-preservation, an urgent search in a threatening world for recognition and validation. It made him think of his own child-hood and wonder if he and his friends, with their unspoken determi-nation to become "good," had only been protecting themselves too, in a way.

Joe began to study law with a wide range of deficiencies —there were no other fine arts majors in his entering class, but a misunder-standing of the relationship of clarity to justice was not one of them. Before the end of the first semester, he perceived that the search for truth and justice had, as its raw material, the words of the English language. At an early age, he had formed an unconscious perception of the fundamental connection between truth and clarity. His child-hood contemporaries understood it too, although like him, none of them could have explained it. If absolutely made to try, they might have observed, in so many words, that truth was not complicated, and it shouldn't take too much talking to express it. The more words it required, the more suspect was the speaker's motive. If studying law had worked any fundamental adjustment in Joe Stephenson, it might have been a reaffirmation of the sanctity of truth and a height-ened awe of the English language. And as though it all needed a final emphasis before Kate came toward him down the aisle, there was marriage counseling with the Reverend Stanley Wiley.

He was a big, unkempt, hairy man in his late sixties. Like Stephenson many years later, Wiley appeared uncomfortable in his clerical collar. Tugging at it as though to keep it from contracting, the Reverend Mr. Wiley regarded them across his desk like a large amused owl. As with many men of a certain generation in his vocation, however, he made up for in perception what he lacked in bearing. He appeared at first to be a relaxed man, but he had an air of alert uncertainty about him, as though he had known scores of young lovers.

"Money is power, control. Time is power, control. They can be tools of compassion and understanding in a marriage, or they can be stumbling blocks. It is how we use them that decides what they are."

"I think I understand, but say some more," said Joe.

"Oh! I understand completely," said Kate, as though nothing could be simpler. "A person who has a lot of money can get a lot of power, a lot of influence. People will do what you want them to."

Wiley looked out the window. "Think of it as a way of communicating between spouses," he said. "You have X amount coming in. You have a certain number of expenses—rent, car payments, insurance. Money is a way of addressing family needs and wants. Time too. You only have so much of it. How are you going to divide it, share it, make the best use of it for the whole family? Both of them need to be discussed constantly, continually, for the common good. Time and money. Each of you will need some personal money and personal time, you'll need family money and family time, and how you divide it all up is where the continual discussion comes in."

"Give us an example of 'continual discussion,'" said Joe.

"You should have three bank accounts," said the veteran clergyman quickly. "One for you Joe, one for you Kate, and a third one for a family account. Put your paychecks into the family account, pay family expenses out of that, and pay each of you some personal money just as though you were paying another couple of bills. You'll need to talk about finances and be open about how much to spend on what and how much personal money to dole out."

Joe cleared his throat in an understanding way.

"And the same way with time. And whatever each of you does with his or her personal time and money is no business of the other's. But can you see what is happening as you discuss all this and abide by your agreements?"

"Trust," said Joe.

"Making sure both get the same," said Kate, at the same time.

"What about underwear?" said Joe.

"Underwear!" exclaimed both Kate and Wiley together. Wiley said the word with a laugh, and Kate as a question, as though she was pronouncing it for the first time. Wiley looked into a middle distance above them. Kate threw back her head and laughed.

Joe grinned. "Is underwear a family expenditure…"

"Or are that and similar things personal? Would it come out of personal money?" said the priest, who had heard it all before. Joe, having never been married, was unaware of how much of an iceberg drifted beneath his point.

"That's where the discussion comes in," said Wiley with a broad smile.

"I guess if a wife didn't feel like discussing buying underwear with her husband, she could just buy it with her own personal money and not say anything about it," said Kate, looking from Wiley to Joe and back. She sat straight up, her hands folded in her lap and her feet perfectly side by side on the floor.

"It's symbolic, Kate, and entirely practical too," said Wiley, shifting forward and planting his elbows on his desk. "How a couple works with time and money leads on to working together on other issues in marriage." Smiling, Wiley took off his spectacles and cleaned them with an old bandana he kept in his desk.

One of the "other issues" in their marriage would be Ted. Joe and Kate loved him dearly, and although they found it hard to agree on other matters, Joe anticipated that his well-being would always draw them together. It was Ted who tipped the decision toward accepting the call to Redeemer.

Kate had loved the idea of living by the sea and made it plain from the beginning that she wanted to go to Shackelford Harbor. Joe believed God had set all three sites before them and that they could fare well in any of the three. But he was concerned about raising a son in a vacation community, no matter how inviting it might be in summer, known for its easy availability of drugs. And although lovely in the warm months, Joe reasoned that Shackelford became bleak in late fall and winter. A retired clergyman in Shackelford Harbor confirmed his suspicions, relating how he had "lost" his own twelve-year-old son in the aimless life of the wayward beach population. By his early teens, his son was failing in school and smoking pot daily. He was arrested for some minor offenses. He dropped out of school. Now he was a construction worker somewhere, paying child support to a girl he had known for two weeks before they attempted to live together. The restaurants, fancy motels, and rollicking water parks drew the wayward from Washington, Baltimore, and Philadelphia. They came in search of jobs and good times. The vacationland trappings masked a lonely society, directionless and unexciting beyond the transient allure of the summer people. It was no place to raise a child, said Joe. Kate had agreed reluctantly, an entirely intellectual concurrence but without any emotional commitment. It would take Joe some time to understand this.

Of the two other parishes, the bucolic congregation of Carrollsville had a long and perplexing history of conflict with clergy. The last priest had been nudged out diplomatically by the bishop, and the one before her had been forced to leave when the congregation ceased paying his salary. It was rural and charming in its way. They both agreed that Ted would get on quite well there. There were job openings for a science teacher in two local high schools, which reassured Kate.

Redeemer was also the hub of a rural community, but with several large cities less than an hour's drive away. The schools were disappointing, except for those in one particular district of the county. Kate could expect to find work in this community too and probably more easily than in either of the other two. Real estate around Catoctin Springs was less costly than in Carrollsville and a great deal more reasonable than in Shackelford Harbor, and taxes were lower too.

Although he dared not suggest it, Joe was as deeply concerned for Kate in this move as for Ted. She spent the winter months of each year in depression. The darkness and cold and seemingly endless weeks before spring vacation had meant tears and sullen moods every year of their marriage. If she had found life so difficult in the lively and pleasant towns where they had lived, what might happen to her in the winter wasteland of Shackelford? He worried too that she would be unhappy in the trendy, fashionable, and socially upscale community of Carrollsville, where their neighbors would all be more affluent than they. Kate's critical nature was aroused by those whom she perceived as more fortunate than she was, better off financially, or more socially savvy.

Joe knew better than to attempt to raise these concerns with Kate. He figured she had accepted that Shackelford would not be a nurturing place for Ted, but what did she think about Carrollsville? Would she perceive what he saw? He had used up his credibility by coming out against Shackelford Harbor, and he sensed she would grant him little latitude in deciding between the other two. It was a choice, he decided, that he should not attempt to control. Either community would be good for Ted. Kate was a grown woman and by now should realize what was best for her. Although his reservations about her long-term happiness in Carrollsville were very real, he knew it would work against them all if the choice were not hers.

Kate was clearly troubled in deciding between Carrollsville and Catoctin Springs. She had reservations about each. She was vague and grew irritable when Joe asked her to explain. If friends asked about the choices, however, she conversed enthusiastically about both as though either would suit her just fine, thank you. By this time in their marriage, Joe was used to all this, but he had learned to recognize the doors through which necessary subjects could be, at least, approached. Kate was fixated upon Ted and upon her job, wherever they had lived. As long as a subject could be brought up in the context of these two obsessions, some talk, however grudging, could follow. In this way, he succeeded eventually in hearing her say that either place could be right for Ted and that her own prospects were about equal in each of them, although perhaps the cost of living would turn out to be better in the Redeemer area.

For his part, Joe was convinced, after much prayer and reflection, that he could serve God in either place. He felt he could work with whatever unexamined baggage existed in the Carrollsville church. Taking it all together and striving to weigh his words so as not to lose Kate's participation, he proposed that they go to the first of the two parishes to issue a call. Kate was silent but offered no objection. The first call came from the Church of the Redeemer.

A familiar pattern emerged. Ted's well-being and her own employment aside, Kate began to make it clear that she was still dissatisfied. Catoctin Springs was shabby, dull, and dirty. Its blue-collar ways promised to afford her some amusement, but she anticipated little more. She found the accents hilarious, the manners disagreeable, and the shopping wholly unsatisfactory. But she would sacrifice herself for the good of her family, for her only child, for her husband's career. She set about packing her own clothes and sorting through her jewelry, raising her voice in irritation when Joe tried to talk with her.

And we aren't even there yet, he said to himself.

Chapter Five

G od does not promise to shield us from the evil of this world. Our prayers to save us from the time of trial are always heard but seldom answered in ways we understand. The radio evangelists, however, to whom Joe listened occasionally in the car with a mixture of amusement and despair, preached a doctrine of protection, material blessings, and earthly hope for those who would get in line behind them. It was a choice, they said. Come in this direction and God will shower you with blessings reserved for true believers, especially if you show how much you believe. And the measure of a person's faith can be determined, basically. It is proportionate to the amount of money each is willing to provide for spreading the Lord's Word. Sending in money means you have got yourself focused upon God. It's a sure sign of how much you care.

"That's bullshit, and you know it," said Roger, a Roman Catholic farm equipment salesman. He shifted his Philadelphia Flyers cap backward on his bald head. "I know it. You know it. And Father Joe here knows it."

"Don't call me *father*," said Joe. The people standing around laughed, and someone gave him a consoling pat on the back.

"And everybody with any sense knows it. What does the Bible say about rain falling on the good and bad alike? Or sunshine or something. It don't make no sense that people can buy their way into heaven," said Gayle, a deputy sheriff on her day off, another Roman Catholic. "If that was the case, then only rich people would get in. Believing in God and all don't mean nothing about having it good in life. What it does do is on the *inside* of a person. My grandma taught me that, and she won't nothing but a country Baptist. Nearly starved to death in the Depression." In spite of these convictions, she had begun attending with a cousin an independent Bible church north of Catoctin Springs that preached damnation for almost everybody, and refused to participate in local ecumenical activities or the community food bank.

"People see that collar and automatically they want to say *father*, don't they?" said Roger.

"Until they get to know me," said Joe.

"Until you come along, we never had a preacher come in here before," declared Raymond, the bartender, looking around for confirmation. "Some people think it means you ain't really a preacher, or least not a good one."

"They're right," said Joe.

Locals referred to the Third Base as a "private club." A private club where Joe came from usually looked like Tara and was enfolded in acres of golf courses, swimming pools, and tennis courts. Jaguars and Mercedes glided in and out like swans, fashionable people called to one another from porches and pro shops, and children in swimsuits raced about in golf carts. Such places were often quite pleasant, but for Joe, the Third Base was every bit as entertaining, especially on Friday nights when pickup trucks crowded the parking lot and lined up along the road. Happy hour lasted until 3:00 a.m. Even so, Joe never stayed longer than two cups of coffee.

"Trouble is, people take religion too serious, or they don't take it serious enough," said Rita, the waitress, mopping a rickety table with vigor. "I mean, just to live it and be natural about it and all. In the Army, I knew the chaplains. They was decent men. They could relate because they could talk English, make somebody feel they could be open and all. Chaplains I met in Afghanistan made a believer out of me. If they was too serious about it, too heavy and all, I don't think I would have listened. They was some good men. One was an asshole, but they was mostly good, commonsense men, like."

"No women?" asked Joe as he sipped his coffee. A ceiling fan whirred lazily overhead stirring the cigarette smoke and warm air.

Electric beer signs from the 1950s winked on and off on the dingy wall behind the bar, advertising beer that was not even made anymore. A jackelope peered earnestly from above the men's room door. The massive head of a whitetail buck, its antlers entwined in twinkling Christmas lights for the past twenty-five years, kept watch from the opposite wall. *Who?* Joe wondered. *Who would get it just right? Thomas Hart Benton? Maybe, but I hate to imagine it. Who painted "High Yellow"? Could Hopper? No, too lonely, too spare. Grant Wood? Ah, an early Philip Guston. It needs an American Toulouse-Lautrec, someone who paints like Dickens wrote. Someone who paints like Raymond Chandler wrote. Black guy over there in the white sweatshirt—Winslow Homer. Rita—Berthe Morisette. Ray—who?*

Whenever Joe entered the Third Base, an amiable crowd gathered about him and conversation eventually got around to God. Sometimes he enjoyed the God-talk, and at other times he did not.

"Joe, *you* take it seriously," said Raymond. "I mean religion. God and all."

"Thanks, Ray," said Joe. "I like to think so." Everyone laughed.

"But see, you come in here and talk like you're right at home with us and all. A lot of preachers can't do that," said Crystal, settling her enormous bottom upon a barstool. She drooped over on all sides like a feed sack. Crystal worked in a liquor store part-time and at the truck stop the rest of the week. She still had a lovely face, and Joe guessed she had once been beautiful, until the age of sixteen or so. He had a momentary vision of Father Hervey sitting here, talking with her, and he laughed out loud.

"Priests do, in Ireland," said Roger. "Ever see *The Quiet Man?*"

"Great movie! Great movie!" said somebody at a nearby table.

"Ward Bond on *Wagon Train* was the Catholic priest," said a voice from a booth.

"It won't him. It was Hoss Cartwright played him," said someone else.

"Well, I'll be damned if we ain't got nothing but a bunch of goddamn movie critics. We ought to get the paper in here. Excuse me, Reverend," said Raymond, blushing a little.

"It wasn't no Catholic priest. It was Protestant," said Rita. "I seen that movie a dozen times on the VCR. Lester, he loves to see the Duke."

"In Ireland! You got to be kidding," said Roger, contemplating an image of his grandmother and great aunts, clad in black, dreaming of the greening plains of Mayo as they trudged to Mass in a blizzard in Pittsburg. "Ain't no Protestant priests in Ireland."

"I'll guarantee you more religion gets discussed in bars and clubs than in half the churches in the world," said Crystal, setting her beer bottle down with emphasis. "Them Catholic priests come in the store and buy scotch and bourbon and all with their overcoats pulled up around their necks so nobody'll see. But I can pick them out."

"'One glimpse of it in the tavern caught, better than in the temple lost outright,'" said Joe, looking down into the baffling clouds of his coffee. They all looked at him in a mystified way.

"If Jesus was to come to Catoctin Springs tomorrow, I know damn well he'd pass by half the churches in town and end up in here having a drink of wine or something and talking with people," said Rita. "Or a cup of coffee, like Joe."

"Damn right," said Wally, a "sanitation engineer," from his usual place at the end of the bar.

"Or maybe a beer. Anybody'd like an Old Baltimore," said Susie, who cooked at the middle school cafeteria. She cackled and raised her short brown bottle in a toast. "To them skins," she said. Nobody paid the slightest attention.

"Damn, Joe. One of these days, I'm going to talk you into having a drink in here, and when you do, it is going to be my treat, on the house," said Raymond with conviction.

"Oh, I'll have one with you sometime. Got some stuff to do first," said Joe, standing up and shaking his raincoat, which had slipped to the floor.

"Ask him what kind of stuff and he'll tell you first he's got to raise his kid," said Rita.

"That and a few other things. Ladies and gentlemen, may the roads rise with you," said Joe, lifting his cup. "I've got to hit the road."

As conversation shifted to the Washington Redskins, he went out into the night and breathed in deeply the cold country air. He thought about smoking one of the small cigars he kept in a box on the back seat of his car. But it would take less than fifteen minutes to drive home, and he was looking forward to his time with Ted. He knew the smell of a cigar would annoy Ted, who, like most of his school friends, was strongly opposed to smoking. He put the box back into its ziplock bag.

He drove toward home along the winding back roads that intersected the county like a tattered web. Driving on country roads was a pleasure for Joe, although he could not have said why. Tonight Ted would return home after weightlifting. One of his friends would give him a ride. Kate was staying late to attend a faculty meeting. So for a few precious hours, he would be able to have a conversation with his good-natured son. He would cook some fried eggs and heat up what was left of the country ham they both liked. They would sit at the kitchen table and talk long after they had finished eating, just as Joe and his brothers and sisters had done with his own parents as he was growing up. After dinner, they might watch the news or part of a video. Ted might play his video games. They might draw. They might sit outside and talk with Cory, who would quiver with delight at their company. Joe would be able to listen to whatever Ted had to say.

It was one of the many things he had tried to work on in family counseling over the years, without success. A conversation with Ted was largely impossible while the three of them were together. From the time Ted had learned to talk, it had become increasingly complicated. He would speak to Ted and Kate, wherever she was, would be drawn to the two of them immediately. He would ask Ted a question, and Kate would answer before Ted could speak. Ted would comment to Joe about something, and Kate would interrupt and provide a response. It made communication with his son very difficult. If he objected to her interruptions while the three of them were together, Kate would indicate her displeasure in a dozen small ways, and Ted, anxious to pacify his mother, would begin to direct his attention to her. Either way, Kate won.

For Joe, it was important to wait until Ted had gone to bed to discuss problems with Kate. He was determined to shield Ted from their arguments. By the time his son was in bed, however, Kate would grow dismissive and act as though he were bringing up ancient history, directing at him her usual refrain of "Get over it." If he persisted and tried to explain how her interruptions, for instance, made him feel, how they spoiled conversation and set a bad example for Ted, she grew irritable and raised her voice. Nothing ever changed. It all happened again at the next family meal.

So he treasured the rare times at home with Ted, a few precious hours here and there that worked upon him like good news, a day off, a good night's sleep. His only child made him feel as though his life had been worthwhile.

As Ted grew older, Joe found that the only way to keep peace at home was to give up the field. As long as she could set the rules, Kate would dominate family conversations and remain even-tempered. Once Ted was enrolled at St. John's, however, she knew she was playing a home game on her own field. The gossip and routine events of the insulated private school became the theme of family life at meals and everywhere else. Joe would listen patiently and attentively, from time to time asking questions about what they were discussing. His wife and son would pause long enough to give him quick answers, Ted willingly enough, Kate in a guarded way as though he was trespassing upon private territory. More and more he assumed the role of spectator. He knew he wasn't handling it well and sought the advice of his helpful family counselor.

Over the years, Kate had grudgingly agreed to accompany him to counselors for a few sessions. Sitting passively, speaking only when addressed by the counselor or Joe, she observed the few sessions like a student required to attend a lecture outside her field. If questioned too closely by the counselor, her attitude changed, and Joe saw her assume a familiar posture. She would not return. This too he had tried to discuss with her. She would tell him he was making too much of things, that he was mistaken, that it didn't matter. If there were problems with their family life, it was Joe's own fault. By the time Ted was in high school, Kate could no longer be persuaded to join him in any family counseling, even for a few sessions. She was extremely guarded among her few close friends, and there was no one else to influence her. Her world, safely contracted to the secure dimensions of her job and summer home, left no room for worrisome pressures. Joe found it particularly hard to sit by while she monopolized conversation with Ted, making him a spectator to gossip between two teenagers.

"Mom, did you see Erika today and the way the hockey team laughed when she came on the field? It was hilarious! What was she *thinking!*"

"There was nothing funny about it. She looked like a little streetwalker. There's no excuse for a girl having her hair like that, even if it is for just an afternoon. If Father had seen her, he'd have had a fit. Of course, knowing him, he would have expected *me* to do something about it. Who does she think she is, doing that way?"

"What in the world did she do?" said Joe.

"Dad, you should have seen her. She did her hair the way they wear it in that new movie."

"Which movie is that?"

"Oh, Ted, you should have seen James Reid when Sharon Wells jumped all over him for getting on the bus late to go on the history tour. He was apologizing left and right and saying all kinds of funky phrases like, 'So very sorry, Ms. Wells,' and 'Please forgive me, Ms. Wells.' It was so faggy."

"Mom! Nobody cares if he's gay. He's one of the coolest guys at school. He has the best sense of humor in the whole class. Everybody likes him."

"Yeah, especially Father," said Kate, with a conspiratorial grin, very pleased with her own wit and perception.

Joe winced. "Kate!" he said.

Both of them looked at him. Ted was surprised at the tone and ready at once to defend his mother. Kate was annoyed, as though Joe was meddling in something of which he had no knowledge or business. Later in the evening, after Ted had kissed them good night and closed his door, Joe tried to talk with Kate.

"Honey, you just can't converse with Ted about teachers and students like tonight at dinner. You are his mother. You are a teacher at the school, talking about other students." Even as he spoke, he knew with regret that she was interpreting what he said as a lecture, and he anticipated her reaction.

"So what, Joe. Ted won't say anything to anybody," she said quietly, not looking up from her book.

"Yes, but talking that way is bound to spill over where other people will know. In the car last weekend, you were talking the same way in front of Randy Stanfield."

"Randy doesn't go to St. John's," she said, looking up at him quickly. "He goes to Hillsville High." He knew that she knew he was well aware of where Randy, one of his oldest acolytes, attended school. But she said it as if she were imparting to him an obvious fact of which he was wholly ignorant. "Randy doesn't even know anybody at St. John's."

"Kate, he certainly does. He knows Ted. They live down the road from the Tracey's. They go to Ocean City every summer with the Traceys and the Crosbys. All those children go to St. John's. And even if he didn't know anybody there, he and Ted are still sixteen years old. When you make cracks about Hervey… He's your employer! These boys are still children."

He was looking at her as he spoke and watched her eyes move from him to her book. She was silent for a moment while her mind shifted totally into defensive mode.

"They do not, Joe. The Crosbys' twins aren't old enough to go to St. John's. You have to be in the eighth grade to get in. We even voted on that again in a faculty meeting this year. Some board members had talked to Hervey about lowering the age to seventh grade. I was right there, and I spoke against it. We voted on it, and you weren't even there. You don't even know what you're talking about, Joe."

"The Crosbys' oldest son and daughter go to school at St. John's," said Joe, wearily, striving to be patient. "And the Traceys' daughter—"

"Yeah! But you said *all* the Tracey and Cosby children. Shows how much you know. And besides, people don't talk about school when they go on summer vacation to Ocean City," she said, as though stating a universal maxim that everyone understood except her dim-witted husband.

"Kate, try to stick to the subject. When you gossip like a teenager with Ted, it is not good for him and not good for your job. If it happened once in a while, well, that's understandable. But when it's all the time…"

"You don't know anything about St. John's, Joe!" she snapped, raising her voice. Joe looked into the hall toward Ted's closed bedroom door. "You've never taken any interest in anywhere I've ever worked. You wouldn't even come to the English Club play last Thursday night."

He looked at her, propped up in bed with her Coke and her paperback novel. She was a good-looking woman, although she would never believe it. Against all his good intentions to the contrary, he was falling once more into an old trap.

"Thursday night was the special vestry meeting, Kate. You know that." He *knew* she knew and wondered what would come next.

"Yeah, but you could have changed it."

"Kate, I can't change a scheduled professional meeting with a dozen busy people just like that. And certainly not for a school play that Ted wasn't even in. He didn't even go to it, he told me."

"Oh! Give. Me. A. Break! Linda Reese doesn't even work. She doesn't do anything all day but sit by the pool and talk on the phone," said Kate, who was deeply suspicious of Linda Reese and had spoken with her perhaps three times in eight years.

Joe might have replied that Linda Reese served as a trustee for the state university, chaired the volunteer Community Interfaith Outreach Council, and was on the board of directors of the hospital. He might have reminded her that the Reeses homeschooled their daughter, who had Down syndrome. He might have tried explaining that the parish secretary had spent two days making telephone calls before finding a date that suited everybody for the special meeting. He might have reminded her that the meeting was necessary to decide on whether to repair the ancient heating system or replace it at a cost of fourteen thousand dollars, and the weather was already cold. He might have pointed out that the topic under discussion was the way she talked about students and faculty with their teenage son. All this he would have attempted to discuss in the first ten years of their marriage. But in the last six or seven years, he had found it harder to remain calm in the face of things that never changed. To the demands of his ministry, the routine events in the lives of their neighbors and friends, the multiple and complex issues of life in adult circumstances, Kate was closed and oblivious. He got up from his side of the bed, shaking his head a little and hoping that Ted had not heard. Kate resumed reading her novel as though their conversation had never taken place. She finished reading a book every week or so. Soon she would turn over and switch off the light without saying a word and within seconds be completely, soundly asleep.

He went downstairs and looked through the mail. He knew he was guilty of mishandling many things. He knew he had made a lot of mistakes in their marriage. He had worked conscientiously to change himself, his behavior, his ways of doing things, saying things. In the early years, at least, at any crossroads, as he hungered for adult companionship and mature support, he had bent over backward to give his wife the benefit of the doubt. Now, he was always tired. His side, which had troubled him for days, was aching again. He wondered if he would be able to sleep that night.

Chapter Six

He loved her. There had been good times. She was a fine-looking woman. When they married, she had a lovely figure. She ran a mile in the afternoons and never worried about her weight. She was lively and adventurous, and like Joe, she loved the outdoors. She liked to travel. She had a sunny look about her, confident and healthy. She appeared younger than her age, and her choice of clothing contributed to her overall teenage effect. Entertainment and an amazing ability to avoid serious news marked the perimeters of her curiosity about the world, an attitude Joe had found endearing at first. For all her expertise in teaching about DNA research and biology, she could not have found the Czech Republic or India on a map and had never heard of the Final Solution or Pol Pot. She read a paperback murder mystery and People magazine every week and followed early evening situation comedies on the television. She preferred talking to other people by telephone rather than in person.

Since she learned to walk, Kate had loved the natural mysteries of the ocean. It was her particular birthright from a fine old family that had spent generations in a summer house on the Atlantic coast. Kate was clever. From an early age, she could distinguish sanderlings from sandpipers, Common Terns from Royal Terns, and identify seaweeds that nobody else even noticed. The children of her southern summer community, especially the boys, knew a croaker from a spot and a striped bass from a puppy drum, but not much more. Loathing even the thought of a classroom during the sacred summer, they did not always appreciate Kate's surfside lectures. From an early age, Kate had understood classrooms as stages and teachers as people to be pleased. The young summer seaside audience, however, grew bored when she instructed them, in front of amused tourists, on the differences between knobbed and channeled whelks. Oblivious to their indifference, she would hold forth until some former playmate, tired of being followed and buttonholed, pushed her into the surf. Chastisements seemed only to strengthen her young resolve. She was learning even then to interpret emotions as a filly wearing blinders observes a narrowed range of the larger world, moving ahead in a comfortable oblivion that obscures both joys and sorrows. By her early teens, she was talking in detail to anyone listening about the slow, imperceptible longshore drift of sand, wind-driven currents, and surf upon the fragile seaside islands of her summer home. Threading her way into the midst of adult discussions, bright-eyed and eager, she aroused admiration and accepted compliments with hungry enthusiasm. Neither then nor by her early twenties could she read the meaning in a bored stare or a glance toward other conversations. The significance of the shallow continental shelf was clear to her. The pain in the eyes of a distracted companion, the fatigue or joy in another's wrinkled brow, all evidence of what lay beneath the surface for those who can read the signs, were unavailable to Kate. Life was more manageable without them.

From the time she entered school until the moment she earned a master's degree, Kate made straight As. Turning in each assignment before it was due, completing every option for extra credit, perched like an inquisitive chipmunk in the seat nearest the teacher or the speaker, she approached the world of grades and examinations with an alert single-minded urgency. She was used to being first in her class and grew to accept it as a duty, a tradition to maintain as she grew older, regardless of the cost. Her academic achievements were badges of honor and proof of an inner worth. She did not suffer fools gladly. Her best friends were a few older, well-educated women with good careers and bad marriages.

Behind Kate's personality was her mother, a petite, unyielding, remarkable woman of iron resolve and eccentric views. She had raised Kate and her older brother alone since their father's death. Kate was seven at the time of his stroke. Upon learning of their father's death, her ten-year-old brother had gone out into the backyard, where he remained alone until dark. He never spoke of his father again. After ten years of marriage, in reply to Joe's recurring questions, Kate spoke of her father on one occasion only, saying she did not remember him and that her family had never discussed his death after the funeral. There was no point in it, she said. He wasn't there anymore.

Kate's mother had tried vigorously to be father and mother in the following years, a difficult itinerary for the whole family. Catherine McIvor had been the rebel in her family, or as much of one as a young rural, southern lady could get to be. Even as a child, Kate's mother had always opted for the most unconventional way forward, an athletic and intelligent loner who seemed to believe that stubbornness on any issue was proof of strength and character. She brought this quality to the role of motherhood, together with a mathematician's sense of logic and a chilly preference for exactness in the face of life's troublesome messiness.

As a child, Catherine had loved her family's old summer house almost as much as she would one day love her children. Her parents had always secretly admired her insistence, even as a child, on getting up on the roof and hammering loose shingles back into submission. She had been among the first women to graduate from the state university, with a rare combined degree in mathematics and physical education. Her brother entered the Navy and became an officer. As though to make up for their oldest daughter's mystifying singularity, her parents saw to it that Catherine's sisters learned to pour tea and sew.

When their parents died, a sizeable estate was settled on the children. Catherine's share had consisted of the old vacation house and adjoining ocean-side lot and a small sum deemed adequate by her parents for maintenance and taxes for twenty-five years. Although each sibling received a bequest of equal value, Catherine's sisters had been outraged at what they considered the loss of their second home. After years of spending vacations and holidays there, neither of them ever set foot in it again.

The twenty-five-year maintenance money had lasted only until Kate's brother's birth. Thereafter, Catherine taught in the local public schools to supplement her husband's earnings. After his death, it grew increasingly difficult to meet the family's expenses, and summers in the old beach house became a job too. A hand-painted sign announcing "Rooms for Rent" was nailed to the gatepost—to the consternation of the neighbors—and with the exception of one room, in which Catherine, Kate, and her brother bunked like sailors, the bedrooms were let out to tourists.

Kate's forebears on both sides were respectable and industrious people, successful at small businesses and farming. Among her kin were a country lawyer, a doctor, a banker, and a career naval officer. All were sturdy small-town Baptists, not especially worldly or given to fancy ways and wholly without pretensions of any kind. They had struggled upward to the fairly comfortable generation of Kate's grandparents, the grandparents whom Kate never knew, the farsighted couple who had built the now weathered summer house. Catherine's own generation had seen their legacy slip away in a series of poor choices in business and love. Her sisters and brother, chafing over the loss of the beach property, turned their backs on Catherine and one another with no second thoughts. As they had never felt much affection or empathy for each other as family, and positively disliked one another for years at a time, they passed up every chance to cooperate in any sort of family enterprise. Kate and her own brother, a bully since childhood, had unknowingly carried on the family tradition, living in a state of suspended argument all their lives. The two of them were in silent agreement on one thing only; each viewed their difficult, strong-willed mother with the same mixture of exasperated love, anger, and humiliation. Catherine's sacrifices for them since their father's death created in them both a grudging sense of duty toward her, but without intimacy or affection. Their bond with Catherine would become an unrecognized lens through which they filtered their approach to every other relationship in their lives. Hardworking loners, socially immature, clever but with little imagination, they led dissatisfied lives in which anger was always just beneath the surface.

Some say life is like a river. Displacement of water in one place has its effect upon all the others, however slight. Somewhere in the past, someone in Kate's line had picked up a beer, a glass of wine, or more likely a shot of homemade whiskey and felt for the first time the seductive mellow warmth of a security they had never known. Whatever the beguiling propensity was, whether conceived at the time of that first drink or lurking in genes for unsuspecting generations, a displacement began that stirred the waters downstream for the current's full run.

A compulsion to drink alcohol had trickled insidiously down the generations and come to rest in the lives of Catherine and her brother and sisters. Staining relationships and personalities in a thousand diminishing ways, it controlled their lives, a subtle and sneaky presence they refused to acknowledge. Through which of their parents, or both, it had crept into them was closed to discussion because the subject did not exist. Nobody in *their* family had ever had problems, *any* problems. Nobody *they* knew did things like that. Drinking was a moral failure, like crime. Anyone who doubted it could come to the Baptist church on Sundays and hear what God had to say on the matter. Worse, it was failing to measure up, a fundamental personal flaw, a deplorable and unacceptable weakness of character.

In the insular, small-town Baptist enclave in which they flourished, such failings rarely occurred and certainly not in the McIvor family. A certain type of person might get involved in things like that—drinking, crime, prostitution, cheating, gaining reputations for dishonesty and deceit, people whose word is no good, who just don't measure up. Some people are free of such diminishing ways. Some people are in control of their lives. Being in control means intelligence and respectability, success and achievement. Such people have no basic failings and certainly no inherent deficiencies—evils that strike at the very heart of self-image, self-worth, and self-esteem. This sort of thing happens. But not with us.

Denial had become reality. The illness that had kept Kate's aunt bedridden for years in New England was the result of an undiagnosed stroke. The doctors should have known better than to let her have a stroke like that. Kate's uncle's peculiar disposition was the fault of his troublesome wife. Kate's brother's arrogance and inability to discuss anything personal or intimate was the result of marrying too early. And his wife was a bit odd too. Besides, he worked too hard. When the local school board fired Catherine for showing up intoxicated at evening faculty meetings, Kate and her relatives said she had begun driving to distant school districts because the teaching was more challenging. After retirement, when Catherine's license to drive was suspended for drunk driving, relatives commended her for choosing to walk to the grocery store for daily exercise. Generations of friends and neighbors, well aware of the truth, had looked at one another and smiled at a thousand such explanations. Years and lives passed by in the lonely control of an illness for which treatment existed and which was no more a moral failing than left-handedness or tuberculosis.

Needy and anxious to please, Kate had learned to play the role of perfect child with an attention to detail that resisted the most careful scrutiny. She developed a reflexive and impenetrable shield. People could never figure out what they could not get close enough to see. Sadly, this pitiable attempt at self-protection, the very distance she created for comfort, rendered those on the other side of it too distant for her to understand. Nobody really knew Kate, and because she refused to examine herself, she would never fully know herself or anyone else.

In spite of her shell, both the inherited portion and the layers she had added on her own, Joe believed that Kate had led a remarkable life. He admired her, even before years of marriage taught him to recognize her barriers and see beyond them. He knew it was not her fault. She had not chosen to grow up this way. As a lawyer and a priest, Joe understood addiction to alcohol as a medical problem, not a moral failure. People who "have" it are no more to blame than those who suffer from epilepsy or color blindness. A disease can be treated, managed, especially when caused by something to which the victim is allergic.

Joe had seen and heard enough in his own family to know that certain of his great-aunts and uncles had been alcoholics. Instead of denial, his family had endured these realities with a sort of embarrassed and bemused exasperation. The problem was acknowledged, talked about, lamented. Arguments, recriminations, and lectures happened on occasion. His parents, who drank occasionally, cautioned Joe and his brothers and sisters about drinking and many other things as well. Examples of lives ruined by drink were available, both in the family and community, to illustrate these lectures. The view his parents took of alcoholics was cautionary, not condemning. Their words were accompanied by grins and shrugged shoulders, as though one could really do nothing more. There was no unkindness or dislike. After all, they were taking about relatives, neighbors, and the parents of some of Joe's best friends.

Besides, how could a person have disliked the kind of people who revealed themselves in later life to be alcoholics, family friends, neighbors, people at church, teachers. Early on Joe came to see them as suffering from something they could not control. This belief had, at first, prevented his understanding the pain that came with addiction, especially for those who live with the addicted. As with so much of life's mystery, Joe would have to get out in the world and live awhile before beginning to comprehend truth fully. And the truth about a life that had become unmanageable would be a hard lesson indeed.

Chapter Seven

Ted's Ikea and video game world was as different from Joe's own youth as the sixties were from the Jazz Age. A new language was needed just to compare them. The world of global warming, terrorism, and the Hubble telescope made Woodstock and the Cuban Missile Crisis seem as remote as the Surrender at Appomattox. Ted's generation couldn't even imagine the Depression, the invasion of Normandy, or Mao Tse-tung. One of them in ten knew anything about World War I or the Holocaust. The high school history books were compiled by people who knew nothing about them either other than somebody else's inaccurate account taught somewhere in a graduate seminar. Teaching history had become a way of sanitizing the past for the benefit of contemporary causes or special interest groups. As long as children had colorful books and were going through the motions of school, learning was happening to everybody's satisfaction.

Their immediate and unpredictable special-effects culture was as alien to old moral and ethical models as *Star Wars* was to Jane Austin. Science fiction and fantasy had blurred the lines of perception; material advantages had replaced everything as goals for which a life is worth living. Joe knew it. He had heard elementary school children talking about the president of the United States as though casually describing a serial murderer or cartoon character. He knew it was what they heard at home or what their teachers said at school.

Parents and other adults said and did anything in front of children these days. Children were the same, behaving like adults of no account who happened to be locked in the bodies of children. Where was restraint, self-control, respect? Where were manners? Who had respect for anything but money? He had not heard "Yes, sir" or "No, ma'am" since college. When he was a child, character was taught and modeled in families, and it made no difference how poor or wealthy people were. Joe and his friends knew respect and had manners, and they grew up wanting good manners for their own children. It was an intention not so anybody could "get" anything, but because they understood that however poor they might be, they were decent people, with feelings, and they knew that God loved them.

God. Faith was dying all across the Western world. It was dead in Europe. It was being replaced in the East by a fanaticism as evil as Western secularism was oblivious and dismissive. He had seen high school students jostling one another and arguing over chewing gum and bottled drinks as they ambled mindlessly through the Holocaust Memorial Museum in Washington. Middle school students discussed the president of the United States having sex in the Oval Office and lying about it under oath. Parents on the sidelines at athletic events talked openly of the Oral Office in front of children who were saying the same thing to each other. Rock stars and basketball players who couldn't spell their own names earned more than police officers, teachers, or social workers.

With the ebbing of faith went a certain perception of the past too. Joe knew that the standards by which he was raised had changed. The seductive screen shine of relativism was fun and profitable; what more was there to hope for. The rejection of intrinsic meaning and the beguiling freedom to which it led was a far more flexible and undemanding worldview for those who expected to assume the lifestyle for which their parents' generation worked for thirty or forty years. The lessons and guidance of the past. Where was respect? Did anybody even know what it was anymore?

Chapel at St. John's began at 7:45 a.m. Before that auspicious moment Kate and Ted must make the drive there from home, Kate must have time to park, and they had to take books and schoolbags to classrooms so there would be room to sit in the pews of the crowded chapel. Each had to get across the campus and be seated with the rest of the faculty and students by the time the Reverend Dr. Hervey made his entrance. Snow or rain added extra minutes. All this meant they must leave home by 7:10 a.m., so they got up at 6:30 a.m. and were eating a quick breakfast by ten till 7:00 a.m.

Such was the school day morning routine for the Stephensons. When Joe thought about it, his admiration for his parents soared. They had managed with six children. His friends and neighbors managed with two or three teenagers and two working parents. They were all of them doing only what they should do. It was the attitude with which they persevered, the patience and kindness, that he so admired.

Joe, who had evening meetings two or three nights each week, came down to the kitchen about 6:45 a.m. He did not want to start the day without seeing his wife and son and hearing their voices because often he would not see them again until shortly before bedtime. Conversation was always vigorously underway when he entered the kitchen, and the eternal topic was high school life at St. John's. Often they would not even pause to say hello. Joe was guilty of it too, taking for granted the myriad small courtesies and kindnesses so vital in family life and so easily undervalued. Joe would swat Ted on the shoulder, and his lanky son would respond with a clenched fist and a momentary look of fierceness. Sometimes he would swat back. He was generally always in a happy mood, especially in the mornings with the school day ahead of him. He liked school. Joe considered this a blessing and easily imagined the countless teens and parents for whom fractious school mornings set a tone for the rest of the day.

"Ted, you'd better not be late to Dan Ohrstrom's class today. He was talking yesterday about really cracking down on anybody who comes in late from now on."

"Mom, I've never been late to Mr. Ohrstrom's class. I'm on time for all my classes. Gosh!"

"Well, I'm just saying. He's on the warpath about it, so you don't want to start now."

"Don't worry!"

"Ted, what do you want for breakfast today? An Eggo? Oatmeal? Cereal?"

"Morning, Dad."

"Morning, bud."

"Ted, we've got to get moving. What do you—"

"Eggo."

"Well, you could have answered me. How am I supposed to read your mind?"

Joe looked at her closely. She avoided his smile and grew stiff as she busily unwrapped the waffle. They both looked up when she snapped the door of the microwave shut with a bang. *Am I supposed to read your mind?* How many times had Joe said the same thing, those very words, to her? A hundred thousand? Two hundred thousand?

"Any tests today, Ted? Special things coming up?" asked Joe.

"Ted, tell Dad about what happened on the field trip."

"What field trip?" said Ted, loudly folding some papers into a textbook.

"What do you mean 'what field trip'? The one everybody's been talking about all week. Where have you been?" said Kate, her arms crossed tightly, frowning.

"Mom, what are you talking about?"

She turned away, shaking her head, and glared into the microwave.

"Anything special coming up today, Ted?" Joe asked again.

"Ted, what do you want on this waffle?" said Kate.

"Mom! What everybody eats on waffles? Syrup and butter," replied Ted.

"Well, eat it fast because it's almost seven, and I don't want to be late again like we were yesterday."

"Why were you late yesterday?" asked Joe.

"Sharon Watson just *had* to pick before chapel to use the copy machine. I think she knew I was giving a quiz first period and needed to copy it."

"We left on time, Mom. I was in chapel on time. You should have copied the test the day before," said Ted as he gobbled down the yellow waffle.

"Oh, don't give me *that*! You sound just like everybody else. I have more to do than the three of us put together. It's time to go. Get ready. Joe, I need the checkbook today. I have to put gas in the van. I'm almost out."

How he wished she would bring up these things at night before when they went to bed rather than seconds before she was to leave. "If that's all you need to do, Kate, would you mind just taking a check? I'm going to the hospital in Lexington today and can stop on the way and pay the storage bill. And I'd planned to pay the car insurance and go by the grocery store for the things—"

"Just...fine, Joe. I'll take a check. Just give me one. Where's the checkbook?"

"Right there beside my briefcase on the hutch." Ted put his dishes in the sink and hoisted up a backpack of books that appeared to weigh fifty pounds. Joe walked behind him to the kitchen door and stepped down into the garage to say goodbye. Kate burst out moments later carrying an armload of pocketbooks, shopping bags, and books and bustled through the garage door toward the van, shouting to Ted to remember his soccer shoes. She did not speak to Joe. She was always hyper in the morning, and he knew that now she was angry too. He waved until her van roared out of sight at the end of the drive. He went back inside and, after a few minutes of searching, found the checkbook where Kate had tucked it, barely in sight between two stacks of magazines on the coffee table in the living room.

When Kate took the checkbook, Joe would take checks for whatever bills he intended to pay, making a list of each one he wrote and recording them all when he saw the checkbook again. Kate never balanced the account. When she took a check, he had to ask for the information every time. She would reply there was a receipt somewhere in her purse, and she would look for it later. In the beginning, Joe had seen it only as a matter of bookkeeping and expediency. The one who had to write only one check would take a check so that the one writing more than one could go ahead and record them on the spot. It seemed so simple, a mere economic allocation of time and effort. He had learned his lesson over the years, however. To Kate, the checkbook represented money, and money meant control. To someone who bristled at anything that could be interpreted as an instruction or command, unencumbered access to money was a sign of sovereignty.

Her refusal to discuss their family money or be honest with Joe about her spending had become a difficult issue. For the first two years of marriage, she had refused to deposit her paycheck into the family account or say what she was doing with it. When he questioned her about it, she grew irritable and silent, but eventually, she would deposit one or two hundred dollars into the family account without explanation or comment. For two years Joe paid all the family expenses from his own paycheck, which he deposited every two weeks into their joint account. He had opened a family savings account but was unable to put in more than a few dollars each month. Kate became evasive and changed the subject when he tried to discuss saving for a house, a rainy day, or for the child they were trying to have. When he insisted, carefully, so as not to excite sarcasm and then silence, she would promise to deposit her paycheck the next day. She never gave him a deposit slip or said whether she had followed through. He asked her to record her deposits. A look at the checkbook later would show another deposit of seventy-five or a hundred dollars. When he lost patience and pressed Kate about what she was doing with her salary, she grew angry in a way that shocked him, shouting and slamming doors and turning off lights, going to bed early and leaving him alone in the dark. In good weather, when the windows stood open, she yelled at him in front of them, positioning herself so their neighbors would hear every word. She professed not to remember anything recommended in their marriage counseling.

They rented a small brick house then, one of six identical brick bungalows tightly grouped around a circular drive, built in the early 1950s. Voices raised from windows or porches could be heard by everyone. Most of the other renters were older and retired. The neighbors on both sides, married for fifty years, waved at Kate and moved on. She moved quickly between the house and her car without looking around. Joe wondered whether she did not see the neighbors waving at her or was making an effort to avoid them. With Joe, they made eye contact and smiled encouragingly, letting him know by a pat on the back or a grin that every marriage had its adjustment period, and they knew what he was going through. He was embarrassed, but he knew they were doing the best they could to be good neighbors. When he asked Kate why she did not wave to the elderly neighbors or otherwise acknowledge them, she grew indignant.

"I do, Joe. You just didn't see me."

In those days, he was starting a law practice, a profession that would support their family for the rest of their lives. He found himself trying to explain to Kate the nuances, as he understood them, of reputations in small towns, the diplomacy of living in close quarters with other people, matters he never imagined would require explanation, and how their behavior affected their family reputation and his budding professional standing. He talked calmly to her, striving not to let his anxiety show. The calmer and more reasonable he tried to be, the harsher she became. She grew increasingly sarcastic, a quality he had never seen in her before their marriage. In the amiable, eager Kate he had known, or thought he knew, in the years before they married, he had never encountered the sarcastic responses and routine scorn for almost everything with which she related to him now. It was like trying to reason with a rebellious teenager. She claimed he was interested only in himself and his precious work. For an adult who had been raised in a small town, she showed no sign of understanding small-town culture, society, or relationships. It was the first few years of marriage. He told himself it would get better. Every couple went through adjustments. Her evening anger seemed to dissipate in sleep. The next day she was composed and agreeable as though nothing had occurred the night before. She remained in a good mood as long as Joe brought up no unpleasant subjects and listened attentively while she talked ceaselessly about her teaching.

When Kate took the family checkbook for a few days, she would write a dozen checks. One of them was always for cash. Together they totaled several hundred dollars, sometimes more. Joe said nothing about it at first, even though she was withholding her own paycheck, assuming it was all just part of settling down in a marriage and in a new community. But it always happened again before the end of the month. These unexpected expenditures made it impossible to follow the family budget he was trying to set up. He began routinely paying family bills and balancing the checkbook when he saw that Kate was paying no attention to the budget. In any case, it seemed pointless to expect her to involve herself with family finances as long as she was withholding her own paycheck.

When they were overdrawn two months in a row, he tried to talk with her again. Her reaction was so severe that he began to fear bringing up again anything likely to upset her. And he was rapidly learning, or thought he was, what those issues were. So long as he did not try to make an issue of them, she was peaceful, pleasant, and affectionate. His common sense told him the issues already existed, and his growing reluctance (or outright fear) of bringing them up with her might be a bigger problem than her angry reaction. He knew he was part of the problem; he had to be as he was new to marriage too. Whenever he spread out the bills on the kitchen table and spent an evening paying them and balancing their family account, Kate would go upstairs to read or turn on the television.

Even after their time in marriage counseling with the provocative Stan Wiley, Joe had to acknowledge that he knew little about Kate's personal finances or the way she managed money. He knew that Catherine had paid all her expenses in college and graduate school. He did not learn until after their marriage that Kate had no savings and that she had withdrawn her teacher's pension and spent it on their wedding. It was all quite different from Joe's limited experience with money, for his large family had had to struggle to make ends meet. He borrowed what he needed for school, paying it back over the years, working even in college at a variety of jobs. Although he worried about planning for their future, it was not dollars and cents that concerned him. It was honesty, openness, truth. It was a hunger for intimacy.

It made Joe feel lonely. When there was intimacy or when they did anything together, he perceived in himself a small cool spot of doubt, as though discovering suddenly that an old friend whom he thought he had known had all along been a heroin addict or gay. A small but intense sense of wonder and disappointment grew in him toward Kate and at himself as well for being so, what, unobservant? naive? dumb? blind? That there was a side of Kate he had never known, had never even guessed at, and wasn't getting to know as the months passed, was becoming clearer to him. He understood that managing money was only a symptom. The real issue was different. It made him feel very foolish, like learning at last a family secret that should have been obvious before, even to a child. Her moods frightened him because he didn't understand them, and Kate clearly saw no reason to talk about any of it. It was about then (he could never be sure exactly when it started) that he realized Kate was using a phrase he would come to hear in his dreams: "Get over it!"

Spending time together, doing things as husband and wife, was more important and puzzling a problem than their finances. He could have all the time with her he wanted as long as he was prepared to participate in her high school routine. Every Friday and Saturday night, she said she was expected to be present at athletic events, school dances and plays, student fund-raisers, faculty social events, and other public school affairs. She told him it was part of her contract. All the teachers worked that way. He went along with it, cheerful and positive because it obviously made her happy to be in the school environment and with the students, and she was clearly pleased that he was there with her. But he soon grew tired of it. The other teachers were pleasant and good company, but conversation never seemed to diverge from school matters. Often it was hard to distinguish students from faculty; they all dressed alike, especially on weekend nights. He tried to fit in, but he found himself hungering for adult company and conversation and for social activities that did not center on teenagers. In trying to discuss this too, he found himself facing an impenetrable wall.

"It's part of my job," said Kate. "I'll go by myself if you don't want to. So get over it!"

He wanted more than anything for her to be happy. He loved her in spite of everything and he never, even when they argued, regretted their marriage. She was his wife. He considered himself fortunate, blessed, that she had married him. It was his duty to do everything he could for her. He began to understand that her happiness depended upon things going her way and his own discretion in making that happen.

They had settled in Jeffersonville, where he had lived for a few months before their marriage and where he was practicing law. He was still getting to know his professional colleagues and his community. He was learning about himself and how to be a good husband. He wondered and worried about how to make Kate happy, staring out the window of his office and claiming to be thinking over cases when someone interrupted. Had her emotional life fluctuated all along, or was he the cause of it? What would be helpful? He did not know where to go for advice. Old Wiley was hundreds of miles away. He knew that the decent older lawyers would have advised him as best they could, but he was reluctant to ask them. He felt he was already in danger of wearing out their patience in seeking their professional guidance with his few cases. It was not in Joe's nature to be intrusive, even as a lawyer.

In his heart he knew that part of it too was plain old pride. Out of loyalty to his new wife, he was reluctant to discuss details of their marriage with anyone, even such relatively neutral matters as family finances. Wasn't it too early to be dealing with troubles? No, they were after all in the period of adjustment. Everyone went through it. It would be years before he understood that seeing the subject as neutral, in spite of Mr. Wiley's good counseling about power and symbolism, was a measure of how much he had to learn. His larger fear, and of this he knew he should be ashamed, was that seeking someone else's guidance would make him appear incapable of managing his own affairs. He feared being seen as an amateur. Who would want to consult an attorney who could not even manage his own family matters? He was ashamed of himself.

He found some comfort in his friends in Jeffersonville. The other young lawyers were struggling too. They talked together at lunch and after work in one another's offices. They were decent, earnest men and women, young idealists with common sense and whose experiences in the law, especially in the courtroom, were strengthening their good judgment and thickening their skin. One of them, like Joe, had recently married, and Joe and Kate joined them several times each month for dinner or drinks. Wade Chester's calm temperament and good humor were soothing for Joe's anxiety. Kate enjoyed Wade and his pretty wife, Nancy, for the same reasons Joe did; they were good company and, as his parents would have said, "down to earth and plain as an old shoe," an estimable compliment. Jeffersonville had been a good place to begin married life all those years ago, and their friends there had been a blessing.

* * *

Soon after Kate's van had disappeared, Joe came out of the house dressed for work and drove into Catoctin Springs. It was a fine, dry day, and he wished he had the courage to cancel all his appointments and spend it on the Appalachian Trail or hiking along the river. A month ago he had heard about an abandoned road that wound from Macy's Glen up to the top of Gold's Knob to what the locals called the Fields, a big bald spot on the crest south of Boyd's Rocks. It was visible from the valleys on both sides of the mountains. They said you could follow the old road up to the top in less than two hours, and from there it was a fairly level hike north along the ridge to the rock outcroppings. The view was said to be worth the effort it took to get there. He thought of Winslow Homer's romantic views of the Adirondacks. Or was it the Catskills?

Three families had farmed up in the Fields a hundred and fifty years ago. There was nobody left there now, and the state had abandoned the road. Such places made Joe want to cancel everything and put on his hiking boots. The history, wild beauty, and rugged loneliness of the mountains reminded him of central Virginia and restored his spirits. Around the old places lingered a character intense as prayer. The vanished people had known all the pitfalls of a hard life. He could imagine the log houses with smoke blowing from stone chimneys, June apples in the yard, dirt paths swept clean daily, the spring, a woodpile, chickens, blackberries. He supposed the Fields had been taken over by redbud and dogwood. The old chimneys stood defiantly still above the uneven ground. It must be lovely in the spring and early summer. Imagining it created a reverie that lasted all the way into town.

What remained of the Redeemer church yard was compressed snugly behind the church and crowded round by contiguous dingy buildings and the old graveyard. Sectioned into a dozen precious parking spaces reserved for clergy, staff, and workers in the church day care center, the small parking lot spread between overhanging trees. Across a half-dozen spaces on this particular morning was strewn a ragged array of soiled underwear, empty food containers, and lumpy plastic bags, all apparently spilled from a damp sleeping bag whose yellowish stuffing had come loose and was drifting about like snowflakes. Joe parked on one side and pulled a crinkled grocery bag from beneath his front seat and began to pick up the trash. Some of it had blown under the bright red Mazda belonging to Milly, the parish secretary, who had arrived ahead of him and already gone inside. Or perhaps she had parked over it. Homeless people and some drunks had taken to sleeping under the overhanging buildings surrounding the little parking lot. Several times each week, they apparently got into fights, and somebody's meager belongings would end up all over the place for Joe to clean up the following day. Milly refused to touch any of it, fearing she would die of AIDS before she got home that night. The sexton worked only at night, and Joe was unwilling to leave the mess there all day. It was a recent problem. Since homeless people had become a local phenomenon four or five years before, none had dared sleep near the church for fear of the old cemetery and its clusters of tilting gravestones. But the homeless had become less superstitious of late and more destructive too. The recent installation of a motion-sensitive floodlight above the parking lot had only made matters worse. "See bettah now, fight mo' easy," said Wilmar the Honduran sexton to Milly, who was not at all amused. Joe had left his card and notes atop the sad evidence on many occasions, advising that he would be glad to meet them, help them find food, shelter. The sight of their pitiful small piles and filthy bedrolls saddened him. Nobody ever responded. After working late on many nights, he would walk around the parking lot before going home, always without finding anyone. The following morning, a dozen beer bottles lay shattered over the parking places. The police had never been able to catch anyone.

"Don't put that smelly thing in here," cried Milly as Joe entered with the garbage bag through the rear office door. After pretending to deposit it on her desk, he carried it to the kitchen and dropped it into one of the big day care trash cans. While he was in the kitchen, two of the women who prepared the children's lunches asked to speak with him. He accompanied them to a far corner of the parish hall and listened again to their lament of how "low on money" they were and how long it would be until the end of the month. He had visited their homes when they were sick or when someone had died and was astounded at their ability to get along, with dependent relatives and endless problems, on so little. In their world, a broken fuel pump or emergency room visit destroyed for months the precarious balance of earnings and handouts on which they survived.

This time, Clarence somebody had dozed off with a cigarette and burned up the sofa, creating smoke damage for which the landlord had raised the rent, and it came at a bad time because Tina's asthma was acting up again, and Carla had demanded twenty dollars to drive her into Frederick to the doctor, and Arthur was not on speaking terms with Marleen, so they couldn't get any more rides from him, and...

He went into his office and spent ten minutes on the phone with the Food Lion manager who promised that his assistant manager would accept the church's check so the women could buy groceries after work. Like everybody else who needed assistance, the kitchen women preferred cash, and Joe knew it, but they had long ago accepted his explanation that he would write no checks for cash from his discretionary account.

He was hanging up when Milly came in to say that Emma Tarbaugh, an elderly parishioner with a hot temper, was waiting to see him, "and she ain't the least bit happy." He reminded Milly to let him know when the chief of police arrived, his next scheduled appointment. Mrs. Tarbaugh was shown in. She advanced fiercely toward his desk, glaring at the floor to avoid looking at him. Milly glanced over Mrs. Tarbaugh's fuzzy gray head and rolled her eyes up as she closed the door.

After announcing that she was "moving over to the Methodists or maybe even the Presbyterians" and threatening other iniquities, the old lady, white with anger, accepted a seat and steamed silently while he gave her a few minutes to compose herself and declare what had riled her so. She began to talk about how God was a "he" and how ashamed Joe should be of himself to dare to say otherwise. Her father had called God "he." Her mother had called God "he." Every preacher that preceded him at Redeemer had said "he." Joe listened to every word, and then they talked.

In a forum on the previous Sunday, Joe had been asked an excellent question by, as usual, one of the teenagers. If God was male and we were made in God's image, how about women? They must not be made in God's image, right?

Joe had begun by thanking the teenager for the question. Inside his head, he was busy thanking God as well. It was what his wise seminary professors called a teaching moment, and a splendid one too. He waited while the exclamations subsided and took note, with regret, of the angry exit in the rear of two very bright young feminists who believed, he knew, that their noisy departure was an important statement. He had then replied that God was the creator of everything in the universe. Human sexuality was part of the universe. God transcended everything God had made and was not bound by it or subject to it. God was not bound or limited by concepts of human sexuality and was, therefore, neither male nor female. He said that Jesus had lived in a patriarchal culture where it was natural to refer to the Lord as male. He had taken pains to explain again that human sexuality was part of God's created order. God had given it to us as a gift. God was not subject to, or necessarily defined by, his own creation because God exists outside God's own created order. Being made in God's image was the biblical way of saying that human beings have free will, we are free to make our own choices, and that we are the means through which God's own will is realized.

This had generated much sincere discussion. As in all church discussions of sensitive issues, Joe paid careful attention to the ones who sat with their arms crossed and mouths tightly closed. Of these few, one had apparently reported to Mrs. Tarbaugh, who had not been present. Joe wondered who else was upset and hoped they would have Emma's character and come to see him.

By the time Milly entered to say Chief Hughes had arrived, Emma Tarbaugh was not wholly mollified, but she had been listened to, and she could tell that Joe had taken her seriously.

"There have been changes enough in the past twenty years to drive all of us crazy, Emma. God is the same, though. If we speak of God in different ways, it means only that we're trying harder these days to understand." Joe felt a special affection for the older parishioners whose faith life, language, and all else had been changed, rearranged, modified, manipulated, and molded by distant hands. It had all been done in ways that confounded their hearts and troubled their intellects. As they grew closer to the day when Joe assured them they would stand face-to-face with Christ, they wanted reassurance and plenty of it. There had been enough changes.

The chief, an affable Methodist, wanted to discuss an idea he had brought back from a sheriffs' meeting in Philadelphia. He hoped to organize community block parties in three or four of the poorest sections of the community, something with food, music, games—a celebration in which the neighborhoods could take pride and work together. His pastor had wanted to form a committee of elders and conduct a series of meetings to determine whether or not it would be a good idea. The police chaplain, who was in charge of a local independent Bible church, doubted he could find enough people to help, "since it might get racial and all." Would Joe consider working with the chief to get it going and hopefully plan the first one for the second weekend of the following month? Was it possible? Could it be done?

Joe told the chief a joke, and he laughed until his face was red. After squirming around to assure himself that the door was closed, the chief told Joe such a good joke that they both laughed until they began to cough. Then they talked about food and music. The chief had brought a town map, and they consulted this and Joe's calendar. Joe made telephone calls, and the chief used Milly's phone for a while, and between the two of them, they arranged to meet with the mayor, the manager of the Food Lion and Giant, and two local black preachers whose small churches were in the communities in question. They would all meet on Thursday afternoon at Redeemer and get started. The chief departed, relieved and encouraged.

Joe followed him out of the parking lot and drove to the hospital to make his rounds. It took twice as long as he had planned because a gaggle of busy nurses surrounded the bed of each patient he intended to visit, and in each case, Joe waited outside in the corridor until they had finished their duties. The nurses, taking no notice of him, ambled out of each room speaking to one another and without saying whether they had more to do, were coming right back, or that he could enter. Hospital visits were delicate matters. If one were preoccupied with other concerns, nobody would detect it quicker than a hospitalized patient who could well interpret it as disinterest. Joe always preferred to sit in order to meet the patient on eye level rather than joining the rest of the world by towering over them. Sitting was not always possible. He prayed with all four patients, raising his voice over the televisions near the neighboring beds so the prayers could be heard. Mostly he listened, maintaining eye contact and holding hands when they would allow him to. Before leaving, he tucked his card into the frame of the bulletin boards on the walls near the beds.

As he left the hospital, he met in the parking lot the grown daughter of one of the elderly patients he had visited moments before. She had just come from Joe's office, and she was crying. A doctor had called that morning to say her father's cancer was inoperable and that he had maybe another two months to live, at most. Joe thought of him, weak and cheerful several floors above, and how he held Joe's hand tightly until a nurse came in to change his drip. Joe and the distraught daughter drank a cup of coffee together in the hospital cafeteria and talked. She wanted him with her when she spoke with her father and was terrified of telling him. More than the news itself, or her father's hearing it, she feared the reaction of her invalid mother, whose heart was weak and who was waiting across town in a nursing home to know what was going on. As they went up in the elevator to her father's floor, the daughter grew quiet, drawing upon all her strength to be strong for her father.

Joe returned to the office to proof the rough draft of the bulletin for the coming Sunday. Milly needed it by early afternoon in order to have time to complete the monthly parish newsletter, which had to be mailed by noon of the following day. The antiquated office copier required much coaxing and patience, and it would be a year or more before the parish could afford to replace it. He wondered which would break down first, Milly or the copier. Joe circled errors in red on the rough draft, noting that the hymns for the coming Sunday were the same ones they had sung the previous Sunday. He called the elderly organist, but there was no answer. He turned to the phone calls he had intended to return that morning when Emma had appeared. Three parishioners wanted appointments. The finance committee meeting had to be rescheduled because the new chair had a hospital board meeting. A local Baptist minister wanted him to call but left no message as to why. The editor of the newspaper, an intelligent, good-natured young woman whom Joe especially admired, had called to ask him to attend a historic preservation meeting with her. The principal of a local high school had called, leaving no message. Three calls were from people whose names Joe did not recognize. As he shuffled through these messages, Milly came in to say the bishop's secretary had just called to remind him he was expected to be at the diocesan Worship Commission meeting the next day in Conyers. Conyers was two hundred miles away. Joe called back immediately to explain he was not a member of the Worship Commission. The bishop's secretary, unusually cool, replied she was just doing what the bishop told her to do, and she would take it up with him when he returned late in the afternoon.

He drove over to Lexington in the rich, elegant sunlight of early afternoon. As he watched the road, his eyes kept drifting over the land, drinking in the intoxicating champagne tones that invaded and caressed the countryside like the light enfolding Renoir's soft model in *La Boulangere,* or thirty years before in *Country Road.* The world was so beautiful, so thrillingly, ecstatically, achingly beautiful. He thought of an indigent mother who had come with her daughter to his office a week before. The woman's rugged face had beguiled him with its resignation, as though she understood the world clearly and anticipated trouble and rejection. It was one of those disconcerting worn faces that, when watched with care, glimmers now and then with traces of a youthful loveliness. A radiance still glowed in the olive look of the morose daughter, perhaps ten years old, whose solemn features and silent green eyes made him think of Portugese children he had seen playing along the waterfront in Provincetown. He could see his beloved art teacher Jenny who spent her summers painting on the Cape. This girl looked like Jen's portraits of the children of Provincetown. The child's face had changed as he talked with her mother like the land brightens and darkens under the shadows of drifting clouds, unexpectedly, relentlessly, and the chief emotion it roused in him was regret, regret at the ugliness of human greed in this world and at the inevitable way we all get caught up in the brokenness. He had put the mother and daughter into a motel for the night and then on a bus to Baltimore, traveling like gypsies, for that was what he thought they were, to their next temporary refuge. He had watched them board the bus quietly, sitting down by a window without looking out at him even though he stood just below them, humiliated, he supposed, to be once again the recipients of a handout. Or perhaps it made no difference to them. He was someone they would never see again. They owed him nothing, not even a look and certainly not a smile. He remembered all this and once again felt only regret, dull and colorless, regret that the world was no better than it was. Why did he dwell on such things on such a lovely day?

He stopped at Potomac Junction long enough to pay the monthly bill for the family storage bin and buy a cup of coffee and a newspaper at the 7-Eleven. He drove on to the hospital near Lexington. One of his parishioners worked there, a radiologist well-known in the area and much respected. He was a very intelligent man, and Joe admired him and his wife for their cheerful, easygoing way with people. He admired them especially for their good manners in all circumstances. Two of their children went to school with Ted and were quite popular. In spite of long years in the community and their success in so many endeavors, he knew that Stuart and Jane

Holloway would prefer a busy metropolitan community, where they might have been happier. But the children were in school, his practice was flourishing, her interior design business was going well, and moving was just too complicated.

At a Christmas party a few years before, the Holloways and Joe had discussed the season and how good it was to see happy faces. Kate had said she had nothing to wear to a Christmas party and had gone over to St. John's to help hang a student art exhibit. Years before, Joe had started going out socially without her occasionally. Stuart Holloway had commented upon an increased incidence of depression in his patients. Joe commented on some mental health statistics about holiday depression and had then admitted to his own depression over the years and how medication had given him some relief from time to time. The three of them had talked for a half hour or so about depression until they were joined by the hostess, who insisted they come and join a group who were making plans for New Year's Eve.

Now the doctor himself was talking. Aware of growing depression in his own life, and at the urging of his wife, he had talked it all over with Joe several times during the past month. This time, they were meeting in his office.

"Stan," said Joe, gazing around at the diplomas, citations, and licenses lining the office walls, "good lord! You're as bad as I am. How many of these things did you make up on your computer?"

"They all seemed worth it at the time. Now I can't even recall getting most of them," said Holloway, who grinned and looked around like someone in a museum. "Sometimes I look around in here and wonder who earned them all."

They were silent for a moment. Joe leaned back and stared at the ceiling. "So little done. So much to do," he said aloud, knowing it had been said by someone on his deathbed but not remembering who.

Stan cleared his throat and said slowly, "Of course, with Jane and the children, looking back is impossible. I mean, I can't even imagine life any different. But I keep thinking what we should have done was go off and spend our lives in Doctors without Borders or open a clinic in the goddam Belgian Congo or somewhere. *That* would have made a difference."

Joe was conscious that this role reversal was difficult for Stan, whether he was aware of it or not. "I think I know the answer to this," said Joe, still looking at the ceiling, "but bear with me. What 'difference' do you mean?"

Stan waited a good three or four minutes before saying, "I could have died and felt I had done something important."

There was another pause. Joe stood and walked to the window. "With me," he said, "it's a house on a farm somewhere. I would get a big old place and fix it up, then Kate and I would move in and take in a dozen foster children. Children who needed a home. We'd raise them, see them through school, celebrate holidays and birthdays, help with homework, take care of them when they were sick, give them a real home, and then send them off when they were ready to live their lives in the world. Then, I think I could stand before God and hear the words 'Well done.'"

"I know," said Stan. "Jane says she knows how I feel. She says it's just our time of life. She has a better handle on it than I do."

"How about Bill Kelley? Have you seen him like you promised?" said Joe.

"Yes, and you were right. He was very helpful. He made a lot of sense. You were right about a psychologist instead of a psychiatrist. I'm going back to see him next week. And I'm going to go ahead and take the Zoloft. You're right. It's just my pride."

"God blessed us with the gift of reason, Stan. That makes it possible for us to create drugs. It's one of the ways God heals us. Medicines, doctors, nurses, psychologists, public health nurses... even radiologists!"

Stan smiled. "I've never thought of myself as a tool of God."

"God works through you in a way that brings comfort to hundreds, hundreds of people. Most of us need to be reminded at times to get out of the way and let God do his thing through us. There is power in it. And I agree with Jane. Look at us, at our age, with children almost grown, launched far into our careers..."

"Yes, some people I know have launched into several careers," said Stan with a grin, looking at Joe.

"And we've lived to tell about it," said Joe. "One day, Stan, you and Jane and Kate and I will be laying back on a beach in the Bahamas, drinking a big cool rum and pineapple or whatever, with nothing but the fun times ahead, saying 'It was worth it after all,' and some little island honey with big tits come up and serve us a fresh cold one..."

"And wearing a see-through grass skirt," said Stan, "and the children at their desks back here in the States ready to send us a goddam check as soon as we call." Stan laughed again, but only a little. And then he said, in a completely different way, "I look forward to some *time*, Joe."

"Believe me," said Joe. "I understand."

* * *

Joe prayed on the way back to Catoctin Springs, as he often did in his car. He prayed again for Stan. When they had prayed together before he left his office, Stan had been visibly moved. Although he had seen them in praying with hundreds of people over the years, tears always rather stunned Joe, like opening a coarse sea shell and finding a pearl. He prayed for all doctors and nurses and healing professionals and then for all decent people who long for clarity. He prayed for Kate and Ted and for his mother and brothers and sisters and their families and for the people he had seen that morning in the hospital. He prayed for the women in the day care kitchen and for the gypsy mother and her lost daughter. Sometimes prayer was cleansing and energizing. At other times, he found it only deepened life's frustrations. Sometimes he couldn't pray at all. But he prayed now as massive tractor trailers roared past him and frantic drivers, as though in a race, swerved their cars in and out of the lanes ahead without giving signals.

Stan and Jane had said many times how helpful it was to Stan to be able to talk with Joe and how grateful they were for Joe's ministry at Redeemer. Stan was reasonable, intelligent, faithful, and decent.

Joe knew Stan had no idea how healing their talks were for him too. The faces of the gypsy woman and her daughter drifted through his mind again, something in them recalling Eakins' *Mrs. Siddons*, a pain so numbing no words could touch it. Once again he felt regret, anesthetizing and serious, at how wrong it all was. Kate's face floated into view with the look of anger she had worn as she hurried through the garage that morning. And he saw something else, Ted's sweet face as he listened to his mother rant about Joe all the way to St. John's. "No!" he shouted aloud in the small car. "She would not do that. It would be hurting her own child." At these words, other images crowded in like furtive owls gliding and banking in his inner darkness, only just seen and then gone. He winced and shook his head.

He felt around on the front seat under the books and newspapers until he found a cassette tape in a broken plastic box. He looked quickly for the side he wanted and shoved it into the dashboard. In seconds, the car was filled with the liquid romantic notes, like pearls falling on amber, of the second movement of Mozart's Piano Concerto No. 20. It was one of his favorite recordings, a performance in April 1978 of the London Symphony Orchestra conducted by Sir Colin Davis. He played it three times on his way over the mountain and then played the whole concerto through until the last movement brought him back to the Redeemer parking lot.

Milly had gone for the day and had left a pile of notes and phone messages on his chair. There was no message from the bishop or his secretary. He tried calling the diocesan office but got only a recorded message. He called a priest in another town who served on the Worship Committee, but her secretary said she had gone for the day. He called her home, but her daughter said she had left for Conyers, for a committee meeting the following morning. He called the church in Conyers. Nobody answered.

He had hoped to have time to work on his sermon for the following Sunday. It was almost five o'clock, and he had to buy groceries before going home. He knew the Food Lion would be crowded. He was getting a headache. He wondered if he would have to get up at 4:30 a.m. and drive two hundred miles to meet the bishop. He wondered if Kate was still mad. He thought about lying down on the floor of his office and closing his eyes. He sat down and leaned on his desk with his face in his hands until he heard the rattle of a key in the office door, heralding the entry of any one of a dozen people. A familiar, cheerful voice called his name, and a smiling Harry Campos, the senior warden, entered. Joe felt better immediately.

Of the many decent people he counted as friends, Harry Campos and his family had special places in Joe's heart. Harry was devoted to the community, the church, and his neighbors. He had served in the legislature and local government for years and knew half the people in the state. He was one of the many who had gone out of his way to make the Stephensons feel welcomed. Kate and Ted loved him like an uncle. Harry was one of those parishioners upon whose judgment and instincts clergy could rely. Of the utmost value to Joe, and to clergy who had preceded Joe at Redeemer, was Harry's willingness to be plain-spoken and prompt in discussing sensitive issues. He was the sort of man anyone would treasure as a next-door neighbor.

Joe listened as Harry apprised him of a curious conversation. Winston McLaughlin, a retired clergyman, had spoken to Harry in the early afternoon and asked him to caution Joe about something he had overheard, although Harry was unable to say from whom or where. The specter of hearsay aroused Joe's natural suspicion as a lawyer, which Harry recognized and acknowledged while waving for Joe to hear him out. Joe knew the way things were handled in the diocese, he knew Harry, and he knew the retired priest, so he listened carefully to every word. Apparently the bishop was very irritated with Joe, believing for some reason that Joe had caused a number of Redeemer's members to leave the church in anger. They objected, it seemed, to the way Joe was mishandling his discretionary fund. So serious did the bishop view the matter that he intended to give Joe a lecture and was planning to summon him to a meeting in Conyers within a day or two. What in the world was all this about? Harry wanted to know. He did not mean to alarm Joe, but he wanted him to know what he had heard, and old Winston McLaughlin felt that Joe should be warned too.

Joe's first response was to thank Harry for warning him. The two of them talked for a half hour. The discretionary fund was of no concern to either one of them because Joe recorded every check with ample annotations. The bank statements were given to the treasurer every month, and Harry himself audited the account four times each year. All this Joe had put in place when he learned, shortly after arriving, that the Internal Revenue Service had audited the Redeemer discretionary fund during the previous rector's tenure. Nobody had left Redeemer and, in fact, attendance had been increasing since Joe's arrival. They talked until, at the same moment, they looked at each other and Harry gazed at the floor and said, in a weary way, "Lottie."

Joe got out a recent issue of the diocesan newspaper and consulted the bishop's printed schedule. The board of directors of the seminary had met on Friday of the previous week. They looked at one another and shook their heads.

Lottie Bascomb, a longtime Redeemer member, had disliked Joe from the time he came for his first interview. She had been the only Search Committee member to vote against him. The other eleven members had chosen Joe over her objections. She had responded by refusing to speak to him during his first year at Redeemer, creating a number of awkward and unpleasant situations. As the months passed and Joe refused to respond to her in kind, continuing to treat her politely, her animosity toward him grew increasingly bitter. She found no comrades in the congregation, and her troops had dwindled down to four other perennially unhappy detractors. Joe counted it as a blessing that there were only five against him in a congregation so large. His self-esteem was bolstered too by knowing that Lottie had treated all but one of his predecessors the same way. One former Redeemer priest, now a bishop in a distant diocese, had gone out of his way to warn Joe about her. In spite of this behavior, or maybe because of it, and her crafty way of ingratiating herself with those in power, the last two bishops had taken Lottie willingly into their confidence and appointed her to a number of diocesan positions. One of these was as a representative to the seminary board. Most parishioners knew that Lottie, at each meeting, poured into the bishop's willing ear a stream of invective against Joe. Joe could always tell when the bishop had recently spent time with Lottie. He would treat Joe like a man with an infectious disease, and he was critical to the point of rudeness. Bishop Spencer in his home diocese would never have reacted this way.

Joe had perceived in each of Lottie's children the signs of depression he had recognized years before in his special education students. Parishioners assured him they behaved the same way at school and in other places, where their perpetual frowns and bad manners generally warned away adults who might have reached out to them. They were especially sullen toward Joe, slouching and sulking their way through their acolyte duties and refusing to acknowledge him when he greeted them. Searching for some way to form a pastoral relationship, Joe continued to speak affably to them and listen when they spoke to the other children in his presence. Lottie's twelve-year-old son had mentioned to a friend in Joe's presence that he was finally going to take guitar lessons, a birthday gift from his parents. Joe had wished him a happy birthday and said something encouraging about the lessons, and the boy had, for the first time, spoken civilly to him. The following day Joe had sent him a check for ten dollars, drawn on his discretionary fund, and marked, "For guitar lessons. Happy Birthday!" He and Harry concluded that this gesture, intended as a pastoral connection, could be traced through Lottie to the bishop's displeasure.

Joe accompanied Harry to the side entrance, thanking him again for the discussion and promising to keep him informed of whatever was going to happen. As he was asking about Harry's wife, he pushed open the office door and an envelope, stuck behind the outside handle, dropped to the floor. Harry picked it up and handed it to him, saying he was sure it would all work out. As he went down the steps to the street, he turned and exclaimed in exasperation how trifling and unfair it all was and how personally sorry he was that it was happening at Redeemer and to Joe. He departed, leaving everything feeling more decent and wholesome for his presence.

He returned to his desk, wondering what to do. His side hurt. He dreaded the prospect of a two-hundred-mile drive to Conyers more than the confrontation with the bishop. His interminable feeling of fatigue had grown over the years until he could hardly remember what it felt like to be well-rested. He would be all right driving over in the early morning, drinking coffee. It was the dreadful drive back that worried him, the struggle to remain alert, the need to pull over and sleep every so often. He sat down and looked out the window. After a moment, he reached for the phone to call Kate.

The envelope at the door lay faceup in front of him, addressed to "Rev. Stephenson" in a clumsy big hand. He opened it and read.

"Dear Rev. Stephenson, I am sending you your check back to you because this is not what the discretionary fund should be used for. You are supposed to use it for poor people who need food or medicine. You are not supposed to use it to give gifts for kids. Please put the ten dollars back and use it for the purpose it was intended. Yours truly, John Bascomb." Joe's check was in the envelope too.

* * *

In the neighboring county was an affluent congregation, an anomaly in the diocese, in a fine old church almost as old as Redeemer. The parish priest was an able, decent sort who had been born in the diocese and served there throughout his career. He was respected and especially well-liked by the bishop, and among the clergy, it was known that the Reverend Walter Lewis had "the bishop's ear." This was helpful to everybody because Walt Lewis was a fair man with a sense of humor.

It was almost six o'clock. Wendy Lewis answered the phone, and Joe apologized profusely for having to disturb them at home, and especially for calling at the dinner hour. The pleasant Mrs. Lewis told him to call anytime and then summoned her husband from the backyard, where he was feeding the dogs. Joe explained his situation. Lewis listened, breaking in a few times with questions. Joe was perfectly willing to call the bishop at home and take the matter up with him by telephone and was willing to take whatever consequences might come. He stated clearly his determination to convince the bishop, once and for all, how destructive his listening to Lottie Bascomb had become and how the bishop was one of the very few people who did not recognize the truth about her. As Walt knew the bishop well (and as someone who could be trusted, although Joe did not complicate matters by adding this), Joe wanted his guidance. Should he clear his calendar and make the long drive the following morning and discuss it all in person, or should he try to do so tonight by calling the bishop's home?

Lewis had known Lottie Bascomb for years and was familiar with her tactics. He agreed that she had probably dictated her son's letter. He advised Joe to go home. He would call the bishop himself and call Joe at home later in the evening and give him a report.

Joe thanked him. He checked the locks on all the outside doors and went down to the parking lot. He had a headache, and he was very hungry. The prospect of going to the grocery store was discouraging because he knew that he would encounter a half-dozen people who would want to talk. The thought of dealing with anyone else right now made his side and head feel worse. They could get along all right for another day or so at home without the groceries, but he knew that Kate would see it as evidence that he had not needed the checkbook that day after all and had only been trying to inconvenience her. But he needed to go home and be with his own family. He looked around the parking lot for a moment and thought of the homeless people who would gather there after dark, seeking, he supposed, the same kind of thing he needed.

He stopped at the convenience store on Church Street, where the old Redeemer had stood two centuries before, and went in to buy coffee. Sometimes caffeine helped his headaches. He stood in the pleasant, cool evening air in front of the store for a few minutes with Sandra, a waitress at the Third Base who lived nearby. Her young son, taciturn and disheveled, would not look at Joe in spite of his mother's earnest threats, and spent the whole time leaning against her with his face mashed into her crotch.

The clerk in the store had commented, with genuine concern, on how tired Joe looked. As he stood in front of the store, Sandra told him kindly that she though he needed a vacation and asked him if he was sick. At this, her grubby child extracted his face long enough to glance quickly at Joe, hoping no doubt to observe him in the act of vomiting.

He drank a few sips of coffee on the way home, thinking how nice it would be to spend an evening with Kate and Ted and hoping Kate had heard a new joke from one of the other teachers. He was convinced that lawyers heard the best jokes, and he longed for the old days when, even in the most tense and trying situations, somebody—another lawyer, a police officer or deputy, some of the judges, his clients, a court clerk, a bailiff—in the system would have a new joke. In the old days, when most law offices had a Watts line, a joke told in San Diego on Monday would be told in Washington on Tuesday afternoon. The clergy were different. Some of them were very different, and Joe wondered at times whether they had a sense of humor at all. When you found clergy however who could tell a joke, and take a joke, they could be as bold and undeterred as the most personable lawyer. In every diocese and at every clergy conference, such amiable people could be identified, and Joe had found them excellent company. This was especially true of some of the old-timers who, like the experienced lawyers, had seen it all and known all types of people and problems. Faces drifted through his mind. Glimpsing them made him feel better. Kate was good at jokes if she was in the right mood. Some people could tell a joke, and others simply could not. He wondered if the internet was responsible. Who needed to tell a joke when you could send it to everybody with the pressing of a key. Like telling stories, jokes might be a dying art.

He got out of the car very glad to see Cory. The happy dog, true to his lineage, could tell by looking and listening that his buddy Joe had had a long day. Cory looked at him intently, wagging his tail and whining in sympathy as Joe took his briefcase and coffee cup out of the car. With Cory leading the way and glancing back at him every few steps, Joe walked around to the garage door. He stood for a moment in the yellow glow of the bug lamp, breathing in the cool air deeply before going in. His forehead felt tight and stretched, and the back of his head throbbed like a small drum.

"Are you ready for this?" shouted Kate, as he entered. "You'll never guess what happened!"

"What, honey…," said Joe, standing in the bright kitchen in his raincoat, holding his briefcase and coffee, blinking like a pedestrian in the path of a bus.

"Well, I go in this morning and check my box, which I hadn't checked yesterday because of the fire drill, and here's this note from Gretchen saying that all department heads have to get their budget requests in for next semester at the end of this week! I mean, I haven't even opened the catalogues yet, and now I have three days to get it in. They must think we're robots or something. They told us last fall that we had till this coming Monday morning, so I had planned to spend all this coming weekend getting it ready, but now I've got to have it ready by Friday. With everything else I've got to do! And do you know why? Because Gretchen and Father decided it would suit them better to go over the requests on Saturday so they can attend the administrator's workshop in Baltimore on Monday. They were going Tuesday. Now they're going Monday because Father's going to be in Baltimore anyway on Sunday, and the poor thing just doesn't want to drive two days in a row. So just because they change their schedule, all the department heads have to change everything too, just to suit them. That's what these are doing here…" And she waved at a small stack of catalogues on the kitchen table.

Joe put his coat and case on a living room chair and set his luke-warm coffee in the microwave and pushed a few buttons. It wheezed like a small vacuum cleaner and finally emitted a prolonged beep. He sat down, and Kate sat down too.

"Sounds like you were taken by surprise," he said.

"You're darn right it was a surprise," she said. One of the many things he admired in her was her refusal, even at her angriest, to use vulgar language. "Darn" was about as far a she would go. Of course, as a high school teacher, she had heard it all.

"Well," he said. "I'm sorry it—"

"But wait! It gets better. I'm glad you're sitting down. Ray called." At the mention of her brother's name, after years of his difficulties and dishonesty, both Joe and Kate tended to wince. "He put Mom on a plane today at four o'clock. She's flying into National at nine fifteen tonight. I've got to drive all the way in there to meet her.

Apparently, we have to keep her for a while. And we have to send him half of the cost of the flight. Can you believe it? Give me a break."

Joe stared at her with his mouth half open, as though he were insane.

"Hey, Dad," called Ted, bounding down the stairs from his room. "Come on, Mom. Cook something. I'm starving."

"Hi, honey," said Joe, squeezing Ted's arm.

"Ted, Dad and I are talking. Have you finished your homework? I told you I don't want you turning in anything late."

"Mom, as long as I've been going to school, I have never turned in anything late. It's crazy to even say that."

"Excuse me?" said Kate, as though posing a question. "How about that time in Ms. Kenny's class when you brought your jar of lightning bugs in on the wrong day? We're forgetting something, aren't we?"

Joe and Ted looked at her and at the same time said, "Who is Ms. Kenny?"

"Remember?" Said Kate. "She was the substitute in your class in the second grade when Mrs. Richardson took time off to have that baby?"

"Second grade!" said Ted.

"Second grade," said Joe, his mouth open.

"Second grade, and you took it in on the wrong day, a day early. Remember? And you had to bring it home again. So you certainly have turned in work late. I remember. You don't."

Joe's headache was throbbing like an engine at high idle. As Ted explained that he could not even remember fifth grade, five years ago, and asked how he was supposed to remember something in second grade, and couldn't they just get back to the subject of something to eat, the phone began to ring. Joe could suddenly see the bishop's face and hoped it was Walt Lewis. It was a telemarketer, but instead of declining and hanging up, Kate handed the phone to Joe, who proceeded to do it himself. He walked into the living room and lay down on a sofa with a cushion over his eyes to block out the light. Ted came in and turned on the television.

"Want to see the news, Dad?"

"I'll listen and you watch, buddy. Trying to get rid of a little headache here."

"Why do you have a headache?"

"Just a lot of things going on today. Something different everywhere I turned. And I'm having a little misunderstanding with the boss."

Ted began a video game. The room was immediately filled with pops, the twangy sound of plucked piano wire, and the report of futuristic firearms. The noise sounded harsh and sinister to Joe, unlike the old commercials for Quaker Puffed Wheat on the Sergeant Preston radio shows of his childhood. He stood and went upstairs to change his clothes.

He put on one of his flannel shirts and a pair of old jeans and slipped on a gray zip-up sweatshirt. He lay down on the bed and tried to think. For the whole of their married life, Kate's brother had treated them like servants. Kate allowed him to do it, giving in to Ray on the telephone and spending the next five days ranting to Joe about how unreasonable Ray was. For years he had called, careful to contact Kate at work or on Sunday mornings, when he knew Joe was at church, and plainly told her what she and Joe were going to do, usually about their mother. Kate would then come to Joe and announce what their instructions were, bemoaning the unfairness of their having to do as they were told. When Joe demanded to know why Kate had not said no to Ray, she grew furious with Joe for adding to her plight. After years of encouraging her to stand up to Ray without the slightest change in her behavior, Joe had taken matters into his own hands.

He had called Ray, but Ray was never available. Ray would not return his calls. His wife and children pleaded ignorance when Joe asked when Ray would return home. Finally Joe wrote him a long letter, carefully explaining how unfair his behavior was and advising him not to manipulate them further. Before mailing it, he sought Kate's approval, asking her to edit out whatever she found inaccurate or too blunt. She returned it to him quickly saying she agreed with it. Ray never replied. There was no way of knowing whether he had even read the letter. Joe expected that he did because, like most bullies, Ray was intensely interested in anything to do with himself.

He always demanded half payment from Joe and Kate for any expenses incurred by Catherine while she was at his house in Georgia. Joe and Kate paid all her expenses while she stayed with them, with the exception of one occasion when Catherine's insurance company refused to cover a very large medical bill. They requested help with it. Payment from Ray never arrived. Finally Joe had written a lawyerly letter without mentioning the medical bill again but warning severely of the need for the two households to make decisions about Catherine together. There had been almost a year of total silence, except for Christmas gifts, until tonight. This time Ray had called after putting his eighty-year-old alcoholic, nearly invalid mother on a plane. Kate and Joe would have no choice but to meet her flight.

From the kitchen, Joe could hear the prolonged beep of the microwave. Ted called from the foot of the stairs that dinner was ready. Joe took some of his prescription headache medication and set the bottle beside his billfold and keys so he would remember to take it to work the next day. He went down to dinner.

Kate had hastily prepared all the leftovers in the refrigerator, and she and Ted were waiting when Joe came in. As soon as Joe was seated, Ted opened his mouth to say the blessing, as he always did, but paused automatically while Kate directed him to say it, as she always did.

Joe knew it was useless to try to discuss Ray and Catherine then and there. Someone would have to meet Catherine's flight, and it was too late to do anything about it. He did not want Kate to drive in alone to the airport at night, and he knew before he inquired that she had asked nobody to ride in with her. She had a few acquaintances but only one person in the community who could be called a friend. She was not particularly close to any of her colleagues at St. John's. She had a good friend, a teacher with whom she had taught years before when she and Joe had just married. Joe was very fond of this friend, but now she lived way off in Northern Virginia and had a family of her own. Even if she would agree to ride to the airport with Kate, the drive to her house in the dark was just as long and worrisome for Joe as the drive straight to the airport. He did not want Kate to go alone.

He began to explain that he would go with her. First he had to call Walt Lewis because—

"Oh," said Kate. "I said he called. Remember?"

"When did he call!" said Joe.

"Right before you came home. I told you as soon as you walked in."

"You did not."

"I did, Joe. You were standing right here in the kitchen…"

"As soon as I came in, you began telling me about your science budget."

"Yes, and right before that, I told you that Walt Lewis called, just after you came in. Remember? If you'd just listen to me sometime, Joe."

But he was already up and searching the notepad for Lewis's number. Kate had not bothered to write it down. As it was in another call zone, he had to contact directory assistance to get it. When he finally called Lewis's home, his wife answered and said Walt had gone over to the church about five minutes before for a meeting and that Joe should call him there. No, he had not taken his cell phone with him. Joe wrote down the church number and called it immediately. Kate and Ted, talking loudly, were getting up and placing their dishes in the kitchen sink. Joe waved for them to be quieter. Ted lowered his voice. Kate stopped speaking altogether. There was a busy signal at Walt Lewis's church. Joe dialed again to be sure he had called the correct number, and the line was still busy. Kate was rummaging around in the hall closet and shouting up the stairs to Ted to finish his homework and not to turn on the television until he had completed it.

Kate was walking out to the garage, and Joe asked her to wait just another moment. His head was splitting. He called Lewis's church again. The line was still busy. He called Lewis's home while Kate disappeared into the bathroom. Gail Lewis did not know whether or not her husband had spoken with the bishop, but he had been in his home office on the phone with somebody for a while before dinner. She did not know with whom. She knew only that he had wanted to speak with Joe, but she had no idea what it was about. Joe tried the church again. It was still busy. Kate went into the garage, and the engine of her van began to roar like the inside of Joe's head.

From the kitchen door, he waved to her to wait while he sprinted up the stairs to say good night to Ted and tell him that they would be back around midnight.

"Aw, Dad. Tonight *The X-Files* reruns are on. I wanted you to watch them with me."

He explained that he had not known about Grandma's flight until he came home and apologized for not being able to watch their favorite show together. Ted understood that Joe did not want Kate driving to the airport alone in the dark. He kissed Joe good night and promised to go to bed by ten thirty. Joe explained he was expecting an important call from a Mr. Lewis and that he would call from the car on the way in to see if he had telephoned. He asked Ted to write down exactly what Mr. Lewis said and added quickly that he might have to leave early the next morning before Ted was awake to drive to Conyers. If he did, he would see Ted tomorrow night.

In the driveway, Kate was blowing the horn. He grabbed a jacket, his billfold, and headache medicine. As he hurried through the kitchen, he picked up a cold biscuit from his untouched plate on the table. He locked the kitchen door behind him and lowered the door of the garage. With his stomach burning, he climbed into the van, and Kate gunned it down the driveway.

Chapter Eight

As a child, Joe had accepted that he was a flawed creature. He felt loved and valued but, just as he was certain of having two hands, he was sure of an inward brokenness that he could no more cure than change his blood type. It was not a source of guilt or anxiety because he perceived the same brokenness everywhere in life. He accepted it in himself as one accepts a food allergy and learns to get along without peanuts or milk. He reasoned that there is so much of oneself and life that is good that the broken parts need not be determinative of the whole. For reasons he could not explain, acceptance of this awareness had turned him very slowly into a hopeful man. As an irritant in an oyster creates a pearl, awareness of his own imperfection developed in him a marked expectancy and anticipation that resulted in a certain uncomplicated courage.

Joe's low side was a want of patience with other people; the trivialities and nonessentials that appeared so important to everyone, and were such a source of emotional drama in life, bored him easily. It was restive enthusiasm more than a lack of empathy that tired him and never so much with individuals as with the human race as a whole. Even as a child, he grew bored and frustrated with self-centeredness and greed. His impatience to get to the point in life and in personalities would one day make him a poor diplomat and a good trial lawyer. In a child, however, his desire to ignore the small stuff could be a wearisome quality, and Joe could wear out the patience of others with his curiosity and imagination. He had many friends but was equally happy being alone. Small talk bored him. He was an average athlete, but his mood did not rise and fall on the winning of games. His love of reading and the outdoors helped shape the world into a manageable adventure.

There was so much to learn. The world was beautiful and mysterious, qualities not confined to externals or appearances but filling and animating everything from the core. Was it something in the way he processed and understood the world that made it a marvelous mystery? Or did he perceive the world as it truly is? What is real? What is truth? And why? Reading at night, or roaming the woods, or arguing with his good-natured long-suffering friends, he thought he might be insane. His friends certainly did.

In the beautiful order of things, what were the deficiencies and imperfections he sensed but understood so imperfectly? He did not know, and others did not see life that way, so no one could tell him. He knew that others found his questions and daydreams curious but unimportant, the way he knew he perceived many of their issues.

In his early teens, he began to scrutinize life from behind an increasingly quiet exterior, creating little stir and channeling his enthusiasms into observations of a world that seemed troubled enough without his contributions. Within him, his own brokenness fostered a hopeful courage and fortitude in the face of life's relentless difficulties and perseverance where wiser heads would long before have given way.

Consciousness of his own ignorance, impatience, poor judgment, and misunderstandings encouraged him, often against his will, along what would turn out later to have been right paths. Arriving at clean and wholesome turning points, he could look back, discerning and intuitive, and see how along the way his own imperfections had made him move in the right direction. Life was an arduous struggle in one direction, while all else seemed to surge the other way. Yet confidence in an eventual, inexplicable denouement forced him forward, as though peace and order waited around the next bend or the one after that. In later life, he would conclude that of God's many gifts to him, hope and courage, unearned and undeserved, had been his most formative.

Being raised in the church by faithful parents had its effect in time. By his early teens, Joe believed that God had set him certain tasks and responsibilities in life. His duty was to discover them and apply himself. This youthful misconception blended rather well into his expectant attitude toward everything. It was not idealism; it was a developing naive confidence in the benevolent intentions of God. Joe's resolve was innocent enough. His misjudgment came in seeing the unfolding of the plan of salvation in much too personal and worldly terms. It was the shortsightedness of inexperience, forgivable in the young, and with it came a blessing. He perceived the danger of talking too much about such matters. Young people can be cruel and ignorant, and adults impatient much of the time. By his early twenties, he had abandoned his primitive analysis of everything and begun to accept life's imperfections. Despite his atrocious grades in college, he took from his studies mental and emotional strength that would have amazed his teachers and that would nourish him for the rest of his life.

His art classes especially enticed him back to probing the source. Far from preoccupying him with the merely obvious and superficial, drawing and painting proved impossible without understanding the underlying nature of things. The vast subsurface reality, waiting for his attention to refocus upon essentials, called to him in the drawings of Leonardo and the Chan paintings of Liang Kai, refreshing his wonder at powerful depths and informing him of the distracting superficiality of the obvious.

He pondered again his own perception. Was the world as it presented itself to him, or did he alter it in the course of his experience of it? And what was the great flaw running through everything, like a fault line on distant mountainsides, indicating hidden forces powerful and illusive, like tectonic plates, silent but trembling? Teaching troubled children after college led him to a critical turning point. He gained a long-overdue understanding that God, except in very rare cases, has no plan for the life of any individual human. God's plan, the grand salvific design, is a plan for the whole of creation. The duty of the individual is to study the divine plan and conform one's own life to it. Far from hiding the truth, life's most unlikely, chaotic situations, of which there seemed so many, far more than moments of relative peace, actually revealed it and with uncomplicated clarity.

He told himself that one is never too old to learn even the obvious. Immersed in the multiplicitous world where humans come and go, blind fish buffeted on all sides by the unexpected, one may never perceive the light from above. It would take him years to get even this far. Dim as his own vision was, and in the muddiest of waters, he began to feel sorrow and kinship for those who seemed to miss the light even more than he did.

The little understanding he had of God's plan was deeply troubling. The contrast between it and his own smallness and limitations, his gnat's breath flickering against the mysterious unity and interrelatedness of all created things, was overwhelming and kindled in him a lostness that even his innate hope could not soothe. The relationships he shared, the qualities he observed in his parents and neighbors, all that was happening around the world—mountains, oceans, atoms, everything—increasingly revealed itself as a unique part of an inseparable whole. An ambiguous perception of this unity was as far as he could go, for many years, in learning how to conform to the plan. Although he felt (more than understood) an instinctive truth glowing through reality, he recognized the limitations of his five senses in apprehending beauty and mystery. Around him he imagined the creation groaning like glaciers, like an ice shelf splitting and crashing, and it was alternately nurturing and maddeningly dangerous. Surviving in one part of it while aware of the wholly other was turning out to be an unnerving adventure for which hope and courage were indispensable qualifications.

God was purposeful. The whole creation, despite the slowness of apparent change, was unfolding according to plan and going somewhere. As a boy, he could not have said where this was, but a momentum was clear to him. Like the difference between lakes and rivers—the lake is still; the river moves one along by indigenous forces in a discernable direction. It was something like this that he felt when he considered conforming his life in the world to a plan that was beyond the world. To his surprise, he was especially conscious of this fundamental, elemental movement in the endless, boring Sunday mornings in church. His parents dragged him and his siblings there Sunday after Sunday, until each departed the nest for college or elsewhere.

As a child who loved to draw ("Even on the goddamn walls," declared his father), Joe had grown to perceive the multiplicitous world as a painter comprehends a still life, landscape, or the human face, unconsciously seeing existence take focus as line, texture, space, form, and color. He looked about him in worship services, when he should have been praying, and interpreted form and content in everything around him. Form held. Content moved. (The lake and the river…) The duality made a whole, or something observed fleetingly in a moment that passed for a whole, a unity—a face here, a folded overcoat there, a fly perched on a pew, a bloom of colored light through stained glass. The two qualities worked on one another, changed each other before his eyes, and changed him because he had observed and were themselves changed by his very observation of them. Especially during the interminable Prayer for the Whole State of Christ's Church, during which he and his friends could have played a game of basketball and returned to their places, he scrutinized the folded hands, closed eyes, and bowed heads of his kneeling neighbors. Young and old, men and women, there was no black and white; they were all white, some vigorously so, and his friends, who knew better than to misbehave here, of all places, all existed in a flow by virtue of being in the world, as though their very existence meant they were going somewhere with purpose.

He understood that his friends also were moved in some way, but only by where they were and what they were doing. How moved, he never knew in those days. They would have to become adults with children of their own before being able to discuss it. But something spoke, certainly, in their faces and postures, their quiet fixations, as though they responded to something nearly tangible, almost audible, as it vibrated within and around them. Somehow he knew that apart from Mr. Anderson, the minister (nobody said priest in those days), and perhaps a few others, none of them could have explained what they were experiencing. As they were so submerged in it, like seashells moved around by an undertow, he wondered if they were aware of experiencing anything at all. It was around them and inside them but impossible to define. He saw it most distinctly in the light in his mother's face.

When he was about thirteen, his parents allowed him to sit with his friends in the last pew, "as long as you be quiet and pay attention." It was a parental concession to having a teenager, a small but initial hard act of letting go by good people who looked at each other and smiled and sighed. Several generations would pass before parents would begin to say, "Well, at least they are here." As everybody went to church in those days, the presence of young people was assured. But as most families had four, five, or six children, getting everyone to church was still an accomplishment.

So large was St. Mark's and so lengthy the service that on some Sundays, Joe and his friends could escape following the offertory, go down to Candler's News Stand on Main Street, and have a Coke and gaze in wonder at the adult magazines behind the counter and return in time to join the lively commotion that reigned throughout the vast building when the service "let out." After about a year, they stopped slipping out and forced themselves, yawning and slumped in the pews like weary convicts, to stay through the whole service. It was not a decision based on parental respect but on an unspoken mutual reaction to something else. They never discussed it, but they would have acknowledged that doing what they knew was right made them feel better in the long run.

For about six months, there was the added incentive of the Meade twins, a year older than Joe and his friends. They sat with the other older girls in the pew in front of the boys, studiously ignoring the young peasants behind them and threatening to get up and move at the slightest tap of a finger or Prayer Book on their backs or shoulders. Lovely, popular, and much more mature than Joe and his friends, the Meade twins occupied everybody's dreams with their blond hair and tight smart dresses and smelling sweet as lilacs. The long pew full of girls giggled and teased and whispered through the service as Joe and his friends, stupendous erections disguised in reverent kneeling, peered at them all over the back of the pew as though they would like to eat them. When the Meade twins moved to Richmond, the focus of worship shifted a little, other girls taking their place as objects of veneration, and the less sensual and unspoken moods of worship returned to claim their old places for a while.

What was it that moved beyond the obvious? Joe dreamed and daydreamed. What was shifting and billowing behind the lines, planes, textures, forms, points, sounds, hues, and the rest of what intruded upon the senses? Joe's father, who would have been the last man in Christendom to engage in any sort of serious religious talk, supplied a piece of the puzzle without knowing it. A man who liked to work on cars, Joe's father's most significant theological moment of the week occurred when Mr. Anderson intoned "thy manifold and great mercies." His father would look along the pew at him as if to say, "Hear that? Now we're getting somewhere!"

There was in the gravity room aplenty for absurdity. And the sheer absurdity of the truth, of the whole absurd realm of possibilities that he was learning to call truth, cried out for the deepest, most philosophical of responses: laughter.

* * *

Joe's family's means were limited, but left over from his childhood and the Army, Al Stephenson had a collection of well-worn camping gear. Several times each month the whole family piled into their ancient Woody, bound for one of a dozen campsites in the mountains.

It was not always fun for Joe. Sibling rivalry was natural and normal in his big family, and as the oldest child, he played his special role in it. On many weekends he would have preferred to spend the night with a friend, especially when there was a party. But again, as with his growing realization of mystery in the church and in the world, the sheer power of the mountains confronted him with further insight into the unseen. And like spring or fall, never encountered all at once but experienced in progressive changes, the effect of the natural world and its mystery advanced in him slowly, sometimes faster, but always stronger and with growing clarity. As he matured, he would find the same light shining in all wild places. He would perceive it on sandy shores, islands and tidal marshes, in cypress swamps and cactus deserts, on vast grasslands and in great forests. He felt it in rivers, lakes, and fields. It loomed up in the microcosmic complexity of the gardens he planted wherever he lived. Even in a houseplant or in one iris or rose, he perceived something shared with the great chopper blues and striped bass running on the coast, in the gaze of a mindless deer in the fields, or the mournful wail of a screech owl.

His friends felt it too. On hunting and fishing trips and in their fondness for dogs and other pets, a companionship existed with something more than what they saw and touched and heard. Beyond an occasional comment about the view or the weather, nobody discussed it. Had they done so, even if one of them had become a poet, they would not have been at all romantic about it. Any perception of the unseen world was never a matter of melodrama or fanciful perception. What sentimentality it held had to be unspoken; to attempt a definition was limiting, dispelling. Awe was experienced and accepted with the same dependable, dutiful affirmation they would accord the birth of their children one day, or the passing of their parents. When a dog died or a favorite old tree was blown over in a storm, they grew silent and felt diminished.

Chapter Nine

Joe was in love with Kate when they married, in love with the happiness of spending the rest of his life with her. He was amazed at himself that she had accepted him. She was a blessing, an act of God, and a gift of which he was determined to make himself worthy. His awe of her was tender and sincere. She made him feel clean and whole, filling life with a newness and wonder that focused his intuitive hope into their relationship for the rest of their lives. Joe idealized her to a degree she neither recognized nor desired. And he was naive. He believed every word she said. He devoted himself to pleasing her. Her carefree disposition, witty and sunny, had been a light in his life before their marriage. When they saw each other every few months, often at her house at Wicomico, her presence worked on Joe like a transfusion, filling the following weeks until he could be with her again with joy and purpose he had never known.

When she grew irritable and easily annoyed soon after marriage, he attributed it to the many changes and adjustments she was going through. Her sarcasm was a complete surprise. But she was in a new marriage, new community, new home, and new job, and it was all bound to be stressful even if she refused to say so. He believed it would pass as their marriage matured and as she grew more settled. Still, in the two years he had known her before marriage, he had never encountered the derision and cutting remarks that he heard now, and it saddened him even though he thought he understood it. The mood swings were especially troubling. But he was prepared to give her whatever time she needed.

When Kate began losing patience with him several times each day, and finding fault with almost everything he said, he began to scrutinize the only possible source of her discontent. He looked at his own words and actions, and he found himself wanting. He desired her happiness more than anything. He believed they had a good marriage and a grand future. Everybody else went through adjustment periods too. And they talked about things. If pressed, he would have acknowledged that Kate never initiated any of their discussions and said little about them afterward. But she was smart. She understood. He would learn how to handle things better. Time would help her grow more comfortable. Both of them would learn. He knew Kate remembered their marriage counseling with Stanley Wiley because on one occasion she quoted him, and quite accurately as far as Joe could remember, to justify something she had done. In his law practice, Joe saw the sad results of marriages in which respect, trust, and communication had died. He had every confidence in Kate, and he knew himself well enough to know he would work at their relationship until she was happy.

When they went out with friends to dinner or parties in their first year together, Kate always drank a lot of wine or bourbon mixed with ginger ale. She would go to sleep in the car on the way home, and on many nights, Joe put her to bed. If it worried him, he told himself she was his wife, he loved her, they were in their adjustment period, and everything in their community was new for her. Like everybody else, she had to unwind now and then. Everybody they knew drank alcohol. Joe usually had one bourbon and water when he came home from work, as well as when they went out socially. There was always white wine, Kate's favorite, in the refrigerator. They bought it by the gallon. Kate had several glasses while she prepared dinner and more during dinner. Sometimes she would have another while watching television or grading papers, as Joe cleaned up the kitchen and washed the dishes.

But after a few months of marriage, Joe began gradually to question his own reasoning. He could not understand why certain things happened and no amount of hope and confidence made them clearer. He wondered daily whether or not he correctly interpreted what he saw and heard. These were mysteries wholly different from the spiritual and philosophical speculations of his early years. They were small matters at first, the sort to which most people paid little attention. He might not have noticed them either except that they kept happening.

At the small house they rented, the front doorknob was loose. He knew the knob had not been loose before. After a few weeks, it became so wobbly he feared it would come off altogether. He asked Kate about it, and she replied that it had always been that way and that it made her feel unsafe to be in the house alone at night. It was a small enough matter, and something he could easily repair, but the thought of her alone at night and anxious about intruders alarmed him. He felt, somehow, responsible. And his own memory worried him. He knew the doorknob had been firm, but Kate said it had always been loose. His failure to notice it made him feel careless, negligent.

One evening they went out after dinner to buy groceries. They left the front porch light on. When they returned, Joe carried the heavy bags to the door, while Kate felt around in her pocketbook for her keys. As Joe watched, she jammed her house key with difficulty into the lock on the doorknob and rattled it vigorously back and forth until it slipped all the way in. She turned the key sharply and shoved the door open, knocking it hard against the inside wall. Joe said he knew now why the doorknob was about to come off and asked her why she had unlocked the door with such force. Did her key fit? Was the knob too hard for her to turn? Kate replied calmly that she had no idea what he was talking about. She denied she had rattled the doorknob or shook the key into the lock. He was imagining things.

He stared at her in amazement. His every effort at reasoning with her was futile. Each time he tried to describe to her what he had just seen, she said she had not rattled the doorknob, and he did not know what he was talking about. He protested that he was not accusing her, merely asking her why she opened the door that way. He felt foolish questioning her over a thing so small. But she was, after all, the one who said she was scared to be in the house alone with a loose doorknob. She grew increasingly loud and irritable and ended by refusing to talk about it further. After a few minutes she took a glass of wine up to bed, read for a while, turned off the light without speaking, and was asleep within seconds.

It was a small matter, but it confused Joe and made him question himself. Perhaps he had not seen what he thought he saw. He had probably overestimated the whole thing. She was his wife. She was bright, accomplished, and talented. She would not mislead him. He would repair the door and not bring it up again.

A few weeks passed, and they received a demand letter from the PenMar Power and Light Company threatening to cut off their electricity because a bill had not been paid. Joe was paying all the bills. It was during the time Kate was withholding her paycheck and refused to involve herself with family finances, except for when she had the checkbook. Joe went to the power company and paid the bill. He could see from the family checkbook that he had made no payment in the previous month, and he could not recall ever seeing a bill. If they had received a bill, he would have paid it on time. He asked Kate about it. She said she didn't know.

Several days later he was in the cellar examining the water heater and discovered a stack of magazines and unopened bills, none of which he had seen before. The unpaid power bill was among them. The magazines were still in their wrappers. He questioned Kate about them, and she said she knew nothing about it and that Joe must have taken them all downstairs by mistake. She explained all this in a natural, straightforward way and immediately began talking about her day at school. Joe could not recall seeing the bills or magazines before. The state bar journal was among them. He glanced at the articles and read the disciplinary decisions each month as soon as the journal arrived. He was certain he had not seen this issue because it contained the obituary of someone he had known years before in law school. He was also sure that he would not have taken bills to the cellar and left them.

Late one evening, as he brushed his teeth and stared into the bathroom sink, he saw what appeared to be a piece of lettuce in the drain. He lifted the stopper, and with it came a small glutinous mass of what looked like partially digested food. He opened the door to the bedroom and asked Kate, who had just turned out the light, if she was sick. In a sleepy voice, she said she was not. He asked her who had visited the house that afternoon, and she told him no one had visited. In the gentlest possible way, because he was beginning to dread her anger, he asked her to look at something he had found. She came in reluctantly, sighing heavily as though he had asked her to lift the rear end of the car. She looked at the mess in the sink and said in an impatient voice that it must have come up through the drain from somewhere. Even Joe grew alarmed at this, and he demanded to know why she had vomited. Was she all right? Had she been sick? Raising her voice, she claimed she knew nothing about it and that she was not sick. She asked him if he thought she looked sick. She did not. She told Joe that things came up from drains like that all the time and asked how it was he had never seen it before. Where had he been all his life? She said she had to go to work the next day, returned to the bed, and was asleep in seconds.

He stood in the bathroom, staring at himself in the mirror. Could the stuff have gurgled up from the line, from someone else's house? He was no mechanic and no plumber, but he felt certain it had not. But Kate was so smart, so bright and capable. She was a science teacher, and stuff bubbling up from the drain was, well, in the realm of science, wasn't it? He went downstairs and sat at the dining room table and thought for a while. It was the first of a thousand such nights to come.

Then on a lovely spring day, as he prepared to go to court, a good friend came to his office, another young lawyer who had begun practice a few years before Joe came to town. He and his wife lived up the street from Joe and Kate. He was well-known and highly respected and served as a substitute judge in the county court. Joe was flattered that he had come by to visit. After some conversation about recent cases and a few jokes, his demeanor changed slightly, and he withdrew from his pocket a blue paper and handed it to Joe with obvious embarrassment. Immediately he expressed his profound apologies for bringing it by. Joe unfolded the paper and stared. It was an official legal notice of a lawsuit brought against Joe and Kate by the owner of an automobile repair shop in a nearby county. It alleged an unpaid bill of four hundred and seventy dollars and sought to recover that sum plus interest from the judgment date, together with costs. It had been served upon the Stephensons in the usual way, taped to their front door by a deputy sheriff, and discovered there by Joe's friend as he walked his dog early that morning. To spare Joe some humiliation, he had removed it and kept it until he could give it to him in person. He apologized a second time, and waving away Joe's profuse thanks and saying that it was the sort of thing that could happen to anybody, he left.

Any lawsuit is a cause for concern. Being served a legal notice on the front door is unpleasant and humiliating for anybody, and especially for an attorney, an officer of the court. Joe, who was struggling to establish a practice, knew the damage this could do. There was no telling who had seen it before his friend had found it. Throughout the morning, Joe's imagination conjured up all manner of devastating prospects. He was certain that everyone he encountered in the courthouse complex knew he was being sued and had been served with a summons. He imagined that they had just broken off conversation about it when he approached. In the clerk's office, where the notice had been prepared, the deputy clerks behaved in their usual friendly way, but he felt certain they all knew. He wondered which one of them had processed the suit and turned the notice over to the sheriff. In the corridors outside the courtrooms stood clusters of deputies and police officers, talking with each other as they awaited their call to testify.

Any one of them could have posted the notice on his door. He could imagine their comments. "Can't keep his own affairs right, and him trying to practice law. Don't make 'em like the old days."

As soon as he returned from court, Joe called the repair shop and spoke with the manager. The bill was for repairs and servicing for Kate's car, an expensive Subaru that had been her prized possession for years. Joe canceled his afternoon appointments and drove to the bank and then over to Lanhamsville to the shop. On the drive there, he remembered, several months before, hearing Kate talking on the phone with another teacher about finding someone qualified to work on her car. She did not trust just anybody, she had said. "And nobody where we live can probably do it. I've got the only one I know of around here!" he had heard her say. There had been no more discussion about it, and he had forgotten about it.

Or at least Kate had said nothing to him. Her car had continued to run as it always had. Her occasional complaints about it had never changed.

At the repair shop, Joe paid the bill in cash and got a receipt. He apologized to the manager and assured him that the whole thing was a mistake. He told him he had not known about the bill. His embarrassment was evident, and the manager took the payment and told him not to worry, that it was all over and done with. He and his office manager appeared mildly amused by it all. They both mentioned that each had called several times about the bill, and the office manager had spoken with Mrs. Stephenson personally. The office manager's hesitancy and exchange of glances with her boss suggested to Joe that they were not telling him something. He decided not to inquire. The office manager said she had not realized Joe was a lawyer and she would have called him personally if she had known.

The payment left less than forty dollars in the household account for the rest of the month. He returned to his office and called the clerk of court. The deputy clerk had already received a call from the repair shop. The case would be removed from the docket as soon as the costs were paid. Joe thanked the clerk, assuring her he had not known about the bill and apologizing for the whole situation. The clerk, who had served in her position for years, was diplomatic and reassuring. She had been very helpful to Joe since he had opened his practice, and he knew she liked him personally. He had always appreciated her help. He hung up the telephone, humiliated and chagrined. He knew she had heard a thousand times the same sort of excuses he had just tendered. This time she had heard them from a lawyer, one to whom she had been especially friendly and helpful.

In truth, Joe's alarm over the situation was overblown a bit. If he had been in practice for years, he would have perhaps chuckled a little and apologized to all concerned and forgotten about it. But he was new at the law and almost as new to Jeffersonville as Kate was. He was truly embarrassed.

At first, Kate denied any knowledge of the whole thing. When Joe produced the blue motion for judgment, she acknowledged, as though only just remembering it, that she had had her car serviced one day months ago "on a school day." She said she had given him the bill. "You were sitting right there, on the sofa, watching television. Remember?" she said calmly, reasonably. He did not remember, and he told her so. He could feel anger churning in his stomach, and he was unsure of what upset him more, her lies to him or her apparent absurd assumption that he would actually believe her. Any sane person would remember being presented with a bill for five hundred dollars, he told her, raising his voice.

But Kate defended herself immediately. "I beg your pardon! That bill wasn't for five hundred dollars! It was for four hundred and seventy dollars! You don't even remember how much it's for," said Kate, with an air of alarm at his obvious inaccuracy. She seemed genuinely hurt that he would accuse her so unfairly.

She was inflexible. Nothing about the situation seemed to concern her except that Joe was wrong about the amount of the bill. So what if he had paid court costs and the whole thing amounted in the end to over five hundred dollars? The bill itself was for four hundred and seventy dollars. "Let's get our facts straight, Mr. Stephenson. You're a lawyer. You should know better than this," she said, indignant. It seemed to make no difference to her that she had caused him professional humiliation. That was all he cared about, really, she said, his precious reputation, and she began to grow angry. It didn't matter to him at all that she drove twenty miles to work every day. And back again too. She had worked hard all day. And now this! It was not fair. How was she supposed to get to work without a car? Why was everything always her fault? He treated her like a child, like a criminal. Why? What had she ever done to deserve being treated like this?

He listened to her go on and on, incredulous, utterly amazed at what she was saying. She got up and flounced around, slamming magazines together on a table and knocking them loudly into a stack, seizing his briefcase and sliding it into a corner like a bowling ball

("It's always in the way and I could trip over it and fall! But that makes no difference to you!"), sweeping up newspapers he had read the night before, and stomping into the kitchen to ram them into the trash can.

She would not back down. She had done nothing wrong. When he suggested that she had simply forgotten to bring home the bill—and even as he said it, he knew it was not true and was ashamed of himself for proposing it—she rejected that possibility with angry denial. There was no question of apology in her mind because the whole thing was Joe's fault. She had done absolutely nothing wrong. She behaved as though she was the victim of a conspiracy, a minor misunderstanding of which Joe was making "a federal case." He did not ask her why she had not paid the bill with her own paycheck, which she kept for herself.

Joe was shocked. He found the whole thing so bizarre and unfair that he didn't know what to say, how to talk with her. Did Kate really believe what she was saying? Who could possibly believe it? Yet his astonishment and hurt feelings were small compared to the exasperation and betrayal he would experience in years to come. In attempting to discuss future bills and finances with Kate, she would flatly and emphatically deny that they had ever been sued over anything having to do with her car. It had never happened.

Even the cumulative influence of events such as these was not enough to break through Joe's romantic concept of the happy marriage they were entering. He swallowed his anger and accepted that Kate was not prepared to discuss certain things in their relationship. He reasoned that years of life with an alcoholic mother and bully brother had forced her to adopt a sort of combative self-preservation. It would take some time for them both to settle down in married life. And maybe, just maybe, she truly did forget to give him bills, to discuss with him the things that wives and husbands talked about, to be open about personal matters.

He was himself no jewel by any means. He had known it since he learned to walk and talk. He had faults as much as any other man. More, really. He was sure she was correct when she claimed he did not listen to her at times. There were nights when he came home from work exhausted, feeling like a slave let loose from the salt mines, weary and craving some peace and quiet. Days in trial, negotiations with determined colleagues, the intense focus and organization on which his practice depended, the high stakes in criminal defense work, civil trials in which minimal damages inflamed the deepest passions, the constant public scrutiny, the ethical standards to which he and his colleagues aspired—it all took a toll and sent him home some nights craving peace, rest, reassurance.

It seemed Kate began to talk the moment he opened the door. Before he could take off his coat, she was reciting details of what had happened in her high school that day. If his face showed stress or fatigue, she appeared not to see it. This unending stream of academic minutia and school gossip, after a difficult day in his own work, sometimes tried his patience to its very limit. The small events of life in her rural high school, from which her every waking moment seemed to draw its meaning, became their standard dinner topic. If he tried to change the subject, Kate listened with her eyes fixed on her food until he paused, and then she resumed her recitation like a radio suddenly switched on again. She never asked one question about what he had done all day. And he knew that toward the end of the evening, she would test him, subtly and unobtrusively, asking small questions about details of what she had been talking about all evening to see if he had been paying attention.

It was clear to him that Kate placed great importance on his listening to her. In a strange way, it made him feel rather good, important to her, but he wondered who had filled this need before they were married. He spent his whole day listening: clients, judges, witnesses, police officers, other lawyers, court personnel, his secretary, friends. There was poured in his direction a continuous flow of discourse, without interruption, all day long, every day. Even when he sat at the counter in the Old Courthouse Square Café for five minutes and tried to read the headlines in *The Washington Post* as he munched a grilled cheese sandwich, inevitably someone would descend onto the stool beside him and begin to talk. He did not find it burdensome; it was his profession. He liked to imagine himself actually getting better at listening. And wasn't it reasonable that his own wife, the one he loved, should expect him to listen to her too when they were together? She deserved it, after all. And he did listen to Kate. He was very interested in what she said, what she did, what she thought, how she felt, her life, her. It was just that he needed a break at times, like everyone else. And sometimes he needed to talk too.

He began to understand something else that he had not seen before. About the beginning of their second year of marriage, Joe began to realize what had been happening for some time, perhaps even from the beginning. When he was with Kate, as soon as their conversation touched upon his own personal feelings or preferences, she changed the subject immediately. She shifted quickly to an unrelated topic with such precision and seamless control that his personal matter had been left behind before he knew it. She might be complaining about how busy she was at school and how tired the students made her and how long it would be before her next vacation. Joe might reply he knew how she felt. He would love a break too. He could see no chance of having one until the summer. Kate's next sentence would be about whether to shop at Food Lion or Safeway and how Food Lion was probably better because she thought their stores were cleaner and how she loathed shopping in dirty stores. And before he knew it, he was listening to her talk about her favorite stores and the wonderful shopping malls in her college town.

Joe could not remember when this sort of one-sided conversation had begun to characterize their time together. He could not remember being aware of it before their marriage, but by a few years into marriage, it had become their routine. At least it had become Kate's routine, and he had acquiesced in it. But when? And why? He had always deferred to her in conversation, allowing her to set the agenda and talk as long as she wanted to. By the time he was conscious of her reflexive avoidance of any mention of his personal feelings, he recognized it must have been going on for a while. It hurt. He knew his unwillingness to confront her, or confront her more than he had in the past, was a major part of the problem.

He began to anticipate it and condition himself to accept it. He even experimented a few times, shifting the talk to his own headache, say, when Kate was going on and on about how many students had left class since Monday complaining of severe headaches, how bothersome it was to have it happen during a lecture, how mystified the teachers were by it, and how some of them wondered if it might be something in the air ducts. At the mere mention that Joe's head hurt at that moment, she would shift in one sentence to how good it was going to be to get down to Wicomico Island and air out the house at Easter. Breathing the fresh sea air would do her a world of good. Joe would respond with surprise and ask if they were going down at Easter. She would reply that they had already discussed that, "Remember?" His headache, nor anything else that might be troubling him, was not mentioned again.

Joe would have been the first to emphasize that there were plenty of good times. They always enjoyed visiting Joe's family. Kate dearly loved his parents and brothers and sisters, and they all treated Kate like a daughter and a sister. She doted on his father, continually amused by his grouchy peculiarities and perhaps finding in him, Joe supposed, the father figure she had so missed in childhood. Joe's mother treated Kate with the love and attention she lavished on her own daughters. Kate thrived under her devotion. Joe telephoned his parents several evenings each week to talk, equally for Kate as for them, because they all enjoyed each other so.

He kept all family difficulties strictly to himself. He was good at keeping confidences. Not only was it a professional duty, but he had also been raised in a society in which a person's personal discretion was bound up with the sanctity of one's word. A person of integrity knew when to keep quiet as well as when to speak up. He considered it his duty to Kate never to speak of their marital differences to anyone. He wanted Kate and his family and all their friends to get along well. In any case, he was convinced that time and experience would heal their marital problems, that Kate would come into the maturity that was, it seemed, still awaiting her. Making an issue of their problems now, while they were still adjusting, would not be helpful later on. In later years, when he had begun to seek the guidance of professional counselors, he would keep them and their advice to himself too.

They had wonderful times at Wicomico Island. In their first years of marriage, Joe missed Kate dreadfully when she went away for the summer, her absence somehow worse than the troubles. When he joined her there during his own vacation, they enjoyed some of their happiest days together. She was usually relaxed and congenial at her beach house, rarely leaving the place except for shopping trips or to visit the public library. She enjoyed sitting on the porch, reading, doing nothing, and especially sunbathing while she talked with friends and the guests who rented rooms.

Kate's mother was in declining health before their marriage, and the income from the summer rentals was significant in her retirement. The house and room rentals were too much for her to manage alone. Since completing graduate school, Kate had worked as a teacher, so she continued her academic summer vacations by going to the beach to live. The Wicomico business provided Kate's own summer room and board, and the earnings from room rentals went into Catherine's bank account. For four or five years before their marriage, Kate had assumed more and more of the responsibility for running the house, but in almost every way, her summers were an idyll uninterrupted since birth.

But in spite of the nurture of family and friends and the thought of going to Wicomico during the summer, the first year of marriage was very hard for both of them. The spring had been especially trying, and Kate had been depressed since January. When Joe's coaxing finally encouraged her to talk about her feelings, Kate said she could not bear the thought of spending the summer in the home they were renting. In what little she said, she made Jeffersonville sound like a prison and talked for a while about how her winter depression was always relieved somewhat by the thought of going to the beach for the summer as soon as school ended. Joe felt he was listening to a child in middle school lamenting having to miss summer camp. She cried and covered her face in her hands. He brought her a glass of white wine.

"Honey, is this what has been bothering you since Christmas?"

She was silent and still, except for reaching for the wineglass. After a gulp or two, she said, "I just love it there so much. I need a vacation. What am I going to do here? I don't have friends here."

"But, Kate, you know teachers at the high school and our friends around town. Certainly you have friends!"

"Do you really think I want to spend the summer seeing the people I teach with all day? You just don't understand. I want to be where it's sunny and where I can hear the ocean." And she sobbed like a small child.

Joe was moved. He felt great tenderness for her. He could not imagine that her months of depression had been about where she would spend her summer. But by this time he had learned to wonder what exactly loomed behind her behavior, concealing again matters she would not discuss. He was ashamed of himself for thinking so, but the prospect of a long summer with Kate moping around the house feeling sorry for herself was distinctly disagreeable to him. He was sitting beside her, leaning against the back of the sofa. Kate was sitting forward with her face in her hands, except for her occasional sips of wine. Joe put his hand on her back. She was suddenly still, and he felt distinctly that she was waiting for something.

"Kate, I don't know about Catherine's finances. We haven't even been able to talk about our own"— *she* had not been willing to talk, but he phrased it in a way likely to minimize her going upstairs in a rage—"and I certainly don't know about hers. But I know she depends on this summer income. You've been doing the washing and cleaning the rooms for several years. Do you think she could handle it alone?"

"I guess she'll just have to. *I* certainly can't help her."

It would have been so helpful to both of them if she had merely opened up and discussed it all with him as one adult to another. He felt a sort of despair. He had never had a teenage daughter, but with Kate, he felt he was learning about what it must be like. If anything more was to be decided, if the conversation was to continue, if a resolution was to be achieved, he knew he would have to take the initiative.

"What would you like to do?" he asked.

She shrugged her shoulders. "Nothing I *can* do."

"Well," he said, adopting a cheerful, positive tone, "we're a family. You need your summer break. Your mother needs the income and can't do it alone. It's a beautiful place down there. It seems the right thing to do for you to go. There's only one thing."

"What?" she said, with a small sob, turning to face him for the first time.

"When I come down to see you all, will you charge me for a room?"

Instantly her whole manner changed. She turned to him with a laugh and put both arms around his neck and hugged him in an almost frantic way. She buried her face in his neck and said, "Of course not! You're family now. You can come whenever you want to." She laughed again and kissed him, behaving like someone who had just won the lottery. He had not seen her so happy since Christmas morning.

Joe telephoned her at Wicomico Island every few days, and he heard the same joy in her voice on the phone for the first week or so she was there. The summer was fun and relaxing. Some of the renters had been coming for many years, and Kate looked forward to their time together. She soaked up the sun, salt air, and freedom like a prisoner newly released from jail. But after about ten days, a portion of every telephone conversation was taken up with Kate's complaints about Catherine. By midsummer, Catherine was Kate's eternal topic as the school had been all winter. The things Catherine did and did not do, what she said, lies she told, poor choices in shopping, bad decisions about caring for the house, her arguments with renters, and her failure to complete certain routine chores—it was frustrating for Kate, and she spared Joe no detail of it when he called. That much of it arose out of Catherine's use of alcohol was clear to Joe and almost everybody else who knew the family. But true to a long McIvor tradition, drinking was never, ever mentioned. It was all put down to contrariness, forgetfulness, headaches, age, confusion, high blood pressure, the relentless faults of other people, and an assortment of other excuses that were pressed into service as needed.

Chapter Ten

They stared at him with narrowed eyes and mouths hanging slightly open, cigarettes poised, and bottles held motionless below parted lips. It could have been a freeze frame from a noir movie or a film based on a novel by Harry Crews. He thought of Thomas Hart Benton figures in a Charles Burchfield building. The superlative suspended drama, mellow lighting, tranquillizing blend of smoke and colors, the striking contrast of the inclined shoulders and erect faces, an expectant tension in the paralyzed eyes and brows—where was Margaret Bourke White when you needed her, or Walker Evans? Immobilized like the critical instant before Dickinson's "my life had stood—a loaded gun—" the whole gaggle of regulars clustered around the end of the bar, spellbound in sudden contemplation of the nonexistence of what they thought they had but didn't after all. Then the magic transfixion shattered, and the still life burst into action.

"I do so have a soul, and I'll be damned if I ain't since I was a little shit," said Pruitt, a truck driver who, although a Baptist, preferred to keep a rosary and crucifix dangling from his rearview mirror. "I mean, excuse my French, Joe. But…"

"Yeah, and now that you a big shit, you still got one, ain't you?" said someone in the rear, trying to be helpful.

"But Rev! Everybody got a soul!" exclaimed Janice, a new waitress who was fitting in just fine. It seemed that everybody in the Third Base had gathered suddenly around.

"Now wait a minute," said Raymond, the bartender, looking off to one side with a frown. "It says so right there in the Bible. It talks about people having a soul. Jesus talks about souls. Don't he?" he said, looking around for confirmation.

There was a murmur of general agreement. Joe could see they were shocked. They took it seriously. He wondered how long their consternation would last. "Think of it this way..." he said.

"I got to hear this," said Dodson, a fat man who sold insurance.

"It is not that you *have* a soul," Joe said. "You *are* a soul. When the Bible talks about our soul, it is referring to our whole, unique nature, every part of us, our sacred personhood, the thing about us that makes each one of us different from everybody else. Body and personality together."

"Listen, Rev., when I die... Let's say I fall down on the floor right here and die of, say, a heart attack right this minute. My soul is going to leave my body and go up to God. That's the way things work. Says so in the Bible," said Horace, who worked for the phone company.

"That's right," came a chorus of voices. "Ain't that right, Joe?"

"That is what almost everybody believes, including most clergy. But no offense to you, Horace, it's wrong," said Joe. "That is not Christianity. That's Greek philosophy. It's what the ancient Greeks believed."

"And you saying it ain't Christianity. Then what do we believe in?" said Pruitt, with sincerity.

"Christianity teaches us to see ourselves as whole, precious creations of God. We are not two entities, not body and soul. We are one sacred, unique, inseparable whole. There is nothing inside you called a soul that will flit up to God like a ghost when you die." Joe drank the rest of his coffee. Raymond reached over immediately with the greasy pot and poured him some more.

"You mean my soul ain't going up to God when I die?" Now it was Gloria talking, a woman from across the road who was raising five children with scant help from their absent fathers.

"No, Christians believe in something different. The Greeks believed in the immortal soul. Christians believe in something different. It's called resurrection."

"Yeah, but ain't that the same thing?" said Janice. She had taken a seat on the bar with both feet planted on a barstool. Raymond made her get down.

"Not exactly," said Joe. "When we die, our lives come to an immediate and complete end. Bang! We're dead, it's over. Life has ended. No soul escapes and floats up to God. We are totally dead, every part of us. That's when the miracle happens. God steps in and gives our life back to us. That's the miracle. And not just our old life. We don't become resuscitated corpses. We get new life, in a new body. That's resurrection."

Everyone was quiet for a moment while they thought this over. Then Gloria said, "A new body?"

Joe smiled and looked at her. She weighed about 250 pounds. "A new body," he said, "as suitable for life in the next world as these bodies are, more or less, suitable for life in this world."

"Will we know each other?" said Horace. "Will I recognize my wife, my daughter?"

"Yes, because when God gives you new life in a new, spiritual body, God also gives you back your sacred personhood, what made you one of a kind in this world, the uniqueness that set you apart. We'll be able to recognize one another, communicate, and join the party."

"Damn if this new body business don't seem like a good idea to me! You don't reckon I could sort of get it early, like right now, do you?" Gloria's enormous bosom shook, and she slapped a massive thigh. Everybody laughed. Some of the men patted their own ample stomachs and growled in agreement. Several people asked Joe to go over it again, and he promised to do so next time. Gradually, everybody began to talk about the Washington Redskins. They had had enough theology for one evening. The wonder was that the conversation had lasted as long as it had.

Some variation of it occurred almost every time he came in for coffee. People asked questions. Each one of them had troubles to spare, and they wanted to tell Joe all about it. They loved to hear Joe tell jokes. It had taken them a while to get used to him. Clerical collars were as rare as orangutans at the Third Base. In fact, Joe had confided to Ted that he could imagine a couple of gorillas shuffling in and having a drink at the bar without arousing the slightest attention, unless one of them wore a clerical collar. Certain customers would sit and talk with them all afternoon without noticing anything. But the sight of Joe's collar had been enough to dumfound the whole place on his first visit. Nobody would talk to him for the first couple of times, which was exactly why Joe came back again. It seemed to be one of those rare places where he could drink coffee and read *The Washington Post* without interruption. Then one day Raymond asked a few questions about where Joe's church was, how he had come to settle in the area, and whether or not in Joe's church they believed in Jesus?

The customer at the bar to Joe's right, on that occasion, was Clarence Sandford, a very old man whose family had been among the first settlers to cross the mountains, sometime around 1725. He had been baptized and confirmed at Redeemer as a child. The center window above the altar was dedicated to his great-grandfather, a Confederate general who had served in Congress after the war.

Raymond, Clarence Sandford, and Joe had talked awhile, and the next time Joe entered, every customer in the place smiled and nodded. They knew all about him. Mr. Sandford, whose family had fallen far, began to attend the early Sunday service at Redeemer for the first time in fifty years, to the immense delight of the old-timers. Two years later, Joe had conducted his funeral. Most of the regulars at the Third Base had showed up, standing silently in the background along the stone wall as the ashes of Clarence Morgan Greene Sandford IV were buried in the last remaining plot in the Old Redeemer Cemetery.

Chapter Eleven

From the beginning, Joe and Kate had wanted children. Knowing they were going to raise a family together had resolved no problems between them but had given them a mutual goal and the promise of happiness. The thought of their children made the future glow with joy and reassurance. Not once in all their difficulties did either of them consider a separation. They recognized the reality of their adjustment period. Everybody they knew had been through it, and they would get through it too and raise a family together. The thought of having children together bound them to one another, as perhaps nothing else would have done. It gave them confidence. As with many men and women who work as teachers, they were certain they already knew something about parenting children. They would have to learn the truth the hard way, like so many other good teachers before them.

From the time he was old enough to walk, Joe remembered having a baby at home. As a boy who preferred to play outdoors, caring for younger siblings was not the sort of circumstance he might have chosen on his own. But he had no choice in the matter, and helping to care for a baby became as natural for him as carrying firewood up to the back porch or mowing the lawn. Many of his friends were growing up in large families too, and they also knew how to deal with a baby even though none of them talked much about it. It would have been like discussing homework or straightening up when company was coming, something that everyone did and that warranted no special comment.

When Joe thought of his parents, there was always an infant in his image of them. The memory of his father changing diapers was as natural as his changing a tire on the ancient two-door Plymouth he drove to work for years on end or washing the dishes after dinner at night. His mother nursing one of his younger siblings or on her knees beside the bathtub, leaning over, bathing a little one and talking sweetly to the smiling, upturned face, would fill his imagination and dreams into old age. He could not remember when, even in winter, diapers weren't fluttering on the clothesline in the backyard or the diaper pail wasn't occupying its corner of their bathroom. As a child, Joe helped with it all. Feeding the baby and keeping quiet during naptime was part of growing up. Above all else, he remembered the continual endearing, soothing voices of his parents as they spoke to him and his brothers and sisters, a constant nurturing conversation that began at birth and was forever thereafter underway, intriguing, inspiring, encouraging, and reassuring the objects of their love.

His friends were growing up in the same way. Groups of them would sit around on front doorsteps talking quietly while a comrade finished feeding or rocking or changing an infant brother or sister before coming out to play. As soon as he burst out into the open air, they all raced for the woods to throw spears and play in their forts. Their domestic duties were never discussed any more than they would have talked about taking a bath or bringing in the groceries from the car. Over forty children lived on Joe's street when he was young, all of them growing up in similar ways.

Kate had grown up in a different way. She was the youngest in a family who lived on a road where their small town merged into the countryside. There were few other children in the neighborhood. She and her brother played together, often an unhappy arrangement. There were some boys down the road who played with her older brother, but they were older than Kate, and Catherine disapproved of their manners and hygiene. Spending every summer at the beach was fun, but it did little to build friendships with other children at home. As a child, she had one or two close friends, and they lived across town.

In her teens, Kate gained a reputation as a good babysitter. Efficient and reliable, she arrived precisely on time and carried out parental orders with precision. She was always available because she did not date or otherwise go out socially. As she grew older, she was very fond of her friends' children, gladly supervising them for evenings and even weekends. She found it fun to be in charge for a short time but appreciated her privacy when that time was over. The children for whom she cared occasionally were not babies but of an age for kindergarten or older. She concluded that a baby of her own would be about the same, only full-time.

They were going into their second year of marriage. Both would interpret the birth of a child as a sure sign that their marriage had been right for each of them all along in spite of the difficult adjustments each had been making. There had been good times too. Both believed firmly that things were improving. They loved one another, and each wanted the best for themselves and for the children they would have.

Despite these mutually gratifying musings, making concrete plans had become a lone endeavor for Joe, and he had gotten used to it reluctantly. Kate did not like discussing plans and responsibilities, but she bristled at having anything decided without her being consulted. It created an unfamiliar dilemma for Joe, who was used to making decisions with others, talking about possibilities, considering alternatives. He made plans and decisions as best he could, determining what he thought Kate's input would be if she had talked to him, and then consulted her about the result. If she agreed, she was noncommittal. If she disagreed, she was equally equivocal at first but soon grew sarcastic. The waiting periods varied in length, and Joe could never be entirely sure if he was in one of them. He felt a chronic but subtle tension, never certain where he stood, aware that with both his wife and his mother-in-law, his judgment was always the subject of suspicion and scrutiny. He felt angry for a while, especially when among their acquaintances Kate covered herself by pretending she and Joe decided everything together. Joe wondered if she was consciously being truthful. Was this difficult pattern her idea of working together?

He grew used to the indecision but never content with it, and he continued to believe that Kate would mature as the months passed. Each of them would learn to adjust. He did not interpret her secretiveness and indecision as avoidance or even denial but as a well-concealed lack of understanding and fear, perhaps, of the adult world. Kate appeared to have little understanding of the natural consequences of her actions, and he perceived a link between this and her inability or unwillingness to plan for the future. Planning for children, the eventual purchase of a home, establishing a family savings account, saving for college expenses, even agreeing to stick to a monthly budget were all matters she said she considered important. She stubbornly resisted the small incremental steps of putting them into practice on a daily and weekly basis, however. An impulse buyer, Kate refused to make lists. It was a small enough matter, except that Joe was the one she expected to run to the grocery store several times each week to compensate for it.

Sex was a joy they approached with different expectations. It felt good to Joe to feel Kate next to him in bed, and on the nights when she didn't roll over and turn out her light without speaking, he could enjoy their time together, and he loved her dearly. But what to make of her habit of lying still, almost unresponsive, during intercourse, as though waiting for their lovemaking to get better or more to her liking, confounded Joe. She was a good-looking woman who would have made any man proud to call his wife, and when they were together, he could almost forget the striving toward secrecy and sudden outbursts of anger that characterized their relationship during less intimate moments. Maybe most married couples took the good with the bad however life may have doled it out and continued to yearn for the better days that must be just around the corner.

* * *

How an educated woman in her late twenties could live almost entirely by assumptions was a mystery to Joe. "Drugstores aren't open on Sundays" and "Insurance won't cover accidents in somebody else's car" were the end of the discussion for Kate. Nothing that Joe said dispelled her assumptions. To change her mind, it was necessary to drive her to an open drugstore on Sunday afternoon or read her an insurance policy, solutions that were not always practical or possible.

He reread his vows every week and more often when frustrations ran high, letting the words sink into his mind like pebbles dropped into a pool. *I, Joseph, take you, Catherine, to by my wife, to have and to hold from this day forward, for better for worse, for richer for poorer, in sickness and in health, to love and to cherish, until we are parted by death. This is my solemn vow.* Sometimes Joe repeated the ancient formula over and over to himself like a mantra, seeking to squeeze from the words another drop of patience, another bead of forbearance, a further pinch of humility or humor.

He saw marriage as a sacred pact among three parties. He was as certain that God would help him in his marriage as he was that the sun would rise the following morning. A wedding was not just a ceremony, like an induction into a club or fraternity. It was not a contract. It was a sacrament; he had understood it this way since he was confirmed at the age of twelve. God was active in a sacrament, doing something inside the people involved while the outward and visible moment was taking place. Joe was absolutely certain that he and Kate were not in their marriage alone but that God, like a good parent or attentive coach, was standing by to support them, encouraging their health and wholeness even in the worst moments. God had brought them together out of the entire world, and God would give them what they needed to overcome their adjustments and difficulties. His own domestic relations practice had exposed him to many marriages in which God did not appear to be fulfilling this reconciling role. His own situation would be different, he told himself. He loved Kate, and Kate loved him. He felt confidence in them and in their marriage. It was becoming stronger every day.

He had learned much from Kate, and he knew there was much more for him to learn. She had taught him the value of sitting down in the evening and doing nothing together, and he had come to treasure these times—watching television, reading the paper. He had developed more patience and become a better listener. He had acquired new skills with in her care for Catherine's old house. Kate had a good sense of humor in many ways, and he enjoyed it immensely when she told him jokes she had heard from other teachers. Whether the jokes were good or not, he loved to hear her tell them. Kate was an excellent cook, cooking by instinct and especially good at preparing the old southern receipts with which the two of them had grown up. Her culinary skills were becoming well-known among their friends. Joe knew nothing about cooking despite growing up in a large family, where his parents and sisters had been good cooks. He had never been interested.

He took his marriage and their problems seriously and, according to his oldest childhood friend, too seriously. He saw Jeff every spring and fall when they met other old friends to fish for a few days at Cape Hatteras. Jeff had been like another member of Joe's family since the first grade. He had been a groomsman when Joe and Kate were married, and Joe had been a groomsman when Jeff had married Sally. His old friend loved Kate like a sister and looked upon Joe as a brother.

"Don't worry about it so much," he had told Joe on more than one occasion. They were walking north along the beach from Cape Point toward the magnificent lighthouse, gleaming defiantly now against the troubled horizon. "You'll do all right. Hell, Sally and I have our times too. There are days I want to go down to the river and jump in, and I'm not kidding. But everybody gets through it. Look at how Kate was raised. Can you imagine growing up with your mother drunk half the damn time? And with an asshole brother picking on her? Just keep at it. You sound like somebody who has read a goddamn book and expects things to definitely get better every day. With some people, it takes longer than others. Shit! There have been plenty of times when Sally and me liked to kill one another. You think Kate can be peculiar? You haven't seen anything till you see Sally in action. Just relax. You all will be okay."

"But what about the..." Joe gazed ahead along the line of crashing breakers. In the east, the November sky, dingy gray as roofing slate, plunged ominously down to the water like a thick curtain, making the midafternoon dark with the oncoming storm. The ocean, always heaving and agitated at the cape, reflected the white light from the untroubled west and ran out against the gathering storm on the approaching horizon, a sea of silver beneath the bulging, threatening sky. They had seen a thousand storms along these islands since they were boys. Behind them, their friends had rigged for drum and were maneuvering for positions along the curving finger of the point, awaiting the elusive copper monsters who might not wait till dark now that the sky was growing inky.

"The what?"

"I don't know…"

"What, goddamit! Spit it out!"

Joe shot his cigar into the surf, took off his weathered glove, and rubbed his eyes. "Hell," he said. "If I had to plead somebody else's case in court, I could explain it all. But when it's my own stuff, me, my marriage, my wife…I don't know." They trudged over the packed sand in their clumpy chest waders, carrying their surf rods with the fireball rigs dancing before them. They were speaking to one another but watching intently the gulls and terns riding in the shadowy sloughs beyond the breakers. "What is it that would make a person, an intelligent, capable person, somebody who wants a good marriage and a good life, knowingly refuse to take part in basic family responsibilities? Family things, social things, chores, the sort of thing that is in her own interest? Do you follow me?"

"Keep talking. I'm listening," said Jeff.

"I mean, just routine responsibilities, expectations. The kinds of things married people do, families do, adult professional people do, neighbors do. She won't help with housework. She refuses to take any interest in the yard, keeping the place looking right. I almost hate to have people in, unless I can get there first and pick up because I know she won't do it. She cooks only when it suits her, even though she's great at it. She won't put herself out any for social occasions. Says she doesn't have anything to wear. We're invited out, but each time she says she must go to the school games and chaperon the damn high school dances. Yet she complains day and night about the other teachers, the principal, the people who work in the office, everybody, our neighbors, even the president. I cannot get her to talk with me about our own stuff. When I try, she goes into her 'poor me' routine, as though she's the most oppressed woman in the world."

Except for an occasional "shit" or "damn," Jeff listened in silence.

Joe went on, relieved at being able to talk to someone. "And as for a budget, saving up for a down payment on a house…talking to me about personal feelings, anything to do with me…forget it. But if you go to her classroom, every single thing is organized and in perfect shape. And when I try to point out how other couples are handling things, she gets sarcastic and argumentative. Her response to everything is that I don't understand her. I don't appreciate all that she does. I'm the problem. Sometimes I feel like I've got a teenager around the house. Even sex. She just lays there with her eyes closed. And the sarcasm every day! It drives me crazy. I don't remember hearing that before we got married. Could she have been that way before and I just missed it? I must be the dumbest bastard on earth."

"Damn right you are! I been trying to tell you that for thirty years!" Jeff coughed and spat into the surf. "It will get better. She just needs time. I mean, you knew about some of this shit when you married her." He paused to light a cigarette. Joe cupped his hands too, to block the wind, a reflexive gesture among old hunting and fishing friends.

"But I *didn't* know," said Joe. "It's been a surprise. And some of it is bizarre. Weird."

"Like what?"

"Like…being what I've been calling selectively honest. What I mean is plain old telling lies. I've never accused her of that, never used *that* word."

"Good. Don't," Jeff barked. It had been among the worst things one could say about another where they grew up. The thought of a man saying it about his wife was appalling to both of them. Even Joe's experience in the law never helped him become used to it.

"You're right. I won't say *that*. The few times I've tried to discuss it with her, I've used the words 'selectively honest.' Hell! Being a lawyer must be good for something, so I came up with that phrase. She'll tell me only what she wants me to hear. Almost never the whole story about anything. I am honest and open with her, and it ends up getting me into trouble. I don't dare talk to her about any of my cases anymore because she'll have a glass of wine and yak about them to anybody around. So now she complains that I never tell her anything. And she must think I'm dumb as dirt to tell me some of the things she says. She's not fooling me. And when I catch her on it, one time she'll be hostile and threatening, and the next time she'll get this sad, sheepish look and pretend I have devastated her. Then she won't say anything, won't discuss it, but she'll give me the silent treatment and get that look. I don't know what's worse, her sarcasm or the silent treatment. Then I feel sorry for her, or I get to worrying that she'll blow up... You don't want to be around when she blows up. So I back off. I think to myself, well, at least she's got the message. But the next day or the next week, it happens again. She does the same thing, as though we had never been through it before. She does not learn. The cycle goes on."

"Women. Who can figure what they're thinking?" said Jeff.

"I haven't talked to anybody about it, not a single soul other than you. Because I know you won't say anything. You're too damn dumb to remember past this afternoon, anyway. But you live three hundred miles away. The priest who gave us marriage counseling has retired and moved to Florida. Where I am, I'm on my own. She's my wife. I mean, I owe it to her to keep our married stuff to myself. I know plenty of people with loose tongues, and I will not be one of them."

"It will change. She's smart. She knows it takes two to make a marriage," said Jeff. They walked another hundred yards in silence then turned and headed south again toward the cluster of jeeps and trucks where their group had set up for the afternoon. The wind had shifted from southeast to east, and the temperature had dropped a few degrees. Now and then a splatter of cold rain blew in horizontally from over the sea. A skimming gull, in a final foray before the storm, flew past them in a trough parallel to the beach with its orange beak inches above the water. On the horizon, three big boats, white against the smoky sky, plowed south around the point toward the inlet.

* * *

Against his best judgment, Joe had begun to hope that three might actually "make the marriage." He wanted a child more than anything. But bringing a child into the marriage before some of the issues were resolved, and there were plenty of them, seemed irresponsible, even reckless. Shouldn't their lives be in order first before bringing in a baby? Shouldn't they get more adjusted? Wasn't it best to finish working out some of their differences?

He thought of Jeff's description of him, "like somebody who has read a damn book and expects things to happen in perfect order." Jeff was right. Joe was much too academic about it all. He felt ashamed of himself. And the one, single conversation with his trusted friend, whose confidence he could rely upon with certainty, had left him feeling like a rookie player who has already let the team down halfway through the first game. It wasn't that Jeff would repeat anything. He would go to jail before he would break his word. It was the feeling that in discussing personal issues about his own wife he had broken a kind of code. *for richer for poorer...in sickness and in health...to love and to cherish.* His duty was to follow through no matter how long it took or how difficult it was. But speaking to anyone else, even to his oldest friend, about these intimate matters felt positively wrong. It had nothing to do with Jeff. He was completely trustworthy and honorable. It was having done it at all. He felt he had crossed a line that represented commitment and trustworthiness to his wife.

His common sense told him that others would see it differently. He had heard jerks talk too much at parties, but that was not what troubled him because he knew himself well enough to know he would never do that. Many men and women had talked over similar issues with him in legal consultations, seeking advice about divorce, mental commitments, counseling. It was something like that, a conviction that their own personal matters, family matters, marital matters were nobody's business but his and Kate's. He could not imagine his father or mother breaking such a commitment. The only exception should occur in a consultation with a professional. Jeff was as much of an exception as his conscience would allow, but even talking with Jeff had made him feel guilty.

People kept suggesting to him that he and Kate ought to have children. Maybe they were right. Nobody followed up by saying that children would help their marriage, but Joe wondered if that could be part of what they meant. People were always asking where Kate was or where they had both been on Friday night. His explanations that they had been at a high school basketball game or chaperoning a school dance drew a few compliments at first. Soon friends began to suggest they forget high school and join them at parties, at the races, at concerts. It was exactly what Joe preferred to do. He wanted adult companionship, adult conversation. Kate and the other teachers talked and sometimes dressed like their students.

Next to his marriage itself, having a baby was for Joe the most exciting, joyful blessing that could occur in his life. He felt that Kate saw it that way too. The way she sounded when she talked about a baby filled Joe with warmth and deep affection for her. She said she was ready and mentioned several times, in her oblique way, that in her late twenties she did not want to wait much longer. Although there were issues yet to work out, and for Joe the progress seemed maddeningly slow, having a baby began to represent all the wonderful promises of the future. Therefore, they continued to try to have a child as though they were as together on all other matters as they were on that.

And the union of body and spirit and all else in them was bliss that made everything else seem unimportant. For months they felt good. Joe suspended his efforts to discuss other problems. He did not allow them to be swept under the rug, as he had watched so many couples do on their way to divorce, but he contented himself by putting them on hold and knowing that there were years ahead in which to come to understanding. He went around for months in a euphoria that blessed everything he saw, all his relationships, every conversation. He was happy and looked forward to the future, and the difference felt good. He longed for the feeling to last, so he found himself letting things go by without comment.

Kate woke up and started complaining about driving to the airport to pick up her mother, a month's visit she had never bothered to mention to him. Bills arrived that exceeded their budget, to which

Kate was contributing a few hundred dollars each month, with no explanation. He was told to change quickly, as soon as he came home from work, to attend a high school affair of which he had never been warned. Money was needed immediately for repairs to the beach house he had never known about. They went out for cocktails at the home of Joe's hunting friends and Kate, without comment, dressed in a T-shirt and denim shorts and berated him afterward about the other women ("your fake friends") in their dresses. He bit his tongue and let them all go by. He told himself she would learn by experience. She was his wife. He loved her. And one evening, she came home late, having visited her doctor without mentioning it beforehand, and announced to him that she was pregnant.

Chapter Twelve

J oe remembered his father saying that his mother had never looked more beautiful than when she was pregnant. He had described Joe's mother's eyes, her bloom and warmth, and the other lovely qualities that made her so beautiful as she awaited the birth of their children. His father's words came back to him in the months before Ted's birth. Kate was lovelier and more inwardly composed than he had ever known her to be. She had stopped drinking alcohol during her pregnancy, and her temperament had been more even. She was understanding and patient. The miracle developing within her took her mind off the world and other people. Criticism of people at work and in the neighborhood grew less and less, as well as complaining about her own misfortune and how nobody appreciated all she did. Everything began to organize around her pregnancy, which provided an excuse, completely reasonable much of the time, to miss social gatherings and avoid some duties at work. Her participation in everything at home came to a stop. Joe willingly took on everything; he had been doing the cleaning, shopping, and caring for the yard alone for many months anyway. Kate's more even temperament and mellow regard made everything pleasant and manageable. It seemed her focus had shifted from herself to the two of them and their child as a family. Joe was proud of her. He loved his wife, and he loved what was happening in their lives.

In their Lamaze classes, Kate and Joe were the oldest and most attentive participants. They made friends with the other expectant parents, a dozen equally excited people who were younger than the

Stephensons. A few were very young, one couple still teenagers and inexperienced barely described them. Kate discussed them in bed at night with Joe. She found them completely unprepared emotionally for what was coming, and she expressed concern for the baby about to be born to them. Neither Joe nor Kate was frivolous or capricious in their excitement. Each felt they had as a couple a maturity that was the gift of years and professional work with children. Others felt great confidence in their future role as parents and told them so. They felt good about themselves too as a family and counted the days until the blessed moment.

All that came with being born, being alive. God did the choosing. God was in marriage too and parenting, but a man or a woman had a choice in them, perhaps even the determinative choice. And, ah, how lightly the choosing weighed in some lives, how casually some experienced the balance between choice and accident. An afternoon carousing around the lake with friends or a date where wine or beer flowed too freely and nine months later, bang. A squealing, needy, demanding, life-changing surprise for which nobody, especially the father and mother, were either prepared or capable. He was determined that his own little one would arrive where everything was ready, hopeful, and supportive. It was a new kind of love, something he had sensed but never really known before. Not sex, no infatuation or visceral longing throbbing up and overwhelming the senses and reason, not even affection. It was deeper than affection. He was in awe of the coming birth of their child and of his own feelings stirred up in anticipation and mostly of the one about whom he and his beloved wife had already begun to rearrange their lives. Their child, their son or daughter, his parents' grandchild, to whom his wife would soon give birth, it was a miracle, a gift of God, and he was moved to the depth of his very being by it.

He figured he knew something about children, at least about the special education students he had taught for years. He reasoned his experience would be helpful, but the closer to birth they came, the more he understood that it was not the same as being a parent. Nothing was the same. Once, when his father was lamenting some trouble in the life of one of Joe's sisters, Joe remembered making the worst possible response. To his father's remarks he had replied, with the best of intentions, "I know how you feel."

"No! You don't know," said his father quickly. "You won't know how I feel until you have a child of your own. People think they know how a parent feels. But you have to have a child of your own to know how all this makes me feel."

In bed at night, Kate talked, excited and happy despite her discomfort. They listened to each other and tried to understand. Unlike Joe, she appeared to have no personal reservations about herself, and she looked at the coming joy more clinically than Joe did. She was confident in the soundness of her own judgment. She had been successful in every academic course she had ever studied and was certain she would master motherhood with the same triumph. Joe had confidence in her too. Regardless of how much he had learned to be wary of her judgment in other matters, he was encouraged and relieved at her openness and honesty about her pregnancy. Participating with her in birthing classes, touching her and feeling the life within her as the months passed, and talking with her in bed at night about the future gave him, at last, the sense that they were sharing their married life together. He knew now it meant something to her. He had hungered for her companionship and participation, and he felt it was happening finally as they approached the birth of their child. Even with his own deficiencies, he felt he could be a good parent with Kate. He talked about their marriage and their family and the future, excited and grateful, beside her in bed in the dark until her deep breathing and light snores signaled that she had heard enough. She complained to him about the odd sensation of waking up to find the two middle fingers asleep on each hand. Joe agreed it was odd and even laughed about it. He awoke the next day with the same symptoms and continued to experience them for days after Kate was no longer troubled by them.

Their classes prepared them well for the night of Ted's birth. He was a big baby, and the delivery took a while. Kate bore up under it all with courage and good humor. Joe was as proud of her as he was of their son. The genial, gentle Pakistani doctor and good-natured nurses were attentive and kind. In a day when men were just beginning to enter the delivery room, Joe was adamant from the start that he intended to be present. Kate insisted that she wanted him with her at every moment. The delivery room staff, who had seen every sort of prospective parent, found the Stephensons to be patient and sensible in everything. Until the moment when Dr. Alkari said "You have a...son," they did not know if a baby boy or girl was about to enter their lives. The nurses cleaned Ted up and handed him carefully to Joe who held him and gazed into his tiny face. He felt the earth tilt.

When he nestled Ted carefully down upon Kate and watched her looking at her newborn son, he was certain that all the best things in the world were happening for them. He would carry the moment with him forever. When Kate was safely in her room and Ted sleeping soundly with his compatriots in another ward, Joe left the hospital and went home. It was almost 4:00 a.m., but he could not sleep. He was so moved and so excited that he sat on the back steps and watched the sunrise, thinking of Kate, Ted, their wedding, the future, and so many, many other wonderful things.

In the days that followed, Joe looked at Kate and thought of Renoir, Watteau, Fragonard, and all the large, lush female figures who descended from Titian and Rubens. He saw in her Renoir's *The Bathers* and the lovely, severe classical girl in *The Plait,* with its Italian premonitions of Modigliani. He saw in her Manet's superb *Blond Woman with Bare Breasts* and Mary Cassatt's intimate, haunted Japanese *Girl in the Garden*. He loved to look at her, to inhale her sweet scent when she came from the shower into bed, to taste the delicate touch of her cheek, her lips. It filled him with awe and humility and excitement to see her nursing Ted and to watch her go about her small domestic matters like the girl in Mary Cassatt's *Young Mother Sewing.* It made him ache with happiness to be together with his wife and their son. "This marriage, beauty. This marriage, a moon in a light blue sky..." He remembered Rumi, Dickinson, the Sonnets. It made him sing within himself.

It amused him to teach Kate to change a diaper, a thing he thought would come naturally to a woman, a mother. Having changed a thousand of them in the past, it never occurred to him that she might not know. In their nighttime routine, Joe went in to

Ted when he awoke hungry in the night, changed his diaper, and brought him to the bed, where Kate nursed him. She was at home on maternity leave, and Joe worked every day waiting for the moment he could go home to them.

As happy as he was and continually excited, he felt tired much of the time. After a few weeks, after bringing Ted in to Kate, Joe lay down too and went back to sleep, waking up when it was time to return Ted to his bed. He found it odd to hear Kate tell callers that "*he* gets to go back to sleep while I have to stay awake and nurse the baby." He questioned her about it. He reminded her that he was doing everything a husband could do and that there was no way he could take part in breastfeeding. Kate replied that the least he could do would be to stay awake and keep her company.

Why this exchange should have stayed in his mind over the years, he could not say. It was a small enough matter, but he thought it odd anyway. At the time he wondered if it perhaps signaled the end of the less critical, more easygoing period he had so cherished with Kate during her pregnancy. He remembered how, in those days, in talking about men in general, Kate referred over and over to a television actor (someone whose name, to her utter astonishment, Joe did not even know) who had "stolen his best friend's wife." It seems this actor had a childhood friend who was married. The friend and his wife had children. The actor began an affair with his friend's wife, eventually "stealing her right out from under his own best friend and their children. Isn't that just like a man," Kate exclaimed in dismay, "stealing your best friend's wife." This always amused Joe, and Kate immediately grew irritable and accused him of not taking it seriously. He tried to talk with her about it, but Kate would not listen. "You're just a man trying to defend what another man did," she would say. The acquiescence of the "stolen" wife in these shenanigans seemed never to enter Kate's mind.

There were nights when Ted fussed after his feeding, as all babies do at times. It alarmed Joe that at such times Kate made more noise than Ted, loudly suggesting that something was wrong, wondering what ailment he could have and declaring she would call the doctor. Her raised voice and agitated manner ratcheted up Ted's tiny wail proportionately, providing Joe's first experience with an exponential emotional equation that in time would affect their lives in ways he could not begin to imagine. He took Ted from her gently in the dark, speaking as soothingly as he knew how to both mother and child as he settled Ted down on his chest, carefully shifting the pajamas he wore in those days so the buttons would not irritate his son's pink skin. He lightly patted Ted's little back and spoke quietly to him, while Kate, exasperated and near tears, fidgeted beside him. Ted would squirm until his little head came to rest under Joe's chin. Then, feeling secure, he would settle down and fall asleep. Joe would hear Kate's faint, relaxed breathing about the same time in the dark, and soon he too would sleep.

Ted's luxurious dark hair fell out soon after birth, and he bobbed about with a bald head for a while. When his hair grew in again, his delighted parents were at first amazed by his beautiful blond curls, until both their mothers remarked that each of them too had blond curls as a child. They wondered if Ted's hair would turn brown like his parents' hair. A pretty baby, Ted developed quickly into a big, beautiful child. He was bright and inquisitive, learned fast, and walked early. At nine months he began to talk.

Joe believed that Kate was a good mother, and he said so to everybody. A few things troubled him, but he told himself they were minor and were certainly outweighed by her total and sincere devotion. In his work in the courts and with the police, he saw children every week, and adults who had been such children, who suffered from the neglect of uninvolved parents. They were children who had to find their nurturing and security in places other than home. Ted would never be that sort of human being; he would know what it meant to be loved, valued, esteemed. The issues Joe was forced to notice had nothing to do with love but much to do with other things, and over time they began to disturb Joe. He would have preferred to ignore them or to minimize them, as he had done with problems in their marriage. He could not because they concerned Ted.

The relationship between Kate and Ted was noisy. Kate talked relentlessly. Joe saw this as helpful to mother and child; children who were talked to learned to talk too. It was not the act of communicating that troubled him. It was the hyperactivity it led to. Kate was a center of noise: talking, the sound of the television in the living room, the kitchen radio blaring at the same time, a blender turned on and allowed to whirr for minutes on end, cabinet door slamming, an egg timer dinging, any musical toy Ted owned yipping away too, and all together in a cacophony of persistent sound. Ted would respond by what Kate and Joe too called singing. But sometimes he would cry. And no matter how calm he was and how content and happy, a few minutes with Kate as she changed his diaper was often enough to make him wail. She did nothing to hurt him, of course. She loved him dearly. But she was hyperactive herself while around Ted, and her ways communicated themselves to Ted so continuously that he would make noise around her too, and often this meant crying. With Kate around, there was very little calm, relaxing down time.

Joe tried to discuss it with Kate, but she could not understand and quickly grew defensive. When he tried to present specific examples of what he had observed, she responded with sarcasm. In a way, it was like picking up again where matters had been left before her pregnancy. Although she would not discuss these matters with him, Joe suspected that she had understood what little she heard before routinely closing him off. In public, she began silently to defer to Joe when Ted needed changing or a bottle or an adjustment to his stroller or car seat, allowing Joe to step in calmly and quietly. When Ted was old enough to sit in a high chair in restaurants, she busied herself with other people or her pocketbook, while Joe fed Ted or placed his food before him. She once attracted the attention of the entire clientele of a big, busy restaurant in Pennsylvania Dutch Country with her furious protestations that Ted would never eat cooked carrots. Joe knew that the reason was her own dislike of cooked carrots, but discussing it with her had always been out of the question. While Kate talked with friends at the table, Joe quietly showed Ted the big round orange disks of carrot and spoke quietly and encouragingly in his ear about how good they were, swallowing a few with a goofy grin to demonstrate his point. When next Kate focused upon Ted, it was in time to see him shove three bits of carrot happily into his mouth and gesture to Joe for some more. Kate sat silently by while their friends, whose little girl was a bit older than Ted, and Joe complimented Ted on eating his carrots. She began to understand that Joe could manage some of these issues calmly and well and that he had skill as a father she had been too distracted to notice. Joe could deal with Ted in ways that elicited no unnecessary crying. Although discussion about it was out of the question, Kate silently recognized it and acquiesced. At least when other people were around, she preferred to do it this way rather than experience the embarrassment of Ted crying under her care. Joe would see calmly to whatever needed to be done, while Kate could be heard telling friends that she had Joe "trained" to care for Ted when she needed a break.

And Kate had begun to drink again as soon as she returned home from the hospital. After carefully and conscientiously abstaining during pregnancy, she found her first glass of white wine powerful and affecting. Within a few days, she needed several glasses to achieve the same good feeling. Soon she had returned to her pre-pregnancy routine, except that now Joe found himself watching her when she was with Ted.

During those years, Catherine spent the winters with the Stephensons, arriving as soon as it became too cold to remain in the unheated Wicomico beach house. She would sometimes leave for a while to visit Kate's brother and his family in Georgia. Kate's sister-in-law, Fawn, would grow weary and hurt by Catherine's drinking and complaining after a week or so and demand that Ray make her stop. Ray always responded by sending Catherine back to Kate and Joe, with no explanation, often telephoning Kate as he put her on a plane. Catherine would return, irked and subdued, and within days, sometimes hours, she and Kate would have an argument. The tension was severe, and Joe worried constantly that it would somehow affect Ted.

Catherine was wonderfully excited about Ted, and she loved to hold him and rock him to sleep. For the first few days after arrival, her presence was pleasant enough, but she and Kate soon fell into a routine that included an argument every couple of days. By the time Joe came home from work, unless a trial kept him in court through the evening, Kate had left the high school and picked up Ted from his sitter. She would have been at home for an hour or so with her mother, usually preparing dinner. The one advantage of Catherine's visits was that Kate would always prepare dinner when her mother was with them. Almost every night Joe came in to find Kate and Catherine arguing, sometimes with raised voices, or they were in separate rooms refusing to speak with each other. Joe's arrival signaled a welcome outlet for Kate, who would begin talking to him as soon as he entered the kitchen. Her complaints about the administration at school had resumed as soon as she returned to work, and the other members of her science department came in for much criticism too. Kate had always seemed to view herself as trapped between the irritations of work and the annoyances of home, and her mother's presence made all this worse. While preparing dinner, Kate often related her mother's latest indignities loudly enough, Joe feared, to be heard in the living room where Catherine sat, pretending to watch television.

Joe found himself continuously thinking of Ted. He believed that infants learned through multisensory means. He worried that Ted's fledgling emotions and intellect were being affected by the constant tension, arguing, and sarcasm that radiated from Kate and Catherine like heat from a furnace. His view of Kate as a better and more capable person than himself caused him to take a sort of personal inventory and wonder what messages he too was sending to his precious son.

Chapter Thirteen

The lively chatter of early Friday evening was especially jovial on payday, and the Third Base resounded with many voices raised in satisfaction. Both county high schools had a shot at the state triple A basketball championship and the weekend would likely bring them closer to a showdown that would make local history. Across the river, somebody had robbed a bank, and an accident on the interstate had sent hundreds of confused drivers frantically along the unmarked county roads. A rattle of glasses punctuated the vigorous discussion of all this as indignant stares, the lone woe on the premises, were directed at the television above one end of the bar. It was tuned perpetually to the sports channel, which insisted on showing from time to time, as it was now, prolonged reruns of the World Cup, which interested nobody but Latino migrant workers. It soon moved to news of the NFL, and the hum of contentment resumed. People hailed each other and laughed at old jokes. From the brightly lit room adjoining the bar came the distinctive clack of billiard balls, unlike any other sound in the world, and the accompanying swell of stimulating expletives. A giant old Wurlitzer jukebox, the last in use in the state, crouched immensely in the wide doorway between the big rooms and somebody stepped forward and deposited two quarters into it. A series of internal noises and movements led presently to the earnest lament of a whiskey-voiced woman crying into a microphone of long ago.

Lord, forgive me while I drink my lonesome wine;

My man's gone again, ain't coming back this time.
I'm lost and broke and lonely as can be,
So, tell me, Lord, what is your plan for me.

"Ain't heard that old song in years," said Donna. She and her companion, Ricky, owned the Third Base and the gas station down the road. What they really wanted was to open a truck stop.

The rent is due and all the kids are crying;
Ain't no one by my side, but I keep trying.
My life's a mess as everyone can see;
Lord, help me understand your plan for me.

Wallace took a long swig of his draft beer and said, "Preacher down at our church was saying last Sunday—"

"Who's that, now?" asked Joe.

"His name…is…damn, Joe, if you hadn't of asked me—"

"What church?"

"Well, now that I *can* tell you. Tabernacle Methodist," said Wallace, very pleased with himself. "Been there since I married Lady, going on twelve years now."

"I don't know your minister," said Joe. "What did he say?"

"Wallace don't know what he said. Soon's he opens his mouth, Wallace is sound asleep. Ain't that right, Wallace?" said Sandra, a waitress.

"No, it ain't right. I wait at least five minutes till he gets going good." Everybody laughed.

"How long does he preach?" Joe wanted to know.

"He ain't too bad. Thirty, forty minutes," said Wallace in a charitable way.

"Good lord!" said Joe. "Forty minutes!" His own sermons lasted about ten minutes, and he grew weary even thinking of sitting through a forty-minute diatribe. At Redeemer, where they liked Joe's sermons, people started checking their watches at twelve minutes.

"'Less it's Christmas or Easter. Then he might cut loose for an hour. Sometimes I doze off but didn't this past Sunday. Lady don't like it when I do. Preacher said Sunday that the problem with the world is sin. You agree with that, Joe?"

"Certainly do," Joe said.

"And then he said sin was not knowing what God's plan for your life was and not trying to find out and all. You agree with that, Joe?"

"No."

"Why not?" asked Raymond, the bartender.

"That's not the meaning of sin," said Joe. "And God does not have a plan for your life. Or mine."

"Wait a minute," said Donna. "I haven't been in church in longer than I care to admit, but the preacher always said God had a plan for everybody's life. Don't most people go around waiting to find out what God's plan is for their life? I though everybody did that."

A murmur of affirmation arose along the bar. Raymond removed some hot glasses from a dishwasher and turned and said, "Don't it say in the Bible that God loves every human being?"

"Just like a good parent loves a child," said Joe. "But that is not the same thing as having a plan for everyone. God doesn't. God leaves it up to us how we want to live our lives. It's called free will. It's a gift to each one of us from God. We are free to make our own choices. You can work your ass off, or you can lay back on welfare. God will let you."

"Well, 'scuse me for interrupting, Reverend, but I've always been taught that God has some special plan for my life. I mean, I'll be the first to admit I haven't been exactly looking for what it is like I should. But don't God have a plan for me?" This was a stranger speaking, one of the many that were always passing through. He sat at the bar just past the bend with a wild-eyed woman wearing a green tank top and no bra. Everybody looked at him and murmured in concurrence.

"God has a plan, all right," Joe said. "But not for the life of any individual. Once in a great while, God makes special plans for people. Not very often. What God has is one great big plan for the whole universe. It's called the plan of salvation. Our duty is to understand the big plan and use our free will to conform our own lives to it. It's called following Christ."

"Well, so a lot of what happens…" said Donna.

"Is up to us?" said Raymond.

"Now that is a new perspective I haven't heard before," said the stranger. The wild-eyed woman considered Joe's clerical collar warily.

"We are never too old to learn," said Joe.

"Well, who does he have a special plan for, then?" said Sandra.

"Who gets their own customized blueprint?" asked the stranger.

A short thin man named Kidd interjected, "I know it ain't me. Don't know all that I been doing since I was a kid." Everyone looked around and agreed. They all knew Kidd, a regular customer who had been in and out of jail since he was thirteen. He looked to be in his fifties, but he was not yet thirty. "I been doin' what the hell I want!"

"At times God does pick a human being to do a special job. Usually it's to serve as God's mouthpiece, somebody God can speak through to warn human beings. The warning is usually to turn around while there's still time."

"Now, that would be your prophets," said Sandra. Everybody looked at her.

"Like Isaiah, Jeremiah," said Donna.

"Just pray it doesn't happen to you," said Joe. "To be chosen as God's spokesman…" He shook his head. "Whatever words God puts in your mouth, you can be certain the world doesn't want to hear. Most of the prophets were killed or driven away. The modern ones too. Gandhi. Martin Luther King."

"Man, that King was something," said somebody in the rear. A murmur of agreement went round.

"So there's one big plan, and I'm supposed to figure out how I fit in?" said the stranger. The wild-eyed woman gazed about in listless irritation.

"Right," Joe said. "And then spend your life following the plan as best you can."

"But how do we know what the plan is?"

"We look at Jesus, listen to him, watch what he does, the way he lives. We get to know him. We spend time with his friends. We go where we know we'll find him. The evidence is everywhere. God's fingerprints are all around us," said Joe.

"Evidence? Fingerprints?" said two or three people at once.

"Science helps us understand how God made the world. Not why but how. Mathematics alone is evidence of God's design. Pi on earth is the same as pi in another galaxy. It's evidence of the Creator."

"So you mean it didn't just happen."

"No. God has a plan. God made the world to be inhabited. God didn't make a mess. God does not create chaos." Joe would have liked to continue, but his pastoral instincts sensed a certain boundary. There would be another time.

"Pie?" said Wallace, as if to confirm Joe's caution.

"Wallace, you dumb bastard, he's talking about—" began Donna.

Raymond interrupted, saying, "Remember from high school? Pie are square?"

"Aw, shit. Let's get back to this plan," said the concrete Wallace. "How am I supposed to learn to know somebody I can't even see?"

Joe was thrilled, but he controlled his feelings. Credibility. Every now and then, he recognized that his years as a trial lawyer had been worth something, after all. He chose his words with care. "That is the best question anybody could ask," he said. "Just a desire to know Jesus sends a signal to God. Imagine a beacon out at the airport shining up into the night sky. When we really want Jesus, we send the same kind of signal. God responds immediately and helps us understand. It begins in private prayer. It continues when we worship with other people."

"Lord!" said the stranger's companion, covering her bare stomach.

Joe got down from his stool, understanding the consequences of pushing a good conversation too far.

"One more thing," said Raymond. "You say God will help us. Give me an example."

Joe put on his raincoat and said, "He already has, Ray. Long ago. Sorry to eat and run."

He went out into the night and, on his way to the car, paused at the window and looked in. Through the wet foggy glass, he could see them all still clustered around the end of the bar. They appeared to be arguing. Somebody waved an arm. Someone else joined them. He wondered if they were continuing to hash it out or if talk had drifted to football or the bank robbery across the river. It didn't matter. He could also see an obese man in the background rigging up a karaoke set. Joe got into his car. He was making his getaway just in time.

Chapter Fourteen

Ted brought unspeakable joy to their marriage. Their loveliest times were when the three of them were together. Both took delight in learning something new from him, about him, every day. He was alert, lively and, even as an infant, appeared to have a sense of humor. He learned quickly and had a clever way about him, imaginative, inquisitive. It was as if he had always been a part of them, not just of their marriage, but of each of them before. Within days of his birth, neither could imagine life without him. Each was moved by the most mundane evidence of his presence, although in dissimilar ways. A tiny shirt or pair of pants from Joe's parents or the miniscule booties Catherine knitted on the dry wrack or folded baby clothes on the sofa made them feel like Christmas morning. Baby powder and a plastic washtub in the bathroom, toys everywhere, became sources of inspiration and encouragement. The expedition of going anywhere, with stroller and baby bags, formula and diapers and right clothing for the weather, became as much fun as vacation travels. They couldn't imagine loving anyone as much as they loved their happy big blond baby. They began to talk about a second child.

With her baby boy, Kate was like a child with a new favorite toy. Until Ted's birth, her career as a teacher had been the focus of her existence. Now it shared her attention with her child. Her choices, decisions, and attitudes were shaped by her high school during the day and by her son at all other times. Joe believed she loved him too in her own way, but he was aware by now that he was chiefly background and backup for her identity as educator and, now, mother.

He was someone, and at times he sensed some*thing*, of which Kate was generally aware, necessary and often frustrating, upon whom she relied for a sort of context. Like a dependable servant, at hand when needed, who should remember his place and fulfill his duty without undue fuss, Joe was useful but not expected to present surprises.

Although their fun together with Ted was genuine and joyful, a new phase of their existence together, each of them would have explained it in very different terms. Joe saw it as evidence of good things to come, proof of progress between them, confirmation that time and patience was leading to a better and more intimate understanding. And to a certain extent, although a great deal less than he supposed, he was correct. Kate viewed her baby and her marriage as affirmation too. What was affirmed was her whole life until that point, a validation of her approach to the world and to her marriage, a reward of sorts for how she had managed it all. Like a student climbing the academic ladder, her successes had brought her to graduation with honors. She was in possession of an award that proved the rightness of all that had come before. Appreciation of her accomplishment strengthened the unyielding infrastructure that had brought her this far, for now she had more to protect.

Regarding himself too highly, never one of Joe's faults, grew less and less a danger as he looked at his smiling son and perceived a gift in trust, and he and Kate as trustees. He was being blessed, trusted. Even then he knew it was for only a while. Perceiving his own faults and feeling the want of confidence and insight that others, especially other lawyers, seemed to take for granted, Joe was left with just enough self-esteem to keep him healthy and not a bit more. He longed to identify with something larger than himself. He told Kate he believed God had no grandchildren, only children, and he felt he was always on the edge of comprehending something about that but forever just missing it, an insight or breakthrough into the mystery of relationship. Kate, who knew all she needed to know about law and lawyers from television, thought this was strange talk indeed for a lawyer. People were defined by what they did. Lawyers "made" wills and contracts for people and went to court on traffic cases. What did this kind of thing have to do with raising a child, changing diapers, leaving school early to rush him to the doctor.

Joe was half crazy at times, one of the few things in life upon which Kate and Catherine could agree. Let him ramble on. Just don't say anything. Life just proceeds, and we go along with it. One day he will learn how simple it all is. When he talks about how the past is always with us in the present and how we are not there but he is here ("and I guess 'he' is God, who knows?"), well, it's better to just let it go, try to ignore it. I have enough to think about. I have enough to do. After all, I have to work.

His natural inclination was at first to defer to Kate in matters of parenting. He did not see it as sexist at the time. She was Kate, and she was Ted's mother, and Ted was her baby. The initiative he showed in court and in professional negotiations was not meant to dominate his role in family life. Marriage is a partnership in which he and Kate were meant to share everything. Leadership and responsibilities were mutual, or should be, in all areas. He desired her love. He craved her participation, support, confidence, and judgment. He believed Ted's welfare depended upon their mutual success as husband and wife. He was certain Ted was learning consciously and unconsciously from their relationship. Having worked professionally with many damaged children, Joe was continually aware of his infant son's delicate, developing sensibilities. The positive duty he felt toward Ted would be fulfilled in being a good husband. A good marriage, always critical, would be determinative of everything from now on. He wanted his son to grow up calm, reasonable, and courageous.

As the months passed, Joe began to understand that nourishing these good qualities in his son would have its challenges. Kate often interpreted his deference as unloading unwanted responsibilities upon her. Joe had been learning for two years how to love and live with someone in denial, whose temper exploded with very little provocation. Ted's arrival on the scene outshone everything else for a while. And though his light still blazed, the old shadows could soon be perceived in new configurations.

Joe's disposition was affected by a streak of conscience inherited from parents whose lives had demanded careful and sensitive stewardship of what they had. By struggling to stretch their time and Joe's father's meager salary over every family need, they raised six children by working together and putting each other and their offspring first. Their sharing and self-denial were never topics of even the most oblique comment. It was the way decent people lived, and it merited no discussion. They denied themselves routinely and never complained, not once, not even to each other when late at night they finally had a moment to themselves. Their sacrifices had been cheerful; they were glad to fulfill their duty because they loved one another, and they loved their children. Their relationship had nurtured Joe's temperament, unconsciously formed over years of growing up with two young parents, five siblings, and one bathroom.

Catherine too had raised her children with care and good intentions. Although she had been forced to do much of it alone, her relatives and their small Southern community had provided as much support as Catherine would allow. Her teacher's salary had been adequate in most cases to meet their needs. But her good intentions had been mixed with chronic drinking and her unyielding denial of its effect upon her, her children, and their family life. No recognition of a disease, no acknowledgment of a need for help, no perception of the accruing damage to personalities and relationships, and no softening of the homegrown anger that was its legacy was permitted to enter her life or her children's. Kate's emotions and intellect had formed in this environment, acquiring layer upon layer of insulating, self-protective, impenetrable denial.

These differences in background, misunderstood by both of them at first, had formed in Kate attitudes toward life quite unlike Joe's. Her upbringing, without the example of two parents at work on the same issues at the same time, had made it difficult for her to understand the role of mutuality in family life. Joe was no psychologist, but he sensed trouble when he saw it, even in relationships among people who loved one another dearly.

As with his attempts to discuss their differences, make long-range family plans, manage finances and time, and attend to all other areas of family life, Kate resisted Joe in raising Ted. When her intransigence became loud and abusive in public or in social situations, Joe at first chose to pacify her in the most destructive way—by giving in. He was mindlessly and sometimes recklessly protective, of Kate herself so that she would not disgrace herself before others, of Ted so that he would not be subjected to bad examples, of his career or Kate's career, of their "place" in the community. He was shamed at times by his own caution and worried at night when he was trying to sleep that he was placing too much emphasis on the appearance of things. But every stage of his upbringing, teaching experience, legal education, and career had made clear to him that a person must avoid even the appearance of impropriety. Its application to his professional duty was plain, but he felt that it was a good rule for family life too. In its simplest relevance, it meant parents must set good examples for their children. It was not at all different from the standards of the world in which he had been raised. Most people were honest. They did their best. They tried to live with integrity. A mature man or woman was responsible, ethical, and respectful of others. And wasn't family supposed to be the birthplace of one's integrity? If Joe or one of his friends had told a lie while growing up, it would have reflected upon his whole family. And family had been important in the South of Joe's youth. Wasn't it his duty as a husband and father to preserve the integrity of their family and its reputation? Was it right to do nothing when Kate said and did things before others that damaged the way people saw them? But how should he manage these differences when she was closed to discussion? She was a grown woman, an intelligent person, and not a child to be corrected and ordered around. How was he supposed to respond to her behavior? What could he do to make her respond? What should his duty be, what was his role? It amazed him that he was still asking himself these questions two years and one baby into marriage. How *should* he react when she became loud and sarcastic, shouting at him in an unaccountable nasal twang, slurring her words, her nose and cheeks red?

She was not completely negative. He knew it was not fair to believe she would react to every challenge with hostility. Usually she would simply listen, pretend to agree, and then proceed to do exactly what she wanted to do. He had found this general attitude extremely difficult to live with but manageable to a degree when it concerned only the two of them. But Joe understood that Ted was being influenced daily by what went on around him. Gradually, Joe became alarmed, and his anxiety for his son was unlike any other worry he had ever experienced. It was increased each time Kate routinely rebuffed his efforts toward discussing their issues.

One night he came home just before dinner to find Kate on the telephone with another teacher, while Ted toddled about holding a box of Girl Scout cookies. He offered Joe a cookie, and Joe thanked him and gently took away the box and placed it on the mantelpiece behind some books. At dinner shortly afterward, Ted would not eat his vegetables and meat loaf. Joe tried to talk with Kate. She denied that Ted had eaten any cookies. Joe went into the living room and returned with the box. Kate countered that Ted must have taken the box while her back was turned. Joe reminded her casually that the cookies were kept in the cabinet next to the refrigerator, well beyond the reach of a three-year-old. Kate became angry and demanded to know why everything was always her fault. As this was occurring in front of Ted, Joe decided to drop the subject until bedtime. By then Kate was in a compatible mood again, and reluctant to reignite a smoldering fire, he chose not to bring it up again.

One evening upon his return home from work, Catherine took Joe aside and complained to him that by the age of three, Ted should be dressing himself. She had carefully avoided discussing it with Kate. Joe spoke with his secretaries the next day, and each confirmed what Catherine had said. Without mentioning Catherine or his secretaries, Joe discussed it with Kate that evening, and she agreed to lay out Ted's clothes so that he could dress himself from then on. The next morning she dressed him, as usual. She grew irritated and sullen when Joe began to discuss it, replying that she had not had time the night before to lay out his clothes. Joe began to remind her that she had watched television for two hours the previous evening, but an instant premonition of her loudly demeaning Joe in Ted's presence all the way to the day care center caused him to remain quiet. After a week or so, Joe began laying out Ted's clothes for the next day each night after Ted's bath, encouraging Ted to choose what he wanted to wear and talking with him about which colors and patterns fit well together. He complimented Ted on dressing himself. Occasionally, Kate, irked when Ted put on a T-shirt backward, cast accusatory looks at Joe, and she continued to dress him on weekends. But soon Ted was choosing his own clothing from his bureau drawers and insisting gleefully to Kate that he could dress himself.

In those days, young children played with popular mechanical toys that could be twisted and manipulated from the form of a car or dinosaur into a robot or alien from outer space. Like many children his age, they were Ted's favorite toys. He had three or four, and it seemed Joe was moving them aside every time he wanted to sit down. Joe began to notice a proliferation of them around the house. One Saturday morning, he counted eighteen of them and was certain he had not found them all. They cost about seven dollars each. It emerged that Kate had been buying a new one for Ted each time they went out together. Ted asked for new toys often, like most other children. Joe tried to discuss with Kate how harmful it was to give in to Ted's every request. She agreed not to buy him any more mechanical toys. A few days later, Joe discovered that she had, instead, over the preceding four days, bought him a different type of toy. He tried to talk with her about teaching Ted patience, the value of material things, and good manners. She listened, eyebrows raised, eyes lowered, and her tongue pressed into her cheek. She made no response. While Kate sat at the kitchen table and glanced through a newspaper, Joe took Ted on his lap on the living room sofa and patiently explained to him that boys and girls could not buy new toys whenever they went out and asked him please not to ask for them. He tried to tell him about the many children who had no toys. He assured Ted he had done nothing wrong and, seeing the unease in his small face, talked to him about his own favorite toys when he was young. Ted listened and asked a lot of questions. After Ted had been put to be that night, Joe managed to wrest from Kate during a heated discussion a promise not to buy Ted any new toys until they could discuss the subject again on the weekend. Joe came in the next evening to find Ted playing with a new set of plastic soldiers and sailors. When he demanded an explanation from Kate, she countered sharply that Catherine had bought them. She had gone out with Kate and Ted to the grocery store and bought them while they were there. Joe became angry and accused Kate of not keeping her promise. He talked with Catherine, who said, with pained surprise, that she had not known Ted could have no new toys. Kate interrupted to say that she had told her mother not to buy any toys. Catherine shouted that Kate had helped choose the army men. Kate shouted that she had not. The two of them proceeded to argue. Joe, who had not yet had time to change out of his business suit, took Ted for a walk in the field behind the house. He carefully explained to him that sometimes adults disagreed and assured him that he had done nothing wrong. Ted produced from his pocket two green plastic soldiers and a blue sailor. Joe sat down in the grass with him. They constructed fortifications with pebbles and dry grass and played together until Joe took him in to dinner. They found Kate and Catherine already eating in silence, seated at opposite ends of the table. As they sat down, even Ted could sense that his beloved mother and grandmother, who bought him toys, were angry and that somehow his father had caused it all. Joe helped Ted up into his seat at the silent table, knowing with frustration and sorrow that he was appearing again in his precious son's eyes as the bad guy in the family.

One evening Joe came home from work and set the table for dinner. Catherine had been visiting for about two weeks. Kate and Catherine were still drinking wine at night, and the great confrontations over alcohol had not yet begun. Joe poured white wine for them. Because he had not had his bourbon and water that evening, he poured wine for himself too, something he almost never did.

A few minutes later, after the blessing had been said and they were eating and listening to Kate talk about a disagreement with an assistant principal, Joe took a sip of wine and found it to be mostly water. His desire not to begin an argument and his proclivity for evaluating evidence precluded his saying anything at the time. Neither Kate nor Catherine mentioned it, even though both had several glasses from the same big bottle. After dinner he discussed it with Kate. She said she had noticed nothing unusual about the wine. It had been so obviously diluted, and he told her so, that she reddened and said that her mother always ruined everything and this was no different. Kate was clearly upset but refused to talk with her mother about it. When Joe discussed it with Catherine, she agreed immediately that the wine was "funny" but denied having had anything to do with it. The big bottle, still half filled, disappeared from the refrigerator the next day. The following few days, prior to Catherine's departure, were quiet and uncomfortable. She left for home clearly offended at the suggestion that she would drink up the wine and replace it with water.

Three days after Catherine's departure, and one day after Joe had bought a fresh gallon of white wine, compelled by what he could not have said, he sampled the new bottle and found it also to be mostly water. When Kate came into the kitchen, carrying Ted, he confronted her. Even Kate was unable to hide the truth this time. But instead of shouting and sarcasm, she presented an affronted and disinterested silence, her face taking on an impenetrable defiance that made him angry. Even his pointing out that she had let him accuse her own mother seemed not to get through her closed obstinacy. Later that night, staring up into the dark in frustration and anger, Joe reminded himself that out of this too, he had come off as an ogre in the eyes of his son and a cad in the estimation of his mother-in-law. Kate, on the other hand, had gone to sleep innocently beside him with no apparent qualms, quickly and soundly in her usual way.

These scenes, and others like them, worried Joe constantly. While driving, interviewing witnesses, preparing for court, even while seated at counsel table during trial, he found himself daydreaming about Kate and their son and how to manage their family issues. His secretaries, whom he considered friends and professional colleagues, knew him well and asked him from time to time how it was going at home. These women were used to confrontation and difficulties. Working for years under pressure, dealing with lawyers, police officers, high-stakes litigation, and pleadings filled with references to evidence and events that would confound most people, they had long ago learned the value of clarity and time. They had met Kate at office parties but saw her only occasionally. They respected privacy and the confidentiality that prevailed in every law office. When an issue was plainly on the table, however, they became as impatient as Joe and the other lawyers with evasive small talk and preferred to cut right through to the facts. They had all raised children. Most important, however, was the sense of humor each had developed to survive in the stressful and contentious world of trial practice.

Joe valued their friendship. He knew that each of them was in certain ways more experienced than he. There was a comfort and dependability in working with them akin to the confidence he felt in some of the older lawyers in town. One day as they all had lunch together in the small office kitchen, they reminded him in their good-natured, no-nonsense fashion that the period of adjustment was behind him now, that he had a three-year-old, and perhaps it was time to take his own professional advice. He knew they were right, and he told them so. He couldn't count the times he had advised clients to see a counselor or a psychologist. He knew the therapists in the area and that he could get a recommendation of someone not too far away. Would Kate go with him? That was the question.

As with the persistent engine noise that falls silent when the car enters the repair shop, that very evening at home there began a period of stability and reason. Catherine had returned to her home to prepare to go to Wicomico for the summer. Kate was elated that school was ending and that she too could enjoy the prospect of relaxing in the sun all summer. Ted was a joy to come home to, with something new to tell Joe about his day as soon as his father entered. Enjoying the peace and coziness immensely and reluctant to spoil a moment of it and aware that their time together was about to be interrupted for the summer, Joe decided to wait. Even if Kate agreed to family counseling, and if a counselor could see them within a week or so, both of which were unlikely, by the time one appointment was over, they would have to wait until September for the next session. They might as well wait until the fall. It was a decision that was for Joe both a disappointment and a relief.

Chapter Fifteen

A few days before graduating from seminary, Joe accepted a call to serve as assistant to the parish priest at the church in Dorchester. A week later, he took Ted there to see the town and the school he would attend the following fall. They had lived at seminary for three years, and Ted was now seven. Most of his memories were of their time there. Joe wanted Ted to understand that they were going to a good place and to soothe any anxiety his son might have about moving. The Dorchester school year had just ended when they made this excursion, and Kate was completing her final days back at her high school. The Patrick Henry Elementary School, the only one in town, was almost deserted. They arrived early for their appointment with the principal, so they explored the grounds and playing fields, peering into windows and climbing all over a vast, ancient jungle gym. It reminded them of the creative playground near the seminary grounds where they had spent so many Saturday and Sunday afternoons scrambling through the obstacles with Ted's friends. Climbing the metal bars in a seersucker suit, Joe saw quickly that too much pressure would cause the whole rickety structure to collapse. Compared to the cramped quarters of his school at the seminary, Ted found the new environs expansive and exciting. He was content and enthusiastic during their tour of the school with the young principal, asking many questions and wanting to check out some books from the library then and there. When it was over, Joe took him to lunch in a local restaurant where they could sit on barstools at a counter, an experience always considered by Ted to be exciting and grown-up.

Before saying goodbye to the principal, Joe had promised to join the parent-teacher association and was very surprised to learn that none existed at the school. He was even more surprised when the young African American principal telephoned him a few days later and asked him to consider forming one. It would take a few more weeks for him to understand that racial tension had discouraged this and other civic progress in his son's new school. He would have preferred to focus solely on his new ministry, especially as St. Andrew's would be his first parish. The years in seminary had nourished his understanding of how God speaks in a person's life, however. He interpreted the principal's request as a sign. He asked the principal for a list of a few local parents who might be willing to help.

Joe telephoned the people on the list, mostly younger mothers and a few fathers, white and black. They were relieved and enthusiastic about working together. He convened a meeting in the living room of the home he and Kate were buying. The parents sat around on the sofa and a few chairs and used the unopened packing boxes as tables and began the process of forming an official parent-teacher organization. In the coming year, they would raise funds for new playground equipment, establish a Teacher Appreciation Day, and complete a half-dozen other much-needed improvements. It seemed that a new face and fresh voice was what they all needed to cut through the racial mistrust. Although Joe did not know quite what he was doing, his efforts felt right to him, and the teachers and other parents were pleased with the progress.

The place they had found in Dorchester was a typical split-foyer, three-bedroom, brick-and-aluminum siding home with a garage. Joe's old friend Ken who had moved them from Jeffersonville to the seminary, came to the rescue again and moved them to Dorchester in his massive horse van. Joe had known him since his first week after law school and had hunted with him every week for years. Ken and his family had made Joe feel at home, and they had gone out of their way to welcome Kate.

Old friends emerging continuously, faithfully, cheerfully from the past, offering their time and good humor year after year, still wanting to be part of things, had been blessings in Joe's life as far back as he could remember. For him their appearance was always a reassurance of stability and hope in a paradoxically lonely and troubled world. When he thought about them, their loyalty overwhelmed him at times, men and women, young and old, wealthy and dirt-poor from his childhood, college, teaching, graduate school, his law profession, and a dozen places in between. It astonished him that they found in him someone to whom they chose to be loyal. This particular old friend and his wife and son had always been special.

The house Ken helped them move into was much larger than the home they had rented in Jeffersonville and three times the size of their apartment at the seminary. Although she helped select it, Kate was noncommittal about it. Although she liked the leafy, pleasant neighborhood well enough, she expressed no real interest in the house until to their immense relief, she was hired to teach at the local community college. The new position put an end to many months of melancholy. The uncertainty of where she would work, where they would go, and where they would live had deepened her annual springtime depression. The closer she drew to the magic moment of departure for summer vacation in Wicomico, the more difficulties and exasperations life seemed to propel at her, and this year had been especially trying. She had always expressed a longing for the day she could end her years of work in her public high school, where she had continued to teach after the family moved to seminary, bravely commuting back there through metropolitan area traffic, week after week. But the approach of that departure had only heightened her anxiety. Leaving people with whom she had not enjoyed working suddenly became a source of regret.

The vast uncertainty of the future was debilitating. Joe too felt it both for Kate and in himself. He believed that God had called him into ministry and had a stake, so to speak, in his career. His personal uncertainty was minimized by his conviction that God was leading them to where they were meant to be. The knowledge calmed and reassured him. Listening to Kate and sharing his feelings with her, trying as best he could to comfort her, was no consolation to her in her turmoil. Although she heard him out, in silence, and seemed to appreciate that he was trying to help, her agitation grew and was, as always, vented upon him without warning. He made the worst possible mistake by telling her that they could live on his salary if necessary, that they would manage, and if it took her a year to find work, it would be all right. The mere suggestion of being unemployed contributed to her gloom, adding an edge of anger to her refusal to talk with Joe about her feelings. It made the process of moving and resettling in a new community exceedingly difficult. They both got little sleep. He made every effort to shield Ted from Kate's moods, fearing his son too would grow alarmed at the newness of it all, the changes.

Ken's presence during Kate's most intense depression was a blessing in more ways than lifting boxes and transporting furniture. Kate put on a happy face and forced a genial bravado for Ken lest he sense her true anxiety and think that something was "wrong" with her. She behaved as though moving was the most natural thing in the world. The suppressed turmoil smoldered all day until Joe could have the full blast of it at night.

In the end, finding a position at the community college proved stunningly uncomplicated. The position proposed was organizing and setting up laboratory experiments for the science department and keeping the necessary materials on hand. It required no lesson preparation, teacher conferences, or any of the other activities that had proved so worrisome in the past. Unlike some surly high school students who counted the days until they could legally drop out, the more mannerly and enthusiastic college students were polite and appreciative. The setting was gracious, landscaped, and a great deal less institutional than the high school. Kate was thrilled. Her initial interview transformed her temperament, and she became happy in a way that inspired Joe as well. In the three days before she was to return to sign her contract, she talked nonstop about the flexible work responsibilities, how much free time she would have, and her astonishment that the pay was more than her high school salary. Her euphoria was tempered on the second day by a sudden preoccupation with wardrobe concerns. She would need a different type of clothing to wear to work. New clothes became a constant topic. Joe was secretly pleased at the prospect of her abandoning the casual high school wardrobe for clothing more appropriate to her age and position. He loved to see her in her shorts and T-shirts but thought it would be nice if she had dresses she could wear too.

As soon as she was offered a contract, Kate set about opening boxes and fishing out her own clothing and other things that she and Ted would need for the summer. Joe continued to unpack boxes, arranging their contents all over the house, and flattening the cardboard cartons and setting them out for recycling. There was a great deal to do, and his own work would begin in two more days. He was reluctant to push Kate to help for fear of spoiling her good mood. A few days later, she signed her contract and, giddy with satisfaction, departed an hour later for Wicomico for the rest of the summer.

Both Joe and Kate were pleased with the school Ted would attend, and they liked Dorchester's pleasant, old-town ambience. As Joe moved about the empty house at night, unpacking, cleaning, laying out shelf paper, and rushing to find the right place for a thousand things, he was presented at every turn with signs of Ted and Kate. The people he loved, his wife and son, spoke from every direction in sights and objects and stuff, small signs of family spilling out of boxes and bags in all directions. He was overjoyed that Kate's employment was settled. More than anything, he wanted Ted to be happy in this new home. He wondered about neighborhood children. He had seen none as he drove around the subdivision while they were considering the house. It was a neighborhood made for children, but in the confusion of the few days they were together there, before the departure for Wicomico, no children had appeared. Joe drove the spacious streets again, searching for any sign of them, halfway expecting a police cruiser to fall in behind at any moment. Visions of his son wandering the streets alone plagued him until he set Ted's small bicycle in their front yard, close to the street. Within ten minutes, two little boys about Ted's age were buzzing like bees back and forth in front of the house on their own bicycles. Joe went out to meet them and, later that morning, followed each of them, at their urging, to their homes in the neighborhood to meet their parents. They continued to visit Joe throughout the summer, talking to him nonstop and following him about while he trimmed trees and planted bushes and flowers, asking hundreds of questions about Ted

("What kind of cartoons does he watch?" "Does he like spaghetti?" "Have you all been to Disneyland?") in anticipation of meeting him when he returned in August. They too attended Ted's school, and the three of them would become cohorts that fall in a friendship that would last for years.

Ted made many friends all over town. The following spring, Kate joined with the mothers of some of them to form a Cub Scout troop. She rushed from the end of her teaching day to wherever the latest Cub Scout project was taking place, a great deal more serious about it all than Ted and his friends. It was a relief for Joe to see her content and sharing projects with people her age. After their marriage, while they continued to live in Jeffersonville, her emotional highs and lows had affected all her relationships. She had found teaching at the local high school rewarding but intensely frustrating, adding to an innate tension that was often sensed by other people. Yet Kate was unable to understand how her moods affected her personal relationships. Everything was always somebody else's fault.

She had come out of those years with two friends, both teachers, good people whom Joe liked and admired. One of the two, Kristin, had divorced her husband and moved to a distant town a few years earlier. She and Kate talked by telephone every week, and Kristen continued to join them at the house in Wicomico for vacations. Their friendship had changed when Kate insisted on driving home from Wicomico early one morning, intoxicated, in the rain. Joe, following in another car, had stopped them and removed Ted from her vehicle. In the passenger seat, Kristin had remained still and quiet, looking away through the side window into the fog. She did not call much after that. Although Kate continued to call Kristin, chatting breathlessly as though nothing had happened, their friendship was never the same again. Now and then, Kate grew irritated, wondering aloud why Kristin had suddenly changed, that rainy morning relegated safely to the secret place in her denial where it shared room with so much else.

It was heartening now to see Kate meeting people at St. Andrews and finding friends in their new neighborhood. She did not go to them much; they came to see her, to pick up Ted, to chat with Joe as he worked in their new garden. Whenever people stopped to talk, Joe made a point of calling Kate out to meet them. She appeared to experience real satisfaction in Dorchester her first fall and spring there. Her happiness was vital to Joe's peace of mind and, together with the ease with which Ted became a part of his school and neighborhood, made Joe feel good about their lives. It reaffirmed his faith in the validity of his call. He was still very new in ministry and needed that affirmation when he was overcome by the doubt and discouragement that hovered along the lonely road of ordination. To come home at night and find her happy and even-tempered made everything else seem imminently manageable.

* * *

Joe had begun considering a career in the church a few years after they were married. Ted was just a toddler. He discussed it often with Kate. Her initial response, reasonable and practical, was a question he would hear again and again for the rest of his life.

"Why don't you like practicing law? What's wrong with what you're doing?"

"I do like it. Especially trial work. It's exciting. It's tough, but it's exciting. I enjoy it more than sitting in an office all day at a desk."

"You aren't at a desk all day, Joe. Whenever I try to call you, the secretaries say you're in court or something."

"Our receptionist's name is Gail. You know that, Kate. Just say her name."

"I hardly get to use the phone at all at school. The office has this new policy that personal calls are not allowed during the workday, but at least they make an exception for emergencies. And we can make calls if we're setting up a doctor's appointment or something like that. But the secretaries in the office are a pain, and they tick me off. I don't even like going in there anymore."

"I understand. You told me about that last night at dinner. I like practicing law. It's a little hard to explain about the ministry. It's more something I feel than what I know, if that makes any sense." He realized as he said it that it would make no sense to her at all. "The law is not unrelated to what I'm talking about. There's a natural pro-gression. I mean, law and theology should never have been separated after the Middle Ages."

"Oh, they were? Wonder why they did that? What about biol-ogy and science? They're important too," said Kate, wheeling around in surprise. "And it shouldn't be too hard, what you do all day, I mean. Filing papers. Writing things."

Joe thought this over for a moment and was tempted to respond but decided to try to stay with the subject at hand. "What I mean is, well…it has something to do with justice. That's what I'm working towards all day, and—"

"What you're supposed to be doing all day is putting people in jail," said Kate, as though reminding him of the obvious. "If more people were in jail, we wouldn't have so much crime." It was said with a dismissive finality, as though there could be nothing else pos-sible to say on the subject. His stomach churned as she lectured him lightly and condescendingly about what he should be doing all day.

"The rules are," said Joe patiently, knowing that an ambiguous inflection could send her in anger to the television, "a prosecutor's duty is to see that justice is done. Sometimes that means convicting somebody on the evidence so the court or the jury can put him or her in jail. Or prison. At other times, it might mean standing up in the middle of a trial and moving for a dismiss—"

"Oh, give me a break! What does this have to do with being a preacher?"

"Well, I'm trying to talk with you about just that. Human jus-tice can go only so far. Even in our system, we can never be perfect. Life isn't fair. The innocent suffer no matter how clean and fair the law is. I see it every day. We live in a broken world. Some people do their best to make it as fair as possible. English-American common law, Magna Carta, an independent judiciary, the Constitution—they're all efforts to achieve justice and order…ah…in an imperfect, unfinished world. Where there's justice, peace is more likely to pre-vail. And there's something about working in it, being a part of a nation of laws, seeking justice and peace, that—"

"Aren't they the same?" said Kate. He felt a momentary flood of gratitude and affection for her, admiration for the surprises with which she charmed him once in a while, signs that she was listening to him after all, taking him seriously, thinking maturely. The question, the insight it revealed, the way she watched him, intent and curious, not wholly skeptical, encouraged him to think they were thinking in harmony, and upon an important matter. At least it was important to him.

"That's an excellent, ancient point. Can you have justice without peace? Or peace without justice? I think I know the answer sometimes, but at other times I know I have so much—everything—to learn."

"That's the truth!" exclaimed Kate, with a smile. They both laughed.

"Justice, peace, faith, compassion, all that gives human life in the world meaning, makes it comprehensible, cannot be found in the law. English-American law can help, but it is not the foundation. It is evidence of the foundation. Maybe even direct evidence. Seeing through to the source is only possible, if it's possible for a human being at all, in God. That's the ground of truth. That's where ultimate justice is. Not in human institutions, no matter how sincere and perfected they are."

Kate was quiet for a moment, looking down, as though studying the red-and-white pattern of the tablecloth.

"All I'm wondering is," he said, touching her wrist, "would you just think about it? Take all the time you want. Talk to other people." He suggested some local people, ordained and laypeople. "See what they say. Get somebody's thinking other than mine. I mean, I think this would be right, but I could be wrong. If you are opposed, I'll accept that as a sign. I mean, you and Ted are first. You are the ones with the final decision."

At this Kate made eye contact with him, and it seemed to Joe that her whole face softened. Had his words touched her? For a moment she looked at him, something like a smile hovering about her face, in silence. She said nothing. After a minute or two, he said, "Will you think about it, pray about it, talk with friends?"

"Yes," she said, "if I can find the time with everything I have to do. I have to work this Friday and Saturday night both. You'll have to look after Ted. I've got the basketball game on Friday night and the dance to chaperone on Saturday. And then I guess I'll have to get up and go to church on Sunday." She got up in a weary way, looking down, tongue thrust into her cheek, and began moving things around on the kitchen counter. She opened the refrigerator and took out the big bulbous green bottle of wine and poured a large glassful. Joe watched her, trying hard to discern her mood. She came over to him and sat down on his lap. In those days, she still weighed less than some of her students. Joe kissed her neck and inhaled deeply her sweet smell, like spring rain. She had cut her hair short recently, setting off ten days of depression and uncertainty. Her new style looked good, and she was finally accepting it as the right decision. The subject was mellow enough now that Joe could safely mention it.

"Your new hair looks better every day. You should wear it this way from now on."

"You keep saying that."

"It's true," he said sincerely.

"That's what they've been saying at school. The girls in third period say they like it too." This bunch was that particular year's class of troublemakers. He knew that their approval was significant.

"See," said Joe. "They are a tribe of little geniuses, after all."

Kate smiled and sipped her wine.

Joe hesitated and then said, "Honey, why not just tell them that you won't be available this weekend to sell tickets or chaperone or anything, and we can just—"

"Can you tell the judge that you won't be there for some trial?" said Kate sharply. He knew there was no point in trying to discuss her comparison. It seemed she felt complete only when a job-related duty, volunteer or otherwise, loomed before her, something to complain about and take up time she would otherwise have had to spend at home. After they washed the dishes and after a little more conversation, they went upstairs to try for their next child. Each of them would have loved dearly whatever they got, but it would have suited each of them fine this time to have a girl.

* * *

Kate never mentioned the ministry again. Joe, trying to give her all the latitude she required, let six months go by before asking her. As was her way, knowing that he was awaiting an answer on this or any other subject was enough to make her keep quiet about it. He knew the way she would analyze it. He had asked her to talk it over and decide. He had not thought to ask her to inform him when she had done so. Therefore, whether out of some deep psychological enigma he would never fathom, or out of plain meanness, it was her way not to say a word. When he finally brought it up again, gently so as not to make her feel she was being pressed, she said she had spoken to "friends" (she would not say who) and spent a lot of time thinking about it, and she had decided that it was all right with her, this going to seminary. Joe questioned her, trying to understand; did she feel it was positively right for them as a family? Or did she feel only that she would have no objections, a much less enthusiastic position although he did not characterize it as such. He needed to know, before such a critical decision, how solid her conclusion was, a thing impossible for him to tell from her manner, even after several years of marriage. Kate found it irritating to be questioned so thoroughly. In her estimation, a discussion of that depth was unnecessary. She had thought it over and decided it was all right, which is what he had asked her to do. That was as far as she would go, and that should be good enough for Joe. There was one thing, however, that she wanted to know. Would his going to seminary interfere with her summers in Wicomico?

He was grateful for hearing that much from her. The following day he went to see their parish priest, a scholarly man who had known Joe since he had moved to the area after law school. He had baptized Ted. The Reverend Michael Neilson, following the policy in their diocese, began making plans to form a committee of parishioners to explore with Joe the thoughts of his heart on his proposal to consider ordained ministry. It would be the first step in a complicated discernment process that would go on for some three years. Sometime following the many months of workshops, examinations, retreats, medical appointments, seminars, counseling, and other requirements, the bishop and his advisers would review Joe's thick file of results and evidence and decide whether to allow him to begin the initial steps toward seminary.

"Do you hear a call? I'm not asking for an answer yet, just stating the issue in words you'll have to get used to. Is God calling you into holy orders? It is not at all a matter limited to intellectual curiosity and definitely not just a question of your own choice."

"I understand, Mike," said Joe. "Or rather, I understand that I don't understand…if that makes any sense."

Mike Nielson laughed and shook his head up and down. "Do you like practicing law, Joe?" he said, the eternal question Joe would come to hear a thousand times in one variation or another. In those days, second or third career clergy were the exception rather than the rule they would become in another twenty years. Joe responded, attempting to make sense of issues he himself was only now beginning to understand. He was successful only in assuring Mike that he enjoyed practicing his profession. Mike was intimately aware of the nature of Joe's caseload, as was everybody who read the newspapers in that part of the state. He wondered aloud if Joe would find parish ministry boring in comparison.

"Doesn't it get to you sometimes, Joe? I mean, dealing with murders, rapists, that sort of thing? That woman who set those Mexicans on fire? The man who dropped his wife off the bridge last year? What happened to those runaway children over at Kettletown? Sometimes it gives me the creeps just to read about it in the papers. I mean, what's it like for you to work with those situations all year long? And it seems like as soon as one case dies down, there's another in the papers. And I've got sense enough to know that not everything, thank goodness, gets in the papers."

"It has its moments," Joe acknowledged with a grin. "The best thing a man can have is a sense of humor. Everybody who works with these cases agrees. You have to know when to laugh and take every chance that's appropriate. I don't mean laugh at what happens to people. I don't mean that. But it is necessary to look at life and understand, or feel, I suppose, that there's far more good than bad."

"You have to learn to—"

"Count your blessings. And as you'll be the first to understand, we see some things, but we don't see the worst of it, Mike. We have it good in America. How would you like to live in China or Mexico or Cambodia or the Soviet Union?"

"Or Africa," said Mike Neilson, who had just finished reading a book on Islam. "I know. But that kind of work must still be hard on you. And Kate too."

"Kate is fairly much insulated from it, by her own choice," Joe said, looking out the window. "It's hard for her to connect me with the news reports. I'll come home from trying a case, and she will begin telling me what the radio said 'they' did in court that day. She heard it on the radio on the way home from work and by the time she gets home knows all there is to know about it. The universal 'they' did this, and 'they' did that. When I try to explain I am the 'they' involved, or one of them, that it was my case, she changes the subject. When I used to try to talk about what I had been doing all day, she changed the subject to her own stuff at the high school. I'm used to it now. It doesn't bother me anymore. I let her have her space. I don't discuss my work very much."

How could he explain to his priest what he himself only halfway understood? It was not the crimes he worked with that distanced Kate. It was that he was the one working with them. She would not discuss his work because she saw no way to compete with it. He had come to understand by then that competition was her mode of relating to him. But he did not say it. She was his wife, and he had made his vows to her. For better or worse. Sickness or health.

Mike was silent. As Joe would do years later in the presence of his closest friends, the priest had taken off his white clerical collar, and it reposed on the desk between them. Mike Nielson rubbed his neck. It was a hot day, and the neckband of his black clerical shirt was dark with perspiration. He cleared his throat and said, "And how's the marriage?"

Joe's protective instincts were on alert. In his best enabling way, he responded by saying they were "doing fine" and that Ted was growing up by the minute. He was absolutely certain he was betraying no unease nor violating his wife's confidence. With the sincerity of a skilled trial lawyer, he looked at Mike and said, "We've had our adjustments to make, like every other couple we know. I love her. She loves me. We work things out as they come along." It was the truth. He could not have said anything else to this good parish priest.

"Good!" said Mike. "Because that is one of the issues the discernment process will investigate. If there are marital problems, they'll become evident if you get to seminary. You're in a fishbowl there, you know."

They looked at each other. Joe was beginning to understand. There were so many aspects of discerning a call accurately, of the whole process toward preparing for the priesthood, that would grow clearer in the coming months.

"How's Kate's health?" asked Mike.

"Fine," said Joe, not knowing how much he sounded like Kate and Catherine.

"Any…health problems?" said Mike.

"No, except we're having trouble getting pregnant again. We've both been to doctors. I have a low sperm count…between you and me."

"And Kate?"

"She's a very private person," said Joe, continuing to look out the window and shifting in his chair. "As far as I know, from the little she will say, the doctor says she's in excellent health and that we should keep on trying."

"I'm glad to hear it," said Mike. "She is a great lady. How did she manage to land a dunce like you?" They both laughed. "And your health?"

"I still run at night. I'm in good shape. I have trouble with diverticulitis a lot, as you know. My side hurts a couple of times a week, but I have medicine, and I know what not to eat to get over it."

"How long has that been going on?" Mike asked.

"The first spell was in law school. A local doctor diagnosed it. I've been dealing with it ever since. During law school, I lived above a garage in a single room. Cooked on a hot plate. It meant heating things up, soup and stuff. After a couple of years of that, I had an attack. When it was over, the doctor ordered me to eat in restaurants more often. It was expensive, but I did it." Nobody could have imagined how little money Joe had gotten by on in college and again in law school. He never spoke of it except to Kate, and he wasn't sure even she understood.

"Does it hurt often?"

"Several times a month. But I've learned to control it with my diet and getting some rest."

"Your work is really…intense. A tremendous amount of tension. Who do you talk to about it?" asked Mike.

"Other lawyers, the police investigators, some friends at Quantico."

"Quantico."

"On some of the sex stuff. It's so hard to analyze the motives, what's behind certain behaviors. The FBI will help now and then. They know about things we're just beginning to deal with out here in the boondocks."

"Kate?"

"No. We usually talk about her work," said Joe.

They shook hands, and Joe went out to return to his office. The middle-aged priest, who had a great deal of experience and was extremely well read, watched Joe from the door as he walked across the parking lot and drove away toward the courthouse. Mike Nielson was aware of how much Joe relied on his leadership. It had made him nervous at first during his sermons seeing Joe in his pew jotting down notes on the lectionary insert. He was flattered to learn that Joe kept the insert with him all week, reading and rereading the biblical texts and his marginal notes about Mike's sermons. Joe filed each insert away in the desk in his office, taking out one or another from time to time to reread the text and notes, inspired to do so by something said or done in his presence. Although Joe had explained to Mike before, sincerely and simply, how helpful his preaching and teaching was in

175

his life, the country priest might never appreciate fully how power-fully Joe heard God's summons through the words of his careful and scholarly sermons, Sunday after Sunday.

Chapter Sixteen

I n Joe's diocese, men and women who believed they heard God's call to ordained ministry faced the most demanding discernment process in the national church. Behind it lay a critical concern. Confused motivations, bound up tightly in ego and temperament, could be misinterpreted by the sincere aspirant as a call from God. The church wanted to be certain that someone unfit did not get through and later go down, taking a parish down too. The stakes were high, and the diocesan authorities took their responsibility seriously. Far from being nurturing or encouraging, the process was confrontational, challenging, intimate, and intrusive.

The church had a duty to know all about those who proposed to spend their lives working in it. Thus began the psychiatric, psychological and physical examinations, criminal background checks, reviews of academic and employment records, interviews by panels of lay persons and clergy, spiritual therapy with other aspirants, careful individual scrutiny by clergy assigned to each candidate, writing assignments, discernment conferences, and regional meetings. Strung out over three years, all this produced a voluminous record for each aspirant and a decision as to whether he or she would go on to theological studies or take another path in life. For those admitted to seminary, the scrutiny continued for three more years with the seminary faculty and staff conducting the surveillance. Upon graduation, each candidate sat for the grueling three-day national ordination examinations. Provided this was passed, and if seminary faculty, advisors, and diocesan examiners were still convinced of a candidate's fitness, the bishop would decide whether the candidate should be ordained a deacon. And after six months to a year in this role, the bishop decided whether a deacon could move through the final step and be ordained to the priesthood. When this happened, the scrutiny shifted from diocesan committees and seminary professors to the whole wide world. Life would never be the same again.

The Right Reverend Carrington Peyton Spencer, the bishop of Joe's diocese, was a theological and political centrist in the oldest traditions of the denomination and widely admired for his common sense and fairness. He was an unabashedly spiritual man in a generous and unselfconscious way that encouraged the faith in others. For a decade, he had led his large diocese with moderation and tact through the controversies that raged through the national church like summer storms.

Years in the law and education had exposed Joe to some arrogant and difficult personalities. To his great relief, he had never perceived these qualities in Peyton Spencer. He had been impressed by Bishop Spencer's professional courtesy and his obvious high regard, untainted by condescension, for the clergy and seminarians who served under him. It had always appeared to Joe, and to others he knew, that Spencer was one of those bishops who remembered the delicate, stressful dynamics of parish ministry. His concern for clergy morale and fair treatment made those who served under him look around at other dioceses and count their blessings.

The coolheaded, cerebral church in which Joe grew up had muddled along nicely through a violent century, and it continued to nurture the faithful with liturgy and traditions that strengthened them to fight the good fight in a broken world. Reason, personal integrity, and a commitment to honor and decency for the common good were all divine gifts acclaimed in the church for themselves and held out as means of drawing nearer to God. In its blurring of doctrinal edges and amiable tolerance for uncertainty, the church had long celebrated reverent wonder and divine mystery as doorways through which seekers could follow in Christ's footsteps through the suffering world. That mystery and wonder were not wholly susceptible to human comprehension was further evidence of their divine origin. This reverence for mystery, never complicated by too much misleading enthusiasm, strengthened Trinitarian faith and promoted a mature embrace of divine ambiguity that was a bit too complex for less catholic Christians. For centuries this ambiguity had been the church's strength in the uncertain world of the human heart. God in Three Persons, a comment upon limited human perception as much as upon the nature of divine identity, an ancient attempt to understand the incomprehensible, was itself a mystery. And unlike much of the rest of the Western world, Joe's church was at ease with mystery. The church revealed divine mystery in worship that appealed to each sensory perception and nourished the blessings of human intellect and memory in ways unknown in other worshipping communities. It was neither reactive in challenges to its orthodoxy nor unduly permissive in matters of doctrinal integrity. Decency and duty, a reverence for order, forgiveness, and a vivid anticipation of resurrection and the world to come had buttressed this portion of Christ's wounded and triumphant body for centuries. Almost everyone believed the Holy Ghost would sustain it all until the last day.

This spiritual home had shaped Joe's thinking and perception since birth. Though he knew it was sinful to do so, he felt a certain quiet pride in his denomination and gratitude for its ministry of preserving and revealing biblical truth. He recognized some issues that would have to be resolved in coming years, and he knew there must be problems of which he was wholly ignorant. He had met people in the church whose entry into leadership he felt was a mistake. But when his limited knowledge of these few difficult areas caused him worry, he reminded himself that God was still in charge, and the Holy Spirit had overcome much worse troubles than these. In any case, as he told Bishop Spencer in his initial interview he was not interested in leadership beyond the role of a parish priest.

"You must know," replied the bishop, "that ordination means a man takes his place in the councils of the church." The bishop was thorough. He was not suggesting that Joe might be destined for any sort of leadership but merely making the responsibilities clear from the outset.

"If that's what the church requires of me, I'll do my duty. I always have before. All I am saying is that my ambitions are all behind me. I will be content to serve a parish for the rest of my days."

"That's good to hear."

"If I get through seminary and the process, I won't waste energy on running for any office or climbing to anything. I'm not interested. I want to serve out the rest of my days and make them count. And I won't need a big city either. I'll pray for a place where my wife and son will feel fulfilled, at home, safe. That is my only criteria. If they weren't part of my life, I would be willing to go to Africa or South America."

"I'm glad to hear that. As I understand your priorities, they sound right to me. Going far away would serve God, but there are dozens and dozens of small churches right here with small and middling-sized congregations just waiting for someone who will go there and do good ministry. I pray that you will keep your resolve. You might find some things along the way to sway you."

"I suppose so," said Joe, not yet able to guess what all of them might be.

The bishop learned forward and offered his hands to Joe. "Well, let's pray for a few moments. Then I'll make some calls, and we'll see about getting started."

The bishop prayed for God's guidance in Joe's discernment. He prayed for Kate and Ted, for the sacred mystery of the church and for the world. He prayed for all seekers after truth. Joe prayed for the bishop and the diocese, Kate and Ted and Catherine and his own parents, and for the emergence of truth in a case that would be going to trial the following day. Then they parted.

Joe's diocese was one of the few where many of the old traditions still held, and new churches were being planted every year. Bishop Spencer modeled a sincere and contagious spirituality. Joe perceived a quality of kindness in the bishop's style of leadership. Although understandably distracted in crowds where people approached him with issues from all sides, in personal conversations with his clergy and laity, the bishop was attentive, sincere, and plainspoken. He maintained eye contact. His interest in those who served under him was genuine, a virtue that parish clergy, given the complicated web of relationships in their own lives, were able to recognize. In the fussy, political leadership of the national church, Bishop Spencer was a moderating presence. For a man whose every decision, sermon, and action were subject to the keenest scrutiny and certain to upset somebody, he lived out his episcopate with even-handed care.

The discernment process generated anxiety in candidates and examiners alike. The candidates were sincere, including those whose hearts would be broken one day by the decision that they could proceed no further. Apart from the spiritual inquiry, the need to determine a candidate's emotional and intellectual fitness was particularly sensitive. In the end, the church had done everything possible to help aspirants distinguish between God's call and whatever else they might be hearing.

There was one additional dynamic at work in this lengthy process of which both candidates and examiners were unaware. Joe himself would recognize it only after years in ministry. Understanding it then would strengthen his faith in the unseen motions of grace and in the intimacy and subjectivity of God's personal care for the trusting. It was the eventual discovery that the discernment process, apart from the obvious goals intended by the church, was one of God's own tests in determining whether a man or woman had the character and emotional strength to withstand what the church would eventually do to them.

* * *

A month before the Stephensons moved into their ground-floor corner apartment in a large housing complex near the seminary, a woman was raped as she unloaded groceries at night from her car in the parking lot. The seminary administration and housing management advised residents to be cautious. Anybody who read newspapers or watched television news understood that crime in the metropolitan area was increasing daily. But no matter how Joe sought to explain all this to Kate and Catherine, he returned home from the library at night to find them watching television in their nightgowns, every light burning, all the windows and blinds raised, and the sliding patio doors standing wide open. He could see them clearly from his car in the parking lot. Anyone looking from a dozen surrounding places could see them. Only the thin screens on the windows and doors stood between them and an intruder.

His anguish kept him awake at night. The danger itself disturbed him profoundly, but he was almost as upset by the perverse, insensitive recklessness of Kate and Catherine in ignoring everything he told them. They became sarcastic, combative, and then dismissive when he tried to explain how provocative and risky their conduct was. They had just returned from a long, relaxing summer at their beach house where they lived with doors and windows open and ocean breezes cooling the rooms, with no demands upon them but doing the laundry and arguing with each other. Such carefree months returned them to the world of responsibility and obligations more strong-willed and inflexible than ever. They were in no mood to oblige Joe in anything. Their minds closed to all of life's hazards outside their own experience, they saw no need to sacrifice their comfort to placate Joe's ridiculous apprehensions. His closing and locking windows and doors in the hot September night and turning on the noisy air conditioner sent them into paroxysms of contempt. They stayed mad at him for days. Highly knowledgeable in the ways of criminals through watching endless hours of crime dramas on television, they scoffed, in an unusual display of unity, at his precautions.

"Robbers don't come into a lit-up place like this, Joe! How come you don't know that?" said Kate to her husband, the criminal trial lawyer.

"And they certainly aren't coming in here when they see there are two of us," piped Catherine, who weighed a hundred pounds and had never lived in a big city in her life.

Joe despaired at breaking through their shells. Years later, looking back with the relative experience of years, he felt he should have shouted at them, shocked them, anything to make them see reason. When he went in to check on Ted (who found it exciting to move to a big city), he found his young son asleep in his bed at an open window, mere feet from the street, along which ambled strangers throughout the night and day.

He did not shout at them, however, and he restrained himself from trying to shock them into changing. He applied his strength to keeping the peace. This meant handling Kate with care so as not to incite her anger and running general interference between her and her mother. A peaceful household was the best thing for his son and for the rest of them as well. As Kate's emotions soared and plunged like a crazy sea bird over the years, and he grew wiser to Catherine's furtive ways, Joe had learned that keeping the peace was closely tied to his own nonanxious behavior. Ted was always on his mind. Therefore he controlled himself, reread his marriage vows, thought about his parents, and reviewed all he had learned from the blessing of family counseling. He carried constantly in mind an image of his son's precious face. He could soothe the pain in his gut by closing his eyes and seeing Ted, hearing his voice, and imagining his future.

Despite his best efforts, however, Joe's anxiety and fatigue began to create in him a sternness that Kate and Catherine had not seen before. The move from the law and the country, with their dependable stability and sensible progression, to this new environment of theology and the big city, with its complicated anonymity and minimal evidence of order, forged a difference in him that he recognized but could not explain. His professional background and common sense began to compel him, in certain situations, to give orders where before he would have sought to achieve a consensus. With Kate and Catherine, it had always been difficult to find peace, whether between the two of them or between either of them and himself. Both women had lived but a few years with a man in the house, and that had been a long, long time ago. Joe reasoned it wasn't him they disliked so much as it was the role he ended up having to play. Their habit of spending every penny until there was no cushion left caused neither of them a moment's concern, while Joe lay awake at night worried about how they would meet an emergency. At times, he wondered if his legal training had become a curse; thinking ahead as many moves as possible had become a lonely feature of his marriage.

Kate and her mother created incessant clutter. Often Joe was embarrassed when friends visited. At least Catherine would tidy up. Kate would not lift a finger. It seemed that Ted was more organized in his personal habits than his mother or grandmother. The clutter would have been less troublesome if Kate had only helped keep things in order. It exasperated Joe to know that her classroom was the epitome of neatness with every single item in its assigned place. The walls were adorned with immaculate posters and charts, laboratory supplies were arranged on shelves like goods in a well-run supermarket, her desk was spare and immaculate, and each cabinet and drawer was carefully filed and organized, their contents labeled. How differently she behaved at home, where closets, corners, shelves, chairs, and every available surface overflowed with all manner of disorganized, dusty mess. Kate knew where in the chaos she had stuck this or that, although nobody else knew, and this measure of control in her disordered surroundings apparently suited her own needs well enough. An exception of sorts was the kitchen, which each of them recognized as her special domain. It was always better organized, clean, and attractive.

To keep from losing his mind, Joe made compromises, sacrificing reason and substance for a sort of peace. Issues on which he knew he should stand firm, arguments he should pursue, discussions he should have absolutely insisted upon having with Kate, or occasionally with Catherine, were conceded over time for the sake of tranquility. His son deserved a calm, well-adjusted home. By personally compensating for the behavior of Kate and her mother and serving as a foil for their perpetual boozy argumentativeness, Joe secured a calm home for Ted. The multiple nuances of dysfunction were still very much there, but in a failure of judgment he would mourn for the rest of his life, he felt Ted was too young to be influenced by them. In classic enabling style, Joe organized a household calculated to minimize Kate's drinking and wrath and Catherine's drinking and meanness. He felt tired most of the time. He was not a social worker, psychiatric therapist, drug counselor, clergyman, or policeman, each of whose expertise were wanted when he opened the door at night and entered their apartment. He knew he was dealing with lifetimes, generations of denial, and other dysfunctional thinking. But recognizing its extent did not mean he knew how to resolve it.

Although he could not imagine life without Ted, Joe caught himself thinking now and then that if it were just Kate and her mother and him, he would gladly allow them the same constructive freedom he had learned about in his years of teaching. He would let them live the natural consequences of their own behavior. With an impressionable young child in the picture, however, he saw his responsibility in a different light.

Kate saw herself the perfect adult, just as she had striven for many years to be the perfect child and perfect student. Accepting professional help was out of the question. Family counseling or Alcoholics Anonymous were for sick people, and there was absolutely nothing wrong with her. Any problems that existed in their household were Joe's. It was Joe's fault. Let him go to counseling if that's what he wanted.

Catherine presented an even tougher case, if only because her denial had been solidifying over so many more years than Kate's.

Joe felt overwhelmed. It became easier to smooth out the edges than try to manage the whole massive, lumpy mess. His instincts told him he was only delaying the inevitable, but with a young child and a fragile wife and graduate school and a new community and all the other countless worries on his mind, he told himself he was doing the best he could.

He was completely convinced that God was at their side, and in those days he believed God would give him no more to bear than he could manage. He believed they were there in the first place through God's leadership. This unshakable belief led him to anticipate that change for the better was just over the horizon. He did not count on change in his home or marriage as inevitable; one could never know the extent and hidden dimensions of God's sacred plan. But he knew that change was possible, and he had confidence that God would either heal his family or grant them strength and courage to grow through their trials. This was his conviction. He knew that God would never abandon them. And while he waited, he battled his own fatigue and loneliness and tried to show a brave face to the world.

That was why he had trouble sleeping and why his eyes were sad much of the time.

Kate behaved as though their differences were always a surprise to her, disparities invented by Joe to suit the occasion. She saw his insistence on talking things over as a calculated affront to her natural innocence and good intentions. When Joe came home and wanted to know why Ted was still playing cheerfully on the living room floor forty minutes past his bedtime, Kate, shocked, would react as if they had never even talked about their son's bedtime. When Joe tried to point out how unfair it was to keep Ted awake and put Joe in the position of causing him to go to bed, she responded that in that case, he shouldn't have said anything about it.

"Ted is supposed to be in bed now. Why is he still up playing?"

"He's just having a good time."

"But we decided that his bedtime is eight o'clock on school nights."

"It's only a little after eight."

"It is fifteen minutes till nine. When he stays up like this, he's tired in the morning and doesn't do as well in school."

"All right, Mr. Lord and Master! Why is it always my fault? Why did you have to go out tonight after dinner anyway?"

"Because my study group meets every Wednesday night at the library, Kate. You know that. We've been meeting every Wednesday night for four months. When you are out at a teacher's meeting, I put Ted to bed on time."

"That's right, Joe. Blame it on me. It's always my fault, isn't it? Well, just get over it!"

She continued to shout at him, stretched out on the living room couch, as he walked Ted to the bathroom to brush his teeth. No matter how soothingly he spoke to Ted at such times, and despite his explanations and excuses for having to enforce the rules, he feared that behind his son's sweet face was a growing misunderstanding that he felt powerless to heal. As Joe tucked him in and kissed him good night, he always told him he loved him and wanted him to have a good time in school the following day. Joe couldn't bear to leave without allowing him to tell about the events of his day, what his teacher had said, the pictures he had drawn, who had pushed whom at recess. After listening for a while, Joe said good night and closed the door quietly.

He knew that Ted loved him, but he saw too the perplexity aroused in his small son by family strife. It haunted him. It hurt him to put Ted to bed with such a scene fresh in his mind. He was no psychologist, and not the brightest man by far, but he understood that some negative consequences must accrue in a small child falling asleep with such unhappy impressions. His efforts at compensation felt feeble. And invariably, as soon as Joe had settled him down, turned out the light, and closed the door, Kate would enter Ted's bedroom without speaking, close the door behind her, and spend fifteen minutes with him. "Just saying good night," she would declare later. He knew if he tried to stop her, she would start to shout and make a dreadful scene. It was not yet in Joe's nature to wonder what she might be saying to Ted in addition to good night.

Pointing out that three or four glasses of wine might have had something to do with ignoring Ted's bedtime made her more sullen and uncommunicative or a great deal louder. Gradually he was learning that the way to create the calm home life he sought for Ted lay in his ability to change himself. He was learning that he could not change Kate, and she was unwilling or incapable of changing herself. The only matters over which he had control were his own actions and reactions.

Kate prided herself on being the most prepared teacher in her high school but suffered a sudden and debilitating attack of inefficiency and procrastination when responsibilities loomed at home. Joe saw it as a refusal to take initiative. She considered it taking her well-deserved rest. She did not clean, seldom got around to ironing, and refused to touch a dust cloth or vacuum cleaner unless Joe began to clean up first. Until the last few years of their marriage, she would not make grocery lists, priding herself on keeping everything in her head. Joe knew that if she shopped for food, her impulses would cost them twice as much as he would spend for the same groceries. The clutter did not embarrass her in front of her friends because the few friends she had lived far away and were not likely to drop by.

There were exceptions. Kate was precise and planned carefully for anything having to do with Wicomico. A true artist with a needle and thread, she would drop everything to make clothes for Ted or costumes for him for Halloween, school plays, or other occasions. She loved to visit Joe's parents, brothers, and sisters. They all adored her and looked forward to her company. This was a family relationship as important to Joe as to Kate. It made him immensely happy to see all the people he loved enjoying each other, and he put great effort into covering up the marital difficulties that might have spoiled it. Any shopping trip, extracurricular activity at the high school, or browsing at the local mall usually appealed to Kate. Going anywhere new—a nearby small town, outlet mall, undiscovered trendy restaurant—she found exciting. She loved bookstores, another of the interests she and Joe shared.

Short, often impromptu excursions were fun and relaxing for Kate, and equally so for Joe and Ted in most cases. She looked forward to spending Friday nights or Saturdays exploring, window-shopping, trying on clothes, or sightseeing. There was a delightful quality about the pleasure she derived from these uncomplicated pastimes. The appeal for her of small adventures had been endearing when they first met. Joe still found it amusing and touching after years of marriage. He knew he was blessed in these reasonable, attainable satisfactions. He had friends whose spouses preferred weekends in New York or Miami and expected them in spite of the cost. Joe was happy in these interims that Kate enjoyed so. And as long as they were doing this sort of thing, she was friendly, reasonable, and loving. The difficult part started when they returned home and took off their coats and returned to the day-to-day activities and obligations of being a family.

There were times when it seemed to Joe that Kate appeared to view any family decision she had to make with him as an imposition on her time and freedom. For her, such agreements seemed to assume the status of rules. Even when they were clearly benefits to family life, such as a routine bedtime for Ted or saving for college, she was soon quietly and furtively circumventing them. Rather than outright defiance or refusal, although this occurred too, her opposition was generally subtle and tricky. Joe might not realize what she had been doing or not doing until long after he thought they had reached an understanding. It did not occur to him to look for sabotage. She was his wife. He loved her. Their interests and Ted's were bound up together. But even in situations in which Kate's own interests or Ted's stood to benefit in the long run, there was no guarantee she would follow through. It bewildered him because it defied reason and common sense. There was no kindness or affection in it. Discussion sometimes helped, new understanding reached, fresh starts begun. But they never lasted.

In trying to understand how to live and what to do, Joe found superb guidance in the professional counselors he consulted. As time went by, he learned from each of them although rarely did they give him concrete answers. Instead they helped him understand his own behavior and Kate's and understand how to manage situations better in the future. They provided a welcome clarity, a fresh insight that was healing and intriguing on many levels. He had enough common sense to recognize that issues he might have analyzed with some success, on behalf of a client, quickly became insoluble for him in the emotional obstacle course of his marriage.

"I keep worrying about Ted, and I don't know how to deal with what keeps happening."

Dr. Amanda Shore Leffler, a clinical psychologist, looked exactly like what she was, an old sixties radical who had settled down and found peace at the last. He could imagine her in India print skirt and black leotards, earth shoes, beads maybe. Pot, definitely. Burning somebody's bra. From beneath her white pageboy bangs, she looked at him and said, "Okay?"

"I cannot get Kate to step back and see what's happening."

"Such as?"

"At the sound of Ted's voice, she drops everything, anything she's doing, and turns her attention solely to him. Immediately. Whatever she is doing, talking to, whatever, goes completely out of her mind."

"And how is this a problem for you?"

"I want him to have manners, patience, self-control, respect, to grow up learning how to relate to people. He's seven years old. By now he should understand that when adults are talking, the polite thing to do is wait patiently until a break in the conversation and then say, 'Excuse me, Mom, may I speak with you?' Maybe I'm old-fashioned, but that's the way I was raised. Most of my friends' children are being raised that way. That's the way Ted does with me, most of the time. But he knows, regardless of what Kate is doing, he can get her undivided attention immediately by butting in and calling her name. She lets it happen. She never corrects him. She encourages it, in a way. I've watched her talking to other people, sometimes much older people, and Ted will cut in and start talking to her, and she will completely drop the other person in the middle of a sentence and launch into listening and talking with Ted. The other people just stand there, glancing at one another. She's oblivious."

"What do you do when this happens?"

"I say to Ted, 'Son, your mother is speaking with Mrs. Nelson, or Mr. Conroy. It is not polite to interrupt. The right thing to do is to wait until there is a pause, and then say "Excuse me."' Then he stands to one side with a look on his face like I've just turned off the cartoons. Kate puts on a little pout. The conversation goes on for another minute or so, and then one of the people will say something like, 'Well, I know you want to talk with your son…' and then Kate will disappear with Ted. He learns that it's all right to interrupt her. She gets to slip out of the adult conversation and go off with him. I end up looking like the enforcer, to my son."

"And the people standing around wonder why you didn't let your wife handle it?"

"They probably do," said Joe wearily. For a moment, he put his head in his hands and elbows on his knees and faced the floor and yawned. He always felt tired. "Except maybe those who've seen it happen before and know what I've learned—she's not going to handle it. Having his attention is more important to her than teaching him manners. But if she were on the job at school and a student dared to interrupt her, she would become little Ms. Emily Post in a heartbeat. Deliver a hot little lecture on manners, then and there."

"What do you do when this happens?"

"Try to talk with her. And Ted too. In the car on the way home or at night, maybe. They both listen. Neither one of them says much. Ted has more to say than Kate does. He says he'll remember and will say 'Excuse me' the next time. Kate will agree and say she's sorry. She won't take part, really, in the discussion. She'll never initiate talking about this sort of thing. And I end up feeling as though I'm trying to speak with my young son and his older sister. Then, the next time, the same thing, the same fucking thing will happen again. And again and again."

"What is Ted learning?" inquired Dr. Leffler, who, at Joe's obscenity, allowed her long solemn face to smile.

"He is learning to avoid behaving that way in front of me and that his mother is on his side in these things. He is learning to interrupt when I'm not around. I hope he's learning that I care about him and want him to have good manners. What he is not learning is manners, self-control, obedience."

Joe leaned back in his chair and stared out the window. In the early autumn afternoon, a few scarlet maple leaves were already drifting in the sunlight, beautiful. A line from *The Wild Swans at Coole* passed through his mind quickly and was gone. Flat-bottomed cumulus clouds swelled into the dreamy cobalt sky. He felt sad and hopeful at the same time. Dr. Leffler waited.

"And when we go out socially, when we meet friends in a restaurant, for instance, while the adults are talking, Kate is always in a whispering consultation with Ted, turned aside and facing away from the table. When I ask about it later, I find they were talking about going to the store to buy something or something else that could have waited till we were on the way home. When we're all three together with other people, unless I sit between them, they will whisper to each other as soon as anybody else starts talking. If you were standing nearby, you could watch it happen. Someone will begin to talk, addressing everyone in the room, say, or at the table, and the moment everybody's attention goes toward that person, Kate and Ted will look at one another and begin to whisper. No matter how I try to reason with her, no matter how often she promises, nothing changes. It is the same with table manners, interrupting people, making sure the light is on when he draws or looks at books, snacks just before meals, saving a little bit of his allowance. Most of the time she will not follow through with any of the things we've been teaching him. I work with Ted at dinner, and he knows what to do. I teach him the right way to sit and use his fork, how to ask for things without grabbing, not talking with his mouth full. Kate will sit right there and agree. But last month, when they came back from the summer at her vacation home, he had lost everything he had learned. I know she let him do whatever he wanted while they were down there."

"When did you last talk with her about coming to counseling with you?"

"She promised before she left in June that she would come with me when they came back in late August. She's been back for over a month. She has a different excuse for not coming every time. When I asked her two days ago, she got angry. I remind her that she promised, and she says, 'Well, I can't right now, so get over it!'"

How had it come to this? What had he done? What had he left undone? Except for her obsessions with Ted, when Kate interacted with others, Joe saw bits of the bright, agreeable woman he thought he knew she could be. But at home, with nobody else but Catherine looking on, she grew hostile or subversive the moment anything ceased to go her way. He knew it was ancient history with Catherine, but what had *he* done? He wanted a wife, not a moody, rebellious teenage daughter.

Joe would need much more time to begin to understand that Kate found the reciprocal nature of marriage to be uncomfortably restraining. Financial cooperation was the most exasperating for her. For years she had spent every penny she earned and relied upon Catherine for additional money when she needed it. She was used to doing what she wanted and when she wanted to do it. She interpreted agreements with Joe as forced compliance with an authority figure, limiting her subversively, annoyingly, in ways she had never before endured. The distress signals she sent him almost daily, always oblique and indistinct, were as confusing to him as the anger that seethed in her continually. She played the role of efficient, attentive spouse for short bursts at a time, but when she did, she performed so well that even her husband came to accept that part of her as the norm. He was the only one in her life to insist upon resolving issues and sharing responsibilities. With few friends to set good examples and without the guidance that counseling might have provided, Kate insulated herself against an adult world she found too challenging. Joe was forced, without understanding it, into the very role she so resented.

By the time Ted was five or six, Joe felt he had lived in this marital storm for his whole adult life. He had learned to anticipate Kate's ways and had begun to take precautions to minimize turmoil. Later he would look back in shame and guilt upon his own inadequate responses, but then he believed that in time all would be well. Kate would grow out of it. He would learn to handle it better. They would both mature. Seminary was stressful for all of them, and once they had settled somewhere, Kate would change. She would agree to enter counseling. She would join Alcoholics Anonymous. Perhaps she would agree to go with Joe to a family counselor. Perhaps she might open up about herself, her feelings.

Although he did not like to think about it, Catherine would die one day. That much of the confusion would come to an end. He could not imagine how Kate would react to her mother's death. They fought constantly, but he felt surely they must love each other, in their own way, of course, not in the way that love was expressed in his own family. Even though his father was grouchy and difficult, Joe loved him; everybody in the family loved him and found a hundred small ways to tell him so. Surely it was like with Kate and her mother.

So Joe continued to shield Kate and their problems from unwanted scrutiny. His love for her and belief in her eventual health and the amiable disposition trapped beneath her disorder, his love for Ted, and a steadfast anticipation of a happy, calm, peaceful future, made him carry on in their family troubles. He was certain life would improve. They had made their vows. Marriage was a three-party contract; God would help the two of them keep their part of it. Everyone had troubles along the way. He had watched his parents solve problems together, seen friends make a success of it, watched his clients overcome all sorts of obstacles. He and Kate could do it too. He was certain that God had called him into marriage with Kate and that God had sent Ted into their lives. He was certain God was calling him into service in the church. God was acting in the broad, over-all scheme and moving in the details. God was personal, righteous, holy, and loving. Because all this was true, and peace would happen in God's good time, his duty was to go forward with integrity, loving Kate and Ted, helping to care for Catherine, being true to his own parents and siblings, keeping faith with his friends, and preparing diligently for his new career.

Their marital problems were his business and Kate's and nobody else's. His loyalty to her was as strong as it had been on the day of their wedding. A few close friends had observed Kate's behavior and talked with Joe in friendly, general terms over the years. He was grateful for their concern. But he spoke of particulars only with their family physician and the licensed professional counselors he consulted. Even in these professional conversations, his conscience bothered him at first, but he concluded that it was his duty as a husband and a father to seek this guidance. The two or three close friends who asked questions were as loyal to Kate as they were to him, an attitude that pleased him and gave him confidence in their discretion. He answered them truthfully but without betraying the details he knew would have mortified Kate. Her own shell, so carefully developed and perfected since childhood, reinforced his belief. She continued to present to the world the same image of self-sufficiency and spunky bravado Joe himself had seen at first. Most people on the outside, looking in, at first might not have perceived any problems. But the secret inner life that Kate hid from the world and her husband controlled her. It generated moods, attitudes, and disordered perceptions that in time revealed themselves to outsiders. Sensing this and preferring the safety of isolation to the hard work of self-examination, she kept her distance, emotionally and physically, from everyone but her son.

Her shell had been strengthened and preserved since childhood by the academic schedule that gave her life structure. It was a part of her personality, intrinsically intertwined with her attitudes and moods. She suffered through the school year with very little social interaction with friends. Many people knew her, but few were able to get close. In any neighborhood where they lived, she knew one or two neighbors while Joe and Ted knew everybody. When school ended, she went straight to Wicomico, where there were no pressures. There she was supremely in control, and fun and relaxation ruled the day. She could entertain friends of her choosing on her own schedule. With several of her own acquaintances from the past and Joe's family, she was a generous and cheerful hostess. At the old ocean-side house, everybody, friends and renters alike, enjoyed her company and admired her easygoing summer mood. As far as they knew, Kate was that way all year long. Her friends, who visited her only in the summer, and whom she visited occasionally at Christmas, without realizing it were seeing only her vacation personality.

As years passed, the guidance of professional counselors would strengthen Joe's coping skills. On a therapist's advice, he began to attend Al-Anon meetings, where friends and relatives of alcoholics met to discuss their lives. He had been reluctant to participate earlier because he refused to betray Kate by discussing her with strangers. He was heartened to find that members only rarely discussed the alcoholic in their lives, focusing instead on themselves, their own actions and reactions, their personal attitudes and ways of coping. Hearing how others managed familiar problems and sharing the healing sense of humor that prevailed among them was for Joe a gift of God. Offering up thanks and pleas with them to their Higher Power was liberating. Joe left most of the meetings feeling cleaner and calmer.

For all these reasons, Joe did not raise his wife's drinking and disposition during the discernment process. It was focused upon him, not Kate. As far as Joe was concerned, he was the one who slept with her, and she was nobody else's business. The few questions asked by the church about candidates' marriages were aimed at clarifying the way a man or woman was fulfilling marriage vows. Unless one were coping faithfully in one's family, and every married candidate seemed to be coping with something, how could he or she expect to serve effectively in the myriad pressures and demands of God's wider family? In this light, Joe believed he was fulfilling his marriage vows with patience and humility. In seminary, he addressed his lingering doubt with his spiritual director, a senior member of the faculty and the father of five grown children. He had confidence in this good man who advised him to keep on with what he was doing. He counseled Joe to continue to gently encourage Kate to join Alcoholics Anonymous and agreed that God would lead her into recovery in due time. In their prayers together at the end of their sessions, they always prayed for Kate and Ted first.

In his work before seminary, Joe had seen plenty of drinkers and had learned something of the insidious nature of addiction. How many times in court had he heard, "Your Honor, I had one beer. Two at the most." He had known clergy and their spouses and at least one bishop who had "problems," as people liked to say. He suspected that some members of the seminary faculty were acquainted with the problem. Most of his friends were related to a problem drinker. The church appeared to accept all these people for who they were, advising patience, treatment, compassion, and support.

Joe remembered the difficult days in law enforcement when he had been one of the few to speak out for the decriminalization of marijuana. He knew its use inhibited maturity and destroyed character, but he had come to see the whole issue in terms of unavoidable economics. Law enforcement had only so much funding and limited personnel to go around, and what they faced was growing relentlessly. He preferred to see the time and resources devoted to heroin, cocaine, and the other hard stuff and to eradicating the animals who provided it. He had examined a dozen drunk-driving fatalities personally, scenes that had the young cops puking—children, teenagers on their way home from the prom, housewives, overworked fathers who had stopped off somewhere after a hard day. He preferred to see drivers smoking pot rather than drinking alcohol. He had said so, and it cost him professionally. And he was dealing with addiction again now, only this time in his own bed at night, at his kitchen table. There was always a cost. How had it turned out like this?

There was one thing more. It came to him now and then at night after he put Ted to bed, while he jogged the neighborhood streets, or sat in the living room enjoying a peaceful moment before bed. The question would come surreptitiously, meanly out of the shadows like a bat or some other odious creature, unbidden and alarming. Against all his natural instincts, for a few trashy little moments in the dark, he permitted himself to wonder if he had made a mistake in marrying Kate. As soon as this thought emerged in his mind like a spider, he clenched his eyes and fists and saw immediately Ted's precious face looking back. He could not imagine life without this wondrous child. And he saw Kate's face as he had seen it countless times, smiling at a joke, laughing at something said, filled with indignation at some mistake he had made, the way she looked at Ted, and the way she looked at him sometimes. This was all the answer he needed to such a shameful notion. Kate was his wife. He loved her for better or worse. He could not imagine life without her. Ted would not be in the world if he and Kate had not married. But even without Ted, and he could hardly bring himself to begin to try to imagine it, this was his wife, the woman he loved, who slept with him, whose life was bound up with his own. He dismissed the reprehensible doubt until it occurred the next time, often when he was abjectly worried and fatigued. And then he would dismiss it again. No therapist, priest, relative, or friend had ever raised such a consideration. Each time he banished the ugly idea from his thinking, it left an unbearable deposit of shame that festered in him like an infected wound. This was because he forced himself to acknowledge that in his protection of Kate, his own interests, however small and cheap and disagreeable, figured as well. He could not separate their mutual welfare, hers, Ted's, their family's, his own. But he recognized that his own identity was wrapped up now in the wife he was trying to support and protect. And almost as painful as the realization that his wife might not love him was the heartache of admitting to himself that he was failing in his duty to her.

* * *

When they moved from Jeffersonville to the seminary, Kate chose to keep her job at her old high school, preferring to commute there and continue in the same work environment. She drove a bit over a half hour each way from their new home. As a science teacher, she could have found work immediately at any one of a half-dozen schools near the seminary. However, the familiar administrators and teachers she had worked with for years became very important to her when faced with the prospect of a new work environment. After years of hearing of their unreliability and peculiarities every evening at dinner, Joe would have guessed Kate would relish a chance to move. She decided to continue on.

As with Joe's friends in the law and his hunting and fishing companions, his classmates in seminary were friendly to Kate and tried to make her feel a part of things. She understood what they were doing and was appreciative. Still, they were new to her, and instinctively, she kept them at a safe distance. She was wary of most of them, friendly when she met them but critical when she talked to Joe at dinner and before bedtime. To Joe's immense relief and to Kate's as well, the wife of another seminarian, who would become one of Joe's closest friends in ministry, took a special interest in Kate, and the four of them formed a genuine and supportive friendship.

Kate's labile emotions were still a constant concern. He worried about her health. He knew she was not happy but believed she would have been unhappy anywhere, carrying the inner distress that he struggled to assuage. Eventually she became so depressed that even she, after long and painfully careful reasoning and reassurance, agreed finally to see a counselor. As he talked with her, Joe felt like an ordinance engineer defusing a bomb, knowing that a wrong word, a fluctuating tone, even the ringing of the telephone, or Ted coughing in his sleep could result in an abrupt abandonment of the conversation or an explosion of anger that would wake their son and be heard by the neighbors. He could make no progress with her until he raised the issue of her job. Her moods were apparently affecting her work. Dinner conversation for many weeks had been recitations by Kate of one argument after another with her colleagues. Recently she had received a note from an assistant principal admonishing her for something she had been overheard saying (she would not tell him what). By the time she reluctantly, tentatively agreed to see someone, he was soaked in perspiration and his head ached, the same way he had felt in years past after particularly difficult days at trial. She was angry with him for daring to speak of her mental state and her job. He would pay for it down the road, he knew. He had no idea whether she would do what she had promised. But the price he would pay was worth it, for this was as close as they had come to her agreeing to seek help. She declared she would find a therapist herself and did not need his help and went to bed without speaking further.

She had no idea how to find a counselor herself and, as far as Joe could tell, made no effort to follow through. After a few more weeks, he contacted Dr. Alkari, her gynecologist, and with his help found a clinical psychologist, an older woman whose office was in a shopping center halfway between their apartment and Kate's high school.

Although Joe did not understand it then, his own act of finding a therapist put Kate into a defensive mode before she ever entered the office. This was not because she distrusted Joe, and she certainly didn't hate him. She loved him at that time as much as she could love anyone other than Ted. But she had entered marriage viewing Joe in the only way she knew to relate to someone close, as an authority figure who represented a threat to her independence. This was not Joe's fault. She would have viewed anyone with whom she was forced to share responsibilities in the same way. Whether or not she recognized this was anybody's guess. She knew of no way to relate to authority figures except combat or surrender. She had found that Joe could stand up under combat that had worn others down eventually. Surrender represented an entirely unacceptable admission of failure, inadequacy, and a threat to her sense of self-worth. Partisan tactics were therefore the natural maneuvers when the campaign called for action.

Kate agreed to see the therapist because she came with Dr. Alkari's recommendation. Joe asked to accompany her to the first appointment, and Kate agreed. Joe's presence provided a certain comfort, although she would not have said so. Dr. Sylvia Ulm, an angular older lady with a long white ponytail, asked Kate how she was doing.

"Fine," said Kate, smiling, alert, her feet carefully side by side, hands folded demurely in her lap, an image of innocence and attention that her teachers, department heads, and supervisors going back to the first grade would have recognized. Joe knew she was struggling. His heart broke to see her, so close and yet so immeasurably far, far away, enclosed in her denial and beyond his reach regardless of how much affection and patience he poured into the distance between them. He looked at her and he loved her, and because of it, her unreasonableness and inflexibility spread frustration in his gut like burning gasoline. Dr. Ulm waited a moment, but Kate, continuing to smile as she looked from her to Joe and back, as though waiting for them to get on with whatever they felt they needed to do, said nothing more. The psychologist turned to Joe and asked if he had anything to say.

"I'm worried about Kate. I love her, and I want her to be happy, but I don't know how to deal with what happens," said Joe, looking at Kate. Kate glanced briefly at him and then looked away to the wall where Dr. Ulm's diplomas hung in their dreary frames. Kate appeared to study them intently.

"Could you say a little more about that, Reverend Stephenson?"

"I'm not ordained, Dr. Ulm. Please call me Jack. I don't know how… There's so much, so many things. We've been married eight years. In my view, Kate is depressed, and she drinks too much." He looked at Kate quickly and said, "But she would not agree with that. Her mother is an alcoholic and lives with us most of the time. I'm concerned about Kate, and I'm concerned about our son too. I'm no medical man, but my day-to-day observation is that drinking increases mood swings in Kate. I think she would still have some issues to work out even if she stopped drinking. I'm seeing a family counselor. Have for several years. Kate refuses to see her with me. She has been very helpful to me—the counselor. I'm hoping and praying that Kate will agree to see you on a regular basis. I think it would help us all." Joe stopped and looked back toward Kate. Her face had turned tomato red, and she was frowning as though smelling something foul. It surprised him because he had seen this look before but never in the presence of a third party.

Dr. Ulm saw it too. She cleared her throat and said, "Well, Kate, would you like to return one day on your own?"

"Yes. That will be fine," said Kate in a monotone. An appointment was scheduled, Dr. Ulm advising that she preferred to see Kate for a while before asking Joe to come back too. They all agreed. On the way home, Kate chatted about her day at work, a ridiculous new office policy concerning the copy machine that had all the teachers in a fit, a weather report about a severe storm in the Wicomico area, and about the traffic that was getting worse by the week. She did not mention Dr. Ulm. Joe thanked her for going and asked how she had felt about it. Kate replied that it seemed all right, and she would just have to see how things went. Over the next two months, she went to see her three times, as far as Joe could tell. It was not the weekly visits he had hoped for, but it was great progress. Then one evening he asked casually how their visits were going, and Kate announced that they had "finished." She said, "Dr. Ulm said there was no need for me to come back anymore." And she didn't. It crossed Joe's mind to verify what she said, but he became busy with preparing for examinations and let it go.

The following month brought a very difficult spell of drinking. Kate was more sarcastic than ever, and Joe feared for what Ted might notice or remember. Fran, a seminarian he had grown very fond of, had confided that she was a recovering alcoholic. In their first few months of seminary, she had told him one day to dig into her backpack for a book they needed for study group. As he lifted it out, he recognized beneath it a small AA manual, carefully disguised in a homemade floral cover. He had smiled at her, and she smiled back and was soon confiding in him. She agreed immediately to come to see Kate, and Kate, protesting that she was not an alcoholic but would see her if it would make Joe happy, met her one cold Sunday evening in their apartment.

Joe took Ted out to the park while they talked. They returned just before Ted's bedtime. Fran had left. Kate was watching television. On the coffee table were several books and pamphlets about AA. Kate did not mention their talk. As they were going to bed, and it was apparent that she intended to say nothing, Joe asked her lightly how it had gone. Kate pretended to be surprised, as though she had forgotten the visit completely. Without commenting on their talk, she said she had promised to go with Fran to an AA meeting at a nearby hospital the following night, "because I don't think she wants to go alone." Joe was encouraged. He slept soundly through the night for the first time in weeks.

The following evening Kate returned from the AA meeting and declared she had never seen such a bunch of drunks and liars in her life. Most of the people at the meeting smoked, which irritated her intensely. They were there, she said, because some judge or probation officer had ordered them to attend. She had nothing at all in common with people like that and had no intention of going back. Joe asked if she would try another meeting, say, at one of the large churches in the area. She would think about it, she said. She never attended an AA meeting again and never mentioned Fran. The AA literature disappeared too.

As she had done since their marriage, Catherine lived with them for weeks and months at a time. She was becoming too old and feeble to live alone. Her drinking and relentless criticism of everyone wore out Kate's sister-in-law after a week or so, and Kate's brother, Ray, always sent her back to Kate and Joe to keep the peace. A mechanically talented man, academically accomplished like his mother and sister, Ray managed personal relationships with the sophistication of a ten-year-old. His head perpetually in the sand, he ignored problems with the acquired understanding that, if he remained inactive long enough, the problem would go away or somebody else would be forced to deal with it. After the third or fourth unpleasant scene between his mother and his wife, he would telephone Kate and plead with her to take Catherine off their hands or simply put his mother on a plane and leave a message on the Stephensons' answering machine. Between Kate and her brother, alcoholism was never even mentioned. Rare references to "making Mom behave" was as close as they came as they talked around the issue with studied avoidance.

When he was consulted beforehand, Joe always agreed to take Catherine into their home. When he was not consulted, he never objected to her coming but pointed out to Kate that he would like to know as such plans were being made. This was because he knew that once his mother-in-law arrived, it would be up to him, as it was to

Kate's sister-in-law in Georgia, to control Catherine's behavior while she was in their home.

* * *

The family counselors had taught Joe that modeling good behavior and controlling his own reactions was the way to manage his situation at home. Ted too had planted the same seed in something he had said to Joe a few years earlier. Eight years of marriage had also taught him that any infraction of family expectations on his part or the smallest failure to abide by the rare mutual understanding, however slight or unintentional, would never escape Kate's ironclad memory. Her denial was reinforced by a vigilance for failings in Joe, which could be tucked away for use against him later.

Joe felt a lonely duty toward his family, and this included Catherine. She was his wife's mother. Kate and Joe's mother loved one another dearly, a relationship Joe struggled to protect. But even if Kate had detested his own mother, Joe could not have found it in himself to neglect or abandon Catherine, an elderly and lonely woman, chronically ill with a disease that her family ignored. Five feet tall and weighing a bit less than a hundred pounds, wrinkled and rattled by years of drinking and poor eating, she was pitifully vulnerable and needy. Her temper and suspicions were as hard to deal with as Kate's. But how could he feel no pity for her? She had isolated herself increasingly in life. She had no friends. He tried to ignore her dislike of him, telling himself that nobody else fulfilled her expectations either. He found her amusing and tried to humor her as old friends might relate to one another. There were many times when he felt she understood that he was doing the best he could, although he knew she would never acknowledge it. She became nasty and combative when intoxicated, and Kate returned her every such indiscretion in kind. It poisoned their home life. When Kate was drinking too, Joe felt like a round-the-clock social worker in his own home. Even after all his education and experience, he had only a vague concept of an enabler's role in the alcoholic family. Catherine's presence overwhelmed Kate, who spent most of her mother's visits quite literally crying on Joe's shoulder. Finally, halfway through seminary, Joe insisted that Catherine refrain from drinking alcohol in his home. It was a draconian imposition to which nobody had ever dared subject her and for which she never forgave him. She had no problems, drinking or otherwise, and his unreasonable refusal to accept that was evil.

All his efforts to get along with Catherine had come to nothing over the years. Their arguments had been hot and nasty at times, with Joe at times behaving as unreasonably as his mother-in-law. Early on the animosity became centered on the care of Ted. During a sudden storm at the beach house one summer night when Ted was less than a year old, Joe had gone to the second floor to close the storm blinds, while Kate was doing the same on the first floor. Racing through the rooms, closing the southeast windows first, he heard Ted's shrill cry as the thunderous wind and rain buffeted the old house. In going into his bedroom, he found Catherine, unsteady and wheezing, clutching Ted in her thin arms. He had slipped from her grip, and she was holding him up by pressing his small head against her stomach. Joe quickly lifted his son carefully from Catherine's grasp and tried to soothe him. Catherine was intoxicated and incensed. Babbling about how Joe had upset him and knew nothing about babies, she attempted to take Ted from his arms. She knew how to take care of a baby! She had had two of them! Joe only had one! Ted had been frightened by the thunder! She was trying to calm him down!

A terrible scene erupted. Even Kate, called upstairs over the noise of the rain, felt obliged to shout at Catherine. For months Joe would wince at the thought of his infant son hitting the hard floorboards, perhaps breaking an arm or leg or, God forbid, landing on his head. He lectured Catherine harshly, but she refused to hear it. She tottered downstairs to the sitting room, where some former neighbors, visiting for the evening, were seated and talking. They knew nothing of what had occurred upstairs. When Joe came downstairs and passed through the room where they were gathered, Catherine began berating him in front of these guests. Angry and shaken, he raised his voice to her and told her she was not to touch his son when she was drinking. Immediately Catherine raised her fists and attempted to hop around like an ancient trembling prizefighter, lightly punching the air in Joe's direction. Had she not been entirely serious and the recent scene so fraught with danger, the whole spectacle might have appeared comical to Joe. The former neighbors departed in confusion, unwilling to see their old friend victimized by her upstart son-in-law. Catherine tottered about on the porch, calling them back and declaring she would have Joe arrested. Kate remained upstairs in the bedroom with Ted, never once coming down to chastise her mother or make an explanation to her former neighbors. Five minutes later, Kate's irate brother telephoned from Georgia, alerted by the departed guests to Joe's outrageous behavior toward his elderly mother. He demanded to know what Joe thought he was doing. Still trying to keep the peace, Joe tried to give Ray as objective and fair a description of what had happened as his lawyerly skills would allow. In later years he would find it hard to forgive himself for not telling Ray to go to hell, packing up Ted and their things, and leaving that very night and refusing to return until both Kate and Catherine were attending AA meetings. He would remain ashamed of himself for many years.

When Joe visited Kate and Ted during their summers by the sea, for his precious week of vacation, renters at the house were cool to him, unenthusiastically acknowledging his presence and warming up only if they spent some time with him. He knew that Catherine, in anticipation of his coming, had taken every opportunity to make known what a cad he was and how badly he behaved toward her and her own long-suffering daughter and her unfortunate grandson. He also knew, although he refused to permit himself to dwell on it, that Kate did nothing to prevent this sort of conduct. She would not encourage it by any means, and if she discovered Catherine in the act, she would admonish her and roll her eyes for the benefit of the guests. But Joe knew she would take no positive steps to defend him or set the record straight, preferring instead to ignore this problem too.

His "vacation," in what was truly a lovely place, with his wife and son was always marred by the troubled family dynamics.

He remembered arriving at the charming old house late one beautiful Friday afternoon following a seven-hour drive through holiday traffic. He was unpacking and could hardly wait to put on a swimsuit and plunge into the cool ocean, swim with Kate and Ted, and rinse away the frustrations of summer in the hot city. He remembered thinking something that had ceased to enter his mind for years now, how good it would be to have a relaxing tall bourbon while he sat on the beach with Kate. He banished the impossible thought, and Kate soon came into the room to tell him about Catherine's most recent indiscretions.

"And you should have heard her complaining about you to those people from Maryland in the front room. The pump hasn't worked right all week, and she told them that you must have been fooling with it last time you came down."

"What? I've never touched the pump. I don't know one end of it from the other."

"I know! And then she came and complained to me about it, just inside the kitchen door where everybody on the porch outside could hear, how you had ruined her pump and now she had to pay for it! It ticked me off, jumping on me like that for no reason. I told her to just *drop* it, that I couldn't do anything about it now."

Joe listened to her with his mouth open. He had been in the house ten minutes and already he wondered if he would lose his mind.

"Kate!" he said, louder than he should have. "You can't do anything about it now? That's like confirming that I did something. Like saying you know she's right! To both her and whoever was listening. Why didn't you tell her plainly that I'd never touched the damn pump? And I suppose those people will be here all week."

"Oh, right, Joe! Why is it always my fault? You haven't been here ten minutes and you're already on my case just like Mom! Thanks a lot! You've ruined the week already." She was still delivering this speech halfway down the stairs as she stomped away, in easy listening distance of everybody on both floors. And Ted, who was coming up the stairs to see Joe, heard it too.

* * *

It was his precious son who first taught Joe that his own behavior was the key to health in their home. Joe would look back on the lesson for the rest of his life with gratitude and regret—gratitude that God had shown him the light and had done so through his son, and regret that he had not figured it out years before on his own.

Ted was a little over a year old. Joe was bathing him, the first thing he did when he came home in the evening. After his bath and a few minutes of playing on the bed, a time Ted especially loved, Joe would then carry him, clean and powered, down to the kitchen where Kate was preparing dinner. While the three of them spent these precious moments together, Joe drank his bourbon and water, and Kate her white wine or bourbon and ginger ale. Joe looked forward all day to this time with his wife and son, the three of them together in the kitchen, talking and enjoying one another.

Ted was a beautiful baby. Big for his age, by twelve months he had turned from an angelic bald cherub into a big golden-haired boy. His perpetual beam and beautiful hair attracted everyone's attention. Giving him his nightly bath, Joe washed and rinsed his son's hair carefully while Ted held a washcloth momentarily to his face. Ted was talking to him.

The day had been routine for Joe but unusually tiring because there had been no time to sit down and clear his mind. He had worked through lunch, as usual. He was in the third day of a trial that might last another week. The charges were abduction, rape, and sodomy. The defendant was an upper middle class white boy from Delaware whose wealthy family had retained the most disagreeable and acrimonious defense lawyer in the metro area. She was defending her client by putting the victim, and Joe, on trial. The complaining witness, a Costa Rican girl with a green card who cleaned hotel rooms for a living, had a motel room full of young children in Greenbelt being supervised during the trial by her mother, an illiterate illegal alien who had suffered a heart attack early that very morning. She had slumped to the floor and remained there while the oblivious young children sat around her, watching cartoons on television. About noon, a cousin had stopped by with a day's supply of fast food and found his aunt dead in the middle of the children. A bailiff brought word of all this to Joe during the trial. He moved for a recess to explain it to the victim. Defense counsel had objected, and a conference had followed at the bench, following which the judge granted Joe's motion for a recess over the objection of the defense. Joe, accompanied by the Witness Protection Program director, had taken the victim into an adjoining room and explained clearly and compassionately about her mother's heart attack and death. The young Costa Rican woman had become hysterical and begun pounding her head on the metal frame of the conference room door. The rescue squad had been called to treat her injuries, the court recessed the trial until the following day over the grudging objections of defense counsel, and Joe had returned to his office. He had spent the rest of the afternoon returning telephone calls in a dozen other cases, one of them a homicide that would go to a jury as soon as the rape trial had concluded.

Before leaving his office, he had received a call from Ted's pediatrician, a conscientious man who knew Joe well and had two young children of his own. He wanted to mention that Kate had brought Ted to his office again for what she believed was an emergency. Ted had fallen and bumped his head at lunch at the home of his day care provider. The provider had made the required call to Kate, letting her know it had happened and assuring her that Ted was fine so Kate would understand if he developed a bruise later in the day. A few times in the past, the same sort of routine call had caused Kate to panic. She had left school immediately, picked up Ted at day care, and raced with him to the doctor's office. Each time on such occasions, the doctor confirmed that Ted was not injured, and he had explained all this to Joe at a Rotary luncheon. He was content to charge the usual fees, he said with a smile, but regretted to see Kate and Ted upset for no good reason. He suggested that it might be easier on Kate, and better for Ted, if Kate would consult with Joe before bringing Ted to his office the next time.

Joe had understood him perfectly and had discussed the situation that same night with Kate. She had agreed grudgingly. A month had passed without further incidents, until today. Joe would now have to go over it again with Kate and attempt to achieve another understanding. All this had occurred just before he left the office.

As he bathed Ted, he was depressed at the thought of trying to reason with Kate. He was alert for a telephone call from an investigator or witness program volunteer reporting to him about the complaining witness. This young woman had suffered just about all one human being could deal with, and he was terribly sorry for her and concerned about her mental state. He was wondering too whether the trial could resume the following morning. He knew he would get very little sleep that night. As he had entered the house a short while before, Kate, without mentioning the visit to the pediatrician, had begun to tell him what she had heard on the radio on her way home.

"Did you hear what happened today? They had to cancel some big rape trial because the one that got raped had a heart attack in the courtroom. People at school were saying she probably faked it to drag the trial out. Too bad they'll have to have a new trial now. Well, Ted is ready for Dad to give him a bath! Aren't you, Ted?"

He was giving Ted his bath now and longing to go down to the kitchen and have his drink. His head hurt. He was tired. Maybe he would have two drinks and just do nothing for the rest of the evening. Watch television with Kate. Read the paper. Go to bed early. Try to sleep. And when would he talk with her about the doctor visits? He had to do it tonight, while the whole thing was fresh.

He rinsed his son quickly, wanting to go downstairs. He heard himself ask Ted absentmindedly about pictures he might have drawn that day. And in the midst of his usual unremarkable musings and comments about drawing, Ted's voice broke into his preoccupation, and he thought he heard his infant son say, "Annette has it."

He was stunned. "What did you say, honey?" he said.

And once again Ted said to him, "Annette has it." The words were garbled and mispronounced, but clear enough that Joe could understand them. He froze, his mouth open and silent, as he stared at his beautiful, grinning child. Ted grabbed for some rubber toys bobbing in the tub beside him and gathered them up in his lap. He then looked at Joe and said, "Picture."

"Ted!" Joe exclaimed, kissing his son's glistening wet forehead. "That's good! You said it! I heard it! Kate! Kate!" he began to call. Kate came upstairs quickly, drying her hands on a dishtowel, with a look of alarm on her face. Joe told her what had happened. Their son, who had learned to say "Dada," "Mama," "ball," and "juice" had just spoken a whole, intelligible sentence. Annette, a big jolly black lady whom Ted loved, an aide at the day care center, had his drawing! He had said so. Joe was ecstatic, overjoyed. Kate was more excited than Joe had seen her in weeks. They stood Ted on Joe's lap and dried him off, telling him how smart he was and how proud they were of him. Pleased with himself and a bit overwhelmed by his parents' excited reaction, Ted laughed and babbled. While Joe finished dressing him, Kate went back downstairs quickly to make sure dinner was not burning on the stove.

Ted's speaking a sentence to him had a profound effect upon Joe. He understood that he had heard his son's first sentence. And he knew he had almost missed it. Preoccupied with many things, worried about matters far and near, rushing through his son's bath to go downstairs and have a drink, he had almost missed it, one of the most precious moments in his life. As he helped Ted gently into his blue sleeper and zipped it up with care, he understood that one day (sooner, much sooner than he could imagine) he would give a million dollars to relive this moment, and moments like it. Bathing his son, listening to him, playing with him, talking with him, reading to him, observing him as he did things—these were life's incomparable moments. Was anything in the world worth the tragedy of missing them?

Joe, neither deeply intelligent nor a man of superior insight was, however, a faithful man as much as he knew how to be, and at this moment, he believed with his whole heart and mind that God had given him a sign, a warning. He was grateful.

He carried his bright, happy child downstairs and spent the rest of the evening listening to and observing the two people who meant more to him than anything else in life. Never again did he intend to miss a golden moment. He drank no alcohol that evening. Everything was usual, commonplace, and completely brilliant. The air fairly crackled with clarity and comprehension. His wife and son, being themselves, glowed with a new glory. He was enthralled, mesmerized, overwhelmed with joy and wonder. Years before he had read a description of *satori*, the moment of enlightenment in Zen practice. He recalled it now as the precious moments of perception passed, and he was filled with wonder at how the usual and ordinary shine with glorious mystery for those with eyes to see, ears to hear.

That night, as Kate read her paperback mystery and finished the last of her wine before turning off her light, Joe lay in the bed beside her, thinking. Life was complicated. Much depended on his clear thinking and attention at home, at work, everywhere he turned. For every reason he could imagine, his own clarity and steadiness seemed suddenly vastly more important after Ted's bath that evening. He got up and went downstairs to the kitchen table, the heart of every home. On a legal pad, he wrote a brief letter to himself declaring that from that evening forward, he would listen as carefully to his precious wife and adorable son as he listened to witnesses and other people as an attorney. He thought he had done so until now, but Ted had taught him a lesson. And he promised God and himself that, except for communion wine, he would no longer drink alcohol.

Chapter Seventeen

In junior high school, an unsuspecting science teacher broke into Joe's daydreaming long enough one day to impart a truth he never forgot: tension is a force that attempts to pull things apart. Why he remembered it was another of the mysteries of life most of us accept and soon cease to ponder, but it had opened a window. Even then his experience of the world was of universal tension. Everything was being pulled apart. History, relationships, plans, civilizations, families, mountain ranges, good intentions, teams, ideas—always there was the relentless pulling asunder that seemed to be the natural way of things. Life was littered with the crumbling remains of the past. The Appalachians once looked like the Rockies. In his teens, he wondered if all human progress was just a sustained effort to hold together, to establish and maintain, to find wholeness in a universe that tended naturally toward disorder. He wondered (strictly to himself) if faith in God was a reaction to the tension in everything, a search for heavenly insurance against the fires, floods, and lawsuits of creation. His science teachers said the universe is flying apart. Would judgment day be the moment God ceased to hold it in unity, withdrawing his staying hand from the primal mechanics and allowing the ultimate unimaginable spasm of collapse? Why does the best we do suffer ultimately the worst rending? Doric. Ionic. Corinthian. Racism. Greed. Treblinka.

By the age of twenty, he concluded that the best we do is always derivative. Our glorious achievements are a rough searching out of secrets already there from the beginning, doing our little bit to polish them up for a while, hold them up into the light for a moment. And in a thousand years? Ten thousand? Hagia Sophia, the pyramids, relativity, the *Iliad. Ah! Brontosaurus migrated across what you call your Great Plains for a hundred and sixty million years. Where are they now? Where is Gondwanaland? What have you done with Mr. Millmoss?*

Like Jesus retiring to a quiet place or Sally Bowles searching out her overhead, people seek a suspension now and then, an interlude of peace and order, a "clean well-lighted place" where they can escape the tension of existence. That such escapes are mere eyes in the storm does not diminish their healing value. And when we cannot go, we can bring them unto ourselves.

In 1888, Vincent van Gogh, long past copying engravings in the *Illustrated London News*, painted *Farmhouse in Provence, Arles*. His orange sun-drenched field on a yellow summer afternoon, an exuberant celebration of creation, symbolic in color and rendered with energetic calligraphy, unites artist, scene, and admirer in an intermission of joy. The following year, he painted the turbulent *Wheat Field and Cypress Trees*, a churning sea of graphic, heaving color, an emotional identification with creation animating artist and admirer together in a windy, roaring updraft of forms and hues. These great paintings are not the measured passions of a true naturalist, but revelations faithful in form and content to a distinctive logic in creation, a radical spiritual integrity that was always there. Participating in them can be refuge enough for a while. It is reality recorded, interpreted, unraveled, and elucidated with sensuality and religious ardor and exposed in a polyphonic rush to an admirer's eyes with vigor that leaves nothing lingering at the source. The undulating motion of grasses, hills and clouds, the trees swelling and rising like brittle blue flames, the hot baked slink of stone fence toward home, the scarlet poppies peeping from their places—all excite the eye as *An American in Paris* or the *Brandenburg Concertos* thrill the ear.

An hour spent admiring these wonderful pictures, even their reproduction in books, filled Joe with joyful, expansive hope for compassion and interpretive order. His confidence in a certain ultimate rightness was refreshed. The generous nexus of intellect, cosmos, and inspiration in these wondrous pictures raised the image of artist as cocreator with God, a blessed insight into human beings that broke a liberating hole through understanding. In spite of his birth at the end of the Second World War, Joe believed that Abelard had got it right. Human reason could arbitrate the conflicts of life. God had created the human race in an act of love and blessed us with reason. One could discern progress in humankind's maturity. God is leading us forward to a time when poverty, want, oppression, and sickness will be no more. He believed this in spite of the Crusades, Black Death, Thirty Years War, colonialism, Nazis, the Holocaust, the Rape of Nanking, Auschwitz, Stalin, Communism, Mao, the Cultural Revolution, Pol Pot, Rwanda, Tien An Men Square, and radical Islam. Although Faulkner did not go so far, Joe believed that humankind would not merely prevail but join its dispirit voices together to sing God's praise in a hymn of reverence and compassion.

But as he read newspapers and history books, he wondered from time to time, in spite of his elemental hope, as he sat alone at his kitchen table late at night, if he had got it backward after all. Are human beings capable of living in peace and justice in *this* world? We will know it in the world to come, but is it possible here? Was Augustine correct in taking one reference from St. Paul and making the Fall the excuse for our reality? Or is it, instead, a matter of maturity? Was Irenaeus correct? And is free will destroying us? What is real? What is true? Is belief real? Is absurdity real? Are space and time real? he wondered. Are they components of objective reality, discernable through rational analysis of empirical data? Or are they constructs of the human mind, superimposed upon the face of the cosmos to render it comprehensible—seconds, miles, light-years? Does belief in God generate rational inquiry? Does rational inquiry lead one to perceive the reality of God? Hindus, zero, Kant, relativity, Pi, quantum theory, Newton, Plato, Aristotle, Wittgenstein, Tertullian, Origen, Einstein, Augustine, Luther, Hooker, Pascal, Barth, Bonhoeffer, Tillich, Rahner, Kung, Aquinas, Erasmus. What? Where? How? When? It didn't matter. They weren't the right question anyway.

In mowing the lawn, washing dishes, ironing Ted's clothes, running at night along deserted streets and country roads, Joe wondered. He wondered about everything. *And here I stand with all this sweated lore, poor fool, no wiser than I was before.* Sometimes it was too much simply to look up at the stars. Wonder and amazement, moving like crazy dancers in his head, overwhelmed him. *It's all straw,* said a voice from somewhere.

And as he meditated, against all the odds, against every reason not to, Joe became amused. For in such meaning as he could grasp an intrinsic absurdity was always and everywhere present. In any degree of comprehension, however imperfect, which he wrested with effort as he searched, at the most inconvenient moments, it was there, a compulsion to smile or laugh. It was all absurd. And for mystified creatures like Joe, the only thing to do (should he part his hair behind? Does he dare to eat a peach?) seemed to be to accept the absurdity, loving, generous, compassionate, trustful, and humble acceptance. He sensed that this acceptance was connected to justice, kindness, and the humble walk, although how was still a mystery. But laughter seemed to bring one closer to comprehension. He thought he knew that much, at least. And yes, there were other ways. *Now I lay me down to sleep... Take and eat this in remembrance...on me, a sinner.* None of them laughing matters, by any means.

Joe had tried to do justice. He had tried to be flexible. He had shown mercy. God knows he had asked it for himself often enough. He had tried to be kind, to his frustrated father, wounded by the Wehrmacht; his loving and patient mother; his sick wife; his son, jewel of his existence; his family, friends, neighbors. He had failed, of course, many more times than he had got it right. He knew it, but he hoped it was whatever was written on his heart that would count in the end. Laugh! he would say to himself, with humility. After all, *it's all straw,* he would say, with humility.

So Joe looked at the pictures the great artists, now dust, had left behind. He read *King Lear* and *Four Quartets.* He studied Hagia Sophia and *War and Peace,* he hiked the Blue Ridge, canoed the New, and he thought about his son. There was majesty in humankind. There was unspeakable beauty in the world. He kept reminding himself of these truths daily, by every means available. He let Van Gogh help him, and Cezanne, Dickens, Mozart, Rembrandt, Tolstoy, D. H. Lawrence, and Bach. They helped him keep faith in the dignity of human nature. Mostly they helped preserve his sanity in a world he shared with the Solovetsky Islands, the little forest of Birkenau, and Sierra Leone.

Chapter Eighteen

Gracious, comfortable Dorchester's friendly ways came as a relief after the perplexing seminary years. Salesclerks remembered customers and said good morning and people held doors open for perfect strangers. Children paid attention and replied when spoken to. Joe did not worry when Kate called to say she would stop by a convenience store on the way home at night. Teenagers on a street corner after dark were not necessarily a sign of trouble. Many families had occupied the same house for generations.

Coming home to a driveway crowded with bicycles leaning on kickstands at every angle and Ted and his friends playing all over the house worked on Joe like a transfusion. It was a double blessing because Kate was happy too. Touchy irritation over having to move again to unknown territory had turned into unspoken contentment that he could read in her manner and silences. When she was moody, she stomped. Now she walked without sighing from room to room with a lighter tread, saying something positive now and then. He heard fewer complaints. He knew it meant a growing satisfaction with her new job at the local college.

Kate had agreed to spend two weeks in their new home before departing to Wicomico for the summer. Joe had emphasized that he needed help in unpacking and setting up the house. The contents of their seminary apartment and storage bin and their storage bin in Jeffersonville and the contents of Joe's law office had all been deposited at the Dorchester house in crates and boxes, and it all awaited sorting and much other attention. Joe would be working every day at his new position, and without Kate's participation, it would take him all summer, working nights and Saturdays, to put it all in order. This was what had happened when they moved to their seminary apartment, and Kate had intended the same thing this time. She planned to leave as soon as she had dug out enough clothing for herself and Ted for the summer, but she appeared to accept Joe's pleas and had put off leaving for the two weeks he suggested.

She spent part of each day at the college. It was closed now between the end of the spring semester and the beginning of summer school, and Kate was vague about what she was doing there. "Just being around, doing a little work, seeing where things are" was as much as she would say about it. But she began coming home from her time there with new jokes, news of restaurants she wanted to try, ideas for making curtains, and some gossip about life in their new town. She heard a few disparaging remarks about Joe's parish, how it was staid and old-fashioned compared to its newer sister church nearer the college, and these comments she carefully repeated to Joe in detail. He could see that she was settling in, and it was clear she had been talking with somebody. He hoped "being around" the empty college would result in some new friendships for her.

Their new neighborhood was an easygoing enclave in the friendly, pretty old river town. People knew each other. It had not yet lost the Southern ambiance that would fade in coming years as it was absorbed into the East Coast's megalopolis. The gracious feel of the town, so different from the anonymous sprawl of the seminary area, began to soothe the whole family. It was easy to drive everywhere. The uncomplicated leafy neighborhoods merged gently into the venerable business district and nestled among the verdant college grounds, old cemeteries, and shady public parks. Kate was pleased to drive across town in mere minutes and without having to plan ahead for rush-hour traffic patterns and accidents that meant fifteen-mile detours. Neighbors waved to one another. Ted could play throughout their neighborhood in safety. Joe talked enthusiastically about planting a garden and growing Kate's beloved English peas.

Contentment in the people he loved stirred up in Joe a humor and optimism he had not felt for years. He liked the town and surrounding countryside and was becoming devoted to the people in his parish. They made him feel valued and welcome, and he carried their good will inside him like a healing tonic. He wanted Kate to feel the same confident goodness. He tried with new longing to soothe the hurtful, frustrating relationship with her, the woman he loved and with whom he would share the rest of his life in this world. With new care, he searched for the right words and actions that said "I love you" without violating that sensitive precinct she defended so mysteriously. To intrude too closely would arouse her dread of annoying expectations. He looked eagerly for signs that satisfaction with her new work would soon include their new home. Although it was much too early, he still watched for signs that she was taking an interest in life outside her job. Perhaps if they could share a similar hopeful outlook, a mutual contentment or excitement, some of the healthier balance Joe felt in himself could become relief for Kate too. In the meantime, he could sleep at night and the extra rest soothed the pain in his side.

He was grateful for another blessing too. His completing seminary and their move to Dorchester had moved Ray and Fawn to prolong Catherine's visit to them for the entire spring. It was longer than they had kept her since Kate and Joe were married. They would put her on a flight to Wicomico the moment they knew Kate had arrived there.

"They said they knew I would have my hands full with moving everybody from seminary to here," Kate reported one evening, perched on a stool with a tall iced tea, as Joe unpacked boxes in the garage. "And I told them they certainly got that right. With all I've got to do, it's just one thing less for me to have to worry with, not having Mom here to distract me."

Joe knew them all well enough to know that this was just the way Ray would see it too. Fawn would be different. Catherine would spend days declaring how much poor Kate needed her, what with that no-account Joe not doing a thing to help her. But until Kate returned with her from Wicomico at the end of summer, their home life would be free from Catherine's meddling. Joe was relieved of dealing with her, of contending with her influence upon Kate, and from trying to shield Ted from the quarrels that constituted the mother-daughter relationship in their home. During this interim, Kate never mentioned her mother again, even once. It was only Joe who brought her up, in determining which bedroom Ted wanted so that the third one could be planned with Catherine's winter sojourn in mind. It was a blessed respite for them, though for quite different reasons.

But experience had shown Joe how quickly Kate's moods could change. He had placed high hopes in fresh starts before and was reluctant to do anything that might upset these two weeks of relative peace. Kate's work at the college would not begin until the end of August. She had most of the summer in Wicomico to look forward to. And although the house was tranquil for the moment while she arranged her clothing and Ted's in their closets and began setting aside what she would take with her for the summer, Joe's new work had already begun. He was beginning the long process of becoming a parish priest. There was something new to learn every waking moment.

Some five hundred people of all ages comprised the St. Andrew's congregation. No assistant had worked in the parish for years, and the priest was counting on Joe to revive the youth ministry, Christian education program, and adult education. He wanted Joe's assistance too with marriage counseling, pastoral visiting, and finances. The remarkable long-suffering parish secretary, a conscientious lady who would become one of Joe's good friends for the rest of his life, was delighted to have him aboard. Together they began a long-needed culling of the parish rolls and mailing lists, and Joe began to address some of the pastoral needs that abounded on all sides. This was his first service as an ordained man, and he wanted to respond professionally and competently. He knew he was being watched from all sides by the parishioners, area clergy, and by the bishop and his staff. Almost everyone was helpful and patient, and he was grateful. He was used to working and living under pressure. Although he soon acquired his own inevitable squadron of angry parishioners, a territorial hazard in every priest's ministry, his Dorchester group numbered only a half-dozen people. The great majority of the congregation more than made up for the trouble these few would cause.

A new community and unfamiliar job, new friends, new everything—it was all exciting and stressful too. It was the nature of transition anxiety, and he understood that some stress rendered one more perceptive, alert, and sensitive to matters small and large. It was this way with him, a source of much stamina and critical discernment in trial work and criminal investigation, and a great motivation in his special education teaching. He thought about what Kate was going through and wished he could find the right things to do or say to help her. Her wagons circled and defenses on high alert, unable or unwilling to break out and join him in facing the world together, she seemed to have a visceral need to do things her own way, without consultation. All over the country, his seminary classmates and their spouses were in their own new communities, doing the best they could. God was not shielding them from anything and refreshing them only when they began to go down. Each time they had to struggle to regain the surface, they became better swimmers. What a world. He was managing his little part of it well enough, he hoped, and in his prayers he asked for guidance several times each day for himself and everybody, near and far. He always began with Kate, then his parents. In Ted's happy nature and in Kate's more compatible mood at home, he felt his prayers being answered. When his classmates called to check in from distant places, their voices on the telephone were inspirations, transfusions, humbling.

Still, the house was stacked with moving crates yet to be unpacked. The garage was a mess of taped cardboard boxes from floor to ceiling. Lawn tools and more boxes leaned against the retaining wall in the driveway. Joe was grateful it had not rained. He came home each night and ate supper with his family, played with Ted and his new friends for a while, and then spent several hours unpacking and putting things away all over the house. He gradually cleared more space, organizing closets and the garage, all of it progress toward a normal home life that could be measured by the number of flattened cardboard boxes that awaited the recycling truck in a pile by the driveway. There was much that either was no longer needed or hadn't been used in years, especially clothing and toys that Ted had outgrown. He would have taken it all to Goodwill or the Salvation Army, but Kate insisted on examining every single piece before it left the house. She said she would get around to it sometime in the fall.

He had talked with Kate cautiously a few times about helping to unpack and organize, and she claimed she had too much to do at work and would get around to it soon. He casually inquired about what she was doing most of the day at the college, as her job would not begin until the end of summer. He pointed out carefully that she would be leaving in about ten days for Wicomico and that any help she intended to give should probably happen now. But for every prior year of their marriage, she would have completed her duties at her high school by now and already departed for her summer vacation. He began to understand that she was vexed about having to alter that longstanding arrangement, and that in a way, she had already begun her vacation. After another few days, he brought it up again, suggesting she unpack the boxes of glassware and dishes stacked against the family room wall. He came home that evening to find that she had done so. Without using the shelves he had lined with paper in the kitchen, she had instead crammed dishes and glasses in a jumble into the closest available space, a closet that happened to be a few feet from where the boxes were stacked. Later in the summer, he would carry them all upstairs to the kitchen and arrange them on shelves in the cabinets. But she spent time with Ted, taking him out to lunch at the fast-food restaurants he liked and exploring the malls for what they would need in Wicomico.

Their house and yard were pretty and comfortable. He hoped that in time Kate would learn to feel at home in them. It was impossible to pin down what her work schedule would be at the college, although apparently she already knew. As with her teaching in the high school, the demands of her college schedule shifted mysteriously when he tried to talk with her about the things that needed attention at home. She was spending as much time each day organizing her college workspace for the fall as she had spent daily at her high school. He attributed it to her natural desire to make a good start. He understood. He was experiencing the same feelings in his own new duties. He could not fault her for it, although it would have been good to have her help in organizing their new home.

Patterns emerged in these first Dorchester days that would mark the future as they had the past. For a teacher's aide and laboratory assistant on a small salary, Kate was already beginning to spend as much time at the college as a dean. Even in these early days, at home she was wholly preoccupied with browsing equipment catalogues, inspecting mysterious papers, and doing other college lap work in front of the television. Their new neighbors watched her get out of her car and walk into the house without looking around. She did not see them waving, so she never waved back. With the exception of one couple up the street whose son was fast becoming Ted's best friend, she didn't visit. People stopped by with welcoming gifts, and Kate, thankful and upbeat, conducted conversations at the door. She invited no one in, apologizing to visitors for a house in such disarray. She seemed to draw no connection between this and helping to put it in order. She was agreeable and lenient with Ted and his young friends, who were preoccupied with one another. Her attitude toward Joe, in this new environment with its fresh opportunities and possibilities, was soon no different than it had ever been.

One exception to this trend astonished Joe. At dinner one night, Kate said that an elderly parishioner, a relative of people whom Joe had known in his law practice, had telephoned to ask if she might stop by with a gift for Ted. She said she knew Kate would be in the midst of unpacking, and she would not even come in. In the time it took this lady to get to her car and drive across town, Kate had managed to find Joe's tin of Formosa Oolong and a porcelain pot, prepare tea, find cups and saucers and teaspoons, clear off a small coffee table, and shove boxes and furniture around enough to make a sitting space in the chaotic living room. The lady arrived, cheerful and apologetic for interrupting and full of welcome and good wishes, and Kate insisted she come in for tea. They chatted happily for about forty minutes over tea and some homemade cheese straws a neighbor had sent over the day before. The lady, completely charmed by Kate, had departed and reported to all her friends about the capable and kind wife of their new assistant and what a delightful conversationalist and relaxed hostess she surely was. She was thrilled to learn of Kate's summer home in Wicomico and looked forward to visiting Kate there in July when she and her children and grandchildren would take a nearby cottage for two weeks.

Kate reported all this to Joe with contagious good humor, joyfully taking him into her confidence about how quickly she had prepared for the visit. She had even braced herself and sipped a whole cup of hot tea, a beverage she loathed, and her reenactment of the scene made Joe and Ted laugh out loud. Clearly satisfied with her efforts as hostess, she seemed to take special pride in having entertained one of Joe's parishioners in a proper way. Joe was immensely grateful for her effort and thoroughly enjoyed the good humor with which she described it all. He was proud of her and hoped that this would lead perhaps to a friendship. He was glad that Kate was pleased with her own effort. He was touched that she had gone to such trouble for someone whom she barely knew. Her elation made for a joyful evening. They sat on the back porch for a while talking before bedtime. Joe smoked a small cigar, and Kate made not one comment about it. She told him additional bits of information about the college.

Their neighbors adored Ted and the other neighborhood children, reminding Joe of the street on which he grew up. Many had young children themselves. A few were retired. Some were parishioners at St. Andrew's. Another teacher at the college lived a few blocks away. Thirty years earlier, this leafy neighborhood, surrounded safely on three sides by a bucolic national park battlefield, had been woods and fallow fields. Vast old oaks and other hardwoods cast a graceful shade upon its lawns and winding lanes, and fragrant pines stood about in clusters.

Some of the neighborhood families vacationed together, and many belonged to the same pool clubs. Their children played in the community sports leagues and attended the same schools. People walked in the evenings and called to one another as their amiable dogs ambled along beside them. Each neighbor knew everyone else's dog just as they knew all the local children, reminding Joe of the protective ways of his childhood. After Kate and Ted had departed for the summer and the house was finally organized, Joe began to work outside in the evenings. He put in a late garden, mainly because it made him feel good to work outside and get his hands dirty. Neighbors gathered at the fence in the evenings to talk. In these casual conversations, he developed friendships that would follow him for years.

Everyone found Kate's summers in Wicomico exotic and enviable. Most of the neighbors had vacationed on that part of the coast. They were glad to know someone who actually lived in one of the historic island houses and accepted Kate's casual attitude toward the place as an appealing sign of her charm.

Settling down in Dorchester meant facing the need for a new budget. A house payment, a newer car, the seasonable repairs and increased taxes on the Wicomico house, a resumption of savings for sending Ted to college, and other important obligations had to be faced. The new house needed some additional closet shelves, bookcases, and shelving for storage in the garage. Joe would have to put in railings on the stairs before Catherine's arrival. They would have to buy a lawn mower, a few bushes, and replace a dead dogwood. All of it had to be paid for together with the usual expenses of living and running a home. Joe had not yet received his first paycheck. The seminary money was gone now, and what little remained Kate would take to the beach until paying guests could begin to arrive. It would take a few months to determine the exact costs of living in this new community. Some planning was needed, a subject Joe had learned to dread with Kate. He knew as he tried to engage her that he could well be setting himself up for confusion and disappointment in the following months.

Joe knew he and Kate should discuss finances before she left for the summer. To wait would mean trying to talk with her about it during the frenzy of her return, when she would immediately disappear into the academic routine, sometimes without even unpacking her suitcases. Following Dr. Leffler's advice, he had tried to relieve Kate of all pressure (meaning responsibilities) during the last two years of seminary. Taking responsibilities upon himself, learning to cope in new ways, and expecting very little from her had made their home life as manageable as he could. Dr. Leffler was a hundred miles away now. Setting up a telephone conference was always difficult.

Besides, he felt he knew what she would say. It was time now to try again, as a family, to cooperate.

As he carefully began to raise issues with Kate, he encountered a variation on another old theme. In the past she had listened, said just enough to make him think they had reached an understanding, and then proceeded to do what she had wanted to do anyway. Joe approached the subject of a budget, touchy enough in itself, with special care now, making everything as clear as possible. He showed her a sheet with expenses added up in one column and income in another. The difference amounted to a slim margin and would have to be carefully managed in order to put anything into savings. She looked over his list and said she understood, but as in the past, he could see she was not interested in discussing it. But this time she surprised him. Focusing suddenly and with surgical precision, she pointed out that he had failed to include any money for insurance and taxes on the Wicomico house and that the insurance premium would increase this year by a hundred and twelve dollars and they could expect to replace the water heater sometime before the end of the summer. Adding these expenditures reduced their leeway to almost nothing, which seemed to concern Kate not half so much as Joe's careless oversight in omitting them.

* * *

A new place, a fresh start, the maturity that comes of growing, it seemed to Joe it would make a difference. People change. Intellects evolve. Conscience becomes more informed. Attitudes mature with new friends and experiences. With Kate, the world might ripen all around, but the unyielding core of her personality, defended in a thousand subtle ways, developed another insulating layer at the hint of each new pressure. Joe's continual striving to prevent frustrations from becoming resentments created in him a turmoil like an infection. The expectations and hopes stirred up by their move and new environment faded. He felt the struggle for balance resume, a strain in which he knew from experience he would alternately succeed and fail with wearying inconsistency. The resulting roller-coaster ride of feelings made him tired.

In coming to understand his own thoughts, words, and deeds as keys to harmony and peace in their household, Joe had succeeded, but only just and not nearly as much as he supposed. He told himself that the wife he loved had a disease, a physical addiction that affected their relationship and family life. It was not her fault, and she hadn't planned it this way. It was not a moral failure. But his emotions had not yet caught up with his reason, and his understanding provided only a limited clarity. Truth did not assuage disappointment. Understanding did little to ease the frustration of relentless denial. He sensed he had become a part of the problem even as he had lived with it. He acknowledged to himself and his counselors that he was not the key to its solution he had once very foolishly imagined himself to be.

His own parents had dispelled any fiction of males as dominant in family life. They had been good partners, sharing responsibilities, work, joys, and sorrows; open and comfortable with one another and each other's faults; and satisfied with each other's devotion. Joe and his brothers and sisters had taken their parents' relationship for granted, discovering only in retrospect how remarkable a match it had been. Joe had entered marriage expecting the same thing, not immediately of course, but certainly in time. Had he been forced into the role he felt obliged to play, or had he come to it on his own? He did not know. He was not even sure he could tell the difference anymore among enabler, caretaker, and husband. Ted was getting old enough to notice things. Could he shield and support Ted without becoming any more of an enabler for Kate? He thought so, but was he correct? He was no psychologist. He had been a good trial lawyer. He had not been inclined then, nor now, to dwell too much on the uncertain analysis that had nevertheless intrigued him in the past and that had made some of his colleagues famous. A career seeking facts, evaluating evidence, inquiring into motives and personalities, attempting to determine the truth of what people do and say—it had endowed him with more perception and acuity than his wife, certainly, and many who did not know him well gave him credit for. What was Kate thinking? Why did she behave as she did? How did she see their marriage, family life, and his attempts to talk about issues? What was going on in her when the same problems reoccurred year after year? Did she even see them as problems? They did not appear to be problems for her, especially as long as he continued to pick up the pieces. How could he not inquire into these mysteries? How could he help but apply his natural discernment to the world around him? And what was more important in a man's world than his wife? And when one's wife is obviously suffering...

"What would happen if you just let things fall where they had to?" Dr. Leffler had asked him one day, in one of the many sessions Kate could not attend at the last minute.

"When I was teaching, we would have called that allowing someone to live the natural consequences of their behavior," Joe had replied.

"Well?"

"It's not just Kate who would live them. We have a son. We all live together. What she does impacts us all. She denies the problem and so denies the impact too. What do I do? Allow the laundry to pile up for a month, the bank to charge us money we don't have for overdrafts, her car to burn up because she hasn't had any oil put in or air in the tires in six months? Should I let the house get filthy? Should I let Ted's nails grow long and dirty hoping that one day she'll take the initiative to trim them? Isn't that plainly neglecting my child and our family life? I have allergies to house dust. What should I do? Allow the place to become a pigsty until she catches on? I have trouble sleeping at night as it is. When she springs plans on me at the last minute and tries to make me believe we discussed them a month before, what should I do?"

"And what happens when you talk to Kate about all this?"

"Nothing."

In his mind, he could hear Kate telling him there would be no problems if Joe would only have the sense to ignore them. If he would just conform himself to her way of going about life, there would be no friction. This was certainly what she appeared to be telling him. Was he hearing her correctly? What was she thinking?

He felt he was either an average man struggling to do right in a difficult situation, or he was a dumb bastard who had misjudged the whole mess from the start and was handling it ineptly. Whichever the case, and probably some of both, he had tried to get help. He was wrong from the start to try to get help for Kate. A person cannot be helped unless he or she desires help. Kate had made it plain she needed no help because there was absolutely nothing wrong with her that warranted any help. His next step, trying to get help for the two of them together, had not worked either. She would not participate in family counseling. He had started to feel better only when he sought help for himself alone and begun to learn about what he could control in his life.

Still, he kept coming back to it like the needle of a compass. Why had Kate refused to budge when it was so obvious to both of them that their marriage was unhealthy and they had a beloved child to raise? He had seen it before, her refusal to take simple steps that were plainly in her own interest. But why? It baffled him. It defied reason. And she refused to talk with him about any of it. None of these issues existed, as far as she was concerned. "You're making it all up, Joe," she had said to him over the years. "I don't have a problem. There is nothing wrong with me. If there's a problem in this marriage, it's you. Get over it. Give me a break."

And what of Ted? He understood nothing of the dynamics. He saw only the effects, and Joe could tell that in his eyes, the effects were almost always in Kate's favor. Joe was the enforcer, the one to insist on chores, cleaning up, bedtime, foregoing big expenditures, denying his desire for this and that, disappointing poor Mom who only wanted to have fun in life, be happy. Joe's efforts to make it all right, calm, and well-adjusted for the son they both loved backfired constantly. He was aware that he emerged out of all this as the bad guy in his son's eyes. Kate was the fun-loving big sister who dropped everything to satisfy his slightest wish. It made no difference at all to her that Joe was suffering by comparison. Why? How could a parent think that way?

Joe resorted to writing letters. He had tried it early in their marriage when Kate had routinely closed him off. He would try it again in this new community. He placed his letters on the seat of her car where she would find them when she left in the morning to drive to the college. She could not claim to have missed them. He knew that her curiosity alone would compel her to read every word. Although she had never acknowledged, not once, receiving his letters over the years, he knew at least that she knew what was in his heart and mind. It amazed him that she could read his letters and never mention them or respond to any of his queries or suggestions.

Still, a change would squeak through occasionally. In the early years on the rare occasions when she grew irritated with Ted, Kate had been in the habit of saying, "Go play in the traffic!" It made Joe furious to hear her say it, and he told her so bluntly. She treated it all lightly, accusing him of being too sensitive and reminding him it was "just an old saying. I really don't want him to *do* it, Joe. I'm just saying it." He had finally written her a long letter explaining "how sick it is to say such a thing to a child" and "how harmful it is for Ted to hear it" and "how far beneath the dignity of an educated woman, a parent, a teacher" it was to speak like that. Although Kate never mentioned reading the letter, Joe never heard her use the objectionable words again. Was it because he had brought up Ted's welfare? Did she continue to say it during the summer when he was not around? He didn't know. But it had been a rare example of his letter eliciting a tangible result.

Joe discovered that a twelve-step group called Adult Children of Alcoholic Parents met weekly at the Dorchester United Methodist Church. Kate's rejection of Alcoholics Anonymous during seminary had been final. Any mention of AA again aroused her anger for days. AA literature vanished as soon as Joe brought it home, Kate refusing even to acknowledge having seen it. As there were only three of them living in the house, and nobody coming in to help Joe with the cleaning at that point, he found it amusing to imagine what Kate would have claimed had happened to it if he had pressed her.

Because Kate refused to discuss her use of alcohol, or her mother's, it had taken Joe years to understand that mother and daughter viewed alcohol addiction as an admission of failure. It was an imperfection, an impermissible personal flaw associated with the very lowest in society, criminals and such. If her back were to the wall, Joe reckoned, Kate would choose her denial over her husband. He was increasingly aware of how much of his life and energy were devoted to assuring that she never had to make that choice.

Among his hundreds of friends and acquaintances and in the many people he had known in the law, Joe had never encountered denial so unyielding as Kate's and Catherine's. Against the impenetrable shield they maintained between themselves and the world, including each other, he struggled to gain a foothold, a crack or chink through which some insight, however small, might be discerned, anything to help him understand. He tried to calm his nerves in prayer and by rereading the vows he made in marriage and ordination. They provided no understanding but instead gave a certain encouragement, an ability to cope, to keep his sanity and sense of humor in the midst of craziness of which he alone was fully aware. Any doubts in the meaning of his vows he might have experienced in weak moments dissolved when he checked on Ted in the night and looked at his sleeping face or heard Kate breathing as she slept next to him. He thanked God daily for the blessings in his life and renewed his determination to be a better husband and father each time he prayed. He thought of his parents. They had worked together at marriage and parenting patiently since they were teenagers, with no money and six children, never complaining. Their genuine, easy senses of humor had softened the hard edges of life for themselves and their children in ways that still made Joe and his siblings marvel. In the careful management of their small income, their care for their own parents and even their acceptance of his father's severe war wound, they set an unconscious example of uncomplicated, steady devotion. The kindness with which they had accepted the hard work of encouraging each other when they were down and trusting one another even when they were angry had worked on Joe's developing personality like medicine. All their lives, they had been decent and unpretentious people striving to get it right in a largely indifferent world. As a teenager, he had observed and analyzed what he thought were their faults, engaging in youth's callow, critical scrutiny of parents who were too busy fulfilling their duty to devote much attention to themselves. At times he had seen them as unimaginative and embarrassing, in their tedious small ways holding him back, frustrating his efforts to be somebody. Now he looked back and felt only shame at his own crude unfairness. Their example humbled him. He wanted to be like them and the others who had lived with backbone and courage through the Depression, World War II, Korea, Vietnam. The only natural direction in life was the way they had lived, forward, together with his loved ones. In that direction, he unconsciously directed himself with the patience and good intentions he had come to admire in his parents and so many others from the past. Their faces came to him in dreams and daydreams, encouraging him to contend fearlessly with the brokenness, to endure the strife locked in the sod wherever he turned.

In Al-Anon meetings, Joe had felt God's presence in the ironic health and wholeness that comes in conversations with other suffering people. On one level, it was there in simply being with others who were going through the same thing. On another, which he supposed most people would have to experience for themselves to understand, it was in the spiritual work of learning to know oneself. One grew more accepting. Life became more manageable. "Keep it simple" was a constant refrain. *If anyone wants to see miracles happening,* he told himself and his parishioners, *leave the nave and go down to the church basement and attend a twelve-step meeting.* In prayer, Al-Anon, professional family counseling, and spiritual counseling within the church, he had felt his judgment mature, his relationships improve, and he had sensed a clarifying growth in his spiritual life. It was all a gift, nothing he had accomplished for himself. All he had done was walk in and sit down. He wanted the same good things for other people in the same way one wants others to have clean air and water and freedom from violent crime. And merciful God, how he wanted them for Kate. His common sense told him that what worked for one might not be right for another. But so many had found serenity. He wanted Kate to have it too. She was his wife. How would she know until she tried?

Despite the good that had come in self-examination, Joe was too emotionally close to Kate and their marriage to understand the flaw in his own thinking. He was troubled. He believed God had gifted humanity with reason so we could live in the world and come closer to understanding the mysteries of faith. In the gift of reason, he saw the potential for healing, the curative compassion and creativity that are evidence of our divine origin. Reason is intended to serve the common good. Revelation informs it. Its application for the relief of suffering, its saving health for the widows and orphans, is the movement of the Holy Spirit in human life. Humankind is progressing toward a compassionate maturity, and humankind will prevail. Despite the hellish regressions of the last century, Joe saw a widening vein of maturity, glittering brighter over time, running through the hard truth of human history. He had faith in sinful humanity. "We are the means through which God's will is being realized," he told himself and anyone else who would listen. And he told himself that his own marriage was a microcosmic part of this greater natural movement. It too would mature with experience and time.

At the most dreadful news from the world's violent places, images of martyrs flashed unbidden upon his inward eye, thousands upon thousands going faithfully to their deaths in other times and distant places. William Tyndale. Latimer and Ridley. Cranmer. The martyrs of Memphis and Uganda. The saints. The Lord's faithful soldiers and servants unto their life's end. The very distance made them somehow more conceivable, the ancient times somehow comprehensible. William Temple walking the smoking lanes of London in the blitz. Nanking, Phnom Pen, shimmering, heat waves. Faulkner's driven Mississippi patois ascending before the Nobel committee with inextinguishable humanity like spring peepers at the last eventide. It overwhelmed his own bit of reason at times and nullified his limited understanding. Images of raging Islamic fleabag despots and banana republic dictators flickered briefly, the current expression of an ancient evil, eyes wild with a terrible revelation, and receded into the darkness. Four million deaths in the Congo. Unspeakable. Faces. Teresa of Calcutta. Terry Fox. Martin Luther King Jr. Gandhi. The bliss of solitude. He could see Elie Weisel, a shocked boy, herded with his family by the Hungarian gendarmes along the streets of Sighet as the night closed in. Reason. Faith. Justice. God.

He saw families as he perceived all other human relationships. If tsunamis threaten people on the Pacific Rim, all humankind should devote itself to perfecting a warning system. If a government murders its minorities, humankind must intervene. Where a health problem exists in the world or in a family, it is reasonable to address it compassionately for the sake of all people. If one's wife is suffering and the raising of a child is involved, duty and reason compel one to act for them and for the common good. Not to act is unfaithful, unreasonable.

In later years, Joe would look back at these naive convictions with a private sorrow. His artless innocence and callow perception would make him shake his head and groan inwardly at his own blindness. Six years of teaching, in which his troubled students shared their lives with him and taught him more than he taught them, had left him confident of progress and hopeful, so hopeful and determined that he had begun to study law with the naive dream of improving public education. Years of work as a trial lawyer had strengthened his faith in reason. Although rough and imperfect, human justice restores compassion in the broken world. He saw at close hand the terrible things people do to satisfy worldly appetites and desires. Day by day he and his colleagues labored in the law, untangling the chaos of human self-centeredness and greed, and years of this had not made him cynical or embittered. He looked upward and forward and heard the summons of the church as a call to the superior classroom, the highest court of appeal, the cleanest service for the common good in the universe. His instincts told him that going there, closer to the source, would be intense and probably deadly for an average man, a completion of his journey by turning off across a frail swinging bridge above a chasm, deep and dangerous, at night, in the wind and hail, a lonely progress. But he believed the direction was right.

Joe perceived, however imperfectly, a divine plan. He saw his marriage, and all else in his life, as minute parts of its reality and rightness. He seldom questioned his own devotion and affection for Kate or the rightness of their union. He was sincere and willing in his search for compassion and empathy in their relationship. He viewed Kate, Ted, and himself as inseparable parts of a blessed whole. In his heart, he knew that God blessed their union. In their marriage was a fundamental rightness that conformed the three of them to the divine scheme of things. He could not conceive of a life without his wife and son. His sadness had to do with himself alone. Kate and certainly Ted were innocent. The problem was his own, himself. In his marriage, he had been scorched so often that he was sensitive now to every heat, like a burn patient. He reacted reflexively. Years of living with anger and denial had affected him. He accepted Kate's behavior as her natural way of making herself feel normal. She had grown into the sort of person she was in the same way all people become themselves, through genes and experience. In her denial, she lived according to her own rules, and he recognized that this meant friction with the world around her.

She did not hate Joe, and he knew it. Maybe she even loved him in her own way. He hoped so. But his role as her husband, the father of their child, the one to whom adult decisions devolved by necessity, made him a natural frustration for her self-absorption. He understood that anyone who married her would have been forced into the same villainous role. Sometimes at night he was sorry for her that it had been him. If she had married a more inspiring sort or a wealthy man able to let her do as she wished, somebody with the time and means to clear up the loose ends, someone with whom she would not have had to count pennies and plan carefully, someone with life experiences richer and broader than Joe's…

What troubled him most deeply, however, was taking place outside his reason, loyalty, or faithfulness. He felt unspeakably sad and completely alone in his creeping, perfidious recognition that his love for Kate was changing, despite his best intentions, into something like duty.

While he tried to maintain balance and proportion in their troubled marriage, his affection and longing for Kate had meant hope and strength even in the most trying episodes. His compassion was still true, but it was changing against all his efforts to shore it up. The fine fabric of their relationship had been stretched and jerked in unexpected, troubling ways too many times. In good times, it had been smoothed and straightened, making it fresh again and durable, for a while. But the wear was showing—he could not say when it had begun—threads were unraveling and breaking, and at each mending, there seemed less fabric with which to work. In Kate's every deception, her selective dishonesty (which Joe now admitted to himself were plain lies), every promise intentionally and blatantly ignored, every scornful word said to him in his son's presence, each outburst of sarcasm, the threads, one by one, had been broken.

He acknowledged his part of it. He was not the world's finest or most successful husband, lover, breadwinner, or anything else. He admitted that he was dull and conventional. He had always gotten along on very little, but it was unfair of him to expect others to do likewise. He was an introvert. His idea of a good time was fishing, hunting, camping, reading, staying home, drawing, sitting on the porch and talking, ways of relaxing that seemed to interest fewer and fewer people as he grew older. Most people found it boring. Kate did most of the time, but when she was in a good mood—during summer vacation, for instance—she was a joy to him to be with. The careful management of what they had saved, it was not Kate's idea of fun. He had borrowed and paid back over many years of self-denial, what it took to go to college, law school, and seminary. Catherine had paid it all for Kate. They had grown up in different ways, and they saw life differently.

Years of being blamed for Kate's problems and procrastination and making up for her disinterest and inefficiency had made him suspicious against his will of her motives. The cumulative rending continued, and months and years went by, and their marriage never reached the plateau Joe had always known was just over the horizon. Perhaps he had no right to expect a brighter day. Perhaps it was another of his faults. But what was dying in him was love, and the symptoms of its demise were the erosion of trust and intimacy. He felt them slipping away, and he could not prevent it. What was replacing them increasingly was loyalty, perseverance, and a determination to fulfill obligations. The way he approached it all included a certain kindness, a determined protectiveness that was in the beginning indistinguishable from the old feelings of being in love. But it was a sorrowful substitute for what had been there in the beginning. He became angry with himself that all this was happening. He believed he could have handled it better if he had known what he was getting into, if he had gone to counselors sooner, if he had paid less attention to planning and saving for the future, building a career. He had devoted himself to knowing his wife and had continued to work at it despite her defenses. It had all seemed right at the time, natural for his family's health, for their life together, for the future. It was what a husband and father did in life. But he could have been better at it and managed all of it differently, more effectively, and knowing this created a sadness that made him quieter and quieter. He had been honest. At least he could say that for himself. But it was little help when he tried to sleep at night.

As in Jeffersonville and seminary, he slept fitfully in Dorchester when he slept at all. He awoke in the night to find the carousel already twirling in his head. He remembered coming home late one afternoon, during their first fall in Dorchester, and finding Kate preparing for a Cub Scout project. Ted was about seven or eight and was playing somewhere in the neighborhood with friends. Joe chatted with Kate for a few minutes and went into the bedroom to change his clothes. Her cheeks and nose were pink, and she was talking faster than usual, and a sense of dread began to spread through him. In the few minutes it took him to change, Kate dropped something heavy (he was not sure what) four times. Her footsteps on the stairs and kitchen floor had an odd, thudding pattern he was not used to, as though she were clomping about in heavy boots. He asked her how she was feeling, and she said she was "fine, just fine." Shortly afterward, she left the house and drove away without saying anything to him and was gone for several hours.

Joe prepared dinner, having no idea where she had gone, and he and Ted ate supper and talked about Ted's day at school. Halfway through dinner, Kate swept in, filled with venom toward the other women who worked with the Cub Scout pack. In front of Ted, she explained how slow and unreliable they were, how several of them had arrived late for the meeting she had just attended at the Presbyterian Church

"Ah, so that's where you were. I wondered."

"What are you talking about? I told you before I left where I was going! Don't give me that!"

She was harsh in describing the obesity and accent of one of them, an uneducated single mother, "on welfare, probably," who was raising her son alone.

"She can't even speak correct English! And what kind of example is she setting for these boys, having a child without being married?"

The whole incident might have appeared small and merely vexing to someone looking on. Joe would have thought the same thing in the beginning. Now he knew it was part of something deeper. It made him think of people and situations he had encountered in the law, each masking or representing a whole separate cosmos of personalities, motives, people, places, things. The interconnectedness no longer amazed him. The clash and flow of cause and effect in the web of human relationships touched every life and flowed through each human being and on into the world in endless complications. Sometimes he was ready to believe that only good criminal investigators and forensic pathologists had a comprehensive view of it.

"What does she mean, Dad?" Ted asked after his mother had stomped upstairs. "Aren't Clarence's parents married?"

"We'll talk about it later, Ted. Better not say anything about it to the boys in your pack."

"Why? Is something wrong with Clarence or his mom?"

"We will discuss it another time."

He recalled the dozens of times, when Ted was a baby, he had gotten out of bed in the early morning, after a few hours of fitful sleep, to close the doors between Ted's bedroom and the family bathroom so that Ted would not be awakened early by the sound of Kate's hair dryer or the light streaming into his room. Her desire to play with Ted, like a child with a new toy, outweighed his need for sleep and the value of a regular schedule. Saying anything to her at such an hour provoked a stormy response that seemed somehow to color the rest of the day. Joe would close the doors quietly and return to bed and try to get another twenty minutes or so of sleep. When he remembered to discuss it with her at night, she listened without comment, and the next morning, or the one after, it would happen again.

On the mornings when she closed the doors so Ted could sleep, Joe found himself waking up anyway, out of habit.

Ted would be nine years old before Joe succeeded in convincing Kate to purchase skim milk instead of the whole milk on which she had been raised. They had sat together in PTA meetings, doctor's offices, school activity presentations, and television news broadcasts while experts extolled the value of skim milk and low-fat diets for children. Joe had discussed it a dozen times with Kate, and on each occasion, he thought she had agreed. Yet she returned from her next stop at the grocery store with whole milk, without comment, as though they had never talked about it.

Over and over he had tried to discuss with her the harm she caused Ted by denigrating Joe in front of him. When Ted was an infant, she had countered by saying she wasn't saying "anything bad" about Joe, and besides, Ted was too young to understand it anyway. It continued into the years when even she would have found it hard to claim it had no effect upon their son.

In this, as in all else, there was no way of stopping her or changing her behavior, no signals or signs she would honor or observe, no appeal to her reason. On the several occasions over the years when Joe pleaded, cajoled, or wheedled Kate into visiting a counselor with him, the hope for change overwhelmed him. If she followed through and arrived at the appointment on time, she quickly adopted the posture of an observer. When Joe brought up anything from the past, she would shake her head slowly and claim she remembered nothing about it. If the counselor scheduled an appointment for her alone, the odds were excellent that something would occur at the last moment to prevent her attending. After one or two sessions, she would refuse to return, saying she was not getting anything out of it.

"Kate! Where were you? We waited the full hour."

"I had something that came up at school, Joe. I have to work. My work isn't like yours. It's demanding. Students need to see me, sometimes at short notice."

"Kate, you promised me!"

"Oh, don't give me that! There's nothing wrong with me anyway. If there's anything wrong with this marriage, it's you, Joe! I don't need any psychiatrist."

"Anne Harrald is not a psychiatrist. You know that. We've been through that. She is a licensed professional counselor."

"She is too a psychiatrist. They even call her doctor in the waiting room."

"Who calls her 'doctor'?"

"Somebody walked in and said they wanted to schedule an appointment with Dr. Howard."

"Harrald."

"I said Harrald!"

"Whoever said that was probably there for a first visit. People call most family counselors 'doctor.'"

"And thanks to you, now I can never be president!" She jerked a can of peas from a kitchen cabinet and slammed it down on the counter. Joe stared at her with his mouth open. One look at her was enough to convince him she was perfectly, perfectly serious.

"What...," he stammered.

"Someone who has seen a psychiatrist can never run for president. It happened to that man Eagleman years ago. Now, thanks to you, I'll always have on my record that I have seen a psychiatrist. I could never be president. Just because you won't be reasonable about anything. There's nothing wrong with me. It's you! Thanks a lot, Joe."

As Kate refused to discuss their marital issues, or any other personal issues, with anyone else, Joe found attempts to reason with her to be a lonely undertaking. He continued in counseling alone. Over the years, he tried every way the counselors suggested to coax Kate into coming with him. Nothing worked. There was no way of changing her behavior short of laying hands on her and forcing her to do this or that.

Joe had grown up in a world in which boys played football, baseball, or basketball, and nobody knew anything about soccer. He still knew almost nothing about it when Ted started to play on a local recreation league team of beginning players. Half of them had not yet entered the first grade. The coach, a decent, overworked phar-maceuticals salesman whose son was on the team, was desperate for help. He asked Joe to serve as his "assistant." When Joe explained his total lack of experience, the coach assured him that with seven-year-olds, he really needed another adult around to help maintain order. Any willing adult could do it, he said, but nobody had the time.

Joe made the mistake of telling Kate in the car, with Ted in the back seat, that he would help the coach.

"You? You can't coach soccer! You don't know anything about it. He must really be hard up to ask you. Don't be ridiculous. You're crazy to even say you would. You coaching soccer is a joke! Give me a break." Joe was conscious of Ted in the back seat, hearing every word, reading every nuance and each hint of scorn.

Joe tried to soften the conversation by saying the coach was hav-ing trouble getting help. Kate was looking out the passenger window and shaking her head as though the most preposterous thing in the world had just been made known to her. Joe poked her lightly on the leg to get her attention, attempting to signal that he needed her cooperation, a gesture that Ted could not see from his seat.

"What are you doing? Stop hitting me on the leg. I bruise easily. I've been that way since I was born. You should know that by now."

* * *

In Dorchester, Joe quickly ran afoul of the wife of his superior, the parish priest. A consistent person, she had disliked every assistant her long-suffering husband employed. On the few occasions on which she appeared at church, she ignored Joe and Kate, and when abso-lutely compelled to address either of them, she was condescending and dismissive. When the bishop visited and she invited dozens of parishioners to dessert and coffee in his honor, the Stephensons were not asked. In greeting people in a crowd, she passed by Joe and Kate as though they were invisible. She spoke to Joe only to complain whenever her quiet, cautious teenage daughter, whom Joe and Kate genuinely liked, joined a youth group activity. No plans of Joe's for the young people, no arrangement was satisfactory, and the rector's wife reacted as though Joe was trying specifically to irritate her.

There were complicated dynamics involved. The rector's wife had behaved the same way toward everyone. Parishioners had warned Joe and advised him of how to minimize her unpleasantness as much as possible. He was grateful for their confidence and valued their common sense. It was a problem that had preceded his arrival, and he understood that it had little to do with him or Kate personally. They both liked the rector. He was friendly and approachable and, like most clergy and bishops, went out of his way to avoid confrontation at almost any cost. Joe figured that this generated much conflict at home and in his vocation.

Joe explained the background of all this to Kate as soon as he understood it himself and secured her promise not to discuss the matter with anybody else in the community. The parishioners, kind and reasonable, shook their heads, rolled their eyes, and gave their new assistant and his wife knowing looks. He worked hard, and the people liked him and valued his way with things. But regardless of how carefully Joe managed his duties and diplomatic skills, or perhaps because of them, the confluence of dysfunction in all directions poured down upon him sooner or later. There were needy people in each direction and on every level in both parish and community at large, and they all wanted to talk. He was polite to them all and listened as much as he could. He was careful not to try to accommodate everyone and to accept the anger of the dissatisfied and move on. He often thought with affection of his younger seminary classmates, many of whom had launched into ministry before learning that lesson. The situation with the rector's wife alone required a special sort of tact, and his every good quality was tested sorely by the inevitable small group of women who despised him. Joe found the successful management of these and other relationships in ministry more difficult than in the practice of law. At least in the law, the many players were governed by a recognized set of rules by which most of them abided. The rules were fair in the law, and even in cases where bad actors refused to obey them, the system at least bore witness to certain standards. In ministry, one was on one's own. What passed for a system within the church, for rules and standards, seemed to come into play only when one had grievously erred. That at least was what the older clergy said, the ones who had seen it all. Although it all made Joe more cautious, he never for a moment imagined himself violating the rules, such as they were. But the stress was surely there. Knowing oneself, maintaining identity and integrity in his vocation, was at the same time excruciatingly difficult and absolutely indispensable. At least in his denomination, ministry was not for the fainthearted. When he came home at night drained of energy and with his head and stomach burning, he expected Kate to tell him to "get over it." He knew from experience that she was waiting only for a pause to open the floodgates of her own day's minutia. But she was not sarcastic at such times, and she did not interrupt him. In fact, she seemed supportive of him, letting him have his say before changing the subject in seconds to herself. He was grateful for her patience and told her so over and over.

Although the stresses were many and some of them cruel, Joe could swallow his frustration with ease born of much practice. He had known a lot of people in the law and elsewhere, characters of every sort, and he had learned how to stand his ground. Confrontation did not frighten him. He did not seek it out, but when the enemy appeared, he became a reasonable strategist, knowing when to stand and fight and when to move to a more advantageous position before going into action. Nor did he shy at fences. When the rector's wife berated him for some trifling arrangement at a youth activity, he listened and explained firmly why the plans had been made and that he would not change them. Being rebuffed by her husband's assistant was something new for her, and unsure of how to respond, she soon left him alone. He knew her personality problems were deeper, more complicated, and bad manners and irritability were symptoms. There was something clinically wrong, just as there was with his own wife. His common sense told him that a disturbed surface meant turbulence below, a simple connection to a mystery he could not perceive. The depths were too great in some cases. Unlike some of his colleagues in his new vocation, he had no trouble accepting that there are evil people in the world. The law had taught him the importance of distinguishing between the evil and the sick.

As with the people and personalities in his legal practice, Joe did not talk much with Kate about the particulars and peculiarities of his parishioners. In both situations, he was honoring a professional duty and a personal standard as well as exercising care with a problem he knew was beyond his control. Kate interpreted it personally, a withholding implying mistrust in her, no matter how he sought to explain it professionally. He knew that anything more personal, any example of her unrestricted chatter while drinking, would arouse her anger and furious denial. A single exception was relations with his boss's wife, because it concerned Kate personally. He knew it would be in their family's interest, and the congregation's as well, for them to have no more contact with his boss's wife than necessary, and he tried to explain this to Kate. She appeared to understand. And yet, as soon as she was in the same room with his boss's wife, Kate appeared mysteriously drawn to her. She approached, smiling, and attempted to start a conversation. An unpleasant snub always followed, and Kate, who had propelled herself into it despite Joe's explanations, complained for weeks about how rudely his boss's wife had treated her.

At first, Joe made himself see these attempts as Kate striving to be mannerly to an obviously troubled person. After a while, he began to suspect it was another example of Kate's drive to appear perfect to the world, although the dynamics of it all were beyond his understanding. He would see it occur with other people in years to come, Kate seemingly seeking out and exposing herself intentionally—her own worst enemy—to people whom she suspected did not like her. When confirmed, her suspicions provided ample material for dinnertime monologues for weeks on end.

Sometimes at night, staring into the dark while Kate slept heavily beside him, Joe recalled a night when Ted was three or four. After a trial lasting a week and another week of deliberations, a jury had returned a verdict late one afternoon, convicting a defendant of abduction and malicious wounding and acquitting him of the very serious charges of rape and sodomy. Relatives of the victim, a young Latino woman, were outraged at the partial acquittal. Family honor was at stake. The family and friends of the defendant, a popular black high school athlete with a limited prior record, were equally outraged at the conviction. In the volatile moments following the verdict, threats were made in the presence of bailiffs and reporters for two national newspapers against Joe and defense counsel. The judge ordered the chief of police to direct a patrol of Joe's home throughout the night and the sheriff to do the same for the defense lawyer, who lived way out in the county.

By then Joe had learned the hard way not to discuss details of his work with Kate, who would repeat it to anyone while drinking and vigorously deny that she had done so. He was reluctant too to worry her or Ted unduly. He said nothing about the police surveillance when he arrived home. But to Joe's amazement, Kate, who did not notice the checking account balance before creating an overdraft or the look on her husband's face when his insides burned, soon saw that a police car was driving around the neighborhood and slowing down when it passed their small cul-de-sac. Peering through the space between the curtain and window frame, she declared that something was about to happen. Joe explained what was happening, hastening to assure her that he considered it an excess of caution on the part of the court. Kate found it hilarious and told him to "get real" and that he was not "a character on some TV cop show." He explained it all again, raising his voice when she insisted on contradicting him with childish and condescending assumptions. The facts of the case had been brutal, the victim was now distraught and dishonored in the eyes of her people, and the trial and the waiting for a verdict had exhausted everyone. He raised his voice. Kate reeled around to the stove as though stung by a wasp. Ted had come into the kitchen to see what was going on, and Joe dropped the subject with no further effort to make her understand. But Ted had heard his father raise his voice to his mother.

* * *

Wicomico was a place of fragile beauty where the wild sea met an enchanting land. Joe and Kate loved it for many of the same reasons. As a child, Joe had been smitten by its rustic, windblown, maritime feel, its extremes of light and space, its roiling weather and lonely beauty, so different from the mountains and valleys where he was raised. His parents had taken six children and a week's worth of clothing and toys and food, wedged into their old Plymouth station wagon, whose ability to get them there and back was ever in question, all the way to Wicomico several years in a row, where they spent a magic week at the Sea View Cottage Court. From these precious days in a three-room salt box with its tiny kitchenette, on the edge of mystery and romance in sea and sky and wind, memories would flow and follow each member of the family all their days. Joe and his brothers and sisters would drift back to Wicomico in high school and college to live and work during summers and vacations and later for a year or so as they contemplated what they would do in life. This early time by the sea had touched them all in mysterious ways, and Joe had found a wife.

The ocean stirred in Joe a thousand wild mysteries, each made more hypnotizing by his youth and romantic dreams. The sandy islands and broad flat sounds thrilled his imagination with richness unlike anything he had known before. It was a bright world of water and light, and it filled him with a certainty that beyond its beguiling allure opened a future equally as enticing. The mountains and sheltered valleys of home diffused their own magic, sculpting of the world a formative temperament that shaped its children in a thousand elusive ways. The blue lure of remote vistas of misty mountain coves and rugged river gorges, the Appalachian Trail, the region's ancient rocks and caves and varied wildlife got into the blood of certain personalities and made them grow in different ways. Joe was one of these, shaped by places and their moods and blessed, or perhaps afflicted, with a powerful memory.

In Wicomico, while young, he wandered the trails through the woods and crossed out over the windy dunes and hiked for miles on the magnificent beaches and tidal marshes. As with the blue terrain of home, he needed little more than to be there. It was enough merely to be in the openness of it all, buffeted by the big salty winds, shirtless in sunny air beneath clouds that seemed to rise for mile upon mile above the long narrow bend of the islands. He fished for hours, content to watch the surf and the birds and to listen to the ocean's intoxicating sounds. He collected shells and sea glass. He learned the fish and birds and local history better than some natives. When the wind and snow howled against his house or dormitory or apartment on frigid nights in years to come, he could sleep with the memories of this place he had come to love. Joe had loved the islands long before he knew Kate.

But by a few years after marriage, Wicomico had become a place of problems. Whatever role he had elsewhere in their married life, at the old house by the sea, he was on the turf of his wife and mother-in-law who made it plain in countless small ways that he was expected to remember his place. They had not set out together to accomplish this, and they were not coordinated, but their positions derived from the same defensive family attitude. Not disposed to cooperate with the world anyway, they were naturally alert to intrusions on their domain. The merest hint of initiative could quickly qualify Joe as an intruder.

He could not prevent Catherine from drinking in her own house. Even if he could have during his visits, the status quo would resume upon his departure. With Kate in charge, Catherine always seemed to manage to find a drink. How she acquired alcohol was a mystery. She had known many of their renters for years and probably prevailed upon them to shop for her. Joe could imagine some of them believing they were doing a favor for a little old lady. Kate poured her mother's drinks over the porch rail when she found them, which was seldom. They faded into the sand while Catherine shuffled about and protested with drama, an agitation that soon subsided into a lengthy gloom. Occasionally Kate would search until she found "Mom's little cache" hidden below a sink or in a closet or under the sandy accumulation of years in the garage or pump house. During the height of difficulty in preventing mother and daughter from drinking wherever they were, when Joe himself had ceased to use alcohol and Catherine's deterioration was causing alarm even to Kate and her brother, Joe encountered his wife and mother-in-law one day, purely by accident, seated in a restaurant in Wicomico village drinking beer together and eating sandwiches. He was exasperated to his wit's end. Concern for their home life was a lonely preoccupation. He confronted Kate later about it, and she responded as she always did, with silence, finally claiming that her mother had ordered beer while she had been in the ladies' room. Kate felt no obligation to explain her own drinking with her mother. It was her business, they were in her town, spending a summer in her house, and none of that involved Joe. She seemed not to connect her own summer behavior to any family issues throughout the rest of the year.

He wondered. How different it would be if life were altered, an unthinkable impossibility that came to him a few times in his lonely exasperation. If Ted were not in their lives and shared parenthood not an issue, if he were independently wealthy and could live without having to parcel out income and planning for this and that, he would stop trying to impose sanity and let Kate and her mother do as they pleased. If. It made no sense to dwell on it. He had a child to protect, whose welfare was his sacred duty. They were all tied together, a family, and his marriage vows were clear. But even if all the "ifs" were truly there, actually realized, could he even then let his wife destroy herself? Regardless of her denial and rigidity, was he that sort of man? When the exasperation passed, he knew the answer well enough.

Joe was agreeable to paying for the unexpected expenses that arose seasonally with the old seaside house, and for Catherine herself, who was living on a small, fixed income. Kate was generous when any of Joe's relatives needed their occasional assistance. She adored Joe's family, and they loved her. Her happiest times seemed to be when they came as guests to the old house during the summer. Viewing it as the only right way to treat a spouse's family, both of them tried to be decent and kind to each other's relatives. Joe was willing to support Catherine. He was ready to do what was necessary to keep the old Wicomico house going for her and for Kate. Next to Ted and her job, he knew the old place was the dearest thing to his wife's heart. But he was aware also of something that no one else bothered to consider, that their family money spent on the Wicomico house was benefiting Kate's brother as well. Ray would inherit the place with Kate at Catherine's death.

In the early years, Kate generally reimbursed the family account for Wicomico expenditures from the summer rental earnings. Within a few years of their marriage, the deteriorating old house became increasingly expensive to maintain. The longtime summer renters had begun to die. Each spring their relatives wrote to Catherine or Kate with news of another demise, expressing thanks for summer sojourns that had been the high point of their loved one's yearly round. In a few cases, Kate and Catherine simply stopped receiving Christmas cards or the occasional phone call, and nobody telephoned in February or March to make the usual reservations. Those who were left were growing too old to take vacations any longer.

The quaint old house was still charming and dignified. People still stopped to take pictures, especially when the clotheslines billowed with sheets like windblown sails. But rustic elegance was eroding with every winter nor'easter and summer hurricane. Spring repairs were increasingly costly, and it was anybody's guess whether the plumbing or wiring or porch roof would last another year. The beach was wearing away too, becoming narrower as the fragile island and its marching dunes continued their ancient progress to the southwest. The surf grew closer with each season, and winter storms drove the angry surge through the pilings and under the house and outbuildings and clear out into the street.

In some ways, the people were different too. Wealthy urban vacationers wanted air conditioning and pay-per-view movies and bathrooms reeking of privacy instead of tongue-and-groove heart pine. They wanted a swimming pool. Some sophisticated families rented the massive new houses up the island and spent their whole vacation in the pool, hot tub, and on the porch, not even going out to the beach. Their fat children spent their time playing video games, never even getting wet. Where other generations had seen the McIvor house as charming and old-fashioned, vacationers were now more inclined to find it increasingly dilapidated.

There were fewer rental earnings from which to reimburse the family account, and after another few years, Kate stopped doing it altogether. Joe began to ask Kate to request some assistance from her brother. On the few occasions when she did so, Ray refused. It was clear that, as soon as Catherine's estate was settled, he would sell his interest. In the meantime, he was unwilling to spend anything. Kate would no more negotiate with her brother about this than she would help with her mother's drinking. She would put enormous emotional energy into complaining about both of them and their stubborn ways, but the responsibility for any concrete action fell to Joe or never occurred at all. Ray would not hear of contributing to repairs. "It's a losing battle," he would say. "The ocean's going to get it. When the time comes, let it go." What was really needed was a move backward, away from the ocean, toward the road. All the surrounding houses had been moved, buying them with luck another fifty or a hundred years of safety. Joe had worked carefully with local movers and bankers and a helpful neighbor who had recently been through it all, and at one point a move had seemed possible. The necessary loan would have amounted to an additional mortgage, but with Ray's help and some further economizing, at the suggestion of which Kate merely stared, in silence, Joe believed they could manage. But Ray was not interested. Joe and the banker went over the financing again, searching for a way that he and Kate could manage the cost alone. During their deliberations, and a month before the move was to take place, one local politician accused a rival of building substandard vacation homes, and the Town of Wicomico suddenly began to enforce an old ordinance that doubled the length of pilings. The added cost put the whole project entirely out of the Stephensons' reach. Having to abandon it actually seemed a sadder reality for Joe than for Kate and Catherine, who never mentioned it again.

* * *

To Joe, alone and desperate for healing in his marriage, any type of conversation Kate could have with reasonable people could only be positive. The Adult Children of Alcoholic Parents seemed to offer much hope. If she would go to these meetings, the onus would be on her mother, not on Kate, in the unlikely event someone found out about her attendance. He hoped she would consider it. Nobody in Dorchester knew about Kate's drinking, but it had been impossible over the years to hide Catherine's drinking. The summer people who rented rooms knew about it. Others were aware that Catherine had lost at least one teaching position for coming to work intoxicated. Her driver's license had been suspended, and she had been seen walking to and from the Wicomico Post Office and Shopsmart. People knew. Joe presented ACAP to Kate as a chance to demonstrate to others that she was sensitive to her own mother's illness and was trying to help. Whatever the motivation for going, Kate would be attending a twelve-step program, and the results could only be good for everybody.

Kate returned from her first ACAP meeting in a sort of triumph. Feeling like a blind man defusing a bomb, Joe asked if she had found the meeting interesting. To his surprise, Kate began to talk about it without any further encouragement. Early in the meeting, apparently, somebody had said something (she would not say what) to which Kate had taken exception. She had proceeded to tell the speaker that she was wrong and had admonished her on several points. It appeared that Kate had held forth for many minutes while everyone else listened. Most of the participants left when the meeting ended, except for one woman who lingered long enough to thank Kate for what she had said. Kate found the others rude for departing so quickly without speaking to her.

Joe listened with a sinking heart. From his own years in Al-Anon, he knew that all twelve-step meetings operated by similar rules. Everyone was entitled to speak as they felt moved. Participants were asked to avoid dominating the discussion. All opinions were valued. Kate was describing an argument and a subsequent lecture. She had talked a great deal and, from the sound of her recitation, had done very little listening. Joe anticipated that she would quit ACAP as she had AA. After one more meeting, she did.

A blessing for the whole family was Kate's new position at the junior college in Dorchester. She liked almost everything about her job. She worked in a small department with three other faculty members. Two of them had PhDs, and the third was completing doctoral studies. They were likable people who lived fairly quiet lives and were more mature than some of the high school faculty Kate had taught with for years. Kate was aware of her own good fortune in being hired for this position. She seemed more content at home. Joe was very pleased for her.

Joe's ministry brought them all into contact with many good people. The rector, parish secretary, and congregation treated him and his family well. Everybody had long understood the temperament and disposition of the rector's wife and reassured Joe and Kate whenever anything occurred. The congregation taught Joe much about ministry and parish life, and he thanked God daily for leading him to begin his ordained life in this place. The few angry people knew Joe was a safe target and that they would not be condemned by the tolerant parish or the wider community for finding fault with him. Getting an early start in dealing with dislike and anger was a blessing for Joe, although he found it very hard to see it that way at first. In looking back with the experience of years, he would come to see it as necessary preparation for a part of ministry faced by all ordained people. The overwhelming number of faithful, kind, reasonable parishioners were persons of a gentler faith, mature and empathetic people of the sort anyone would want to have as neighbors. Their friendship and common sense more than made up for the spoilers.

Ted was on Joe's mind constantly. He took great pleasure, as he always had, in his son's life, his new friends and enjoyment of school, his love of soccer and music, and in collecting just about everything. Ted was a happy child, not at all given to moodiness or sulking, and he had a marvelous sense of humor. This especially delighted Joe and Kate and particularly when it was expressed in Ted's detailed and busy drawings. As a former art teacher, Joe had watched children confine their tiny drawings to a narrow band at the foot of a page, scratching out miniscule scenes and relegating the rest of the page to "sky." Ted was a big, bold recorder and inventor who used all his space, depicting flying dinosaurs, complex battle scenes, the usual fantastical regions of outer space, involved cityscapes peopled by all manner of wild creatures and fantastic complex constructions that defied identification. He used color with a Fauvist's daring energy. Joe was amazed and delighted by his artistic abilities, as he was by everything else about his son. In the family file cabinet, together with folders containing wills, savings accounts, birth certificates and other valued documents, Joe saved collections of Ted's drawings and schoolwork, precious evidence of his son's journey through childhood. It was a beloved archive that would soothe his heart long after the author of these treasures had grown up and gone his way.

Their home and community were pleasant. Joe knew he was blessed and thanked God for it morning and night. He strived to dwell on the gifts, the positive and wholesome aspects of life, of which there were so many. But in many ways the anxiety only grew, like waiting for the other shoe to drop or the knock on the door that was guaranteed to come. He was ashamed of himself for his lack of faith. Things had an equal chance of getting better just as they might, well, get worse. Kate could change. He would change too, learning to manage it all better, and serenity would replace the anxiety not only for a few hours or days now and then but forever. Despite these hopes and good intentions, each episode of confusion and chaos sloshed Joe's sadness within him like trapped sewage. Ted was still a bit young to read the signs of it with certainty, for which Joe was continually thankful. He labored under an impossible belief that before Ted was old enough to perceive what was happening, Kate would change.

Chapter Nineteen

"I never really wanted to move here in the first place. Even if you couldn't have stayed at St. Andrew's, we could have stayed at Dorchester anyway on my teacher's salary. I want a divorce. We might as well have gone to Africa than coming to this place. The biggest cultural thing here is that they built the second-largest cloverleaf up the road near the truck stop. It's all your fault, Joe. How am I supposed to make friends in a place like this? All to make you look good. Just so you can have your own church. You got one all right, and I hope you're satisfied. Like a slum in downtown New York. The prices are high around here too. I can't find a dress I like. It's hicksville! And it's your fault, Joe. If you had just been satisfied to stay where we were, we would all be better off. And I'm farther away here than I ever was from Wicomico, and I told you that when we came to look at this area. It's a dump, and it's your fault. The trouble with you is you don't think about anybody but yourself. Catoctin Springs is the last place we should have come. And I want a divorce."

At the other end of the house, the back door was pushed open suddenly, and the reason Joe would not consent to a divorce could be heard singing. Joe frowned at Kate and held up his hand. She fell silent for the first time in a half hour.

"Ted!" Joe called. "We're in here, bro. What's going on?"

"I'm going down to the pool. You guys want to come?" Ted shouted, on his way up the stairs to his room.

"Ted, what about the geometry test today? How did you do?" Kate called toward the stairs, her eyes shut and head tilted back. They could hear the bathroom door close and the muffled hum of his radio coming on.

"Oh, it gets to me when he does that," said Kate.

"Does what?" Joe asked.

"When he knows I'm waiting to hear about an important test and he comes in and acts like I'm not even here. And don't shush me! That school he's going to is substandard, and it doesn't make any difference to you. If it weren't for me, he'd be failing everything."

"But just last week, after the PTA meeting, you said—"

"I did not! Don't give me that! It ticks me off when you do that."

"That he's doing well, that you like his teachers. He's making As and Bs."

"He could be making all As if he just applied himself. When he's in high school next year, he'll have to do better if he expects to get in a good college anywhere. And as soon as colleges see that he was in *these* schools—"

Ted bounced down the steps in black-and-white board shorts and a triple X green T-shirt with World Class Snow Patrol spelled out boldly in orange across the front. He came into the living room making swimming motions and gargling the way people suppose fish sound underwater. He smacked Joe lightly on the shoulder. "I'm going to meet—" he began to say.

"I said, what about your geology test?" declared Kate, her head thrown back, with a tiny pause between each word.

"Mom! I just got home. When did you say that?"

"If you'd just listen to me sometime, Ted. As soon as you came in, I asked you about it!"

"I don't even take geology!"

"Who said anything about geology? For the third time, what about your geometry test?"

"I only took it today, Mom. I won't know till I get it back. Probably be next week. Gosh!" He went into the kitchen and opened the refrigerator door. "It takes time to grade papers, you know."

"Oh, don't give me that. I've graded more papers than all the teachers at that school put together. How do you think you did on it? You must have some feeling about it. What did Carson say when you turned it in?"

"*Mr.* Carson," Joe whispered.

Kate closed her eyes and said loudly, "Tell me what Carson said about it."

"Nothing. The bell rang. We all booked." And he was gone.

"Oh, it makes me so mad when he does that," said Kate, examining her fingernails. Joe watched her. His side hurt.

"Where's your mother?" said Joe.

Kate's eyes rolled back in her head. She looked back at her nails and said, in an indifferent way, "In her room, I guess."

"I thought you had a half day today."

"I did. I've been home since one o'clock."

"Has she come out of her room while you've been here?"

"No, and please don't... Let her stay in there. Reading, I guess."

Joe was quiet for a moment. "I got the results of my tests today. Dr. Goldman's nurse called just before I left work. Believe it or not, they still can't say whether it's irritable bowel syndrome, Crohn's Disease, or ulcerative colitis."

"So what are they going to do?" said Kate, leaning over the coffee table and sorting through the mail.

"I have to have another colonoscopy."

"You had one just last year. Why do you need another one?"

"Well, that's what Dr. Goldman wants. Until then, he is following Pete Wyler's diagnosis of irritable bow—"

"Well, none of them know what they're talking about. All you have is diverticulitis. That's what they said the year after we were married."

"But the tests these days are more exact. And Wilson and Henry have already diagnosed it as Cro—"

"Well, sounds to me like none of them really know what they're talking about." She picked up the remote control and turned on the television. "There's supposed to be reruns of *I Dream of Jeannie* on channel nine. But I never get to see it. I have to work. Oh, I wish you could have heard Hervey today in chapel. Talking about the Jolly Green Giant, like the kids even knew what it was. The Jolly Green

Giant hasn't been on television since Ted was born. Bob Custer was sitting in the pew in front of me, and he turned around and gave me the biggest look, like 'Gaaaaaaaaaa.' And coming out, Doris Short was saying how much she enjoyed listening to him preach, and I heard her say just the other day how boring she thought he was. People are so fake!" She found her rerun and fell silent.

"You say Bob Custer gave you 'the biggest look'? Do a big look for me, Kate. Come on," said Joe, smiling.

Kate's face lit up in a lovely smile, a sight Joe treasured. "Oh, be quiet!" she said. Without a pause, Joe told her a joke a lawyer had told him at lunch that day about an old maid teacher whose third-grade student brought a condom to school for show-and-tell. Kate laughed happily and genuinely. She laughed even harder when Joe, getting up, suggested she tell the joke to Father Hervey. "In fact, call him right now," he said. "He might want to use it in his chapel talk tomorrow morning."

Before going upstairs to change, Joe tapped on Catherine's door. Hearing nothing, he opened the door a half inch and peered through. Catherine was in bed, covered with an afghan, facing the wall. He opened the door and went in quietly. She was sleeping with her mouth open, making small bird sounds. On the bedside table were some crumpled tissues and a peanut-butter-and-jelly sandwich. He touched the bread and found it stiff and stale. Beside it, a sweating glass of iced tea stood in a small puddle. Joe pulled the afghan up around Catherine's thin shoulders and closed the door softly behind him.

In the bedroom, he changed into shorts and T-shirt for mowing the lawn. He lay down on the bed. The burn in his gut troubled him. Sometimes lying down and closing his eyes helped. Pollen season had ended, and two days of rain had washed the residue from the air, so the windows were open, and the sounds of early summer drifted in from the lawn. Gregarious birds, which he and Kate both loved to watch and hear, made music in all directions. Chickadees, cardinals, Carolina wrens, mockingbirds, and finches were busily building nests in the trees and shrubs. The feeders were still out while Joe used up the remaining winter seed, and two pairs of mourning doves had strutted about beneath them at dusk for the past few days. He could hear one of them now making its rueful distant hymn. *Lamenting its own lack of skills,* he thought. *Nest building is not high art among doves. A few sticks dropped haphazardly into a pile…as sophisticated as they get…disgraceful as killdeers, scratching little wallows in the gravel and letting nature take its course…* He could hear a catbird. He had seen goldfinches near the big butterfly bush, a glorious Isle de France he had put in two years before. The place was alive with titmice, a million sparrows, house finches, and a few he wasn't sure about. They would enjoy the new row of sunflowers. He had nailed orange halves to the cherry tree because he though he heard a Baltimore oriole, although it was still early June. Maybe tonight he would put out some jar tops with grape jelly. He was sure he had seen an Orchard oriole. And what was going on with the crows? Not a single crow had been heard in the neighborhood all spring.

He thought he heard Catherine cough in the room below. She was going down. Last week he had carried her to the front seat of Kate's van, and together they had driven her into Catoctin Springs to Joe's doctor. He had carried her into the office, and when her name was called, he carried her into the examining room and left her there with Dr. Wyler and Kate. As he left the room, Pete Wyler began to ask questions and flip through Catherine's thick file.

Joe had telephoned the week before and requested that her doctor near Wicomico send Wyler copies of Catherine's extensive records. He had taken that matter into his own hands a week before the appointment after waiting six weeks for Kate to make the call herself. During that time, Catherine had grown weaker and weaker, alarming Joe. Kate had grown more irritated each time Joe asked her if she had called Dr. Bell for her mother's records. "I'll do it, I'll do it. I have to work, Joe. Remember? They don't like us to make personal calls from school, just like in Jeffersonton."

He lay on the bed with his eyes closed. He should get up and work on the riding mower while the advice of the man in the repair shop was still fresh in his mind. He had made notes, drawn a picture, while the man told him what to do this time. Still, he should go on and do it while he could remember. It would be so easy to lay right here until "the silken garments of the night" wrapped everything in restful protection. The moonlit scenes of John Atkinson Grimshaw, which always made him think of ghost stories, began to emerge like specters in his resting mind. Night. He thought of Granville Redmond's *The Rising Moon*. What had Charlie Chaplin said about it? "You feel you ought to whisper..." He could see Grimshaw's *A Moonlit Road.* Catherine coughed again.

Joe had known that neither Kate nor Catherine would tell Pete Wyler about Catherine's lifelong drinking. He recalled the time he had driven Catherine inland from Wicomico for an appointment with the doctor who had treated her for twenty years. The doctor had taken Joe aside and urged him to make Catherine eat more.

"She's skin and bones," said the old doctor, an experienced man whom Joe would have liked to know better. "She has always been thin, but she's got to gain a little weight. Tell Kate I said so."

"It's hard for us to get her to eat," Joe responded. "She says she has no appetite."

"Well, I know they're good Baptists and all. But she is dangerously thin. Do you think you could talk her into drinking a little wine, say, about thirty minutes before dinner? Could you and Kate get her to do that? They'll both put up a fuss. But it might improve her appetite. Just remind her that Jesus drank wine in the Bible or something."

Joe was dumbfounded. He looked at the doctor with his mouth open. "Do you mean you..."

"Oh, I know, I know. They've always been that way about drinking," said Dr. Bell, shaking his head. "Lot of Baptists are. Methodists too. Kate told me just before you all got married"—a big grin brightened his tired old face—"sorry I couldn't come, took Eula Lee somewhere, Hot Springs I think, that she didn't know how her family was going to take to you because you and your family took a drink now and then. You know how these country Baptists are. For God's sake, now, don't tell Kate I told you that, Joe. Those women would be all over me like ducks on a June bug." And he slapped Joe on the shoulder. "Like hens on a hot hole." They both laughed.

Joe took a moment or two to explain a few things, and Catherine's doctor of two decades leaned against his office wall and shook his white head, his eyes closed and both hands pressed together over his face. As Joe left to go out to Catherine, who was waiting impatiently in the hot car, Dr. Bell leaned on his desk and continued to shake his head, emitting a series of exasperated sounds.

"How long have you been seeing Dr. Bell?" Joe asked as he got into the car.

"Going on twenty years. What in the world kept you so long?"

"Oh, just chatting with him, passing the time of day, you know."

Catherine gave him a quick look. "Well, he better not charge me for you taking up his time. If he does, mister, guess who I'm going to send the bill to?"

"Who?" said Joe, feigning consternation.

"Who? You know who! Fact is, I'm seriously considering changing doctors. In twenty years, Bill Bell hasn't done a thing for me to make me feel any better. Maybe it's time I went to somebody new."

She had gone to somebody new, but the new doctor, a young man starting a family practice, had the temerity to question her about "very personal things that no doctor needs to know about." So she had returned to Dr. Bell, who had apparently asked her some annoying questions of his own and then proceeded to change most of her longtime medications. The result was that Catherine began to consult him only when she was so sick she couldn't get out of bed.

Given all this, Joe himself had alerted Pete Wyler. After examining Catherine and reviewing her records, Dr. Wyler spent a half hour with Kate in his office, while Catherine remained in the examination room. He eliminated several of Catherine's medications, prescribed a special diet, and asked a lot of questions about her daily routine and how long she would be visiting this time. He told Kate it was time to consider some permanent long-term plans for her care. Later that night, Kate told Joe only that he had prescribed new medications and that she hoped Catherine's insurance company would not be difficult about paying for them.

With the new medications, Catherine became more alert and began to eat again. She resumed watching television during the day.

Kate assisted her to the bathroom every morning and made a sandwich for her for lunch, which she placed with a glass of iced tea on her bedside table. After another two weeks, Kate and Catherine decided that Catherine was well enough to endure a flight to Georgia for a visit with Kate's brother and his family. It took several more weeks to gain her brother's agreement for the visit, which Kate managed to do by calling him at work between her classes at St. John's. Ray could be more easily persuaded to cooperate when he could discuss Catherine's visits outside the presence of his wife. After knowing Kate's family for years now, Joe knew he would subsequently inform his wife that Joe and Kate were sending Catherine to them, and as hard as he had tried to stop them, there was nothing he could do about it.

Kate's mood and temperament became less fractious the moment Catherine was aboard her flight. Like a patient newly released from quarantine, she became more enthusiastic, expansive, cooperative. She and Joe could talk a little more. It was easier to reason with her. While Catherine was with them, Kate (although she would have denied it) depended on Joe constantly as both listener and helper. She could complain to Joe at length about Catherine, and Catherine could complain to him in private about Kate, and this arrangement saved daughter and mother much relentless bickering. Joe did not find it hard to care for Catherine. She never demanded much, and except for critical observations about everyone in her life except Ted, she kept her complaints to herself. Joe's family knew Catherine well and was very much aware of her "problem." They were always happy to have her as a guest when Joe, Kate, and Ted visited. As with everybody else, however, they had no idea about Kate's own drinking.

Catherine's presence meant having no alcohol in the house. Joe had long ago taken to hiding all the alcohol prior to her visits, something Kate would not bother to do. Years before, when Ted was about seven, Joe had hidden the liquor bottles at the bottom of the clothes hamper in his bathroom before Catherine's arrival. In dropping in some soiled school clothes, Ted had seen the bottles. Joe had sat down with him on the bed and carefully explained that Nanny was allergic to alcohol and that it was helpful to her if they hid it during her visits so she would not be tempted to drink it.

"But, Dad, if she's allergic to it, why would she drink it?" asked his intelligent, reasonable young son.

"Because at first it makes her feel good. A little later on, it makes her feel terrible. And each time she drinks it, it makes her health worse and worse. We can help her by keeping it out of sight while she's here."

"I guess I better not talk to her about it, huh?"

"I agree. You can talk to me about it anytime." Joe was waiting for what came next.

"I can talk to Mom about it too. Because Nanny is Mom's mom."

"Yes, you can."

"They argue, Dad, during the summer while we're at the beach. A lot."

Joe looked at Ted and smiled and waited, giving him time to say anything more he had to say. Joe knew Ted was a perceptive, inquisitive child but was certain that he had not perceived anything about Kate. After a little more talk about Nanny and her health and some encouragement about what Ted could do to be of help to Nanny and Mom, his son ran outside to play with his friends. Later that evening, after Ted had gone to sleep, Joe told Kate about the conversation. She listened with a slight frown and then returned to her paperback novel without comment.

That had been six or seven years before. Ted had never asked any more questions about Catherine or her drinking. Over the years he had learned in school about drugs and alcohol and brought the subject up from time to time in conversations at dinner. Joe asked him every evening what he had learned in school that day. One evening at dinner when he was about eleven, he replied that his class had talked about alcohol in health class that day, and one student had said his uncle was "an alkie." Ted went on to relate what the student had said about how much trouble it caused his parents when the uncle came to visit. Ted was an affectionate, considerate child who doted on Kate and would have done nothing to hurt her. Joe guessed that he had forgotten their discussion about Catherine years before and was certain that Ted still knew nothing about Kate's own drinking. During his description of the class discussion, Kate had remained utterly silent in Ted's presence for the first time Joe could remember. She did not interrupt or otherwise shift attention to herself until it was time to get out the ice cream for dessert.

That had been two years ago. As he lay on the bed now in the cool bedroom, these and other thoughts crowded out the birdsong and swirled in his memory like clouds and leaves before a coming storm. Recollections, scenes, bits of sound and color, they fit together on a background of rough and dun emotion like faded terrazzi in a weathered mosaic, making the apse of his imagination shimmer with memories. It still unnerved him, saddened him like nothing else in the world, to hear her say the word *divorce*. Whenever she brought it up, he reminded her that they had a son to raise and that his upbringing in a stable home, with two parents who loved him, was their primary duty.

"If that's still what you want when he gets out of high school, I'll talk about it then. But he deserves a decent home while he grows up. God gave him to us. We brought him into this world. He didn't ask for it. Both of us, together, have to do right by him until he's on his own."

What he did not add, and in denial she could never have said herself, was that Joe had no intention of leaving Ted with an alcoholic mother. Even if he could have counted on the courts to resist the invalidated presumption in favor of mothers, he knew that Ted doted on Kate. Separation from her would break his heart. Either way, divorce would do Ted more harm than any relief it would afford Kate.

Although he had rejected divorce, and he knew Kate was too lazy to gather up her things and leave on her own, her occasional references to it depressed him. As exhausting as it was to live with her, as difficult as she could be and as much emotional and physical distress as her moods and denial caused him, he was still hopeful. He believed their relationship could be saved. Anyone can change. He was willing to continue to change himself. He would have gotten up then and there and gone with her to a counselor if she would only agree. Even as the months and years passed by and his expectations faded that she would join AA or enter family counseling with him, he still regarded divorce as a betrayal of her, their son, their family, and his vows. He did not even like to use the word in their home, believing its every pronunciation there was like a spreading stain.

"What are you doing up here, Mr. Stephenson?" said Kate, coming in silently from the carpeted stairs.

"Just thinking, m'dear," said Joe in a W. C. Fields voice.

"Well, don't think too much. It'll wear your brain out." She lay down beside him with her head against his shoulder.

"Not much left to wear out after today," he said.

"Why? What happened?"

He would truly have liked to tell her. A very well-known lawyer had asked him to lunch for what Joe thought was a friendly visit. They knew each other's reputation and belonged to several of the same civic groups but had never spent much time together. His name was Fred, and he was a member of a big church in another denomination, the largest congregation in Catoctin Springs. After some pleasantries, he began to talk to Joe about his wife and his marriage. They had four children between ten and fifteen. His practice was vigorous and lucrative, as everybody knew who read the local newspapers. He and his wife were no longer in love the way they had been at first, a revelation that caused him to cough as he talked about it. But they cared about each other and loved their children. His father was a politician well-known throughout the state, a man of influence and charm (and, everyone said, much more charming than his successful, driven son), and in a day or so, everybody would find out that on the previous Friday his father had been diagnosed with an inoperable tumor on his liver. It had spread too. He was overwhelmed by grief. But what kept Fred awake at night, what was causing him the most profound anxiety he had ever known, was his fifteen-year-old daughter. He had surprised her a week ago coming into the house through her bedroom window at about 4:00 a.m., and it was clear that she had been with someone. There had been a terrible scene. She refused to tell him anything but became almost hysterical and implored him not to tell her mother, claiming it would never happen again. But of course it had happened again two nights later. Her grades had been falling for six months. She was increasingly sullen. His wife was already in therapy for "her nerves." He was torn between telling his wife, whose relationship with their daughter was strained, and in trusting his daughter to stop whatever she was doing. He was afraid it would push his wife over the edge. He had been checking on his daughter throughout each night, and as far as he knew, she had not—

Here they were interrupted at their corner table by a husband and wife, parishioners at Redeemer, who wanted to say hello to them both and ask about Fred's father. They had heard that he had had an accident or something. Fred assured them he had not, and after some small talk, they left. Before Fred could continue, he received a cell phone call from the clerk saying that his next case would be called early. Could he come immediately? They made plans to meet the following day and continue their conversation, and Fred rushed off, while Joe finished his sandwich. Joe had returned to his office in time to deal with a belligerent homeless man who was berating Milly, his secretary, who was near tears, because she had refused to give him—

"Joe, are you awake?" Kate's voice in his ear interrupted these recollections, which were playing along like a compact disk.

"I'm sorry. I'm really sorry. You got me thinking about something today, and—"

"Well, you'll never guess what I had to deal with," Kate was saying. "Guess who called?"

"Who?" said Joe, coming into focus.

"Candice. My roommate from my first year in college. Remember? I told you about her summer before last while we were sitting on the beach when the Richardsons came by, the time they brought their dog that made a mess in two different places right where everybody was sitting and you had to clean it up after they left?"

Joe looked around at her and said, "Ah. Oh. So...she called." He had no idea who Candice was and could not recall Kate having mentioned her.

"She called me. I haven't seen her or heard from her for like fifteen years! I mean, I didn't even know who it was at first. She wants to come to Wicomico as soon as I get there next Monday. I mean, I won't even have time to get the screens hosed off. I asked her if she could wait till the next weekend, and she said no, that Hank and Ginger want to come too, and they're going to Atlanta for a wedding that next week so they all have to come then, and I'm thinking, give me a break. But guess who didn't have their schedule book with them? I told her I'd have to wait till I got home to call her back. And now I'm not sure what to do."

Joe considered all this for a moment and said, "How many rooms do they want? You say, Hank and Ginger? Now, who are they?"

"She's Candice's cousin that I told you we went to South Carolina with during Thanksgiving my first year in college. I don't really know her. I only met her that one time. And Hank is her live-in. He teaches shop. They're coming down on a motorcycle. He's like a big biker type. Wait till the neighbors see *him*! That's why I'm trying to decide what to do." He knew it was not a rhetorical inquiry. She wanted him to say something practical.

After a minute, he said, "Tell her you'll be there Tuesday afternoon, not Monday, and that they can come Wednesday morning. Explain to her that you will have just arrived and that the rest of the house will not be ready. Open up the house and unpack Monday evening. Clean two rooms for them Tuesday afternoon. Don't kill yourself getting ready for them. They'll spend their time on the beach or on the porch anyway. And maybe motorcycle man will let you take his hog out for a spin."

"Hey! I'll have to get me a black leather outfit to wear."

"Hell, you don't need no leather. You're sexy enough. Just ride the damn thing nude."

Chapter Twenty

I n his freshman year of high school, Joe had a history teacher who aroused the silent admiration and respect of most of his class. She had taught their parents, and in a few cases their grandparents, and her personality and style had entered local legend. Grown very large in old age, with her hair in a bun and dressing after the fashion of earlier times, she did not give the impression of one who connected magically with teenagers. But she was a phenomenon, in love with history and the teaching of it, and the beguiling thrill of her absorption was silently, and famously, contagious. Moving formidably about her classroom like a great battleship maneuvering amongst tugs, she touched even the dumbest jocks in the back row with her passion for the human story. She talked of ancient events with the excitement and exhaustive detail of one who had been there. She taught with a wholly unconscious drama and a great deal of reverence that arose from her love of what she was doing. The cathedral hush that filled the room when she spoke was the sound of young people who did not want to miss a single word. Even those condemned to study mathematics in college were in awe of history when she finished with them. One had to work hard to do well with her, which was the way in schools of those days, but nobody minded being in her classes. She sent forth generations of students more perceptive of their world because they understood something of its past.

When they came to the War Between the States, she sometimes spoke of her grandfather, but with no more emphasis or immediacy than she brought to Charlemagne or Patrick Henry. A Confederate officer wounded in the Wilderness, he was brought back home flat on his back in a railway car while maggots mercifully ate away the gangrene of his shattered legs. She had his sword hanging above the dining room fireplace at home beneath the tattered banner of the Bedford Light Dragoons, and every few years she brought them in to show her spellbound students. Her grandfather had survived and, after the war, founded a private school where he taught history and English until his death in 1891. He had spent a lifetime memorizing poetry, Latin and Greek in the original and translation, and the great English poets, especially those of the Lake District. He told his students that memorizing verse strengthened the brain like exercise built up one's biceps, propelling passages of Homer and Aeschylus coursing through the lives of generations of poor, rural Virginians. For as long as she had been teaching, his granddaughter had taken after him, illustrating her lectures with apt passages of verse that elicited wonder in students who couldn't have recited "Mary Had a Little Lamb." Bits of Gray's *Elegy* and Coleridge's *Ancient Mariner*, used with discretion and perfect timing, never overdone, always appropriate, imparted a unique inspiration in young minds probing the mysteries of life before the Revolution and ships and the sea. And there was Shakespeare for all occasions, and Milton.

Her grandfather's advice had made an impression upon Joe and his friends, although it would be years before they could admit it to one another. The habit of memorizing poetry had been predictably short-lived in most of them. After a few lines of *The Raven* or *Song of the Chatahoochie*, most had moved on quickly to more practical interests. But the practice stuck with a few of them over the years. With Joe, always drawing in the margins of his notebooks during lectures, snatches of great poems were like the paintings he admired in books, windows on other worlds. The words intrigued him with something like the wonder and pleasure he derived from movies, comic books, and the exploits of Flash Gordon and Captain America. In addition to a passion for history, his formidable teacher had united him for life with the *Oxford Book of English Verse*. With his six-week course in typing during his sophomore year of high school and an understanding of geologic time learned in his college geology class, this introduction to poetry had influenced the rest of Joe's life. In his twenties, he memorized poetry the way other people learned the lyrics of songs. It was mental work as strengthening and physical and pleasurable as running or swimming or climbing rocks, although he could not and would not have tried to explain it. It was all interior. He had the common sense to keep his mouth shut even on occasions when a beer or two set loose everyone else's youthful tongue, a discipline he would one day look back upon with gratitude. He could say that for himself, at least.

He had learned most of Eliot's *Four Quartets*. He played the sterling lines over and over in his mind like a recording of music while he did routine things, running at night, mowing the lawn, washing dishes, driving. Sometimes, near the end of memorizing Yeats or Matthew Arnold, he would walk for miles before bedtime, stealing silence and privacy for his final effort the way he would go off by himself when he reached the last dozen pages of a novel. In the same way, he memorized the law in his thirties, Greek and Hebrew in his forties, and in his fifties, whole chapters of Scripture.

It had proved a valuable skill for an ordinary intellectual who, despite of years spent in schools, disliked the academic regimen. It had seeded his adult life with a legacy of verse that fit its moments perfectly, coming to him unbidden and often unremembered, flashing upon his inward eye and imparting clarity and grace to the events and circumstances at hand. Joe accepted it gladly as an operation of grace, nourishing the daily struggle with drops of joy and insight *like snow upon the desert's dusty face.*

As Joe fumbled to understand his life and the world, the great deeds and immortal descriptions of them he had come to admire began to reveal by contrast an increasingly focused and bitter view of reality. Somehow the sublime made the depths more apparent, as the beauty of moonlight calls forth predators of the night or the magnificence of the sea discloses sharks and killer whales. As a child, he had marveled at his father's brave tales of the Normandy invasion and the bravery of the Americans in the Bulge, but a look at his father's tragic wounds was enough to make him want to vomit, and the glories were rendered sullied and diminished. He memorized portions of *King*

Lear and *Macbeth* and found himself meditating as much on greed and betrayal, or megalomania and disloyalty, as upon the glorious language. Consternation at the contrasts of life was not new to him, but admiration and wonder came increasingly at a price. By revealing light, they forced him to face darkness. The Brandenburg Concertos impelled him eventually to Anne Frank. His wonder at Angkor Wat led to the Khmer Rouge, *Dover Beach* to a secular Europe, and Velazquez and Zurbaran to the death of Lorca. For Joe, all of Western civilization came to a standstill with the holocaust. He perceived it, if one can be said to "perceive" such an unimaginable horror, less as a historical event than as a revelation of terrible, inevitable truth. *We have been warned*, he said to himself.

He saw there was no end to it when he began the study of law. The law made him ponder human greed and self-centeredness in a fresh way, and at least it amused him to imagine the multiple misinterpretations of that new conviction that would arise from the Greek chorus waiting in line for fast food or buying lottery tickets at convenience stores. In the law, great deeds and immortal language did not get in the way of reality. He came to see greed and self-centeredness as human constants, inevitable and overwhelming, diffused in mortal hearts and minds like a viral fog, penetrating and enfolding the broken world with malice that lowered like one vast perpetual thunderhead. In the rare moments when comprehension twinkled against the darkness, a voice inside him said with a sort of amused resignation, as though once more having to explain the obvious: *Humankind cannot stand very much reality.*

He had a recurrent dream in which he was in a big lifeboat on the open sea. Crouched in the midsection with their backs to the horizon was a circle of diverse, noisy people, playing cards and arguing vigorously with one another. In the stern, a slow leak bubbled. As the boat took on more and more water and settled deeper into the sea, Joe squatted in the bow, bailing with his cupped hands, shouting for help. No one listened. When he shook a few of them by the shoulder, they barked at him for interrupting their game. He sloshed about, ignored by everyone as he flailed the rising water over the side. He awoke in panic. As with his classic anxiety dreams of college, in which he found himself on the night before a final exam and realized he had forgotten to attend any classes, he spent the following days trying to wrest some meaning from it all. He had many similar dreams during his marriage. In most of them, he was trying to talk with Kate about something critical. She would not listen, or she was dismissive or sarcastic. Sometimes she merely smiled and walked away. He awoke from these dreams soaked in perspiration, Kate snoring lightly beside him, and he found it impossible to go back to sleep.

Self-centeredness. Greed. One of his deep concerns was shared by many of his friends, smart people on both the left and right. It was the anxious conviction that America's next generation will face a catastrophe, a monumental national debt and soaring interest rates that will lead to an unprecedented calamity. While the world around him lamented the price of gasoline and discussed the Middle East or the Tour de France, Joe worried about Ted and Ted's own children, who would face a disaster prepared for them by their forebear's greed. He knew the implications for civilization, such as it is, were beyond imagining. Power. Covetousness. Self-absorption.

The future of fresh water was another preoccupation, causing him to ponder for hours during long drives or while sitting alone at night at the kitchen table. Sometimes he laughed out loud at himself, knowing that anyone who caught him meditating on water in a lonely kitchen at night would think he was insane. Perhaps he was, and he acknowledged the high likelihood to himself daily. But occasionally he watched the evening news and saw the polar regions birth icebergs the size of Manhattan, while politicians and church people argued about how to discuss critical issues without offending anybody. He contemplated the dislocations of another "Little Ice Age" in a world already too disorganized to conquer malaria and influenza. Water. Life. They were dying—the Mediterranean, the Chesapeake, the wetlands, and rivers of the world. Who remembers Biafra? Who can find Sierra Leone on a map? There are high school students who have never heard of Tulsa, Nanking, Dafur. Certain Muslims worship God by cutting the throats of children in Algeria and blowing up commuters in cities around the world. A ship full of Jews, all doomed, tries to land in New York, Cuba. The traffic of the prosperous and indifferent swirls about the empty cathedrals and churches of France and Germany, relics of a superseded past, and intellectual disgrace shines in every greedy face. Strange fruit hangs from the ragged trees in Africa. In America, the deist's God is trotted out for mention at great events until returned, quietly, to where they keep him.

In the quiet of his midnight kitchen, Joe tried to imagine a new influenza pandemic spreading from China or Iran, where the authorities for political reasons would cover it up until too late, and the response of a world that will not prevent the murder of its minorities. He thought of Ted. He thought of his grandchildren whom he might never know. He loved them already. What could one do? What must God be thinking?

I made the world to be inhabited, said a voice unannounced.

Yes, but humankind cannot stand very much reality.

Oh? Well achtung, Herr Prufrock! Tell me! Where were you when I laid the foundations of the earth?

By this still hearth, among these barren crags, matched with an aged wife—

Abomination! Just ask anyone, anywhere, from the eastern deserts to the islands of the west. You will find that no nation has ever abandoned its gods even though they were false. I am the true and glorious God, but you have rejected me to worship idols.

If I may be so bold as to say so, I know Thou art right. I know Thou art in control. And yet I know, where'er I go, that there hath pass'd away a glory from the earth.

But you know, of course, that the darkness has not overcome it?

What? Is there some blessed hope whereof he knew and I was unaware?

Unaware? Really! I have shown you, little man, what is good and what I require—

Oh, but begging your pardon, Sir, if you would just tear open the heavens and come down again! Come again and make it right, heal—

But lo, I am with—

If you are coming down through the narrows of the river Kiang, please let me know beforehand, and I will come out to meet you, as far as Cho-fu-Sa…

Human beings intend the natural and probable consequences of their behavior. They had taught him that in law school, but life had been teaching it to him since birth. He knew that no republic in history had lasted more than three hundred years. Whether couched in the rhetoric of tax cuts and increases, or entitlements and spending, he perceived that greed and self-centeredness are leading humankind insidiously, malevolently forward. And in all history, out of all the world, we are one nation. He sat alone at night and pondered it all. Where are the rugged frontier builders of yesterday? What has happened to the willingness to sacrifice for those who come after us? There used to be a concept called the common good. A reckoning looms. All the best minds agree. But what is all that compared to entertainment and instant gratification? People seeking comfort and well-being throng the off-brand megachurches to hear the exclusive feel-good gospel of the clean and the comfortable. Celebrity trials, natural disasters, new electronic games, the stock market, the flavor of the month and their romantic intrigues—the stuff of interest and immediacy.

Some cared, of course, and prayed, searched, questioned. Joe knew some of them, intelligent, decent, creative, spiritual, aware of the forest as they climbed their tree, conscious of connectedness (even with the unseen) and alert to the interrelatedness of phenomena, a world of multiplicity. Kind people. A sense of justice. Generosity. Openness.

*****

Dave and Tonette Gallagher were members of St. Andrew's, Dorchester, when Joe served there after seminary, and Joe and Kate became friends with them soon after arriving. The Gallaghers loved Ted, who became a big brother to their three slightly younger children. Joe and Dave shared a love of the outdoors; they had gotten on very well from the start. Kate and Tonette were quite different personalities, but their children and community provided a wide basis for friendship. The year after the Stephensons moved to Catoctin

Springs, the Gallaghers drove up from Dorchester for a weekend visit. They arrived late on a Friday afternoon in April.

While Ted and the three younger children played outside, the adults sat in the den laughing and catching up on news of one another. Dave and Tonette drank very little alcohol, wine occasionally with dinner, so Joe had made tea. Kate did not like hot tea and preferred a soft drink instead. When Joe returned to the kitchen to make more tea, Tonette followed him as Kate and Dave continued to talk. To Joe's complete surprise, Tonette asked him quietly and bluntly what was wrong with Kate. He replied that nothing was wrong with her and asked Tonette what she meant.

"Can't you smell it?" she replied, crossing her arms and leaning against the kitchen counter. "It's vodka or wine or something. You can smell it all over her." She waved her hand back and forth as if clearing smoke or insects from in front of her. "And look at her, her face, her hair. She looks awful. What's going on?"

Joe was astonished. He fumbled for words. He had seen nothing unusual in Kate's appearance or manner, and he said so. Tonette looked at him full in the face then down at the kitchen floor. She closed her eyes briefly and shook her head, almost a shudder.

"Is this what you've been trying to tell us all along?" she said.

Joe could not remember ever being so surprised. Even so, as bizarre as Tonette's questions were, as he stared at her with his mouth open, he recognized he was listening instinctively for Kate's voice in the next room. He could hear Dave speaking in an excited tone. Tonette was looking at him, waiting. In his hand, Kate's grandmother's teacup began to rattle in its saucer. In an instant, he recalled something from a few nights before, a small matter that had made him wonder at the time. Kate had set up the ironing board to press something for Ted. Ted had grabbed the warm garment, a pair of pants or a shirt, and pressed it to his face, feeling the warmth. He had heard Kate raise her voice and say, "Ted, don't do that. I just ironed it! You ruin everything!" It had struck Joe because it was a tone of voice, a choice of words Kate almost never used with their son and reserved mostly for him, and he found it unusual. It was a sign, but he had not recognized it. He stared at Tonette now as she informed him, in so many words, that he had not been as successful as he supposed in covering up the family secret. The most dedicated enablers take on an unconscious transparency as time passes, losing their skill, as Joe had lost his, to understand reality, to recognize the obvious in his own wife's breath and complexion. In his best lawyerly voice, for the first time ever to a family friend, he heard himself say, with a sense of crashing betrayal, "Yes. There is a problem."

"So this is what it has been all along?" said Tonette, with a sound of dawning comprehension. In her way, she was as surprised as he was, and she could hear it in her voice.

"What do you mean?" said Joe, the clergyman-trial lawyer who sounded suddenly like a naive schoolboy in the presence of the principal.

"Oh, come on, Joe. Most everybody has wondered. But we could never put a finger on what it was."

He could not believe what he was hearing. For over ten years, he had covered and maneuvered and contrived, thinking he was playing faithful husband, protecting his wife, and here was evidence blurted out in mere seconds that none of it had worked. He felt like a coil of bailing twine was tightening around him. Kate would be crushed if she knew what was being discussed a few feet away from her, in her own kitchen. She would be mortified. Could she hear them? Had she picked up a word or two as they had talked and figured out what they were discussing? Was she about to fall apart in anger or tears or shame? Would she blow up? Or melt down? His mind, which would have assessed the moment calmly for a parishioner or client, raced ahead with the strength of emotion. Had Ted glanced through the window and seen him talking with Tonette and perceived, through some weird divination, that they were discussing his mother? She would die if she thought he knew, not because it was so bad, but because it wasn't perfect, and it didn't exist at all, and what cruelty—he could hear her, her voice rising—to discuss her with such falsehoods, lies, hateful deceptive fabrications. He knew that his side would begin to ache soon. He switched horses and began to prepare himself for weeks of internal distress. Ted burst in from the garage with the three young Gallaghers close behind him. They raced between him and Tonette and into the hall and up the stairs to the bedrooms. From the den he heard Kate call to him to slow down.

He turned to Tonette and asked quickly and quietly if Dave had seen it too. Tonette said that he had. Joe replied that Kate would probably go to bed, even with company in the house, by ten o'clock. They made plans to meet quietly in the kitchen at 10:45 p.m., after the children were settled down and Kate was asleep. Tonette said that Dave would want to join them, to which Joe agreed. The initial feeling of betrayal of Kate grew in him in the few minutes it took to make their plans. Listening to Tonette and watching her face as she talked, however, dissolved some of his irrational fear and made him begin to see what was happening as a medical emergency. It was a matter obviously outside his control or even his understanding, as though Kate had just been wheeled by strangers into emergency surgery. He was left alone, seeking glimpses of her through the swinging doors. His head ached.

As they went about dinner and the rest of the evening and talked with Kate throughout those seemingly endless hours, the pain in his head and his gut stung like acid, corroding his attention and rendering his forced smile a strained and ludicrous imitation of ease. He did not want Kate, and especially not Ted, to know that something was up. But before the end of dinner, he began to think that if she discovered their awareness, it was just too damn bad. Throughout the evening whenever the anguish rose within him like steam, Ted would appear in his line of vision or speak to him from across the room or from Kate's end of the table (where she had been sure to seat him so they could whisper), and with the sight or sound of his son, his innards would cool and his composure return.

As sad and lost as he felt, he was aware also of the first intimation of a feeling that surprised him—relief. It came, he decided, in knowing that someone else knew too. The slight comfort it began to generate was eclipsed, however, by the anxiety that had always accompanied life with Kate, a distress and uncertainty that was screaming now like a fire alarm inside him, growing louder and louder as the evening wore on. And in this current sequence of an old scenario, the nearness of Ted and old family friends brought some peace to him despite his alarm. He looked at them, enjoying one another, and he smiled. Kate sat across the room, yawning and watching Ted like a dazed hawk, instructing him every few minutes in whatever he was doing. A time that could have been so pleasant was once again turned into a bad dream, and this time it was a nightmare. No trial for homicide in his past, no appalling crime scene, none of Kate's anger or broken promises or lies, no fit of rage by his former students had ever boiled up pain, mental and physical, as acute as he felt on that evening. As he talked with everyone and helped put the children to bed and lock the doors, he wondered if he would lose his mind. So close did he feel to her, and so bound up in her were his life and dreams, that a crises in her disturbed him to his very core.

Hearing Ted's voice, holding him on his lap and feeling the comfort of his warm lanky body, spread healing and hope through Joe like a medicinal balm. He would do anything for this beloved child. He would die for him. He had felt the same way about Kate years ago and still harbored for her a love that burned again no matter how many times it was dashed and stirred to ashes. Somewhere in him was a balance that forever returned in his wife's direction, an internal instrument that swung back continually toward hope, toward the benefit of the doubt, toward the most charitable interpretation of her words and deeds, toward the promise of a peaceful future when there would be peace in their home. When he looked at himself in the mirror and tried to see if he saw a fool or an enabler staring back, his faith and reason convinced him that God was good and that God had called him into this marriage, given them their child, and God would empower him to bear with Kate in her addiction until they arrived at a place of health and serenity. He knew there were better times ahead. He knew that his efforts to make a decent home were right and honorable. He loved his family. God was good. He should be patient.

With hope and confusion battling despair and resignation inside him, he carried his struggling son up the stairs behind Dave, who preceded him with a daughter draped over each shoulder, as Dave's small son raced ahead to lock them all out of the bedrooms. Ted's soccer team was scheduled to play the next day at 10:00 a.m., and it would take a while to get there, so Ted was going to bed at nine on Friday night with a minimum of complaining. The three younger children were content to go to bed when he did. Joe tucked Ted in and kissed him good night, while Dave's son snuggled into his Cub Scout sleeping bag on the floor beside the bed. In the next room, Dave and Tonette settled their little girls into the twin guest beds. After a half-dozen trips to the bathroom and drinks of water all round, the children settled down to whispers, and the house grew quiet.

As the three adults came downstairs, Kate was coming up the basement steps with a stack of paperback novels for Tonette, books she had read and now wanted to pass along. The four of them talked for a while, listening occasionally for sounds from above, giving the children time to fall asleep before they too went up to bed. Kate, visibly tired and stifling yawns, announced she would see everyone in the morning and went up to bed about 9:30 p.m. The Gallaghers went up with her, everyone whispering good night as they closed their bedroom doors.

Joe sat at the kitchen table and waited. He tried to read the newspaper but could not concentrate. The merry-go-round in his mind filled him with sad music and woeful images. He went out to the driveway and checked the car windows. He spent a few minutes in the cool evening air with his dog. Cory's presence and warmth were reassuring. In a strange way, they nearly brought him to tears, tears that "rise in the heart and gather to the eyes," he heard himself say, half aloud. Joyful as his little dog was to have had the companionship of the children all evening and to visit with Joe alone for a few minutes, Cory sensed his friend's deep unease and was moved to whimper a little as he burrowed his face beneath Joe's arm. It amazed Joe at how accurately Cory could discern his feelings. He felt like hiding his face too.

When he had locked the garage door and returned to the kitchen, Dave and Tonette were already seated at the table, Tonette in her nightgown and Dave in a T-shirt and boxer shorts. Joe offered tea or soft drinks, but neither wanted anything. As he filled a glass with ice and water for himself, they began to ask questions. Dave too had found something about Kate to be alarming and wondered if it had been there all along. Neither had seen her for over a year, but both had been thinking back all evening to when they had lived in the same neighborhood in Dorchester. Joe began to tell them quietly about Kate's drinking, amazed that he was discussing it outside a therapist's office. He talked about how he had tried and failed to control it. They listened, interrupting now and then to ask questions. They had noticed a great deal more than Joe would have imagined, and he began to understand that others had as well. They asked about Kate's excessive secretiveness, which had always struck them as odd, and about her perpetual cheerfulness, which people had never found quite convincing. They told Joe that other people, after getting to know Kate, had the distinct feeling that she was keeping many things to herself. Dave had wondered at first if she was happy in her marriage to Joe or in his decision to study for holy orders. Joe was shocked to learn that until they had lived in Dorchester for some months and people had come to know them better, some had wondered if Kate went away to Wicomico during the summer to get away from him. It was a long time for a wife and child to stay away from home. Tonette and others had wondered about Kate's childhood after meeting Catherine. They had concluded that it was her mother who made Kate seem disconcerted, and suspicion had shifted from Joe to Catherine. People had been heard to comment that Kate became distracted and moody when her mother was with them.

They told Joe a few things about Kate's relationship with other people that astonished him. It was well-known that Kate did not get along well with the other mothers who were Cub Scout sponsors. Many of the soccer parents had found her difficult. People had speculated that she was having difficulty at work, but nobody had heard anything to confirm it. She was not especially sensitive to the feelings of others, although not at all to a degree that had caused alarm or even much comment. Still, it had been noticed. Generally people liked her, but nobody felt close to her. Even Tonette found her "hard to read," as she put it. None of it was enough to worry anybody, and only occasionally was it even a topic of conversation. Still, it was what people thought, and they had all wondered at times what truly "made Kate tick," as Dave said. They both agreed that many things made sense now.

Joe listened to all this in perplexity and a growing grief. Most of it was familiar to him from his own experience. Some of what they said made him think back to the early years of their marriage, when he was learning about Kate's inner life the hard way. Some of it was real news; he was hearing for the first time, for instance, of the widespread knowledge of Kate's touchy relationship with others. He had not known there had been friction with other soccer parents. Nor had he seen any marked difference in Kate's temperament when her mother was with them. Or had he? Yes, in the beginning, definitely. And he remembered their real estate agent, when they were trying to sell the Dorchester house, insisting that Joe be present at critical moments. Joe recalled him even delaying certain things until he could be present, when Kate was readily available. He was surprised to hear that people found Kate different at her Wicomico house in the summer. He knew, of course, about the mellowing effect of her summer-long idyllic beach vacations, with no responsibilities and complete relaxation, where she was in charge and not forced to share power and everyone responded to her wishes and directions. But he had not known that others perceived it, and he felt very foolish for his own blindness. ("Who wouldn't be a different person," said Dave.) He expressed his surprise at some things, agreed with them on most of their observations, questioned them on others. He took perhaps a bit of wholly unwarranted satisfaction in learning that nobody had ever suspected Kate of abusing alcohol. In fact, according to the Gallaghers, it would come as a surprise to many of their mutual friends to know that she drank at all. Everyone assumed that her mother's drinking had so devastated Kate's family life that Kate would be the last, the very last, person to get involved with it herself. Dave and Tonette, for instance, had never seen her touch alcohol. He was beginning to understand now how thoroughly and tragically she had learned to hide what she was doing and how he had fulfilled the role of enabler.

"I never wanted Ted to know. He dotes on her. I never wanted to do anything to hurt that relationship," said Joe, with his face in his hands.

"What makes you think you would have hurt him by letting him know his mother had a medical problem?" said Tonette, with a reasonable touch of severity.

"Joe, this is the…maybe the tenth time you've mentioned Ted. It's Kate who has the problem," said Dave.

"But look at his age," said Joe. "He's just a little boy, just turned twelve a few months back. I want him to have a good life. He is our child. Our only child."

"What does that have to do with her drinking?" said Dave.

Joe looked at him, surprised. The question made no sense.

"Why do you keep coming back to Ted?" said Tonette. "I mean, I think I know, but it would help to…"

"Because he is my son. Kate and I brought him into the world. I want him to have a good life, a stable home, a happy childhood. Every time Kate took him out in the car since he was born, I've worried about what might happen. I've taken him out of her car when she's been drinking. I've tried to hold us all together…as a family. I've kept waiting for Kate to change. I go to Al-Anon. I follow the advice of family counselors, whom Kate refuses to see. I want to help her, but she refuses… She lives with her head in the sand. Don't I have a duty to protect him from the fallout of all that! It goes on and on, and she doesn't change. So I have tried to change. I work on my own issues, my own serenity. I change my own habits. I leave alcohol totally alone, except for communion wine. I try to do what the counselors have said. I've tried to model the kind of family relationships that…"

Joe was so agitated that he did not hear the door open and close upstairs. Dave held up his hand and looked toward the door. They all fell silent and waited until they heard the feint gush of the toilet overhead. The sound grew louder as the bathroom door was jerked open and small footsteps pounded away down the hall. A door closed.

"It's Luke," said Dave with a smile. "Every night, about an hour after that last drink of water."

Tonette reached across the table and placed her hand on Joe's wrist. "What can we do?" she asked.

"Would you help me talk to her?"

"An intervention…," said Dave.

"Tomorrow night," said Tonette. "After the children are in bed."

"And we have to… We must not let her know that something is up," said Joe. "And if it comes across as criticism, she'll blow up. Or more likely, she'll be understanding and agreeable with you all and drop out of the discussion the minute she can and blow up at me after you all leave on Sunday."

They talked a little more and decided to try to get Kate's agreement to enter a twenty-eight-day treatment program. Joe would drive her to a hospital as soon as services were over on Sunday. The Gallaghers would stay with Ted until he returned, and then they would return home on Monday morning. The three of them held hands as Joe led them in a prayer for Kate and for all people troubled by addiction, and they ended by saying together the Lord's Prayer. Dave cried. Tonette hugged Joe. He hugged them both, and they went up to bed.

Chapter Twenty-One

Alone at the kitchen table, his mind retraced the past few hours, and the house and its sleeping tenants awaited whatever he would do now. His mouth was dry, and his face had assumed the sad perplexity that for years his friends had come to recognize and ponder, unconscious evidence of a private turmoil. He drank water and got up several times to refill his glass, standing at the sink with the water running as he searched his mind for a way forward. He knew there was no answer in himself and that resolution, if there was one, lay beyond him, with others. The influence he had never had, and never would have, had been in other hands all along, or it might not exist at all, and the loneliness folded around him like a heavy blanket. He knew he should go to bed, but sleep would be impossible now. He thought about the future. He pondered a dozen different contingencies, each a confused daydream of protecting Ted and Kate entering treatment, all of them familiar territory explored a hundred times before, and none of them likely to happen. What would come of their talk with Kate tomorrow night? Would she be honest? Would she face reality? Could she relent and agree to enter treatment? He knew her first concern would be for her job. He could handle that; all those years in the law must be worth something. He would explain it in a way that preserved her privacy and her position and assured her of the time she needed. Hervey's first concern would be business as usual, with no inconvenient or unpleasant interruption and no damaging gossip. Joe could reassure him, and he would.

Years of experience warned him it was far more likely that Kate would react defensively, retreating deeper into her denial. He dreaded the slow anger that would begin to smolder and the dozens of ways it would flare up at him over the coming months. The few times he had succeeded in getting her into treatment had always ended after a visit or two. He had always paid for it. She manipulated him and situations with an inventive dexterity that met every challenge, justifying almost anything, with a straight face and convincing manner. One way or another she would maneuver until she got what she wanted. In that case, what were the options? What would he do? If she were determined to shield herself regardless of the cost to those around her, he would act in Ted's best interests. He had always thought that doing that meant keeping them all together as family, providing a nice home and planning for the best future he could manage. But how does one do that alone in a marriage? They could continue on as they were, of course. That would satisfy Kate until she left him. She was good to Ted despite her bad examples and spoiling him unmercifully. Continuing on would mean renewed effort on his part to adapt, finding new ways to cope as calmly as possible. Could he continue on alone as a single man with a defiant teenage daughter and twelve-year-old son? The hard part would be accepting the frustration and converting it to…what?…without losing his serenity, his sense of humor, his patience and respect for her. Could he do it? He didn't know. She refused to budge. But Ted would change. He was growing up, personable, perceptive. Soon he would notice things. The experts assured him that Ted already knew more than he imagined.

He would not consider leaving Kate. It would be cowardly, an abandonment of his marriage vows to her and to God and a failure to live up to his vocation. God had blessed him with a wife, a child, family, responsibilities, and all of it clearly "in sickness and in health." And even if he did leave her, he knew the risks of trying to win custody of Ted in court. Who would believe him? He had kept her secret so well that even he was blind to it now, as the events of the evening had made clear. He could imagine her on the stand, playing the role of innocent, good-natured, put-upon wife and mother and playing it with an expertise and timing as though her life depended upon her performance. And in her world of denial, it would. That is how she would see it. If keeping her secret, son, and job were at stake, her performance would put Helen Hayes and Meryl Streep to shame.

And if they continued as they were now, even if Ted never understood, how long could he handle the loneliness, the social isolation? Having no one at home to confide in, talk to, the prospect of more years of it was depressing. He could only listen now to her complaints of being unappreciated and misunderstood, of how difficult and unfair her life was, and of how unreasonable the people around her were. He could only listen and look, drained of things to say to her, wearied of trying to make her happy. Their friends were all more fortunate than she was, and with each of them, there was some sort of problem. Everyone in authority was unfair, and Joe had come to realize finally that he was one of them. She was not about to cooperate with him. Despite all her ill-defined beliefs about equality for women, she still refused to live together as partners, and he was coming to realize that she didn't want to. Maybe criticism was the only way she knew how to relate to others. He was ashamed of himself for not understanding these things more clearly after fifteen years of living and sleeping with her. He knew he would not be able to heal their marriage or himself on his own. She refused to participate. How long could a man go on changing himself?

He sat at the table and drank his water and explored the chaos in his head. After a while, he needed health and wholeness, and he began to pray. He prayed for Kate, Ted, and the Gallaghers. He prayed for healing. He prayed for his sick father, for the people of Redeemer, and for old friends. He prayed because he knew his prayer was being heard, and the assurance of that connection between him and the Creator of the Universe comforted him in ways he could not describe. His mind and heart spluttered like his old lawn mower when he fired it up for the first time each spring, hungry for attention and adjustment and tuning. It was a physical longing, like thirst or starvation. His prayer was fitful and uneven as always but especially now as he trailed off into tangents and expressed himself poorly. Even in his distraction, he remembered the advice he always gave others in counseling; it is not our praying but Christ's listening that cleanses and clarifies our relationship with God. Christ knew his heart long before his troubled words ascended like incense to heaven, and Christ would receive them and correct anything amiss and make them acceptable and whole. Truth, compassion, clarity, rightness. They were there, built into the moral structure of creation. Would he ever know them on this end of things? *Come unto me, all ye that travail and are heavy laden, and I will refresh you.* God had promised to share our journey and raise us up on the last day. There were no promises that life would be easy or comprehensible, that bad things would not happen or that evil would not appear to triumph in the short run.

He got up and walked around the kitchen in distraction, and his eyes fell upon a series of Ted's soccer photos on the refrigerator door. In his blue-and-white uniform, his son gazed into the kitchen, smiling. *And when in time to come your son asks you, "What does this mean?" you shall say to him, "By strength of hand the Lord brought us out..."*

His motivation was sincere, but his hope and patience were decomposing like road kill in the summer sun. He was used to praying with all sorts of people, in every sort of crisis. But alone now in his own crisis, in his own home, with his wife and son asleep above him, it took all his focus and concentration to keep his attention from straying in a thousand directions. He dug the heels of his hands into his eyes and saw Kate's face emerge in the blooming purple that rose in the darkness. Dreams. Plans. Hope. External circumstances. It had been a hard week. People wanted time with him. Not with him but with his collar, with what he represented. He had done the best he could. He loved them all. He was certain he had made mistakes, that was a given, but it was not all up to him. He was a mere turnkey. He had so looked forward to a peaceful, congenial weekend with his family and old friends.

He got up and stared for a moment at his reflection in the window above the sink. A man looked back at him, preoccupied, weary, resigned, angry. Who was it? Sometimes he did not know. He went down to the cellar and in descending the stairs heard in his head, *The seeds of love in madness stretch their roots,* and he sat down on the bottom step. He did love her, and that truth gained clarity like a gold nugget emerging from the silt in a panning tray tilted to and fro, washing away all but the precious treasure. Prayer did that to him, revealing truth and organizing his understanding in following hours and days as he turned and tilted in the flowing dust around him. He knew it was a gift, pure and uncomplicated and easily missed in its quietness and simplicity. He was certain that in his ego and distraction he missed such moments more than he caught them, and maybe that was meant to be. And even when he caught them, he did not always understand. He loved her, but it was different now. He wanted the best for her, he wanted her to thrive, but there was a distance now, and he knew it, and it made him ashamed of himself. Was it pity he felt for her? Yes, but not exactly pity; there was something more or less. The quality that was slipping away was tenderness. What was replacing it? What was a word for compassion and lamentation blended together with sympathy and, what else?

He shook his head, almost a shudder, and got up. He went to the corner where Kate had heaped her sewing supplies in a disorganized pile. He searched, being careful to replace the clutter exactly as he found it. As haphazard as it looked, he knew she would know instinctively that he had been going through her things. He searched the dusty boxes containing the accumulation of years of teaching, carefully lifting and replacing bundles of old tests given to students no longer recalled, instructions for office equipment that had become obsolete a decade ago, and stacks of outdated laboratory supply catalogues. He had tried for years to get her to sort it all out and throw some of it away, but she met his requests with silence, whether out of attachment to such things or in defiance of him, he did not know. He was about to go back upstairs when he saw a pile of books heaped up on the floor like kindling, their backs and pages bent open and twisted. He recognized them, some of his art books. He pulled out a copy of Janson's *History of Art* and a large paperback folio of Robert Crumb's cartoons and smoothed the wrinkled pages and assembled the rest of the pile into a stack. Behind them, on the bottom shelf of the bookcase where the books had been, was a collection of paper sacks and canvas tote bags. The first two sacks he examined held what appeared to be the dusty old contents of desk drawers: pens and pencils, pennies, colored markers without tops, rusty paper clips, and small wrinkled pads bearing the name of the high school where Kate taught before their marriage. Behind these was a large canvas tote bag bearing the legend Got My Stuff Together in big block letters. In this was a paper shopping bag containing a large gallon box of white wine with a plastic spigot on the bottom and a small jelly glass wedged into the bag beside it. A sales receipt was in the bag too showing the name of the convenience store where Kate routinely bought gasoline, stamped with yesterday's date.

He closed his eyes, and instantly a chaotic, angry vacation week at Wicomico, years before, came to mind. Kate and her mother had almost come to blows over Catherine's drinking. Catherine had violently denied having any alcohol all summer. On his last day there, Kate had come to him and said, with triumphant resignation, "Well, I found Mom's little cache. It was under a pile of stuff in the storage room." Here he was now, feeling his own resignation, and not at all triumphant.

Sadness and anger clashed inside him like rams butting heads, with sadness still dominating by a little. It was pitiful, he thought, pitiful. Some white wine, it would gladden hearts in other times and places. Such a small matter, pitifully small, but with implications no one would understand who had not lived with denial, hostility, subterfuge, fear, and all the other characteristics of the self-destructive life. People died of it. Love, relationships, reputations, intimacy, respect, careers, self-esteem all died of it, and there was nothing small or pitiful about any of that. He felt so dreadfully sorry for Kate, so unspeakably sorry, and exasperated and lonely all at once. And for the three of them as a family, he felt the same fear that came with news of his father's cancer or parishioners who were confronting Alzheimer's in themselves or a loved one, and the despair of loneliness chilled his heart. How could he help her? How could he help her help herself? What could he do for the three of them as family? In the melancholy and sympathy he felt for Kate and his uncertainty about the future, he could feel already the heat of pain and trouble that lay ahead. The agony of the past flooded in again, and he stood up and coughed a few times. After a while, he put the receipt into his shirt pocket and lifted the wine box and balanced it on one hand. He judged it to be half full, maybe a bit less. He put the box and bag back in their hiding place, replaced the books around them, and went upstairs.

It was almost 1:00 a.m. He could feel his genuine sorrow for Kate turning into anger. Once again, for the ten thousandth time, she had made a mess and left it to him to clean it up or live in the filth and turmoil. It was his choice, and if it caused him grief, well, that was his problem, not hers. The whole thing was his problem, he could hear her saying. Certainly not hers. She slept soundly now up in their bedroom, and here he was at the kitchen table again in the middle of the night, wondering what to do. In the morning, she would present herself to Ted as a rested, cheerful, innocent alternative to his chronically tired, distracted, colorless father. He became furious as the familiar scene played out again in his mind.

He knew it was wrong to feel this way. In Al-Anon, they worked on resolving anger and restoring serenity. It had saved his life, his sanity. But what made her denial so ironclad? Why did she refuse to do anything about it? She would complain to him relentlessly about her own mother and how terrible it was to be responsible for someone like that while refusing to see her own effect upon her own husband and son. It was genetic. It was not a moral failure or a character defect. But none of his hard-earned knowledge softened the concussion of her ironclad denial. Was she *that* afraid of appearing less than perfect? Was her desire for her own image truly more important than the erosion of trust and intimacy that had been progressing day by day, year after year? Was alcohol worth all the arguments, lies, misunderstandings, manipulative secretiveness, sarcasm, anger, maneuvering, depression, meanness... She must be suffering, but from what? Was it him? Was it genes? Was it her job? He thought she loved him. He knew she loved Ted. She seemed to like her job as much as she had liked any other job and complained about the people and the students no more than she had in other places. They had a wonderful son. They had a beautiful home. Joe did all the work; all she had to do was enjoy it. She had her family vacation home and spent all summer there. They were getting on their feet financially. She could have friends if she wanted them, but having close friends came with certain risks. They were taking care of Catherine, and Joe was protecting Kate from her brother's meanness as much as he could. His own family loved her and was more faithful and caring toward her than were her own mother and brother. Joe knew she loved his family too.

He was no prize, and he knew it. He was not the best-looking man by far. He had made his share of mistakes, certainly. He knew he was growing more and more tired, and he knew that made him impatient and less and less attractive. At times he knew he made Kate angrier the harder he tried to get things right. She had contempt for many of his friends although they were always nice to her. Maybe if he had stayed in the law... If he could have earned more money, so she would not have to work. But he could not imagine her not working. As much as she complained about it, next to Ted, her job was the most important thing in her life. He had accepted years ago that her validation came from Ted and her teaching. Although she was not terribly obvious about it to others, and it slipped out in subtle ways usually between the two of them, he had accepted long ago that she found him frustrating, embarrassing, and dull. She would not listen to him explain himself, turning the conversation immediately to herself whenever he tried to talk to her about his feelings, thoughts, dreams. Still, he should pay more attention to her, be more affectionate, and listen to her more. He thought he heard, in the back of his mind, somebody singing over and over, *You were always on my mind. You were always on my mind.*

Joe found his briefcase in the dining room and brought his address book and the telephone to the kitchen table. He called Kate's oldest friend, a woman who had taught her in college and with whom she had kept up a friendship for many years. She now worked at a junior college in South Carolina. Kate saw her in the summer and when Karla visited them during school holidays during the year. It was too late to be calling anybody, and he apologized as soon as Karla answered. He could hear her television in the background. She assured him it was all right. He was used to speaking in tense situations, but he surprised himself, having to struggle to control the emotion in his voice as he told her he needed her help for Kate. He explained what had occurred earlier that evening. Karla said she knew Dave and Tonette; she had met them several times in Wicomico. She listened for a few moments and then began to interrupt with questions in a tone of voice that confused him with its sharpness.

"Why are you calling me? Just what in the world do you expect me to do?" she said, severe and alarmed. "You are talking about my best friend!" She said it as though he was doing something very wrong. For a moment he considered reminding her that he was talking about his wife too, but he let it pass and went on.

"That's why I'm calling you," he said. "You are her oldest friend. Was she in trouble with alcohol when you first knew her? Would you help convince her to get some treatment? She might accept it from you."

"I'll tell you one thing, mister!" Karla shouted. "If Kate did have a drinking problem, the first thing you'd have to do would be to get *yourself* into treatment! Anybody who is married to an alcoholic is sick, sick, sick!"

Analytical skills honed through years of listening to testimony were beginning to hum in Joe like a reliable old engine. The emotion he had felt a moment before was rapidly being replaced by reason and surprise. He sat back in his chair and smiled. "I've been a member of Al-Anon for years," he said calmly.

There was a pause. He recognized the sound of a scene from the old movie she must have been watching on her VCR. He waited. Her hostility amazed him. What had he said? He was seeking the help of Kate's best friend, in a matter of Kate's health. Was Karla shocked? Is that why she seemed to grow angrier as they talked?

After a very long pause, he heard her say, "You can't tell me anything about alcoholism. I am an alcoholic. My ex was an alcoholic. I have a son and a daughter who are alcoholics. I can tell you a few things, and the first thing is that you need to get yourself into treatment!" There was utter contempt for him in her voice, and she made no effort to disguise it.

"I already told you I am a member of Al-Anon," he said calmly. "And if you know so much about alcoholism, Karla, why didn't you know that your best friend is an alcoholic?"

There was a very long pause, so long that Joe thought she might have left the line. He listened intently and could still hear the dialogue of *Terms of Endearment* from her television. "All I'm asking," he pleaded, "is for you to back us up. Call her Sunday afternoon and urge her to get treatment, go to AA, enter family counseling, anything. Just support us. It will make a difference to her. She'll listen to you. Aren't you in AA?"

It was hard to tell if Karla was bitterly angry now or confused or what. She snapped at Joe that she didn't know what she was going to do, but she certainly would not decide until she spoke with Kate first. She was not a member of AA, she said, because it was not for everybody. She was handling it on her own. She would make no promises to him, she said, and frankly didn't know what else she could do for him. Without agreeing to help, she hung up.

He was stunned. He had experienced countless surprises and unexpected reactions in teaching, the law, ministry. But Karla dumbfounded him. Was her reaction harsh because the whole matter was personal to her or to him? He had always suspected that she had never liked him, but he was never sure. She had taken issue with his views and career choices. Like most people, she did not conceal her dislike of lawyers, and she appeared to have no faith, living a wholly secular life. Her disfavor had never exceeded a mild sarcasm, however, and he did not see her often, leaving him in doubt as to whether he was interpreting her attitude toward him correctly. In all the time Kate and Karla had spent talking, shopping together, traveling, had they never discussed drinking? And both alcoholics? Such a revelation would not confound him in later years, but for now, he was astonished.

He thought back to a few weeks following their wedding, to the lengthy trip Kate and Karla had taken together. He couldn't go anywhere with Kate because of his trial schedule (his office had to rearrange cases for months before each lawyer's vacation could take place), and he and Kate had put off their honeymoon till the summer vacation. But eventually Kate had cried and complained that she never went anywhere and assured him that she could make the trip with Karla for fifteen hundred dollars. So they had gone (he was never told where; she didn't even telephone), and Kate returned after three weeks, grumpy and angry at having to return to her new home. On this trip, Kate had run up thousands and thousands of dollars in credit card expenses, which she proceeded to pay off in monthly sums from her salary, carefully hiding the fact from Joe until, after a couple of years of living on his salary alone, he figured it out for himself. Approaching it as gently as he could, without anger, he finally convinced her to let him have her bills, cut up all but one of her credit cards, and begin depositing her earnings in their family checking account. He had never discussed it with anyone and never mentioned it to her again, fearing her wrath.

He drank a glass of water and stared at his reflection again in the blackness of the kitchen window. Beyond the cold glass, Cory came into focus, sitting on the terrace and watching Joe intently as he stared from the lighted window. Cory began to twitch, and his tail started to thump as soon as Joe became aware of him, as though the little dog knew the moment when he had entered Joe's thoughts.

The incident of the credit cards made him angry after all these years. He supposed it was the ridiculous telephone discussion with Karla that had brought it all back. He sat down again at the table and flipped through his address book. What was the right thing to do? Was he betraying Kate in seeking help? He felt guilty but knew it was foolish, a feeling completely unwarranted in the current situation. Perhaps he should feel guilty for not having approached those closest to her before now. Yes, he was a shit for not having done it, for imagining all those years that he could save her, protect her, and rescue their family. Maybe his way of dealing with it had even made it possible for her to continue in denial. He sat still for a while with his eyes closed. He was such a fool. Such a bastard. Then he picked up the receiver and dialed the number of Kate's brother's home in Georgia.

With this call, he had no doubt he would wake up whoever answered. They went to bed the way Kate did, at nine or ten o'clock every night, including weekends. On the fourth ring, the sleepy, startled voice of Ray's wife, Fawn, said "Yes! Hello!" Trying to control his voice, Joe apologized sincerely and told her it was not an emergency but that he needed to talk with Ray, realizing as he said it how ridiculous it sounded at 2:00 a.m. It was, he added, a medical problem… that had just come up…sort of.

Fawn was a pleasant, good-natured sort who told him it was all right and that Ray would be glad to speak with him. They both knew this was hardly the truth, and he silently appreciated her good manners. She told him to hold on and then put her hand over the speaker. After a minute, he heard Ray's flat, indifferent voice say, "Yeah?"

Joe explained what had happened that evening and told him that he had dealt with alcohol problems with Kate, as well as Catherine, which Ray knew already, although they had certainly never discussed it, as long as they had been married. He apologized to him for not saying anything earlier and assured him he had tried to get Kate into treatment for years, that he was trying to do the right thing for her, and that he knew she would want no one to know. He talked calmly for three or four minutes. He concluded by saying that, as Kate's closest kin, he thought Ray needed to be involved. Joe felt he should know what was going on and help make some plans for addressing it. He asked him for his support in encouraging Kate to enter treatment.

Ray listened in silence, except for twice saying, "Well, my, my." He asked no questions, offered no advice, and made no observations. He did not mention Kate's name. At the end of Joe's recitation, he said immediately, as Joe concluded his final word, "Well, let me give all this some thought, and I'll get back to you." He thanked Joe briskly for calling and said goodbye and hung up. His tone had been detached and noncommittal throughout. Joe could not know then that it was the last time Ray would speak to him in his life.

Joe sat at the table for a long time. He thought over the words of his wife's brother and her best friend. Their reactions made him feel worse for Kate than he already felt. If a call for help went out among his own family or friends in the middle of the night or at any other hour, a half-dozen people would have hit the road or gotten on an airplane immediately. But not for Kate, or Catherine either. Each was alone in so many ways. Much of their isolation was of their own choosing. He was conscious of how very much alone he was too at that moment, and he thanked God for the presence of Dave and Tonette and their children. He thought of Ted. His love for his son was love of a different kind, of course, from what he felt for Kate, but still, the two most important people in his world were sound asleep above him.

He got up and turned out the lights. He found his flashlight and checked on the children. Little Luke Gallagher had nuzzled his sleeping bag tightly against the side of Ted's bed. Ted was sleeping in his usual position, on his stomach with his arms crossed under his pillow. Joe kissed him on his cheek, and the touch of his sleeping son was reassuring, calming, affirming in a nourishing and humbling way. Whatever messes existed in the world and in his life, and however much his own mistakes had brought them about, he and Kate had brought into the world this loving child. Everything about him was good. He was the delight of Joe's life. Bumbling and clumsy though he was as a husband, and as inept as a father, he supposed he was doing something right for God to have blessed his life with Ted. The thought made him feel clean and whole, and he stood in his son's dark bedroom for some minutes and experienced the sensation, so different from what else he had felt in the preceding hours.

He went into his bedroom and undressed in the dark. Kate's closeness in the room made him feel exhausted, confused, and sad. He was so tired he felt he could go to sleep standing straight up in the dark but suspected that a sleepless night lay ahead. The thought of confronting her the following evening terrified him. What would she do? How would she react? She was a convincing, practiced liar. He knew her denial would only make her disclaimers more convincing.

Suppose Tonette and Dave believed her? He considered the evidence. Tonette had smelled alcohol and had brought the matter up in the first place. He had found Kate's supply. The Gallaghers had known for years—others had too, apparently—that something was not quite right. Was this enough evidence to pierce her denial and make her speak honestly about what had been going on? What would happen when they talked with her? She could maintain her denial, as she had for so long with him, about drinking and so many other things. She could acknowledge just enough of the truth to satisfy the

Gallaghers and minimize the rest. He was familiar with this tactic. It could easily sidetrack the whole discussion. Or she could open up and talk about it all and go into treatment. People can change. Miracles happen every day in AA meetings. It could happen for Kate. He prayed it would.

As these thoughts churned in his mind, he became aware of the sound of Kate's relaxed breathing, interrupted by an occasional small snore. It was almost three o'clock. The children would be getting up in another four hours.

* * *

The next day should have been a relaxing and happy time with family and friends. It passed for Joe as had so many others, filled with the distracting struggles and anxiety that had marked his marriage. The uncertainty of life with Kate and the relentless vigilance he had learned to exercise in all things about her had taught him to search out peace when he could find it like a miner prying diamonds from the soil.

Cleaving to an old practice, he was determined to enjoy the time with Dave and the children despite the anxiety of family life. Today the first step was to stay awake and alert. As they drove over to Conner's Corner Park for Ted's soccer game, he drank coffee from a large thermos bottle propped up between the front seats. Kate had taken Tonette to St. John's School for a personal, private tour. Although his mind was malignant with fatigue and distractions, Joe silently, continually told himself to pay attention to the good things around him.

He listened to Dave talk about their mutual friends back in Dorchester and about his colorful family in New Zealand. Ted asked Joe a dozen questions about his game and renting a movie for later in the evening, what they would do tomorrow, and why he had to conduct services every Sunday. The three little Gallaghers, thrilled to be in unknown parts and excited about seeing Ted again, chattered away with abandon. In response to Ted's pleas, he spun the radio dial searching for a rock station. Dave wanted to stop at a convenience store to buy a newspaper so they could review the racing results from Bowie and Charles Town. Five minutes after this stop, Polly Gallagher announced an immediate need to use the bathroom. Hovering in the background for Joe, and certainly for Dave, who was a fair, decent man, was the ominous shadow of the coming evening confrontation. As he paid attention to the world around him, Joe's thoughts returned continually to his wife. Would she blow up? Would she agree to treatment? How would Dave and Tonette handle it? Would she sweet-talk them into believing her? How should they begin? How would she behave after the Gallaghers left for home?

Joe had learned in dozens of trials how to divide his attention conscientiously to focus on his thoughts and listen to others effectively at the same time. Throwing Kate into the mixture, however, affected his concentration in ways that the facts of no homicide, crying rape victim, or molested children had ever been able to do, stirring up his emotions and fragmenting his reason with fiendish magic all her own. He recognized the trap and shook his head and drank coffee and refocused repeatedly on Dave's easygoing monologue about taking the children on a white-water rafting trip. Did Joe want to go? Would Ted go too? Joe said it sounded like a great idea.

The fields below the mountains were brightening in delicious shades of green across swelling vistas that would have thrilled Cezanne and Monet. Dogwoods and cedars lined the road like sentinels, and on both sides followed the paths of vanished fencerows out across the fields to distant dark woods. From tree to tree ran undulating hedges of blackberry and bittersweet, dividing the broad slopes into greening fields where it was known that hunters could find deer or flush quail any day of the year, in season and out. The land shimmered with the new spring colors of wild flowers, and the air was alive with birds. There had been enough rain in recent weeks to swell the creeks, and in low places the fields were covered in thin transient pools of standing water that blazed in the sun. The rising land receded in the distance into the smoky shadows under the trees, the lower fringes of an ancient forest that swept up and over the mountains like a vast blanket draped over them as far as anyone could see.

They drove up through the low gap called Chester's Hole between Coldstream Ridge and the endless mass of Massaponasette Mountain, an escarpment that meandered southward for thirty miles in an even slope that faded in the blue distance. Indians had crossed the high ground here for centuries, following the migrating buffalo and bound for their weirs on the great valley rivers. The gap widened out on the eastern side a mile below the top, and the road ran down through a descending series of small level fields that locals called Johns Flats, after an early settler who homesteaded there before the French and Indian War. Joe told the spellbound children about the Seneca war party that scalped the settler and his son and kidnapped the wife and daughters and took them all the way to Ohio. He pointed to the far side of the overgrown fields to hollows where old hardwoods towered like rugged giants, some of the largest and oldest trees in the east, where the forest floor was a carpet of packed leaves as soft and silent as industrial felt. They all wanted to stop the car and hike into the woods immediately. Even Ted, who had heard Joe talk about such things all his young life and endured them now with bored patience, finding them much less intriguing than video games and special effects, was willing to forget his soccer game and explore the woods for signs of Abraham Johns and his vanished family. Joe talked about the deer and fox and occasional bear that wandered across the road and gave startled travelers something to talk about for years. He told them about the coyotes, invading now from the west. He said he was sure that from the gap southward down the mountains, cougars lived in lonely secrecy, coming back carefully into their ancestors' territory in recent years with stealth and courage.

Halfway down the gap on the eastern side was an ancient white oak standing in its own meadow with a few dead limbs protruding from its massive crown like antlers, victims of the polluting haze that swept through the mountains from as far away as Pittsburgh and Cleveland. This towering tree never disappointed Joe, always harboring a big red-tailed hawk, which sat on the same dead limb with folded wings, scrutinizing the mountainside with keen and deadly eyes. A mile before the great tree loomed into sight, Joe alerted everyone to the possibility of seeing a hawk and the little Gallaghers strained in their seat belts and began to shout a dozen frantic questions. Well knowing that if he saw the hawk fifty times in a row, this would be the one time it would be nowhere around, Joe was beginning to comment on the unpredictability of wild things when the tree appeared up ahead, and they could all see the big hawk perched in conspicuous, imperial grandeur. The children squealed as if beholding a pterodactyl, and three-year-old Mary, overcome with excitement, began to cry out loud. Ted was skeptically unimpressed in the way of those about to become teenagers, and Joe remembered with delight the days when his son had also been intrigued by the wildness of nature. Dave wanted to stop for a picture and leaned backward over the seat to comfort Mary. Joe parked the van well off the road, and the children, getting out quickly, clamored out and over the tumbled stone fence into the meadow like a pack of young hounds. To Joe's amazement, the big hawk held its perch during the commotion below long enough for Dave to take a half-dozen photos from different angles. Regarding them all with great interest, the big red tail shifted slightly on its limb, and they could see its white belly, tinged with a pale rufous wash, and the pink underside of its shortish tail. Dave clicked his last picture and said something about running out of film, and as if waiting only for that, the big bird emitted a screech like a teakettle and sailed southward to a more secluded place.

In its springtime flush, the countryside was drenched in beauty that intoxicated Joe, and his cargo of son and old friends was a joy and a blessing. He talked about the surrounding land and answered Luke Gallagher's many excited questions. He found it comforting, a way to calm the anxiety that churned in him like a rotary mixer. In the few seconds now and then when he thought about it, his inner turmoil made him furious, and he felt anger toward Kate for it. The act of admitting his own resentment increased his anguish. It drained the joy and cleanliness from the day. His side, which had been hurting since the night before, was burning now less from the conflict he felt than from his desperate, bumbling efforts to resolve it.

So he chatted and steered the van carefully down the winding mountain road and tried to put up a good show, trying to make himself sound enthusiastic and grinning until his face hurt. He couldn't tell if he was bringing it off. He thought he might be because Ted had said nothing to him to indicate he could see into his father's preoccupation. How often had the same cares driven him to debilitating distraction, destroying peace of mind and much of what could have been good times. He was disgusted with himself for not handling it any better.

As a lawyer and a priest, he had known families with rebellious daughters, good girls in whose young lives something had gone terribly wrong. Increasingly defiant, moody, and withdrawn, sneaking out at night, descending lower and lower into a pit of drugs or sex or emotional illness, and often all of them together, running away and seeking out the most dangerous lifestyles and companions, they drove their parents and others who loved them to mind-numbing despair. It was always worse when a girl went bad. There was something safer perhaps, less fragile, with a boy, although when boys were lost, the anguish of love must be equally as painful, horrific in its own terrible way. He could not speak from experience, thank God, because he had never raised a daughter or lost a son, but he imagined that nothing could assuage the pain of a daughter drifting away. The loss of innocence, trust, intimacy, and all the other precious qualities, as a daughter receded beyond reach and her sacred personhood changed to something hideous and foreign, must be unlike any other sorrow. He had seen it reduce good men and women to bitterness and death, a living death in which, with rejection by a daughter, the heart had been ripped out of their lives. With Kate, Joe felt he knew something akin to the sting of that terrible pain.

His marriage had made him the surrogate father of a rebellious teenage daughter. He had not felt like a man with a wife since the earliest years of their marriage, when he began to understand that Kate was shutting him out of her thoughts, withholding her paycheck, hiding bills, neglecting their home, and lying whenever it suited her. He was married to a forty-five-year-old child who demanded adult respect and behaved like a spoiled teenager. If he did not like it, he could "just get over it," as she had pointed out to him briskly so many times over fifteen years. He had long understood she would have been relieved to see him go, leaving her in peace with the two parts of her life that mattered, her son and her career. It would have been so much simpler for her without his annoying insistence on discussion, counseling, sharing responsibilities, saving for the future, making decisions together. She would be free, he could hear her saying, of the cause of her unhappiness. He could imagine her saying all this to herself, and perhaps to Karla and a few others from her past, and then turning to the world with her deceptive friendliness and careful disengagement, a calculated, guarded image of composure, innocence, and efficiency.

He was beginning to accept that Kate, when her world ran counter to her desires, controlled it all with half-truths and lies. He was not willing to believe her motives were evil. He saw addiction as a medical problem, not a moral failure, regardless of its moral consequences for others. He was certain her behavior was wholly defensive, conditioned by her upbringing, calculated to protect herself from scrutiny and achieve her own desires. If the impact on others was destructive, it was a secondary consideration for her, if she considered it at all. Apart from Ted, he supposed she didn't consider others, however, because to do so would bring her face-to-face with the consequences of her own behavior. It was all painful and unpleasant and much too personal. So she lived in denial. She hid her inmost reality from almost everybody, and that included him. She had manipulated him for so many years that it had long ago begun to feel normal to both of them. Like a fool, Joe had joined in her denial, believing that in time life would change, she would mature, and he could help her change.

Ted adored her. He was her little boy, and his experience of her was different. Kate saw to that. She was good to him and loving, but even with Ted, her denial served her personal aims. As long as she was unwilling to face reality, all Joe could do against her inflexibility was bend, conform, adapt, and pray. He had married for better for worse, in sickness and in health. His marriage vows, and those he had made at ordination, confirmed a sacred duty to carry on and pursue healing. In living toward that blessing, he was meant to make a decent home, be a good father, and try to make a good marriage.

He believed that beyond the disorder existed a stupendous calm, a place of justice and fairness, and with the right vision, one could see the reality of it already breaking into the present. Once in a great while, he sensed the barrier grow thin and felt the cool tranquility of the other side. He thought of *Six Persimmons* by Mu-chi, the Chinese Ch'an painter. He could have coped forever, he believed, if there had been any sign, even the smallest one, that Kate recognized their plight, was dedicated to working on their issues, and valued his patience while she moved in that direction. Such a sign would have energized him, restored him with patience for another hundred years. Instead, an immovable denial as rigid as cast iron was leaching the life out of him. He took heart at each small hope, anticipating change, health, love. Each time he found himself in a new version of the same old story. After fifteen years, he knew the plot well.

At the park, a dozen clean, bright soccer fields lay in all directions, the municipal legacy of a wider tax base and more efficient state government than Catoctin Springs would ever know. Players were everywhere, running about or huddling with their teams and coaches, their colored jerseys and the concession stands and acres of parked cars giving the whole scene the atmosphere of a county fair. They found Ted's team a few minutes before the game and took up their position with the other team families on a long set of new red bleachers as Ted fell in with his buddies. Joe looked around and introduced Dave to the other parents seated nearby. Dave and one of the team mothers recognized each other from a sales conference in Chevy Chase the previous January, and they began to chat. The Gallagher children ran up and down the sidelines, keeping pace with the players on the field. Joe watched Ted's every move, marveling at how tall he was becoming and the new speed he was showing this season. He liked to walk the sidelines too but stayed in the bleachers this time in case Dave wanted to say anything about the evening ahead.

Chapter Twenty-Two

They were all going to church the following morning, so the children were in bed by nine. Ted turned in at the same time as the three little Gallaghers. It had been a long busy day, and by a quarter after nine, they were all quiet. The four adults drifted downstairs, and Tonette went into the kitchen and sat down at the kitchen table. The others, yawning and rubbing their eyes and laughing over something young Mary had said, followed her in. Dave sat down opposite her, and it seemed only natural for Joe to sit down too. Kate was about to say good night but seeing everyone sitting down, she lingered for a moment while the four of them discussed plans for the following day, and as they chatted happily, she sat down for a moment too. Joe felt the adrenaline and tensions that used to flood through him at the start of a trial, and for the first time in his life, he found that his palms were perspiring. The blistering pain that had developed in recent years seared like a third-degree burn in his gut.

The moment Kate had settled into her chair, Tonette took the lead, speaking sincerely and quietly, so deftly that Joe might have guessed she had a lot of experience with interventions.

"Kate," she said, staring straight at her old friend, "I'm concerned about you. I'm worried about your health. I wonder if you have any health problems that are getting you down?"

Kate became very still, and Joe could read the familiar small signs that her guard was assembling. With her eyes fixed upon Tonette and her face and voice expressionless, she said, "No. None that I can think of."

"Do you feel all right?" said Tonette.

"Yes, I'm fine," she replied without a second's hesitation and with no trace of emotion. There was a pause, and everybody looked at her, expecting something more: "What do you mean?" or "Why do you ask?" or "What's this all about?" Something. Anything. She kept her flat, inexplicable gaze directed at Tonette for a moment and then dropped her eyes and examined the tabletop.

Tonette said, "I know this is a surprise, and I don't want to alarm you, but I have a real concern that your health is not as good as you let on."

"Well, I'm fine," said Kate, with a shrug and the faintest hint of a smile. Another pause.

Dave spoke up. "Kate, I come from a family that has had its share of drinking problems. How about you?"

Kate shifted her eyes to Dave without turning her head and said, "No. Everybody's fine."

"What about your mother?"

"She's fine."

Tonette said, "But everyone seems to recognize that there's something. She's as cute as she can be, and we all just love her, but it's easy to see there's something—"

"Oh!" said Kate, sounding lighthearted and surprised, as though just reminded of something so small it had slipped her mind. "She had a little problem years ago, but we have been handling that, and it's not a problem anymore." Joe had been gazing at the place mat in front of him, and he looked up at her now, incredulously. She was careful not to look back at him. All four of them sat in awkward silence for a couple of minutes, Joe watching Kate, and the other three looking at the table.

"It may be none of my business, and I hope you'll excuse me for asking. Have you been drinking alcohol lately?" said Tonette.

"No."

"When is the last time you had a drink?" asked Dave, with great caution.

"I don't drink. Haven't for years. Really. I'm fine." She did not look at Joe but turned her eyes from Tonette to Dave and back again as she spoke, her head and body rigidly still.

For another fifteen minutes, the conversation went on like this, the Gallaghers asking their quiet sincere questions, in tones of pleading and concern, and Kate providing succinct, equivocal replies. Joe watched in amazement as these old friends confronted his wife about her use of alcohol, the only two persons to have done so, as far as he knew, other than himself. The same old familiar pattern was unfolding, and it couldn't be described as a conversation. They tried to get Kate to talk, and she turned away their every statement with a noncommittal, indifferent word or two.

Something in Dave's voice made him look up, and he saw that Dave was crying. Joe was moved by his old friend's tears but not wholly surprised. The frustration of the present situation was familiar, and he remembered the years when his own futile efforts to engage Kate and the sad loneliness that surrounded them had ended time after time in his own idle tears. Beyond tears now, he looked at Dave and Tonette and felt great empathy for them. They were decent people with the rare courage to do what they believed was right. How many others would have stayed out of it and spared themselves this troubling scene and waited to talk about it all in the car on the way home? Joe reached across to the old hutch and set a box of tissues on the kitchen table. Dave plucked one quickly without saying anything and pressed it to his eyes.

"Kate," said Dave. "You and Joe and Ted have been best friends to us since we met, and we feel you are family to us. If there is a problem in your life, it affects me just as much as if you were my own sister. Please, let's talk about this…"

At the mention of Ted's name, Kate's head turned for the first time since sitting down, jerking toward Dave as though he had made a loud noise. "I'm fine," she said, with a sound of determination, finality.

"When we arrived late yesterday afternoon, it was about four, four thirty, I think. I know I smelled alcohol when I hugged you when we came in," said Tonette.

"You didn't. I haven't had any," said Kate, looking at the table.

Dave blew his nose loudly and stuffed the tissue into his shirt pocket. "Kate, please let's talk. We're all the closest friends. I am truly worried because I smelled it too."

Kate looked at him, her bland face immobile. "Well, there's some alcohol in my cologne." She shrugged slightly and smiled, as though there was nothing more to say.

They all fell silent. Kate stared at the tabletop, her face still and expressionless. Joe had seen the same look more times than he could count, but seeing it directed at others was a new experience for him. Completely different from her look of anger and sarcasm, it was somehow more impenetrable and difficult. He felt for Kate a sort of protective sorrow that screamed inside him for her to open up, that these were people with the best of intentions, that here was a chance to turn and go in a new direction. He said nothing and did not move, unwilling to upset whatever delicate progress was being made.

For another half hour, Tonette and Dave continued to try to talk with Kate, coming at the subject gently from a dozen different directions, speaking respectfully, quietly, sincerely. Watching his wife's face, Joe felt the most profound conflict in his heart. Recollections of dozens of times he had approached her this way flooded back to him from many years, and for all the anger and frustration of those failed efforts, he could not deny the feeling of tenderness that arose, even now, when he looked at her impassive face. She was positioned defiantly on the far side of a widening chasm, and his every effort to reach her withered before tectonic forces he knew nothing about. Whether respectful and loving or frustrating and loud, all his attempts to cross the divide had been smoke in the wind. Kate's responses had been hostile, defensive and combative, or quiet and detached as they were now. He too had cried in trying to communicate with her, but she either took no notice or seemed to grow more difficult at his tears. She appeared to take his emotion as a sign of vulnerability and went on the attack like a foe smelling blood. After a few such confrontations, his alarm and surprise had turned to disgust, shame for her that his sincerity meant nothing to her and pity that her compassion and understanding were so terribly blunted.

Kate, he pleaded inside himself, as he had implored her in person so many times, *please talk. Let's discuss this. We can deal with it. We have a marriage, a child. Talk with me. Level with me. Let's get it out on the table and do something to make things better for all of us. Please. Why won't you face what's happening? It's a disease, not a moral failure. It's nothing to be ashamed of. Would you be ashamed of yourself if you had tuberculosis?*

For another fifteen minutes, Dave talked with Kate, telling her that everybody present loved her (to which Joe and Tonette loudly agreed), that it was her health that most concerned them, that we were family and friends and were meant to help one another in difficult times, that God's will for each of us was health and wholeness, and describing in some detail the terrible times his own family experienced during his father's drinking days. Kate listened patiently, nodding her head at intervals, smiling occasionally but still immovable, inscrutable, cautious. Joe and Tonette were moved. It was clear that Dave's heart was in every word as he hunched forward over the table toward Kate, his hands moving in the air for emphasis and dabbing at the corners of his eyes. Dave and Tonette, good-humored, outdoorsy and kind, in their own way were better ministers than some bishops he knew. They were certainly better at what was happening than he had ever been. Here they were, late on a Saturday night, doing what many others would have ignored or left to someone else, courageously and compassionately making a blessing of being a neighbor.

At the conclusion of Dave's final appeal, Kate said, without changing expression, "But I don't drink. I'm fine." They looked at each other in silence for several minutes. Tonette stared at the table, dabbing at her eyes. Joe watched Kate. Her expression never changed. Except for turning her head at the mention of Ted's name, she had remained fixed in the same position since they had all set down, her wagons circled, and her guards posted. Her hands remained exactly where she had casually placed them when they had all sat down.

Joe sat and watched. He was aware of his own heartbeat, wild and weary, his head pounding with tension and the ache in his innards. It was all familiar. Dave was visibly emotional, obviously searching still

307

for some way to break through. Tonette, chin resting in her hands, looked quietly down at the tissue on the table between her elbows. She straightened up and gazed for a moment toward the wall above Dave's head and finally put her face in her hands and rubbed her eyes. Joe was watching a reenactment of his every attempt to communicate with Kate, reason with her mother, and appeal to her brother. Regardless of the energy and emotion expended by others on their behalf, and despite the value to themselves and loved ones of what others were trying to say, they remained insulated in their denial, safely beyond the influence of love or reason. In such a process, the fatigue factor was always high and eventually defeated the most concerned patron. Dave and Tonette had reached that point.

He withdrew from his pocket the sales slip from the wine purchase and spoke up for the first time.

"Kate, last night...I was so worried...I tried to find...I didn't even know...what you had been drinking. It's gone on so long I didn't even know it this time. I found the box of wine downstairs and this sales receipt. It's dated yesterday."

"All right. It's mine," said Kate with the same flat tone and bland expression. For the first time, she looked at him.

"I love you, Kate. You're my wife. Ted is our son. We're a family. But I don't know… It's not the physical consumption of alcohol. It's the change in the way you act, think, the attitudes it seems to harden, the secrecy, the anger, your disposition. For years I've tried to get through to you. I feel bad about it all the time. I'm no expert in what makes life the way it is. It doesn't do you or me any good for me to go through life trying to figure out the motives and stresses that burden you. In the early days, I really wanted to know because I loved you, and I thought I could help. I still love you, and I always will, but this is something beyond me. One of the best things about Al-Anon"—at this, Kate shifted her position for the first time, pushing her chair back an inch—"has been how it helps me look at life in a different way. It has been as good as anything in church. If you would just do something for yourself, for us as a family, to sort some of this stuff out, I won't interfere...I'll support you...it could all be so different."

Kate dropped her gaze to the tabletop. He heard himself saying words he had said so many times before, and in his sinking heart understood that now, as then, they were making no difference. At the other end of the table, the same ironclad doors were sealed. Behind them, where he could not go or understand, the same resentment and rejection his words always stirred up were churning like a storm. Kate studied the table before her. He had watched her cautious scrutiny of Dave and Tonette. His instincts told him that his own approach was useless. She had heard it all before. Her guard went up at the mere sight of him. But Dave's and Tonette's presence was a blessing from God. Everything about their involvement was new, fresh, clean, innovative, penetrating. They were bringing to Kate's denial an influence that, as far as Joe knew, she had never encountered before. No such intrusion had ever penetrated her defenses. However tightly her doors were always closed, a fresh intervention was in progress for the first time. The relief Joe felt was like a transfusion.

Tonette spoke up. "Kate, you've said almost nothing."

Kate gave a small shrug. "What do you want me to say?"

Dave and Tonette began to speak at the same time, and Dave gestured to Tonette as though shoving something in her direction and cleared his throat. Joe got up and filled a glass with ice and water and gave it to Dave and poured some ice tea and set the glasses before Kate and Tonette. Tonette asked Kate if she would be willing to get some help.

"Sure," said Kate, as though nothing in the world could be simpler or more obvious.

Tonette turned to Joe with a look that he could not interpret. He wanted her to keep talking with Kate. He wanted Dave and Tonette to carry the conversation, conscious that they were making some progress and that Kate was conditioned to rebut his every word. But Dave turned to him too, and he understood that they were waiting for him to suggest some sort of treatment. Or perhaps they were too drained to try to go any further with her.

"Kate," Joe began, watching her as she examined the place mat in front of her. "There are all kinds of good ways to...get through this. AA is a fine, healthy program. There are excellent counselors who work with these…issues. They are all bound by law to keep their work with you private. There are excellent treatment programs at the hospitals in the metro area. There's no harm in any of this, no danger. Lives are changed every day." When it was clear he had ended his sentence, she folded her arms and looked down. Nobody spoke. After a moment, Kate took a long swallow of iced tea and leaned forward and folded her hands tightly on the edge of the table before her. She appeared to be waiting for whatever else they felt they needed to say. It was the old pattern. Joe knew she was waiting for them to finish so she could go to bed. It was almost eleven o'clock. He looked at her and felt a sudden flush of fatigue and anger that made his ears redden.

"This is wearing me down, Kate. It has been years. Speak up. Say something. We're doing the best we can." His voice was not so much angry as tired and exasperated. Tonette and Dave looked at Kate.

"What am I supposed to say?" said Kate matter-of-factly, with a small shrug.

He was conscious of his heavy heartbeat, and he could feel his face getting hot and tingly. He was as angry at his own ineptness as he was at her total and unabashed self-centeredness.

"We have a child, Kate. He is intelligent, perceptive. Right now all he knows is that you and I disagree on a lot of things. But he's growing up. He'll soon know what's going on."

"He won't unless you tell him," Kate shot back immediately, with feeling in her voice for the first time the whole evening. She stared at him, not dropping her gaze, a focused beam of challenge and denial. He looked back at her, searching for words that would make any difference. Over the many years, it seemed he had tried them all.

"I know I'm no prize, Kate. But I've always loved you and Ted, and I do the best I can. I try to keep a nice home, I've taken care of Catherine, I've…" It seemed so useless. "What exactly do you want? What would you like to see happen now?"

Kate paused a moment and said, "I guess that we'd all be happy."

"Do you see anything you can do to make that happen?" said Tonette.

"I guess I can just keep trying like I am now," said Kate with a shrug. She looked at all three of them with a small innocent smile and looked with interest at a napkin ring in front of her as though never having seen one before. They sat in silence for another few minutes. Then, stifling a prolonged sleepy sigh, Kate stretched and said, "Well. It's late. I think I'll go on up. I'll see you all in the—"

"Kate!" said Dave, hitting the tabletop with his palms. Tonette closed her eyes and shook her head from side to side. At these expressions of alarm, so dangerously close to disapproval, Kate shifted in her seat and grew quiet. She appeared to shrink a little bit. Joe searched quickly for words. "I've had a bad dream for some time now, Kate. Maybe five times. I dreamed that I've been sick in bed, not able to get up for months. I am too sick to do anything for myself, always need medicine, can't even get to the bathroom. I depend on you for everything, even a drink of water. It's a nightmare. You're surly with me, sarcastic, impatient. Every time I speak to you or need something, you become contemptuous and nasty. There's nobody else around and I have to rely on you. Your treatment makes me feel worse than my sickness. I wake up in a sweat and can't go back to sleep. I get up and change boxers and check on Ted. I come down here and drink water and sit in the dark. It's awful."

Nobody spoke. Then Kate said, in a flat, emotionless voice, "You don't have to worry, Joe. I'll take care of you." He would think back to those words many times, wondering exactly how she had meant them.

Everyone was exhausted. They talked a little more, Kate listening and occasionally saying a few words. She would not engage or contribute and expressed no enthusiasm or even interest in anything they said. She showed no anger or other feeling, replying in a flat, controlled monotone when she felt forced to say something. She refused to let Joe drive her to a hospital, informing him, "I have to work." She would not jeopardize her job. When they pressed this point, and Joe told her that nobody would fire her, she showed a little determination in saying that leaving her work would only make things worse for her because she would feel terrible later on. She refused to participate in AA, saying it wasn't "right" for her, and that in any case, she wasn't "ready" for that sort of thing at this point. The only thing she would promise to do was see a counselor. To Joe's surprise, Tonette asked if she meant a family counselor. Kate replied yes, a family counselor. Dave spoke up, asking if she meant sessions together with Joe. She said, "Yes, both of us." It intrigued Joe that his friends were bringing up the very points that his own experience with Kate had taught him to regard with care. Maybe they had perceived more over the years than he had suspected. He wondered if others had as well.

In his work, Joe knew of almost all the counselors in the area. He suggested they contact someone outside the area, someone whom he did not know, so Kate would not have to worry about any prior relationship.

"No. I can find my own. I can get Father Hervey to recommend somebody."

They all fell quiet at this, Dave and Tonette because they did not know who Hervey was, and Joe because something in the idea aroused a profound suspicion, although he probably could not have said exactly why. Had he been dealing with a parishioner or examining personalities and motives in a case going to trial, his instincts and intuition would have served him far better. He would never have acquiesced in Hervey's participation. In this sensitive, difficult conversation with his own wife, whose welfare consumed him, the mother of his child, his emotions and affections overcame the common sense he could have relied upon in other circumstances. They were all tired. It was very late. Joe must get up in another five hours and conduct three worship services before noon.

"What exactly would you say to Hervey?" he asked.

"I'll just tell him that I'm having some problems dealing with Mom. He'll recommend somebody. He knows people."

Apart from how Kate would connect with a counselor, Joe was concerned that she would leave counseling after a session or two, as she had in the past. He said so plainly. She agreed with all three of them that she would remain in counseling with Joe until the counselor decided they should stop or recommended further arrangements.

"When will you talk with Hervey?" said Joe, rubbing his eyes.

For the first time, Kate grew animated. "Monday morning. No, wait. He's in DC all day this coming Monday with the social studies teachers at a big meeting. They won't be back till after study hall. I have to cover for one of them. I'll talk with him Tuesday. Probably not in the morning because I have to work, and I don't get a break on Tuesday mornings. It'll be Tuesday afternoon sometime, when I finish putting away the stuff from lab." After this, the longest statement she had made all evening, the four of them held hands around the table as Dave led them in the Lord's Prayer. Then they all stood up and hugged one another, each taking an extended time embracing Kate, kissing her and patting her on the back. The Gallaghers and Joe were emotional. Kate submitted to all this with patience and silence, standing rigidly and giving her own brief little hugs in response. Her expression never changed.

With Kate leading the way, they all went up to bed. After a little while in the bathroom, Dave and Tonette closed their door and turned out the light. Kate came out of her bathroom, got into bed immediately and said good night, turned out her light, and faced the wall, and within seconds, Joe could hear the deep slow breathing of her sleep. In the darkness, he collected his clothing for the following day by the weak light from the closet and carried everything down to the living room, where he could dress the next morning without waking her. He pushed aside some toys and games and sat on a sofa in the dark, watching the distant lights of the neighborhood stream through the windows and move on the walls and ceiling.

His insides were churning but with a remarkable blend of relief and happiness. For the first time somebody else knew. There were witnesses. She had acknowledged the truth in the presence of other people. She had given her word before others to enter treatment. There were more people involved now than just him. For the first time since early in their marriage, he did not feel the old sense of loneliness. He went upstairs wondering if he could sleep. He was exhausted by the long day and the stressful evening, but most of his exhaustion had been there for many years, developing in the very subject and nature of what they had sought to confront. He had gone to bed exhausted on countless other nights and been unable to sleep. His side hurt. If the evening brought nothing else, it was guaranteed to mean for him a week of severe constipation.

He lay down and listened to Kate's relaxed breathing. How could she sleep so quickly and soundly after such an intervention? Perhaps sleep itself afforded a safe measure of denial. He lay awake in the dark, trying to empty the chaos from his mind. He tried going over his sermon for the following day. All sermons were certain to put somebody to sleep. With luck, he just might be the one; he might benefit from a dose of his own medicine tonight. Others would get their turn tomorrow. He smiled in the darkness.

Chapter Twenty-Three

Joe conducted three services at Redeemer every Sunday morning. A quiet, reflective celebration of Holy Communion in the old style began at 7:30 a.m. About fifty dependable older parishioners attended, early risers all their lives who were not about to change now, and some younger farm families with their quiet, orderly children. After the service, the people went cheerfully from the Lord's Table to tables in the parish hall for breakfast. From the big room and antiquated kitchen, the voices of children and adults and the aroma of pancakes and homemade sausage drifted like incense and hymns through the building and into the street, scents, and sounds of community, signs of the Spirit in people who drew strength from their time with one another in God's house. Sundays were sequences in the liturgy of lives knit together by worship, a fragile unity few could have defined but everyone felt. The services of Holy Communion that drew them all together in the nave were like Sundays themselves, focusing hearts and minds on the eternal in the midst of things that were passing away.

During breakfast, worshippers began to arrive for the second service, a less formal observance that began at 9:15 a.m. Dozens of families and all the Sunday school participants came to this service, where children and adults prepared the Holy Table, lighted candles, and escorted newcomers and the elderly to their seats. It was here that visitors and church shoppers, sometimes intimidated by a grand and often unfamiliar liturgical tradition, felt especially comfortable. If they stayed on at Redeemer, they attended the other services too

315

as they began to experience the spiritual and emotional movement of liturgical worship.

After the Christian education hour, a third and slightly longer celebration began with acolytes, choir, a procession, and often guest musicians and soloists. Coffee and further refreshments followed in the parish hall. One Sunday each month, Joe celebrated Holy Communion at a fourth service in a parishioner's home, where fifteen or twenty people gathered in the early evening to sing less traditional hymns with banjos and guitars, and the Eucharist was celebrated around a dining room table. The time would come when Redeemer's lay leaders, perceiving a drift of their growing parish into several distinct congregations, would advise Joe reluctantly that they wanted to return to two services. At the time of the Gallaghers' visit, three services was the custom, however, and it was to the third of these that Joe was expecting Kate, Dave, Tonette, and the children.

The crowded Sunday mornings were condensed scenes of the following weekdays. Outreach ministries, a community day school, daily morning prayer, and a midweek Communion service, meetings of parish organizations, and some civic groups made a busy crossroads of the old church all week long. Like all clergy, Joe hoped and prayed that in the midst of all this, the children were gaining faith and the adults learning what it means to be forgiven sinners.

Each Sunday service was preceded by intervals in which Joe's attention was needed in all directions. Everyone had questions or observations. There was the last-minute confusion of people introducing him to guests and seeking seats. There were always special situations with certain worshippers, pointed out to him by their friends or the ushers, that needed a moment of immediate attention. The acolytes were often nervous and had questions about their roles, evidence of how seriously they took their duties and their determination not to be embarrassed in front of family and friends. There were last-minute consultations with lectors about the pronunciation of biblical names, although the training Joe had provided, along with a dictionary for pronouncing biblical words, were gradually making the lectors more confident and resourceful. Joe made a point of welcoming all the visitors and guests in person, getting around to them before the services whenever possible and as soon as the retiring processional hymn had ended. There were often last-minute conferences with the choir or organist and ushers indicating those to whom communion should be brought in the pews and very young apprentice acolytes who craved a word or two of reassurance.

In each small conference and every word spoken to individuals, a parish priest was expected to demonstrate an unhurried diplomacy and encourage good cheer meant to help people feel valued and welcomed. With his ordination came the expectation that Joe would remember the details of everything said to him or whispered in his ear and every face and ailment of those whom he served. He made brief mental notes on these encounters and confidences and made notes on each of them on a legal pad the moment he returned to his office. It was typical Sunday routine familiar to all clergy. The issues were many and inevitable, regardless of how much delegation and training was devoted to lay ministry and worship life. After ten years, Joe was still training himself to manage gracefully the inevitable few people—including one of his most influential lay leaders, an affable former naval officer with an astonishing lack of perception and timing—who chose the busiest moments to attempt to talk to him about matters wholly unrelated to anything going on at the time. Certain people would approach him as he counseled the acolytes while the procession was forming, or while he was speaking with a clearly distressed walk-in, and obliviously begin a conversation about a regional conference that someone was thinking about planning for the following spring or the details of a financial issue that was likely to arise sometime next fall. Such moments made him value the relative discretion and judgment that prevailed in the law where orderly procedure made possible a focus upon substance. His relationship with Kate had taught him something about responding appropriately in these situations, but it was as a priest in the church that he was gaining the bulk of his experience.

Joe could manage these distractions because he truly loved the people he served. Together with the time he spent each day on his knees and his family life and his day-to-day service with parishioners, he was continually being shaped and renewed for ministry.

No amount of training ever seemed enough. He made mistakes and often lost his way, and no one was more conscious of it all than he, but he had been stamped early on by something that had gotten into him and become a part of his maturity. He yearned to serve like the clergy in his own life who had blessed him with a formative kindness. Even as a child, or perhaps especially as a child, he had perceived a mysterious value in what they were doing. People had respected ordained ministers when he was young. The clergy maintained a composure and attitude that at its best generated hope in people and a certain patience for their own personal limitations. The clergy he had known had been imminently decent people, and most of them in those days were men, well educated, pastoral and kind, sometimes dull but never irrelevant. When they became the subjects of disagreements, often a sign that they were fulfilling their vows with integrity, they were not despised personally. Their collars and calling inspired good manners in those around them. Joe understood that such measures of this deference as still exists is respect for the One who did the calling, much as ambassadors are accorded a certain homage in respect for the sovereign they represent. Even when he and his friends as children had joked about their ministers, they had always reserved a certain serious esteem for them like the approval they rendered favorite teachers and neighbors.

With a few exceptions, the people of Redeemer responded to him warmly, and the whole parish had the feel of a true family. Because Redeemer was a large parish of influential citizens, Joe's favorable reputation spread throughout Catoctin Springs and the surrounding county. There were few factions. Whenever the parish gathered, Joe knew something about the story of each person, young and old. Because each story was that of a human being, it had therefore its own measure of tragedy and pain, and Joe was unconsciously inclined to be kind. It was no territory for perfectionists, and a sense of humor was theologically indispensable.

And the world he had grown up in was gone forever now and turned into something less diplomatic, more secular. There had always been people who disliked their priests, but they had been somehow less vocal about it, or at least it had seemed that way. Now there were few reservations about expressing it. Old standards of good manners and decorum had gone the way of white gloves and the Hudson Hornet. Joe pondered his own small opposition just long enough to make a prudent judgment as to whether he had done something to provoke it. Earlier in his vocation, he had wasted much valuable time working to win over his detractors. In coming to know other clergy, he found that all of them had their slanderers, and they had all tried to do something about it. This was harder to do as a clergyman than as a leader in other, secular fields. The clergy were meant to set examples, work things out peacefully, and live in community with everybody as much as possible. In most cases, they had to take it and move on. There was an expectation that it was to be done in ways that never allowed one to be walked on, treated like a doormat, demeaned, but sometimes it was a very delicate balance to achieve. More experienced clergy told him that bishops felt obliged to side with parishioners, regardless of how cruelly or unfairly they had behaved, in confrontations with their priest. Joe was grateful his own troubles had never come to that.

Joe had a good relationship with the children at Redeemer, as he had at St. Andrew's. He considered the nurture of children in the faith as important a service in ministry as any other area. As he was serving alone at Redeemer and had no subordinate to work with, he tried faithfully to serve as youth pastor along with his other obligations. He looked upon it as God's will. He had taken to heart the good training at the seminary, where the nurture of the young and effective teaching skills qualified as invaluable tools for evangelism. He had long understood that when children were rude to him, and he counted it as a blessing that there had been so few, the cause lay with one or both parents and their dislike for him. In such cases, he examined his own behavior first, certain he was at fault somehow. But the great majority of children and teens truly liked Joe, and these relationships encouraged him to be less critical of himself. They expressed their friendship in small ways that he treasured, inviting him to their birthday parties and school functions and returning from family vacations and camp with small gifts for him. These souvenirs always occupied places of honor in his office for a time, and one of his desk drawers was filled with school pictures presented to him year after year by children, proud that they were growing up.

He could not change his detractors' attitudes. If they could be turned into friends, it had to occur naturally, in getting to know him as he went about his ministry, being himself. If that did not suffice, he understood that he had to live with it. He watched Lolly Bascomb and her several cohorts thread their way past him on Sundays or whenever they encountered him, never speaking, averting their faces like sensitive people avoiding an unpleasant odor. They conferred with one another in a small group and fell silent when he passed. He was polite to them, but not so much as to make an unwanted issue of it all. Why their children were rude to him ceased to be a mystery. He could imagine what they heard at home about him. He was aware too that, for reasons he could never fathom, it was to this group that his bishop listened with special care. The Bishop was always available to them by telephone and through one means or another saw to their election or appointment to positions of leadership in and outside the diocese. Thus, Lolly had been able to bring her devious anger to the seminary board of directors. Another member of her coterie, always indignant toward the world and particularly toward Joe, served with him on the diocesan retreat center committee. Joe could not understand it. Taking guidance from the example of the judges he had known as a lawyer, he refused to accept that bishops took the side of such people for their own safety. Like judges, bishops were persons of integrity as far as Joe was concerned. Maybe some of them believed they could assist clergy by keeping close contact with the chronic malcontents, but Joe found this too hard to accept. If loneliness was the chief mark of clergy life, it was bound to be even more of a hazard for bishops. Why would they want to seek out the companionship of the mean-spirited? And yet it seemed to be happening in his diocese, at least at Redeemer. Hearsay and backbiting were the activities for which Lolly and her few friends were known. They had mastered the techniques of insinuation and intrigue and appeared to gain strength from using them to achieve their ends. Could bishops be as susceptible to this kind of influence as everyone else? Judges were not. He could not imagine such a hold on chief pastors of the church. Yet he had learned it was a factor, at least for him, in his own diocesan life, and he was certain it had contributed to his bishop's cool regard for him. It troubled Joe, but he had learned to live with it, as he had with the rudeness of certain people's children.

Now, as Lolly strutted past him focused upon something over his shoulder, he felt the small flush of anguish she and her few always generated. He told himself that medieval ascetics would have accepted her behavior as a gift from God meant to keep him free of self-righteousness. Why couldn't he see it this way and be grateful?

Kate and Ted were a part of most of Redeemer's Sunday morning festivities. Everybody knew them and missed them when they did not attend, as was the case whenever a special weekend event or service took place at St. John's School or his soccer team played a Sunday game. Ted knew many young people in the congregation, and everybody liked him. To her credit, on most Sundays when there was no excuse to stay away, Kate dutifully brought Ted to Redeemer for Christian education and church. She spent her time on Sunday mornings following Ted around and talking to him about whatever he was doing or sitting alone in the library, often with the light turned off, or parish hall, while he was in Sunday school. She was friendly and polite when spoken to and answered questions when asked, but otherwise her interaction with parishioners was limited. She always insisted on leaving the moment the service ended. When Joe prevailed upon her to stay and join the people in the parish hall after the service, she made a token appearance and then departed, insisting on taking Ted with her. Joe would have liked her to join in the visiting at coffee hour, a place where friendships were affirmed and people got to know one another better. He would have enjoyed having Ted stay with him while he locked up and the two of them go out to lunch or perhaps to the movies. Kate almost always had other plans, and Ted seemed prepped to concur with them, even on the few occasions when he appeared willing to stay with Joe. In his whole career in ministry, Joe could not recall a single time that Ted had stayed with him at church, except for occasions when all three of them were joining other parishioners for lunch. It was hard negotiating such plans with Kate during his Sunday morning duties. She always had an excuse, was always ready with a reason why they must leave and why Ted must go with her. After their move to Catoctin Springs, Joe had come to understand gradually that in spite of her concurrence in accepting Redeemer's call, Kate did not like anything about moving there, not the old-fashioned blue-collar town or the poor rural county or the entire state with its poverty and suspicion of outsiders. The grass was always greener across the river where she worked, the people in the St. John's community wealthier and somehow even better bred, and society more affluent and savvy. For all her rural and small-town roots, she was a big city girl at heart and preferred urban conveniences to rustic challenge. Joe did not at all begrudge her these preferences, and he knew she had liked Dorchester and her position with the community college there. But he wished she could experience the many wonderful qualities of life in their new home and get to know the people better. And although Ted had many friends in their community and loved the local public schools, he could sense his son's very gradual adoption of his mother's mild contempt for the area and her preference for where she worked. Ted was much influenced by Kate's choices in everything, and Joe perceived in him the rudimentary formation of her attitudes in politics, society, entertainment, and everything else. He would look back one day in consternation at his blindness to the extent of it.

It was during the complicated time before the third and largest service that he first saw his family and the Gallaghers on Sunday morning. They came through the narthex like everybody else, chatting and looking around. Kate smiled as people greeted her and immediately returned her attention to Ted, who was speaking with several of his friends. Standing halfway down the center aisle, listening as a parishioner introduced him to her cousins from Seattle, Joe observed Kate's entry like a policeman on a stakeout, his every nerve alert for any contingency. The events of the previous evening had kept him awake all night, and his nerves were on edge. All sorts of questions circulated within him: How had they all gotten along that morning? Had there been an argument? What was Kate's mood? Had she slept well? Was she already planning some retaliation? Would she be angry with him, or more so than usual? He watched her face carefully, and he glanced several times at Ted. Had she told Ted that something had happened? He suspected she had not, so paranoid was she that their son would discover her secret. Joe watched Dave and Tonette as they spoke to their children and looked about the nave for him. Kate, preoccupied with whatever Ted was saying to his friends, was not introducing the Gallaghers to anyone. But she might not have done so in any case, especially with Ted around to engage her entire attention, so it was probably not a sign of a difficult morning. He figured she had sailed through the morning in breezy denial, carefully avoiding any reference to the night before, pretending that none of it had happened. She was reserving her anger for him and would let it out in unexpected bursts for months and months to come. If she would only go to counseling with him, he thought. *If we could only talk.*

With perception and reckoning honed during years in the courtroom, Joe processed these thoughts and images rapidly, trying to allow none of them to disturb what he thought was a calm countenance. He spoke politely to the Seattle couple and went up the aisle quickly to his family and old friends. If Kate was aware of his presence, she never showed it, staring intently at Ted as he talked with his friends, interrupting every few sentences to correct him on something. Joe began to introduce the Gallaghers to the parishioners who were standing nearby. Stan and Jane Holloway stopped to meet them, as did Harry Campos and a guest, and Linda Reese and her children. Campbell Collins, a local lawyer and lapsed Roman Catholic who attended services at Redeemer so as to argue with Joe occasionally at lunch about the theology of his sermons, introduced his wife to Joe and the Gallaghers. A confirmation class from the Luther Memorial Lutheran Church, visiting to learn about liturgy, shuffled in slowly as though arriving for a weekend in jail. Joe greeted them and introduced their sponsor to the Gallaghers.

Seeing a group forming around Joe and the Gallaghers, Kate came over quickly, grinning and telling Joe that she had just been introducing everybody. The prelude was ending, and the processional hymn would begin within minutes. The choir was lining up, and the acolyte sponsor was lighting the processional candles and straightening crumpled collars. Over his shoulder, an usher pointed out a worshipper on a walker who would need to have communion brought to her pew. In all this, Joe searched Tonette's face for some sign of how the morning had gone, but each time she seemed about to speak to him, her youngest daughter, wrapped around her arm like a spider monkey, gave a fierce tug. Everyone in the narthex turned and hurried down the side aisles, searching for seats. Joe would have to wait until coffee hour to find out what had happened.

He would find that nothing had happened. Kate had risen before anyone else and prepared coffee and begun to set out her wonderful sausage and egg casserole and homemade coffee cake for a light breakfast. Dave had been the next to come down, and she had greeted him and talked with him in her friendly morning manner as though nothing at all had occurred the previous evening. Dave certainly didn't bring anything up, nor did Tonette when she came down, calling up the stairs to the children to finish in the bathroom and put on their clothes. The morning proceeded uneventfully with the adults studiously avoiding any reference to last night's intervention and the children oblivious of anything having occurred. No one looking on would have observed any sign in Kate that a few hours before, for the first time in her life, she had been confronted about her addictive behavior by people other than her spouse.

Whatever unease the Gallaghers might have felt, they managed themselves and their children pleasantly and deftly throughout the morning. At the communion rail, where Kate always insisted in drinking from the chalice, ever a difficult moment for Joe, he was the only one who attached any uncomfortable significance to what should have been a moment of grace. Two dozen people in the congregation either routinely refused the cup or touched their bit of consecrated bread to its lip. Some of them had discussed with Joe their reasons and others had not. He had made it very clear in announcements and in print that for those taking medicine or allergic to red wine, or for any other reason, receiving the bread alone was full and complete communion. None of it had ever seemed to register with Kate, who took the cup knowing the issues it raised in her and between her and Joe. It seemed to him that on this day when the server approached her, she had lingered an extra second or two over the cup, taking a larger gulp than usual. He decided it was only his imagination and she would not have turned an act so sacramental into a personal cut at him.

In the moments it took Kate to return from the chancel to her pew, an overwhelming feeling of guilt and shame came over him for allowing such thoughts to occupy his mind during the ministration of Holy Eucharist. He watched her over the heads and upturned faces of the good people kneeling at the rail, walking away from him among the other worshippers along the aisle, wearing a familiar blue-and-white flowered dress and looking straight ahead, and tears rose up inside him suddenly and tenderly. His tears filled his voice more than his eyes, and he had to clear his throat several times as he continued to say the words of distribution and serve the consecrated bread. When a face was turned up toward him, he made eye contact and smiled.

He loved her. She was his wife. He was her husband. What would happen now? *The body of our Lord Jesus Christ which was given for thee…* He prayed in his heart as he said the words that the previous night would be the beginning of her recovery…*preserve thy body and soul unto everlasting life…* A new time for her, a new start. Whatever debilitating scourge marked her inmost being would begin to be resolved…*take and eat this in remembrance…* He believed in miracles. *that Christ died for thee…* Life can change. God is in control…*and feed on him in thy heart…* There is healing, wholeness, mercy, forgiveness, strength. *by faith…* He looked down. The top of Ted's head was before him. Next to his son, the upturned faces of the Gallagher children met him with smiles and giggles. *with thanksgiving.*

So it proceeded for the rest of the day, through a coffee hour in which the people of Redeemer were delighted to meet the Stephensons' old friends, through lunch at a nearby pizza restaurant, which delighted the children, and through the long and affectionate goodbyes said in the restaurant parking lot before the Gallaghers began the two-hour drive back to Dorchester. In their words and hugs, they lingered for an extra few seconds, a final silent sign that they were hoping and praying for Kate and Joe and Ted. As they drove away, Joe thanked God silently for their visit, for their uncomplicated decency and courage. Kate gave no sign of her own feelings, whatever they were. While Joe was still watching their car and waving goodbye, she had begun to busy herself with Ted, making sure he rode home with her, in her car. They had plans.

Joe suggested that they go to the movies or to a new video store that had opened in town that weekend. He was so tired he could almost sleep standing up, but he wanted the three of them to do something enjoyable together. Ted wanted to see the new video store too. But Kate was in a hurry to change and spend the rest of the day at St. John's "doing some work." When Joe said he did not realize she was planning on going to the school for the afternoon, she said she had told him about it earlier in the week. By now he knew this was not true, but he also knew that any comment on it would cause an argument, especially now, and that any disagreement would escalate quickly. He lightly suggested that Ted go with him to the new store. Kate reminded Ted that he had promised to help move some supplies into her storeroom at school. He was willing to help but protested, not strongly, that they had never talked about moving any supplies. She corrected him severely, another indication to Joe of a storm on the horizon, and they got into her car and departed for home.

Joe followed Kate's car home. As they were all changing clothes the reason for Ted accompanying her to St. John's seemed to shift to some of the boarding students who were suddenly expecting Ted to join them in a soccer scrimmage. Kate was searching for excuses to keep him with her, another of the signs of defense he had learned to recognize when she felt threatened or angry. He knew he should keep Ted with him, take him somewhere, and spend time with him. He felt overwhelmed with fatigue. The intense morning and the more intense night before and the strain of the whole weekend all led to rekindled hope that brightened his heart with the promise of health and recovery for Kate and for their marriage. But the temporary price was real too, as much as he wanted to ignore it. His head hurt, his stomach burned, and he felt physically drained and profoundly sad, small payment for a great breakthrough that would lead to wholeness and sanity for all of them. His son was singing in the next room, a sound that of itself was balm to his mind and body. He knew he could prevail, eventually, in the fight it would take to keep him with him for the afternoon, and as he stood in the bedroom with his mind racing, he knew already he would feel bad for days and probably end up spoiling a nice afternoon for Ted if he did not lay down on the bed immediately and close his eyes. He let Ted go with Kate. Ted usually took her side in such disputes anyway, and at that moment, he felt he could not stand having them both against him.

He followed them down to the driveway and watched the van speed away, seemingly putting as much distance as quickly as possible between it and him and their home. As soon as they were out of sight, he went back inside and lay down on the sofa, the first place he came to, and closed his eyes. He was asleep before he could lie down completely and was unconscious for a fitful half hour until the telephone woke him up.

Years in law enforcement, answering his beeper and the telephone at all hours of the night, had conditioned him to wake up from the dead and pick up the jangling phone. It was Ted calling at Kate's direction to say that they had decided to stay at the school for supper that evening and would be back before bedtime.

Deeply depressed and hopeful and fearful at the same time, he lay back and tried to fall asleep again. His mind was racing, and he knew he would not sleep. He drank some cold water and walked out onto the lawn and lay down on the grass and stared into the sky. Flat-bottomed cumulus towers were swelling and shifting in the darkening vastness above him with quilted tops like colossal florets of cauliflower. He watched them gathering slowly, magnificently upward, soon to merge into the great anvil forms that would herald storms in a day or so. He had seen and felt the signs yesterday and the day before, the subtle changes before a storm. A light wind was stirring from the flattish land beyond the river. He could imagine drifting upward at will into it all like the way he imagined *satori*. How wonderful it would be to hear the thunder and feel the rain approaching through the trees. As if influenced by his thoughts, the great white pine nearby began to stir and quiver.

As good as it had been to see the Gallaghers, the weekend had been dreadful. Almost unnoticed by him because it was happening so often now, his side had begun to hurt soon after Tonette had confronted him in the kitchen on the first night. Against all his best instincts, he felt a knot of anger in his gut over another good time ruined. More than anything else, he would love to have hugged his son then and there. He put his hand over his eyes and sighed. From the far side of the house, Cory came trotting in his direction. The inquisitive little dog licked his cheek and hand lightly and lay down next to him and burrowed his cool nose between Joe's arm and side. Joe spoke to him quietly, and Cory lay his head on Joe's chest and regarded him with concerned eyes.

Chapter Twenty-Four

"How about a Coke, Bro?"

"All right. Stop at Sheetz."

"I've got a better place."

"Where?"

"It's a good place. You'll like it."

"Where, Dad!"

"It's not far. I'll give you a hint."

"*Where*, Dad!"

"Think of sports."

"Sports? All right! We're going to an Orioles game! Or the Capitols!"

"That's close. Very close. Orioles is closer."

"You want to go all the way to Penn National?"

"No. Keep thinking Orioles."

"Dad, *where*!" Ted seized his math textbook and struck it on the dashboard with violence.

"Ted! I never saw anyone get so agitated about a Coke."

"Dammit, Dad. This better be somewhere good. It better not be like the movies you bring home."

"Hey, now. You liked *Hogan's Heroes*. And *Bladerunner*. You liked *Lonesome Dove*, didn't you? And *Witness for the Prosecution*."

"Yes. But how about *Freeze, Dry, Come to Life*? You can't tell me that was a great movie. I don't care what you say."

"Well, I brought that one home for me. I didn't know you and your mother would come home so early. And you didn't have to watch it."

"It was the worst single movie made by human beings, ever. Mom was asleep in two minutes."

"Oh, come on. It wasn't that bad. For the bloody communists, at least. Think of it as an artifact from a failed, catastrophic world. I mean, it certainly showed the bleakness of Soviet—"

"It sure did!"

"And Mom always goes to sleep if it's one of my films. Except for *Rumpole* and *Prime Suspect*. Often it's better if she does. Otherwise..."

"She makes comments every two minutes. It does sort of ruin it. But nothing could have ruined that backyard Russian flick."

The windshield wipers chopped away at the sleet, and the late afternoon grew darker with every mile.

Joe grinned and said, "Then glut thy sorrow on the morning rose, / Or on the rainbow of the salt sand-wave, / Or on the wealth of globed peonies; / Or if thy mistress such rich anger shows, / Imprison her soft hand, and let her rave, / And feed deep, deep upon her peerless eyes."

"Dad! I hate it when you do that."

"Quote Keats? You're right. Let's switch to Wordsworth."

"Don't quote anybody! And what are we stopping for? Don't tell me we're going here."

The gravel lot around the Third Base was almost full. Joe managed to wedge his vintage Honda between two pickup trucks with tires the size of Ferris wheels with just enough room on each side to open the doors. Slight cold rain peppered the warm car. A scrim of weak ice covered everything, catching each colored light of the lofty road sign in moist beads that glowed in the late March twilight on the parked pickup trucks like jewels. Joe went carefully through the muddy puddles between the cars and trucks with Ted following, head drooping in misery. As they approached the entrance, they could hear Bob Dylan winding up the final verse of "Knocking on Heaven's Door."

"Country music?" growled Ted in a low voice and followed it with a death rattle. Joe opened the door, and they stepped into the smoky gold light in time to hear the big Wurlitzer begin to play "Six Days on the Road." Joe turned to his wide-eyed son and said, "This must be your lucky day!"

Joe settled himself on a stool at the long bar and nodded to Raymond, who came along fumbling with a dish towel and stuck out his hand and said, "Rev. Where've you been? We ain't seen you in here for two, three weeks. Thought you'd forgotten us till Lilly said she seen you at the Safeway." He paused and looked at Ted, who slumped on the stool beside Joe with his elbows on the bar.

"Ray, I'd like to introduce my son, Ted. Ted, this gentleman is Mr. Shifflett. He runs this restaurant." Ted shot out his hand immediately and whipped off his baseball cap, looking the bartender in the eye.

"Mr. Shifflett," he said politely.

"Well! You're the one your old man's always talking about."

"Damn! Ziss your boy, Joe? Well…Cora! Come here and meet the reverend's son," said someone on the other side. As Ted turned to shake hands, he got a generous hug around the neck from Lilly, a waitress.

"Well, darlin', if you ain't something to see. You look like one of them young movie stars on TV! Reverend Stephenson, shame on you. Why didn't you tell us how good-looking he was? Lordy!" said Lilly.

They came at Ted from all sides, shaking his hand, patting his shoulder, hugging him, asking about his health, wanting to know if he knew their sons and daughters who went to the local schools. He remembered some of them from middle school before entering St. John's, and each parent at the same time began to bring him up to date about their offspring. The crowd questioned and complimented Ted with interest, talking over one another and vying for his attention. He responded in a gracious way, open and sincere, trying not to ignore anybody. Joe could see that they all admired Ted, and it made him feel good. Ray brought him a Coke in a frosted beer mug. Lilly brought him a cold root beer, a new brand just delivered by the distributor that day—"You can be the first one here to try one, and I hope it's good"—and somebody brought over a plate of cheese fries that weighed about ten pounds. There was an old-fashioned pinball machine on the far side of the room, and soon Ted was over there with a group of young men from the highway department, poking in quarters and playing as if he had known them for years.

"Fine boy," said Carl, an off-duty fireman. Everybody agreed. Joe thanked them all and sipped his coffee.

"You don't remember me," said an obese young woman as she heaved herself onto the stool beside him. Joe looked around and had to acknowledge that he did not.

"I'm the one from up at Tollytown came to see you that time about my baby? I didn't weigh so much then. My baby'd just died, and I was all tore up, and the preacher at Grandmaw's church told her it was too bad we ain't had her baptized and all yet, 'cause she won't going to heaven and all, and it upset me so I couldn't eat or anything, and Sissy Tolly—at the Sheetz?—said she knew you 'cause you came in there to buy gas and all, and I should go by and talk to you. It's been like year before last. You talked to me that day and really helped me. I was gonna kill myself till I talked to you."

Joe looked at her heavy face. She was about nineteen, maybe twenty, and he could imagine her as a young teenager, not beautiful, but pretty and slender. She had beautiful eyes. Four or five times a year they came to see him, sent by someone he had met somewhere and couldn't remember. The story was always the same, and he had gotten to where he could recognize it as soon as they began. Unmarried, poor, with no education, grieving over a dead child, they had been told by an illiterate preacher somewhere that their baby would never go to heaven because they had never had him baptized. Occasionally where the baby had been baptized, a "preacher" had even told them it was too bad but their little girl or boy would still probably go to hell because she hadn't been *really* baptized, by *him*.

"I remember right to this day what you said. You said that what we know about the nature and character of God from knowing Jesus Christ and all—them was the very words you said, and I ain't forgotten—shows us what God is like, and Jesus is not going to turn away an innocent little baby like my little Crystal just because I hadn't gotten her baptized yet when she died. She won't even a month. And you said God is kind and merciful and all, and I shouldn't worry because my little Crystal was with God and happy, and God's taking care of her and that every time I cried for her, every tear was a prayer, that was just what you said, every tear was a prayer saying, 'Thank you, God, for taking good care of her and all.' I went home and could eat and sleep at night for the first time since she died. Remember? Preacher said it again at the funeral when he preached his sermon, and it nearly made Mama and me and my Grandmaw sick in the funeral home, and Grandmaw got sick worrying about it and ain't been back to church since. I told her what you said, and she and me felt better and been doing pretty well since. You sat right there with me in your church and talked with me over an hour."

Joe cleared his throat and took a long sip of his coffee. "I'm so glad it helped. But all I did was tell you the truth. That's all I did. I'm just so sorry you had such terrible things said to you, and especially at your baby's funeral. God is good. It broke God's heart when your little one died."

"Excuse me, Dad. Can I have some quarters? Please?" Joe gave Ted two dollars, and he went over to the restaurant side to ask for change. A bearded young man called from the entrance, saying he had the truck waiting and it was blocking the drive, and the girl got down heavily from her stool, and Joe held her enormous Army overcoat while she struggled into it. She hugged Joe and kissed him on the cheek. He told her he was very glad to know she was so much better and that he would pray for her and Crystal. He wished her well.

He drank another cup of coffee and paid his bill. It took a while to speak with people on his way out and even longer to pry Ted away from the old pinball machine and his new buddies. The young man who hated country music and had entered the Third Base with all the enthusiasm of a convict on the second week of work release was suddenly incensed at having to leave. As they headed home over the wet cold roads of early Spring, Ted wanted to know who this person was and that, why the girl in the yellow sweatshirt was dancing alone, why the big black guy had to sit down while playing pinball, who the blond girl was in the red blouse, and why the waitress had named her daughter, whom he had known in middle school, "Babygail." Joe tried to provide answers.

Chapter Twenty-Five

Wistful gray rain had set in like a blessing, buoyant and whispering against the windows and rising to a low clatter when the wind came scuttling over the lawn. Being at home with family and friends on a rainy Saturday with nowhere to go was a joy so exceptional it could inspire poetry, music, singing, as evidently it had with Ted and his un-self-conscious friends, who had begun harmonizing upstairs as they drifted awake (some new song with incomprehensible lyrics by a young "artist" whose name nobody would recognize this time next year). Grinning at the cacophony overhead, Joe peered from the window into wet misty vistas like Pissarro's *Diligence at Louveciennes*, but mercifully without its promise of a brightening horizon. He loved such a day here or anywhere, the mysterious and confined wet blend of freedom and security it provided, as if all life's problems had been put on hold and a time-out called like the calm at the eye of a hurricane. The wide, empty lawns and what he could see of the lonely road were gloriously deserted. In the languid blues and olives and tender greens, he could imagine Manet's or Monet's draped figures, hurrying aslant in the drizzle beneath umbrellas in the flooded lanes of Port-Marley. How unpleasant it would be to see a car turn into the drive bearing someone bent on talking business or discussing personal problems.

He took a long sip of his coffee and declared aloud it was the finest coffee he had ever tasted. Arab princes had never known such coffee. Turkish sultans would have traded a regiment of Janissaries for a single cup. Amused and probably confused by the references,

Kate looked up from the bowl where an omelet was being whisked and declared for the thousandth time in their marriage that she had no idea how anybody could stand the taste of coffee. She didn't mind making it, but she was never going to drink it herself. Leaning over her shoulder, Joe kissed her cheek and reassured her that he understood.

Outside, the rain puddled around the neighborhood in the low places where the driveways met the streets, ran in clear, noisy rivulets in the ditches along the roads, and made the needles tremble in the lofty white pines that bordered the greening lawns. When he went out after breakfast, the sod was spongy beneath the soles of what an English neighbor called his Wellies, which had been known as barn boots during his years in horse country. Shrouded in a camouflaged hunting slicker and hood, with the bill of one of Ted's baseball caps protruding above his expectant eyes, Joe roamed from his house through the deserted neighborhood and down the long wooded hills toward the river. He was thrilled by the rain and the clean cool air and the myriad small signs of the late spring that was arriving at last.

Ahead of him, the river lay hidden by the distant rise in its bristle of swaying trees. He imagined the easy persistent cascades of rain blowing over its wide surface. He thought of rain falling on distant fields, along the slopes of the budding mountains east and west, on the steep slate slants of Redeemer's glistening roof in town, spilling opulently into the streets where old cobbles appeared here and there through the worn hardtop. Rain was falling all round, and it was good, swelling the feisty brooks and streams and placid farm ponds, gracing the countryside and giving life and relief to a thousand wild creatures. He imagined it falling all along the eastern seaboard, drumming down into broad river valleys and the rolling Piedmont, picking up intensity along the coast, pelting the wide salt marshes with cold clean water and splattering over the roofs and empty porches of the elegant old houses of Wicomico.

And all mankind that haunted nigh had sought their household fires. Children too, amazingly. Not one to be seen. Through the wide family room windows of his neighbors' houses, clumped in foggy solitude at the ends of deserted drives, the irritable glow of overhead lighting blended with the flicker of computer monitors, where young and old alike sought the vicarious adventure of virtual reality. *When they could be out here,* he said almost aloud, *in this spellbinding gray light, hearing the sounds of a world waking from winter, smelling the luscious drenching life vapors, tasting the cold cleanness, the fine silences.* Bad poetry, bad, he admonished himself. When he was young, every child in his neighborhood would be out and on the prowl on such a day, stomping barefoot in the running gutters and puddles, swirling menacingly the great black umbrellas of parents, from each one of which protruded lethally at least one stray wiry stay.

A big yellow utility vehicle lurched round a corner and bore down upon him in the drifting rain. He stepped into a bank of last year's brittle honeysuckle as it flew by, making the silver rain coppery as it passed, the hiss of the big tires fading away behind him. *There was a time,* he said to himself, *when every driver would have slowed in passing a walker on a wet lane. No more.* That was years ago and in a different society. Some of the older people still slow down. They've lived long enough to know what it means. The image of everybody else, especially the teenage girls who looked too young to drive anyway, oblivious of everything around them, flashed through his mind at the speed with which they raced along the roads with cell phones mashed to their ears, inattentive, unconcerned, dangerous.

Old people. Back at the house, there was an old person who hadn't gotten out of bed, except to use the bathroom, for weeks, and when she did, she required assistance with everything. Catherine was using diapers now, a precaution Joe's doctor had recommended, and someone else had to maneuver them on for her. She was very much in her right mind and had not objected to the diapers at all. This had surprised Joe until he considered that being alone all day meant an intolerable alternative. Even with the diapers, he had many times found her in unavoidable distress. He had asked her permission at first, patiently and kindly, to assist her when Kate was not around, and he was surprised and a little touched when she readily accepted his help. He changed her diapers, trimmed her nails, and even, on one occasion, trimmed her hair, because there was often no one else around to do these things. He would arrive home and discover that Kate, home before him for some time, reading the newspaper or watching television, had not even entered her mother's room. When he checked on Catherine and found she needed immediate attention, he had found it necessary to argue with Kate to get her to move. Eventually she would get up, heaving a sigh as though he had asked her to split firewood, and go heavily into her mother's bedroom. When this happened, she would go about her duties in silence, with neither mother nor daughter speaking to each other. He had been at a hundred bedsides and assisted at many of them and knew there were dignity issues. Some people were not built to handle it. And it was probably especially hard on Kate and Catherine after their difficult past. Still...

In the silvery distance, he could see the crest of the long white roll of fog nestled along the river like smoke hovering over a hidden fire line. Overhead, everything was a swirling immensity of gray and the trees on the high land before the final slope stood out against the sky black and brittle as old cast iron. The wooded land began to descend toward the river bottom in a series of slanting ledges like waterfalls in quick succession, and soon he began to see below him the silvery, silent water through the trees.

Far in the west, this river was still a swift, stony stream, chuckling through deep pools and shallow riffles in places unchanged since the Indians had the land. He had loved his precious days exploring those wondrous narrow mountain rivers in a canoe with old friends, negotiating the rapids and riffles and fishing from the bars below the whitewater falls. These rocky mountain streams and their rugged country had filled him with happiness, refreshing his spirit and returning him home a calmer, cleansed man. They were closer to the origin of things, wild places where creation was fresher, like a canvas still wet and glistening, appealing to all his ideals of beauty and order. And true to the universal pattern he had begun to perceive as a child, the glorious obvious concealed yet more stupendous wonders below the surface, a depth of miracles for those with eyes to see and ears to hear, a spiritual comprehension, an apocalyptic denouement.

The waters concealed wonders like the quantum world within conventional reality, a wilderness of sand, gravel and rocky bottoms, the intriguing world of trout and hellgrammites and colored stones like wet jewels and quivering, waving waterweeds. To the astonishment of his friends, he drifted for long periods, gazing down, inches above the water, into the wild world gliding below him, the shapes, colors, and patterns at once resting and exciting his psyche.

Entering stands of great trees always roused good memories, and they came now, welcomed. Camping, canoe trips, hunting, spelunking, old friends, good times with Kate, and always Ted and his fatherly desire and regret that they could have spent more time together in such places, outdoors, free of tension and complications. Ted was at home now, ensconced before the TV screen, playing the video games with his friends that the young preferred these days to canoes and fishing rods, and speaking a language Joe did not always understand. They had not wanted to ramble with him along the river.

And Kate. If she was keeping her promise, she was reviewing glossy brochures of the half-dozen nursing homes in the community. He had tried to talk with her about it for months, but she had put him off. He had urged her to take a Saturday and drive around and visit the available places so they could discuss their options and her preferences and what was most likely to suit Catherine, but she never got around to it. He tried approaching her at different times, when she had just emerged from Catherine's room with a soiled diaper or when she was happy and laughing and in a good mood. Neither had worked. In this, as in all life's issues that in her mind did not touch directly upon her work or her son, she preferred to deny its existence. He was used to it.

Finally he stopped talking about her mother's welfare and told her that in another state, not the one they were in, but everywhere else, a social worker would refer them to Adult Protective Services for the manner in which Catherine was living. It was wrong to let it go on like this. She required more help than they could provide. It wasn't working, and it was cruelly negligent. Who would approve her working with children knowing she was allowing such a situation to continue at home? He knew this last point was a weak argument

339

and unfair in some ways. He was ashamed of himself for saying it, but allowing the intolerable situation to continue under his own roof shamed him even more.

Placing a parent in a nursing home was a traumatic decision, and he felt for Kate. But he felt great sympathy for Catherine too, and the experience of years had taught him that Kate would take no initiative to act. As she stomped away from him, he had pointed out—because her anger sometimes forced some clarity upon her—that the more needy Catherine became, the more difficult grew Kate's own moods. They had to act, he told her.

And still nothing. Kate began to grow furious with him if he tried to bring the matter up. In desperation he had contacted every nursing home and adult care facility within fifty miles and had their admissions material sent to Kate. It had all arrived several weeks ago, and she had placed the packages in a stack, unopened, on a dining room chair where they remained.

The intervention with the Gallaghers two months before had encouraged him to look for change in Kate, some different attitude toward their family issues. She had not yet begun her promised therapy. He had waited in vain for her to say that she had started, to say anything at all, in fact, about the intervention. She had not. She acted as if it had never occurred. Finally, just yesterday, he had yielded to the old pattern and asked her lightly how her "appointments" were coming along. She had replied, as though only just then remembering it, that Father Hervey was taking his time recommending somebody, so she hadn't started yet. He knew that inquiring when she had approached Hervey would quickly place the whole conversation on a downhill slope. Anyway, he knew from experience that whenever she had talked with Hervey, she would consider it her own business and not something to share with her husband.

She was at home now, incensed with him for bringing up again the untouched catalogues as he had left the house. "On Saturday of all days! My only day off! You seem to forget that I have to work, Joe!" They had had a loud argument in their bedroom as he was preparing to go out and she was settling down with a new paperback novel, and he had finally wrested from her a promise to review the material and see if there was anything around they could afford. Even if they found something, he knew the next step, getting her to communicate with her brother about it, was when the resistance would become impossible.

Her brother. The one who was going to think it all over and call him. Joe had never heard another word. He tried to imagine himself and his own feelings if someone had approached him about a crisis with one of his own sisters. Ray's response, or lack of one, dumfounded him, and at the same time, he knew it should not have come as a surprise. It was the McIvor family way. In trying to understand such paralyzing denial, he had admitted defeat years ago. He was no psychologist.

Karla was different, however, and she had certainly taken action. She had contacted Kate almost immediately, just like he had asked her to do, by telephone he supposed, although when and where he did not know. Karla had confronted Kate, all right, with a recitation of all the mean things Joe had said to her about his poor wife, his many exaggerations and half-truths, his shameful lies, his wicked insinuations, his ill treatment of poor Karla herself, so unfairly roused from precious sleep in the middle of the night after working all day. Kate had been keenly alarmed upon learning that Joe had called his own parents before calling Karla and had told them about her drinking. She had questioned Joe about it and would not say why she thought this, but it was evident that only Karla could have suggested it. Ray had certainly not talked with her. The Gallaghers were the only others who knew, and they had never said such a thing. He had reassured Kate that he had spoken only to her brother and her best friend and to nobody else. He tried to make her understand how desperate he had been to get help for her. He reminded her that the Gallaghers had brought the matter up to him. It had gone on for so many years that he had grown numb to it and sometimes couldn't tell whether she was drinking or not. He had begun to see it as normal. He reassured her that he had spoken to nobody else and had always faithfully kept her confidences. He reminded her that she was his wife and he loved her, conscious as he said it of the want of an old enthusiasm in his own voice. In the following days, he had wracked his brain constantly, going over his telephone conversation with Karla and trying to recall saying anything that would have led her to believe he had called his parents. He was certain he had said nothing. But would Karla lie? Would she make up something hurtful and tell it to her best friend? There were times when he despaired of his own failing sanity; should one who had spent a career cross-examining difficult witnesses really be surprised that people lied? How could he be so naive?

She would not give him specifics of what Karla had said to her, so he could not reassure her or defend himself beyond saying he had not revealed anything to his parents. Nothing he said would convince her of the concern and anxiety her conduct aroused in him. In this as in so many other things, it was clear to him that she could not relate to his feelings and had little understanding of how her ways affected him or anyone else.

He went through the tall brittle grass and weeds, and he shook his head and shoulders, clearing away the troubling thoughts. Anyone watching might have thought he was shaking off the rain, but the tempest in his head was more engulfing and obscuring than any storm of wind and lightening. The skies would clear. The storm within seemed never to disappear, always in his heart or waiting on the horizon to resume its place.

The land sloped upward slightly as he approached the stands of vast oaks that followed the river gorge for miles. Some of them had crowns like whole groves of trees. They had stood nobly for centuries along the ridge top where the land began its rugged descent toward the bottom. He was amazed by all great trees, and the savage size of these oaks was inspiring. Above him, their tops rocked in the wet wind and made noises like distant waterfalls, showering down drifts of spiraling dried leaves that had hung on through the disappearing winter. They towered above a sea of shrubs and mountain laurel. Here and there among them, great rocks broke from the ground, vestiges of the receding ice that had once covered the land. Some northern conifers grew in the rocks, and red maples. Beeches, witch hazels, pines and smaller oaks advanced down the slope toward the old floodplain as though they might one day cross the river and escape to the sea. He thought how magnificent it would have been to see it all with the first settlers. He wished that Ted and his sleepover buddies had wanted to come with him. Theirs was a different generation, more urban, technical, with commercial imaginations, and becoming more so daily in the artificial, isolated environment of St. John's. Where was it all going? Would the glaciers return? Would the clean wilderness survive? Would human hearts evolve? The Ice Age and Pleistocene were easy in comparison to changes in the human heart. He stood still for a moment and smiled, the only rational response to such uncertainties. When he considered the world, it was not the loss of faith that troubled him. It was the want of sanity. From his childhood, he could hear himself and people around him praying, *Lord, have mercy upon us and incline our hearts to keep thy law.*

Through the trees, he descended a rugged riparian slope that would brighten in coming weeks with bloodroot, Mayapple, partridgeberry, and the occasional, illusive Trillium. Such woodland places were like the mountain rivers, restoring hope and refreshing something within that was growing dry. He loved being outdoors in old clothes. Wicomico meant a chance to be with Kate and Ted but also to walk for miles along the open beach, watching and listening in the endless ocean light to the surf and wind, gulls and sandpipers, and witnessing the patrols of serene pelicans that drifted over the waves. He had marveled at the sea lettuce and patterned algae, the egg cases of whelks and skates, and had kept watch where the big loggerhead turtles had returned to lay eggs. Once, on the deserted beach at Ship Island, he had found a whale. In exploring the sand, he was in the mountains too, every grain having come down from the Smokies and the Blue Ridge. His time by the sea had cleansed him for years of the tensions of the trial court and the much greater tensions of ordained life. It had always troubled him that Kate did not understand why he insisted on roaming the beaches and dunes when he could be sitting on the porch talking with her and her summer guests. What a shame for them both that he had not been able to make her understand. Perhaps she understood it to some degree academically, in her intellect, but she could not understand it emotionally. It had to do with personal feelings, an inner need of his own, not a fault but a reality because of the sort of person he was and the way he spent his life. Although to suggest so would evoke a burst of self-righteous assurances to the contrary, she did not understand. It had to do with feelings. Insulating herself from life's stresses and demands had made her unable to empathize with others, even if that person shared her bed in life. She hoarded her legacy of freedom and privilege with little comprehension of its cost for others, checking her watch impatiently when he returned from his rambles. He sat on the venerable wide porch watching the waves and passersby and listening to her complaints about school semesters that hadn't even started yet, wishing he could make her understand that he needed a break too. She interpreted his need, despite all his efforts to explain himself, as a personal rejection of her. He knew the problem was not all hers. He, who had argued convincingly in court for years and preached sermons that people said they understood and appreciated, was a failure at communicating with his own wife. Although his efforts to do so had been consistent and honest and he had sought the help of experts, his common sense told him that fault was never wholly on one side alone.

As much as he wanted her to apply herself to plans for her mother, he wished she had come with him now. She had in her a natural love of the outdoors, and she could have marveled with him at these wondrous wooded places. They had rambled and hiked when first married. Now Kate preferred her nature at a comfortable remove, in textbooks, in a rocking chair on her Wicomico porch, or peering from the passenger window of a car parked at an overlook. She took her older students on a biology field trip every spring, a hands-on, outdoorsy, three-day expedition that was fun for her and them and their chaperones. He had chaperoned one of the trips and had enjoyed immensely her less circumscribed, more cheerful special event nature.

The wooded slope leveled off into a narrow floodplain that was littered and tumbled with the detritus of the ice meadows of winter floods. The wreckage of high winter water lay on every side, and bunches of small driftwood clustered as much as six or eight feet up in the lower branches of the sycamores. Logs and boards lay in piles against the rising slope and shoaled up crazily against the leaning trees. Pieces of destroyed piers and docks protruded from the jumbles and the odd occasional scrap of canvas or busted Styrofoam cooler appeared here and there between the sycamores and raggedy river maples. Here in the warmer bottomland, sheltered from the wind, the buds had swelled along the branches like small cocoons and were breaking open in small yellow sprays. In one place where the sun broke through, the mud was dotted with emerging fragile slips of Twinleaf, or perhaps Mayapple. In their early stages, he found it hard to tell. In another place, he spied what he thought were the heart-shaped toothed leaves of a Marsh Marigold beginning to appear. The big river eased by in ponderous silver motion, the surface warped now and then by streaks of windy rain. In the shallows here during the two previous summers, he had found yellow pond lilies floating and wondered if enough had survived the winter floods to reappear. The far side was obscured in the pearly fog, and from somewhere over there, he could hear the lonely thwack of an axe cleaving wood. The same sound might have been heard here two hundred years ago, nothing having changed except the white intrusion of an upturned utility bucket washed down from somebody's flooded fishing camp.

He sat on a log and continued to look around, enjoying the stillness. Immediately he thought of Catherine and what they would do. He knew he would have to push Kate to do anything at all and that no help would be forthcoming from her brother. He could not imagine any of his brothers or sisters behaving that way toward his own parents. They would all move heaven and earth to do right by them. He knew the dynamics were different and that life with Catherine, without a father, had been sterile and difficult for Kate and Ray. Still, if Joe was willing to take up the slack, it was hard to understand their defiance toward him. He supposed it made them feel guilty for him to do for Catherine what neither of them would do themselves. Whatever it was, they despised him for it. It was that way in everything. But why couldn't they just relent a little and coop-erate with him in planning for the care of their own mother? Even in things that were to her distinct advantage, Kate resisted the practical and routine. And to hear her talk, one would think her life had been an unending, persistent sequence of personal misfortunes. Thinking about it made him yawn.

They would have to find somewhere for Catherine to have round-the-clock care, consistent balanced meals, interaction with other people, and monitoring by a doctor. As a lawyer for the state, he had seen to all this for other people and gone to court to enforce the right thing when others would not cooperate. But what to do now, alone, in his own family? And how would they pay for it? Despite her years of hostility toward him, he felt responsible for his mother-in-law, as he would have felt for any elderly disabled person living under his own roof. It was another problem Kate did not want to recognize.

He was highly conscious of Ted in the midst of it all. Joe had been part of the care and anguish that his parents had felt toward his own ailing grandmothers and several other older people during his childhood. He had helped at their bedsides, visited them in their nursing homes, and sat by as his parents discussed plans and grieved for them. Although he had not thought about it at the time, these experiences had made a difference in him as he grew up. It informed his work as a lawyer and priest, and it had made a powerful difference in teaching his handicapped students. He was continually mindful of it with Ted. It was a chief reason why he struggled so to make their home secure, comfortable, stable.

He pulled down the zipper of his parka and withdrew from a shirt pocket a rare and treasured joy, a dark fragrant Havana Montecristo robusto cigar in a crackling wrapper. One or two of these prizes was presented to him occasionally by a parishioner's husband, a taciturn agnostic who liked his sermons and worked for Amtrak and made occasional stops in Toronto. Joe peeled off the cellophane and, ignoring connoisseur tradition, carefully removed the red-and-gold band, which he tucked carefully into his pocket. He sniffed the pungent aroma for a while and then clipped it carefully with his pocketknife and lit it with a stove match from his pants pocket. He could still strike a wooden match with his thumbnail, one of the many talents of the Boy Scout years that had lasted over time. He smoked slowly, knowing it might be months before he might do it again, watching the pale blue smoke hang for a moment and drift away behind him through the wet air. In observing the smoke, he became aware of a movement in the distance, beside the water. He froze and waited. Beyond a great sycamore, whose brittle bark was peeling in strips like old veneer, he saw it again. A vigilant turkey was stepping forward with care, followed by another, and another, their dark aerodynamic shapes advancing over the ground with the jerky progress of tadpoles in a woodland pool. He watched them casually as he smoked his delicious Cuban, sheltered from the brunt of the increasing downpour by the tall leaning trees. A tom turkey's beard was visible through the bushes, and someday, he thought, somebody would shoot that other bearded critter, that communist bastard, and he could buy these heavenly cigars in Catoctin Springs. He could imagine the bishop's reaction—and most of the clergy's—to such a sentiment, and he smiled. As if alerted by his grin, the wary turkeys beat a noisy retreat upriver and were soon lost in the gloom.

After a half hour of sitting and watching, he headed back up the slope in the direction of home, sheltering the last nub of his precious cigar from the rain and anticipating how good it would be to get back indoors with his wife and son. It was one of the pleasures of a woodland ramble, the getting back and enjoying the presence of loved ones. Would Kate have touched the brochures? To argue about it a second time would ruin the balance of the day. He wouldn't mention it. He would offer to go get a movie and could foresee the tedium of trying to satisfy Ted and his friends and Kate with the same film. He would let them discuss it and tell him what to do. While in town, he would pick up what Kate needed to make a key lime pie. Even people in the Keys could not make pies to match hers. She was an artist, a genius in the kitchen.

He climbed the hill and looked around at the wet gray world with joy. He remembered the magazine ads from his youth of hunters relaxing before blazing fireplaces, having a drink, boots off, hounds lazing by, while through the background window, a cold twilight loomed. "An Old Forester kind of day," said the caption. And hadn't Horace Kephart mentioned Old Forester somewhere in *Camping and Woodcraft*? Or was it in *Cabins in the Laurel*? He couldn't remember. But how nice it would be to get home and sit down with everybody in the warmth and enjoy a drink. A hefty bourbon on the rocks would make the mysterious, romantic weather outside even more appealing for having come in out of it. It had been so many years since he had last tasted whisky. He tried to remember the warm glow on the tongue, not totally unlike the pleasure of his dwindling cigar. He took a final drag and flicked the stub safely into the wet grass, along with any further thoughts of a drink. Willingly, not at all grudgingly, he let them both go, the butt and the thought. It was little enough sacrifice for the peace he figured it brought.

He returned to an empty house, the back door guarded by dutiful, drenched Cory. On the kitchen table was a note in Ted's narrow, angular handwriting: *Gone to get a movie. Bringing Pizza home for dinner. Don't go anywhere.*

Every light in the house was on. He looked quietly into Catherine's room and saw that she was asleep, her mouth open and a large-print *Reader's Digest* upside down on her stomach. He went up to the bedroom to find his shoes and noticed the stack of nursing home brochures on the bed beneath Kate's folded St. John's sweatshirt. He could not tell if they had been examined and knew that Kate would not mention it to him if she had. It was just as well. He could deal with it tomorrow.

He returned to the kitchen and checked the telephone answering machine. An acolyte had called, down with the flu, who could not serve the following day and could not reach the Sponsor. Two parishioners had left their names and numbers, asking him to call. His old girlfriend Diana had called, wanting them to come to a party the following month. He winced because Kate did not like her and was miffed for days when she called. A family with an unidentifiable accent, seeking overnight emergency lodging, had asked him to call them at a pay phone in town. Both of his sisters had called, just to say hello. From the time of these calls, he gathered that Kate and the boys had left shortly after he did. He wondered what they had been doing. Wandering around the mall, he supposed. Catherine began to cough, quietly at first and then in earnest; he thought he heard her trying to call. He went in to see what he could do.

Chapter Twenty-Six

They were lined up in rows on a prominent display a few feet inside the entrance of the region's best bookstore, radiating an aura of bucolic security and positioned as though every customer coming in was there just to buy one. Unfortunately, this was largely true. These days people waited for the next one in the series like news from home. A wide restful advertisement in the style of Grandma Moses glistened above the display. The ranks of sugary covers, dozens of them side by side on a series of horizontal shelves like an odious early Warhol, duplicated its rustic panorama in elfin scale. On each glossy volume, an overhead angular view of a small town stretched like a patchwork quilt toward distant hills. Prominent in midforeground rose a white steeple topped by a cross. The whole exhibit radiated devotional comfort and spiritual nourishment without anybody having to resort to the Bible, drawing forward entering customers like the allure of a free strip show. A closer look at the covers revealed the village streets adawdle with good country people. One could almost hear "Aw, shucks" and "Gee whiz" as Minnie Pearl bumped into Andy Devine at the five-and-ten. Comfort oozed from the big display like the aroma of chicken soup and apple pie, inviting browsers to be kind to themselves and take one of these books home and explore a simpler, saner existence. Read these easy novels and see how beneath its worrisome surface the world is really an uncomplicated place of good intentions and cheerful virtue, and all for just fifteen dollars and ninety-five cents.

There is no harm in them, you cynical bastard, he told himself. He should be glad if they provided comfort, escape, and some temporary relief from worldly fears and earthly anxieties. Let their readers have a break from twenty-four-hour news of terrorists and hurricanes and pandemics. Let them escape into make-believe and find rest for their souls. Who cares how fallaciously art depicts reality? So what if it reinforces stereotypes like old minstrel shows? Be reasonable. What harm can it do? Whatever makes people read has value. What does it matter that no one has gone out into the world from this store today with Dickens, Flaubert, Melville, Tolstoy, Hugo, Hardy? Does it matter? Faulkner, Bellow, the O'Connors (he was fond of imagining a conversation between Flannery and Frank), the amazing Mavis Gallant, Oates—you think the customers should read *them* and learn to understand. *Miss Lonelyhearts? The Catbird Seat?* Cormack McCarthy? *Everything that Rises Must Converge?* Does anyone understand anymore? He wanted to get up on a chair and rouse them all, tell them of *Lie Down in Darkness, The Wind in the Willows, The Horse's Mouth.* Is anyone there? *A Good Man Is Hard to Find.*

Humankind cannot stand very much reality, said a patient voice in his head. Really, now. What could they hurt, these colorful Grant Wood characters in their Thomas Hart Benton landscapes and Norman Rockwell worlds? After all, anything that makes people read has value, a worth that transcends depth. D. H. Lawrence, Hemmingway, Welty, Hardy, yes, but…it's today. It's *Jeopardy, USA Today,* and *Star Troopers.* The getting and spending, the anxiety, it's about all most people can handle. But the majesty is still among us.

Yes, it's pretty to think so, a patient voice said. *Now, get over it! As one's lady wife would say.*

People drifted in and out and milled about the big display, thumbing through the books and reading the back covers.

"I'm going to get this for the beach!" a woman declared.

"Godammit, I'm going to read a book next year if it kills me!" exclaimed a man, suffering a public attack of good intentions.

"I'll wait till it comes out on DVD," said another.

How many of them, he wondered, saw the church and her clergy, if they thought of them at all, the way they were presented in these popular novels? He supposed that nobody else in a thousand square miles was troubled by that question. He bought a cup of coffee and went outside and sat on a bench in the early fall sunshine and gazed across the vast parking lot. His literary incursion had subsided, and now his head was full of church, the blessings and hazards of which hovered beyond each experience, every dream, awaiting their time. At every moment a half-dozen parishioners were in crises, and today there were a few additional ones. Together with his own family, they were always on his mind.

One of the middle schoolers was depressed. Probably a half dozen were, struggling silently at the edge, but this one was alarmingly obvious. He had noticed this slight, moody child growing quieter all summer. Several parishioners had expressed deep concern. The principal of the boy's school had called him. They were all hoping Joe could "do something." The child had always seemed to like Joe. His parents were peculiar loners who sensed a conspiracy in life's every complication. "They'll talk to you if they'll talk to anybody," people said. Joe had invited the parents to meet him later that afternoon for coffee at a restaurant near their jobs. He had no idea how they would react, regardless of how carefully he brought up the welfare of their only child. If they became defensive and left the congregation, he would have succeeded only in further isolating their suffering twelve-year-old. In that case, he and the principal would refer the matter to the understaffed, inundated mental health agency and pray for the best.

One of his parishioners, at the age of ninety-three, was still maneuvering her ancient Buick around Catoctin Springs. Peering myopically over the steering wheel beneath the artificial flowers of her hat, she drifted slowly through jammed intersections and parallel parked at alarming angles, postponing day by day an inevitable tragedy. Her only local relative, a granddaughter, had sought Joe's help in explaining that her driving days must end, and they were going to have that talk—churning with issues of dignity, autonomy, and death—at the end of the week.

He had participated in dozens of such reckonings, the nervous relatives reluctant but resolved, Joe himself striving for the right balance of clarity and tenderness, and the elderly subject of the matter perceiving the darkness deepen with every word and glance. However lovingly the matter was approached with them, even the most resolute felt the ultimate frailty as the good night came on. Joe had great esteem for this generous, practical, bold old lady. Her sense of humor was warm and zesty. She had supported him fearlessly when he began the community racial dialogues and dinners four years before. She still attended each one, bringing friends and always sitting with people of color. She was one of those who responded immediately and quietly when his discretionary fund was low and he was seeking help for someone or something. He admired her good manners, distinctions of a lost time, and her kindness, and the coming confrontation was heavy on his mind.

He had agreed to speak at a Department of Human Services employee awards banquet. He could not bring himself to refuse. He believed in giving front line troops all the support they could stand. Social workers, police officers, schoolteachers, public health nurses, the military, mental health counselors, doctors, nurses, fire and rescue personnel, the National Guard, people who taught English as a second language, animal control officers—the saints among us. Channels of grace. The date was approaching, and he had to prepare.

The choir members were angry with the choir director. The previous Sunday, only seven joined the procession, while the rest sat in the pews. The director was a capable, aged professional, a good organist, raised in a different denomination, whose temper vexed everyone. He had threatened to resign in the past but had never followed through. It was just as well. There was nobody around to take his place. His choice of music reflected his upbringing in a distinctly gloomy spiritual tradition. Unless Joe selected the hymns and included the glorious, uplifting music of the congregation's ancient traditions, the director's choices sent everybody home depressed and prompted a dozen telephone calls in the following week. Occasionally during an especially busy week, Joe left the hymn choices up to the director, cheerfully urging him to plan with care. On every such occasion, like a compass needle swinging round again to north, he returned to dreary hymns that nobody had ever heard before. Everybody leaving church shook their heads and told Joe they knew he was busy, but he just had to plan the music for the following Sunday himself. There were deeper issues involved than taste. Music is an expression of spirituality in any congregation, and Joe felt a positive responsibility toward the congregation. The dignity of this troubled old choir director was important too. Thus far, he had been able to keep them both in balance.

The day care center that occupied the church basement was always, always in need of something, like a demanding child. It was one of Redeemer's outreach ministries, and most of its young, noisy clientele came from families who were just getting by. It had been the first day care opened in the county, and none of the newer facilities served the very poor, of which there were so many. It was a service, a ministry, not intended for profit, but the affordable costs to clients had long ceased to pay for its operation. Every year they raised the rates, juggling subsidies and expenses and striving for a balance of some sort that would keep the center open and pay the workers their meager salaries. The cost of everything was going up. Several times each year, Joe and the board of directors resorted to bank loans to pay the staff. A new director was needed, and encouraging the old one to retire with dignity was proving difficult. She had helped start the center and had directed it on a fragile budget for twenty-five years. The previous week it had become necessary to let one of the teachers go. The board of directors wanted to meet with him.

To everyone's amazement, the venerable furnace had warmed Redeemer, though barely, through the preceding winter, wheezing and throbbing like the bowels of an old steamship. It had been impossible to know what the next day would bring, and Joe had come to work each morning expecting to find the compressors dead or the pipes frozen. They were still trying to raise twenty-seven thousand dollars for a new one, and winter was in sight again.

For the past month, the burglar alarm had been activated in the middle of the night once, sometimes twice, each week. Joe had to get up at 3:00 a.m. and drive to Redeemer to meet the police. The technicians who showed up the next day to examine the system could find no explanation. Joe suspected a bat.

His discretionary fund was low, and in the past week, he had received calls or visits from seven people needing money for food, prescription drugs, diapers, transportation, utility bills, or rent. Each had used up the quota at the community assistance organization, where the needy could apply once every six months. The needs were endless. People came for help each week by the dozens. Most of them had nowhere else to turn. Some of them were con artists who knew how to work the system. Verifying what they told him took a lot of time. It would have been so much easier to respond to every need, asking no questions. But he knew he held the discretionary fund in trust and that careful use of it was a duty. The more care he took, the greater the number of needy it would serve. He never provided cash to anyone unless it was out of his own pocket. Every check he wrote was to a business he had contacted ahead of time, whose manager had agreed to provide food or medicine or gasoline to the bearer who handed it over with Joe's business card attached. It took time and forced him into the role of social worker. In a poor and depressed community, the demands were constant. Each request for assistance was the discernable tip of an endless residue of interconnected troubles and unresolved misery in which the chronically unprepared lived and died. Each time he grew weary of dealing with it all, a voice reminded him that these were the least of Christ's brethren, and the patience it took to minister to them was a duty.

There was a meeting tomorrow of the Senior Center board of directors. He was helping raise the funds for a new building, and his assignment had been to solicit donations from local clergy. He had mailed out eighty-five letters six weeks back to local clergy of all denominations and within two weeks had collected enough contributions to exceed the clergy quota. He was proud of his colleagues but felt a little awkward at the same time. He was the only representative of his denomination in the county, and people still believed the old stereotype that his was a wealthy church. He suspected that his own salary, such as it was, was one of the highest among local clergy. Many of the other clergy and their families were just getting by, especially those who served part-time and had to work at second jobs. He knew many of them, but their traditions and backgrounds were very different from his own, and with limited time together, he had found it hard to form close friendships. He kept them in his prayers.

Time. In ministry and the law, there never seemed to be enough time. Through each of them ran the eternal discomfort of knowing he was keeping someone or something waiting. And even on chaotic days off or the occasional vacation, the eternal footman was at hand nearby, around the corner, peering from the next room, and there seemed to be no peace his low snickering did not interrupt. He had always juggled his calendar daily as priest and attorney, trying to respond fairly to the demands. His office door was always open. He liked people. He did not always like what they did, and at times, he grew weary of their problems. But he knew that most of them were doing about as well as they could, and when he grew tired of them, he knew the issue was not them so much as his own fatigue. He thought of his elderly friend in her immense Buick and how her waiting would take a new turn after their coming conversation. Time. As in the law, his most valuable resource, next to the minutes he spent on his knees, was time.

He recognized exasperation and fatigue as signs of trouble down the road and like most clergy, he tried to pace himself. Saying no to this or that, being with his family, keeping the house clean, bills paid, and the yard in good shape and faithfully serving his parish—there seemed never to be enough time. In most other dioceses, Redeemer would have had the service of two clergy. He knew the difficulty lay not just with him and his small, unimportant life. Clergy everywhere, working against much greater odds, contended with the same limitations. He was no different, except that he knew he managed it all with less grace than others did.

He had no illusions about himself as a special case. His blessings far outweighed his pain. God had been good to him. But Kate and Ted, the greatest of his treasures, were always on his mind, and he felt guilty for not being with them more. With Kate especially, it seemed there was never enough time. What time there was could be a difficulty itself because he felt guilty for somehow not making it count for more. It was not always time spent with her that was wanting but time spent for her or because of her, covering family responsibilities she did not appear to understand. He found himself compensating continually for her obsessive need to be at work, her teen-like disregard of domestic issues, and her avoidance of adult social interactions.

The contrast about her job, at least, was not lost on him. He had discussed it often with his family counselor, trying to understand it. Both the law and ministry had required a great deal of time, and Kate's work as a schoolteacher had always expanded mysteriously to match or exceed every minute demanded by his own professions. It was as if they were engaged in a competition he had not recognized, and Kate was determined to win or, at least, stay even. When trials lasted into the evening hours or weddings kept him at church on Saturday afternoons, Kate's work at school somehow expanded proportionately, and he paid a price. It was a cycle he had not perceived until recent years.

The bishop expected clergy to work every weekday and a couple of nights each week, a half day on Saturdays, and make hospital calls on Sunday afternoons after conducting morning services. He expected clergy to take one day off each week. Joe had vowed at ordination to serve under the direction of bishops. He had tried to remain faithful to that promise, but it had been a difficult and lonely way to get along. More than anything, he was determined that his family should not suffer for his ideals. It was a question of balance, and clergy had to get it right. If they did not, their children could grow up and turn their backs on the church. He had seen it happen, and he was determined that Ted's own faith should have the freedom to mature rather than suffer. And he had made his vows to Kate before making them to God. She should not suffer for the demands of his vocation. None of it was her doing. This too demanded a constant sense of balance.

God understood it all, and that very assurance strengthened him. He was certain that God would give him the grace and power to live with integrity. That was why his eyes always reflected equal measures of hope and sorrow. Constantly balancing family life with service in the church required a steady supply of hope, like the slow drip of an IV providing necessary nourishment. There was never adequate time, regardless of his best efforts. He knew it was a mistake to try to meet all needs. Yet no sooner had he said no to something then somebody was rushed to the hospital, or a crisis occurred with somebody's child, or a perennially cheerful parishioner showed up at the door in tears, or an emergency meeting was called over something or other. It all eventually required more time than what he had said no to in the beginning. He knew that God understood his good intentions and would help him in ways that surpassed his rational understanding. It was not so with human beings, however. This was why ministry in the broken world was so lonely and why his eyes let a sorrow through.

In balancing it all, he felt a particular duty toward the parish children. Invitations from the children to attend their band concerts, school plays, and scouting banquets were signs of the breaking in of the kingdom, evidence that church and parish life had meaning in their young lives. Next to time with Kate and Ted at home, the spiritual formation of children was the most important gladness in his life. He sat now in the midmorning sunshine, and images from the past few hours glowed in his mind with a light of their own. He had attended an elementary school talent assembly. The little girl who invited him had looked around as her class marched into the auditorium to take their seats in the front rows. She had smiled and waved when she saw him. After the short ceremony, her parents, genuinely pleased by his presence, had found him and thanked him for coming. On his way back to the office, he had taken a detour and stopped at this bookstore. He was tired and hoped that coffee would make a difference. It was more expensive here than in the convenience stores, but it tasted more like the coffee of years ago. He needed to sit alone now for a moment and do nothing, a necessity that came upon him frequently these days. He should have called Milly to tell her he would be a few minutes late. Right now, he needed to sit still for a few minutes more.

Parishioners were struggling financially, considering divorce, wanting to get married, having trouble at work, drinking too much, mourning wayward sons and daughters, celebrating accomplishments and milestones, and many of them wanted to talk. They were the same people who smiled and wept at the children's Christmas Eve pageant, went to work weary, enjoyed a good joke, and were lucky now and then at cards. They struggled their whole lives to keep a sort of balance. And whether consciously or unconsciously, he was often unsure, most appeared to sense the scales permanently tipped toward chaos, requiring a periodic readjustment. God was good, and life was unfair, and a great mystery yawned eternally in between. The people could not be blamed for hoping that the man God had assigned to Redeemer to make it all a little clearer ought to be able to provide some answers, some direction. In their eyes, his deputation implied a certain capability. Ambassadors come with credentials.

One twenty-year-old had come to him about leaving college and entering the Army. Her parents would be devastated. She was the first in her line to go to college, and her parents had struggled to make it possible. Her older brother had run off years before and as far as anybody knew was lost somewhere in the drug culture, or maybe dead. The elderly parents were not affluent. They had not completed high school. They had married and had their children late in life and known nothing but hard work since childhood. They had never had a vacation and had driven the same car for twenty years. They would not understand how their very success in raising an intelligent, decent daughter was leading her to conclude that the Army would better prepare her for college than she felt herself to be now. How could he assist the daughter in helping these good, uncomplicated people understand the dynamics of a different world? And how would they explain to them that their daughter was gay?

Several adults were dealing with depression. After meeting a few times with each one, he had received permission to refer them to counselors. Another family was in denial about what Joe thought might be their son's Asperger's syndrome. He took it as a healthy sign that they had asked about his schedule recently. A couple who had tried for years to have a child had adopted a baby, and suddenly they were pregnant and wanted to talk about what God was doing in their lives. Two parishioners had died in the past month, and both families were dealing with remorse over things done and left undone. The additional tension had made an always-difficult time very hard for everyone, including Joe, in the weeks since the burials. Now one family was angry with him, people said, for insisting the coffin be closed during the funeral. The real source of their rage would reveal itself in time. There were always calls from parishioners who were lonely or who wanted to talk but were unsure why or whose faith was being sorely tested or who no longer felt nourished by corporate worship. For all of them, Joe knew he was not a fixer, and he never tried to be.

Joe served on the committee to rebuild the diocese's shabby, beloved conference center, an immense undertaking that required time every week. He was on the finance committee of the diocesan executive board, which met monthly before each two-day board meeting. He served as dean of the regional clergy, and as trustee of a charitable foundation that served four separate dioceses. He had vowed at ordination to take his place in the counsels of the church, and however faithfully he served, the needs seemed to renew themselves every day.

Usually the bishop had understood, aware of the size of Redeemer and the unlikelihood of the parish affording the salary for an assistant. In his finer and more rested moments, Joe could not bring himself to blame the bishop for anything. As lonely and demanding as his own ministry was, he knew that bishops faced far more complicated anxieties. Their responsibilities were wider, deeper. For this reason, Joe had summoned up all his lawyerly composure and tried to accept the bishop's rudeness and indifference. He had never been certain what it was all about, and the bishop's close friends among the clergy appeared not to know either. At least if they did, they had not taken the trouble to explain it to him. He was learning to live with it, like a disfiguring birthmark or poor vision, and it no longer hurt him as it had in his early days in the diocese.

He could never stop thinking about the subtle signs that Kate and Ted wondered why it was all necessary, why he insisted on being away from home so often, and why he didn't just get a real job that didn't require so much time and involve so many people. Ted used to ask him why he had not continued in the law, as though there must have been some disappointment or crises there that had driven him into the church. Kate made no secret of her disappointment that he spent so little time in important places like St. John's School or the other schools that had always been the center of her universe. His wife and son saw him "working" only on Sunday mornings and then only when they attended. What they saw of his ministry did not appear to them particularly difficult, and they could not understand why it required so much time. He suspected that most people shared a similar view, that serving in ministry was largely a matter of showing up on Sundays and keeping everybody happy.

When he tried to explain his ministry to his wife and son, they listened politely and changed the subject at the first opportunity. More than once Kate had reminded him, with weary impatience, that she worked harder than he did and had more to do than he had, presenting it each time as a truth she was compelled to clarify because obviously he could not figure it out on his own. She used to say it too in their early years of marriage while he was still practicing law. There had been so many other issues to address then, and he was still learning his way through the mystery of her rage. He had chosen to let this particular point go and work on more important matters. In retrospect, he had learned that letting anything go meant facing it again sooner or later in the arsenal of her anger. It was too late now. Throughout their marriage, she had continued to see herself as the overworked sufferer and him as the one who had it fairly easy. Whether the implication was that he should be ashamed of himself for not doing more to help her or was proffered as an excuse for her neglect of their home and domestic matters, he was never sure. It was probably no more than exactly what she said it was, an assertion that her job was more demanding than his and that she was a harder worker. Work was her point of reference and personal hardship her incessant refrain. After many years of marriage, she still responded to anything he tried to say on the matter with dismissive annoyance.

Occasionally Joe wondered if Kate was talking this way to Ted when he wasn't around. Ted spent a lot of time with Kate riding to and from school, and she had always talked endlessly about the demands of her job to anyone who would listen. Ted was a captive audience. Occasionally he surprised Joe by asking what he had been doing all day. Joe had always heard it as a child's expression of natural interest in his father. Joe remembered asking the same question of his own father and wished he had paid more attention to how his father had kept food on the table and shoes on everybody. Life had not been easy for a man who dropped out of school in the ninth grade. Joe's mother had taught her children the meaning of respect by the supportive way she talked about their father. He was difficult, impatient, quarrelsome, suffering from a war wound that turned every step into pain. He devoted himself to providing for his family. As children, Joe and his siblings often needed help in seeing through their father's irritable disposition. In helping her children understand their father's basic goodness and remarkable honesty, Joe's mother had taught her children much about life's essentials. Together with his mother, Kate was the most important woman in his world. He could not imagine his mother damaging her husband and children by ridiculing him before them, driving a wedge between him and their impressionable young minds. Good mothers did not do such things. And Kate was a good mother. She would not tear him down before Ted or do anything to mislead Ted about his own father. She loved Ted and would do nothing to hurt him. Ted's occasional curiosity about his work was bound to be natural and well meaning. Whenever circumstances made him wonder, he was ashamed of himself for days for even thinking about questioning Kate's motives.

Because Kate was his wife and he loved her despite and in some ways because of her impenetrable denial, Joe found it hard to be objective about her. When Kate's behavior bewildered and angered him, as when she immediately did something or failed to do something that they had discussed and agreed upon, Joe could make sense of his incredulity only by questioning his own understanding and memory. They had agreed at noon to keep the windows closed while the oak and pine pollen was at its worst. By midafternoon, Kate had opened all the windows in their bedroom. The furniture was covered with a fine layer of golden powder, Joe was sneezing and clearing his throat, and Kate was saying, in distressed astonishment, "It's only one room!" or "I just wanted some fresh air! Can't I even have that?"

Had he made his point clearly enough? Had she forgotten his allergies? Had he forgotten what they had agreed upon, or had she? Was he losing his mind? Confronted, she grew testy. Pressed for an explanation, she grew angry and changed the subject in seconds to something he had said or done or failed to do months, years before that he could not even recall. Suddenly he was trying to reason with her about it, and the issue of the pollen and open windows was lost altogether. Tactics he would have recognized in court and could have managed reasonably within his profession confounded him in living with his own wife.

Yet his mind was sound, and he concluded his memory was far better than Kate would have him believe. His legal training had taught him something, after all, about weighing evidence and expecting contingencies from the most unlikely directions. He was alert to significance in the seemingly unimportant. He recalled an incident when Ted was eight or nine. His sister was planning a birthday party for one of his nephews. Most of the family would attend. Kate and Ted loved to visit his family and had looked forward to going. He had been trying for weeks to clean the patio furniture and move it into the garage for winter. The gutters should be cleaned and the first-floor windows winterized before bad weather set in. The first winter storm, ominously gathering over the Carolinas, had begun its slushy progress northward. A deep, wet snow was suddenly predicted for early in the following week, although the weekend itself would be merely cold. He had stayed at home to complete the necessary work before the snow came, while Kate and Ted went without him to his nephew's party. Kate's excitement about taking a brief trip and seeing Joe's family had quickly turned to fury at having to go alone. "I have to drive all that way, Joe, just to make you look good," she had told him. He had tried to reason with her and finally suggested that she and Ted stay home too. He would call his sister. She would understand. Kate had gone, however, put-upon and fuming. When she and Ted returned home on Sunday night, she spent an hour telling him to his delight about what they had done and the news on everyone in his family. She appeared to have forgotten her anger at going without him. She took no notice of the work he had done around the house in her absence, or if she did, she never mentioned it. And she never said a word about what she had said about him to Ted on the long drive to and from his relatives' home.

During the following week while they were clearing snow from the driveway, Ted told him again about the fun they had had and added casually that, even so, it had been a lot of trouble for Mom "driving all that way just to make you look good." Joe had explained to Ted again with great patience the work required around the house and the winterizing needed before the snow came and that sometimes such things just had to come first. He explained that he regretted missing his parents and family and had stayed at home because the snow was coming.

He waited until after Ted's bedtime to take the incident up with Kate. She denied talking about him to Ted and claimed to see no significance at all in Ted's choice of words matching her own. When he tried to reason with her, she told him he was paranoid, and she had never said anything about him to Ted and to "get over it." She had turned out the light early and faced the wall and fell asleep immediately. Short of grabbing her and turning her over and holding her face in his hands so she could not turn away from him, he despaired of finding any way of getting through to her.

The encouragement and support clergy were expected to provide in endless flow and the diplomacy and energy needed to overlook slights and resolve misunderstandings were difficult to explain to outsiders. And although some of their dynamics were the same, clergy from other traditions—nonliturgical, independent, congregational—did not always understand either. Many of them worked with an assistant or in teams of clergy who could share duties and expectations. Many served in small rural congregations where clergy were accorded much deference. Preparing people for baptism, communion, reception, confirmation, and marriage required time and care. Preaching required time and care, especially with several different sermons each week. Service in the community, diocesan work, the eternal budgetary issues, conferences and endless meetings, personal counseling, and unending hurt feelings to reckon with, it was important to be strong yet vulnerable, compassionate but not sentimental, open but completely above unfair influences. Care must be exercised in everything against crossing somebody's boundary in one thing or another. The constant interaction with people of all kinds, for every conceivable reason, required a mental and emotional energy every bit as critical as physical stamina. It was hard to explain to those who had never served in a vocation. Other professions required the same alertness and attention to detail, and some of them demanded more. But in none of them was one the paid professional in a sea of volunteers. It had been different in the law. Then he had worked in a whirlpool of colleagues and related professionals who shared the pressure and understood it.

Maneuvering through the latest minefield of political and cultural expectations in the church was like running an obstacle course where the obstructions had been designed and erected by those with no knowledge of the race. Neither did they know anything much about the runners or the course before and after their particular obstacle. They felt entirely competent, nevertheless, to shout instructions and correctives to those stumbling by, as if they knew the course from start to finish. At times it was all wearying and hazardous. To many, especially those who had been running for bishop since high school, clearing the hurdles in good form had become the most important function of life. The special latitude the church accorded feminists and African Americans could be dangerous, confusing territory, with simmering emotions beneath the surface that could overflow with even the smallest pressure by the unwary or uneducated. Good intentions were often misinterpreted, especially in the rarified realm of ecclesiastical politics. Joe had seen good men and women condemned for honest mistakes, inadvertent errors or the wrong choice of words. He was especially sorry for the closeted gays and found it painful to imagine the relentless caution in which they were forced to live their faith.

Joe saw himself as a man facing the dawn. The darkness was behind him; he knew the direction of the light. Despite its hazards and loneliness, it was privileged, often joyful labor, and through its difficulty and beyond the world's brokenness, one could feel a personal connection running all the way to the Creator. As in all else in his life, he knew he had no cause to complain. Others suffered for the faith in wretched, lonely places and in the end gave the only thing left to them, their lives. He knew that God understood the working conditions when no human being could. He knew he was a sinner, a pinch of dust, and nothing more. The blessing was that he knew it. He felt the itch of forgiveness tingling in him like a drop of strong medicine, soothing his innards and empowering him for another try. He knew his mistakes were many and disappointing, and knowledge of them weighed him down awkwardly at times and threatened to discourage him. His good intentions were often frustrated, and those that came to fruition in time revealed themselves to be entirely self-serving. Despite how depressing it all was, he knew that God could use his efforts for good. God had blessed him with a reasonable understanding of himself and his labors, and the blessing included a willingness to wait. Impatient as he could be in the working details, he was serene and composed in contemplating the great plan and its final triumph. He knew that his effort would bear fruit down the road, long after his time had ended. Others would see the benefit. That was all right. If benefit and reward in life were his goals, and witnessing the results of his labors, he would have remained in the law. God's gift to him was like a sense of humor, enabling him to see the world with different eyes. He longed to appreciate life without undue solemnity. And while he was struggling, there were decent companions, good people like his senior warden, Harry Campos, and his junior warden, Tom Downes, and hundreds of other parishioners and old friends in every place in which he had ever lived. He could feel God working through them to encourage him, heal him, and shore him up. And he knew the gift was there even when he least perceived or appreciated it.

He sat in the warm sunshine and knew he should be on his way to the church. He should call Milly and let her know where he was. The midmorning light enthralled him. The immense parking lot with its clusters of bright cars, spread out beneath an endless blue sky, quiet and lonely as an Edward Hopper, was strangely soothing and restful. The quiet and stillness were pleasant. Small shifting clouds drifted over in windy rhythm, and the wings of gliding seagulls made white flashes in the intoxicating light as they caught the sun. A sky like Renoir's *Pont Neuf*, it made him long for the scintillating blues and greens of the sea at Wicomico. In dreams he had soared in such a sky for years, over sea and mountains, climbing and gliding in a freedom cleansing as a long drink of cool spring water. He had flown in planes through towers of clouds, peering into their snowy canyons and watching the land race by below in anecdotal panorama, and he had recognized the familiar perspective of his dreams. He went to sleep many times trying to conjure it up, make it happen, but such dreams had a life of their own quite beyond his control. The wonderful lemon light before him moved in waves, transforming the angular pedestrian storefronts into receptive palettes of gold in all its expressions—white, green, yellow, and rose, glowing and warm, joyful and reassuring. He thought of Monet's *Rouen Cathedral in Sunlight*.

The restful hush, more in him than his surroundings, was split by a harsh voice and followed quickly by the pang of a slap and a wail of pain. He glanced over his shoulder. An obese woman was trudging forward on the sidewalk pulling a little boy by the arm and jerking as though to yank it from its socket. From her threatening words, probably audible across the parking lot, Joe gathered she had brought the blond toddler into the same bookstore in the spring, and he had dared to misbehave. Now she was reminding him of his transgression and giving him a swat or two beforehand in case it should cross his mind to "do like last time when we get inside. You mind me, goddammit! You hear? Answer me. What did I just say?" A young Latino man half her size stood with them, saying not a word.

In the broken world, where innocents suffer and evil appears to triumph, Joe had learned a thing or two about anger. Now and then he contemplated Titian or Raphael interpreting chaos in broad allegorical scenes, or its monstrous mysteries portrayed by Keats or Byron in odes, or in free verse by Ginzberg, or songs by Bob Marley.

His inward eye discerned faces at the door appearing and receding in the confusion of freedom, the troubled—so many—seeking the chief whom they cannot see and forced to settle for a deputy whom they see only imperfectly, like an image in a dusty mirror. Faces at the door, reflecting rebellion and wrong choices, arouse the unease of compassion. Behind them the noise of the great battle, to which they must return, clangs and roars. Stung by unfairness, betrayal and want, they bring their hostilities in rough bags slung over their shoulders or, striving for preference, raised forward on silver salvers that twinkle and gleam in the lurid light. A door like the theater entrance at the Barberini in Rome, Caravaggio people like *The Raising of Lazarus*, expecting God or the church or the government or a cop or a social worker or a lawyer or doctor or somebody to fix things and make it all fair, reasonable. There are books torn and trampled and bones and shells in pieces on the ground. The fossil record goes back eleven million years. How can one comprehend even a small part of it in eighty or ninety of them? How does one unlock the complexities for others? He sat on the bench in the warm sunshine, and the studio receded, and he thought of Greece, China, Rome. Eleven million years. Nothing. Nothing at all when laid against the monstrous immensity of geologic time. And God was bigger than all that!

The child with the stinging cheek had been jerked, crying through the heavy double doors behind him, and his wail was lost in the din of horns and motors, for now.

While he worked as a lawyer, Kate had assured him that she knew exactly what he did all day: "Filing papers and stuff," she said blithely, with total self-assurance. It had amused him then, and he had loved her for it, knowing that her perception was innocent and shared by many who were not lawyers. After the years had matured and educated them both, and he had served for five years as a clergyman, he heard her tell a summer guest on the porch in Wicomico that Joe spent all day "picking hymns and answering the phone and things." By then, he understood it was a personal characterization, not an attempt to describe his profession or vocation. After their years together, he thought he had a right to expect a fairer assessment from her. He knew she loved him, but she loved herself more and could not abide anything that threatened to portray her career as second to his. She perceived her worth and work as bound up together, and everything else in life assumed its relative value around them.

It hurt, but it explained the thinly veiled competition by which she related to him.

Joe was secure enough in his own identity to believe the problem was not in him, at least not that particular problem. He knew he had many faults, made more mistakes than he even recognized, but Kate's chronic need to be class champion was not one of them. Her view of him fit in with the way she saw the world: a threatening place where one stayed safe through excelling in everything. He supposed her complete self-assurance in her own views and opinions was a form of self-protection. Was her view of him a function of that or of her anger? And anger at what, exactly? Him? Some fault in his personality he was too blind to see? His waiting for her to change? Her own limitations? She believed that most of life's problems could be untangled in an hour or so, like the plots of television shows. Honor, character, a person's word, sin and forgiveness, redemption, reconciliation, atonement, the plan of salvation—what was all the fuss about? Ministry? Anger? A capacity for intimacy? *Come on, Joe! Lighten up. Being a preacher is no big deal. A lawyer was a little more, ah, important at times, maybe. But you just try being a teacher with five classes each day and only one free period! You just try working with some of these kids. You'll see!*

He despaired of her ever understanding him. Her reference for judging others was what they did in life, and it was all she needed to know to understand everything about them. That she had very little knowledge of what others did, it made no difference in a life lived by assumptions. There was no fault involved; she could not be blamed for it. How she was raised, the choices she had made, the way she grew up... No two minds are alike. If fault must be ascribed, he had only himself to blame. His was a rough road, and it had been his choice. She was just being herself, after all. She had so many good qualities. He was not about to fault her for not understanding him or his vocation. Any unhappiness he felt was his own problem. In fulfilling his vows to Kate and the church, he would concentrate on the practical realities before him and count his many blessings. God would be with him in his marriage as in his calling, and the blessings in both far outweighed the difficulties. When he closed his eyes, he saw faces again: Kate, Ted, his family, old friends, and behind them the ones who touched his life in the church. With so many, how could one feel so lonely? The travel time alone was wearying beyond reason. He thanked God he had always awakened at the final second when he went to sleep at the wheel.

He stood up and finished the cold coffee and dropped the paper cup into a trash bin beside the bench and raised his arms over his head and bent backward and stretched. He was no different from other clergy. Despite his good intentions and the care he tried to take in pacing himself, he became overwhelmed. He never felt adequate, and he knew his feeling was a truth in itself. It was God's work and only God could do it. He was deputized to deal with a small portion of it, and God was with him, regardless of how it seemed at times. He supposed he was effective in about half of what he tried to do. Whether that was average (whatever *that* meant) among his brothers and sisters in holy orders, he did not know. How can one know the minds of introverts when there is so little time to talk and who are not very good at discussing themselves anyway? He thought he had learned what all clergy know, at least the realists, that God doles out no special assistance or latitude to the ordained. From his own experience, he knew the paradoxical and enigmatic joy in serving, apparently not intended for human understanding but only to be experienced, as a reminder, to keep one going. There was no guarantee of worldly success, a truth he had learned intellectually and emotionally. The standard is higher.

God had shored Joe up especially in one way, however. Whether through his upbringing or teaching or years in the law or through some other means he did not yet appreciate, God had taught him early that he could fix absolutely nothing and nobody. He did not have the answers to anyone's problems. It was an ultimate truth he had learned long before seminary. He could not save anybody, including himself. He offered very little advice, and only when asked. As he grew older, he had gotten better about speaking from his own experience, but he was careful to define it as such. Joe had a trial lawyer's impatience with philosophy offered as a substitute for fact. He could listen well, a blessing for which he was grateful. He was capable of helping others sort out the obvious and gain a measure of clarity. But he was no psychologist, professional counselor, social worker or expert on anything, nor was he a theologian. The blessing was that he knew it.

Ordination late in life had spared Joe and his parishioners the trauma of hyperactive youth. His seminary had been quite good at helping students distinguish between their skills and mere enthusiasms. Now that he was in it, he believed that parish ministry was what God expected of him, but he still wondered if he had been wrong about his call. He wondered if his colleagues wrestled with the same doubt. Many of them seemed so confident, so certain of their direction, as though they had been born to their vocation. He knew he was too impatient and spiritually shallow to be entrusted with such work. Whatever he had been born to, life was never going to be easy. Who was he to be so involved in peoples' lives? He could not even manage his own. He would have been happier living in a cabin in the mountains or on an island somewhere, fishing and painting. Who was he to carry moral theology and biblical ethics to anybody?

When he closed his eyes and wondered about it all, the answer that came again was a series of faces. Like someone on an escalator going up or down and observing the faces moving past in the other direction, he saw them coming closer and disappearing above or below with but a moment to relate and connect and understand. When he meditated on his possible alternatives to ministry, he heard in his mind the metronomic ticking of a clock, and his understanding of God and his common sense brought him back again to time and life's brevity. Since childhood, he had known an unexplained and instinctive revulsion toward wasting things—food, water, time, resources, opportunities, fuel, anything. Wasting life was equally, viscerally unacceptable. It was a betrayal of God and an affront to the widows and orphans in their tens of millions. *While we have time, let us do good and especially unto those who...* he recalled, words from his childhood church, the minister intoning them as everybody began to dig around for the gift they would return to God. A lifetime is so short. Ninety or a hundred years did not even figure in geologic time, which itself showed up as less than a pinpoint on the scale of cosmic existence. And God was bigger than all that, the creator of all of it. How does one connect? He had some skills, some abilities, all gifts, none of them earned. How would he account for himself when God reviewed his small résumé and said a word or two about how he had managed his life? He could reassure others. It was not always easy to reassure himself.

While we have time... And so little of it too, as if everything depends upon us, and trusting as if everything depends upon God. So many people with needs. And the eternal administrative, diocesan, and community duties were vital to the church too. He knew that everybody else in parish ministry faced the same balancing acts as they served their congregations. Like all clergy, he was lonely but not alone. He was in good company. He was not fulfilling his calling as well as others, but it was the best he could do, and that was all.

He had great empathy for other clergy in all denominations. They exasperated him, showing up knowing that plans involving many people had to be finalized and schedules planned and, after much small talk and many tangents, announcing cheerfully that they had left their calendars at home or at their church, and they couldn't exactly commit to anything, "but go ahead and set a date and I'll get back to you. I mean, anytime is fine with me, if I'm here, I mean, if I don't have anything planned, you know." How many times had he agreed to meet one of them for lunch and ended up eating alone? Sometimes they wouldn't even call to say they had forgotten. Nobody made notes or carried calendars, and most seemed satisfied with planning things on the run, without writing anything down. Clergy in his own denomination usually were better about it all. And lateness didn't bother him so anymore, as it had when he began his ministry fresh from the law and theology school. He himself had to apologize often for being held up. At times it truly could not be helped. But punctuality seemed always relative with other clergy, and it mystified him. Most of his black colleagues especially, in every denomination, appeared to set no importance by schedules and time. During seminary, in a consortium program of students from many theological schools, the angry African American director had felt the issue important enough to engage a black PhD from New York to explain it all to Joe and his fellow students. His message, thundered forth in old-time religious sermonizing, was that time was just not reckoned the same way in the black community. There was nothing white people could do about it but adapt, and they had better get busy adapting.

He knew his years in the law had conditioned him to expect too much. If disorganization among his colleagues troubled him, the problem was his, not theirs. He believed in being prepared and on time as much as humanly possible. He played by the rules and expected others to do so as well. Others, perhaps most others, had similar expectations. It just seemed that somehow life didn't happen that way. Everybody was busy. Personality types differed. Some thought hierarchically, some analytically; others focused on form and cared little for content. He believed that people generally tried to do their best. Everyone had different gifts. The thousand weekly demands of pastoring, as some of his colleagues liked to say, must always be mixed with the inevitable surprises and balanced with family life and its own responsibilities. Was it any wonder that so many burned out so soon, that faith got so buffeted in the business of church, that the comfort of love could suffer so? It had little to do with a loss of faith. He never condemned himself so severely as after losing patience with his colleagues. They faced what he faced daily, and he knew that many of them, maybe most of them, managed their lives with more grace and patience than he did.

The dazzling Delph blue above him was clear now, the little clouds having drifted over and out of sight. He looked across the immense parking lot and was cheered to see a flock of Herring gulls wheeling over the asphalt. They began to land and strut about like stiff, jerky old men. What attracted them to these asphalt barrens? He thought he saw a laughing gull among them. Hundreds of miles from the sea, they followed the great river inland, alert but not inquisitive, hearty, beautiful in flight, elegant in their obstinacy as they stood their ground with shoulders hunched and tails turned against the breeze. He wished the laughing gull would call. For years he had marveled at gulls as they flapped and dove behind tractors plowing fields in inland valleys, hundreds of miles from the sea, or perched in cacophonous choirs on pilings, laughing their raucous calls as the big ferries eased into dock on the thin coastal islands in the hot sunshine. Winter and summer, in good weather and bad, their behavior was the same.

A tractor-trailer truck the size of a small house drifted ponderously to a halt between him and the birds, and his thoughts shifted to more pressing matters. He must go to the savings bank and withdraw enough from family savings to cover an overdraft and deposit it in their checking account in Catoctin Springs. For a week Kate had had the checkbook. He had been reluctant to ask for it because it was a very stressful time for him, and he knew what he was likely to find, and he wanted to avoid an argument. When she kept it for a week or more, knowing he needed it for bills or gasoline or groceries, it was always a sign. He wasn't at all surprised when the overdraft notice appeared in the mail. He had called his friend at the bank immediately.

Still, he was encouraged and inspired because life would be more manageable now that, finally, after so many years of trouble, Kate was seeing a therapist. At last there would be another responsible player on the field now.

It had taken her four months, apparently, to get her referral from Father Hervey, schedule an appointment, and actually walk through the counselor's office door. She had taken the time, a week ago, to tell him the counselor's name, an older woman, a Dr. Wallace, who said she wanted to see Kate alone for a while. She would let Joe know when he could come in too. This was good news, and he thanked Kate tenderly for telling him. Then in his excitement he had of course made the mistake of asking how her first visit went, meaning how she had found Dr. Wallace? Did they seem to get on well? As soon as he said it, he knew he was committing a boundary violation, as the other priests liked to say these days. However much it concerned their marriage and all he held dear to his heart, he knew that it was Kate's appointment, Kate's therapist, and Kate's business. This was certainly how Kate would view it, and she was right, of course. The whole matter was hers. The fact that he had worried endlessly over her health and waited for years for her to agree to consult a professional, she would see as his problem, having nothing to do with her. Her conduct over the years had made her position clear; she owed him no explanations. He was forbidden to trespass; she had guarded what she had determined were her boundaries tenaciously, single-mindedly, viciously when challenged, from the time she had said, "I will."

She responded as she always had when she felt some obligation to talk to him about anything personal. She described how impossible the traffic had been on the way to Dr. Wallace's office and how inconvenient it was to leave St. John's with so much to do, even though classes had ended for the day. She had to work, after all. She was supposed to be monitoring a study hall and "the history teacher" or somebody had to cover for her, and she told him she had a dental appointment. And Dr. Wallace's office was in one wing of a big medical building where there was little room to park. She had been compelled to drive around the lot four times while a rude woman, her car idling, had brushed her hair and arranged something on the passenger seat of her dilapidated car before finally pulling out so that Kate could park in that space. People were so inconsiderate. She described having to wait for the elevator and how she had stood facing the doors after pressing the orange button, only to have the doors behind her slide silently open and close again the moment she turned around and noticed them. She mentioned the doctor's receptionist, how impersonal she was—"Like she didn't have the slightest interest in my problems! What does she work in a doctor's office for?"—and how the telephone conversation that absorbed her while Kate sat and waited was obviously personal, not at all related to business. The copies of *Newsweek* were several months old, and she had already read all the issues of *People* and *Reader's Digest*, and all she could do was sit there and listen to the receptionist. She had thought of informing the doctor about the receptionist but had decided against it. On the way home, she passed an accident. A man was standing outside a pickup truck arguing with a police officer, and he looked like somebody Kate used to know (the man, not the officer), but she had been unable to remember who, and it had been on her mind ever since. She returned to St. John's and found she had missed an important telephone call from a textbook supplier. She had been waiting for the call all week. And that was it, she said with a shrug, her eyes downcast, as though nothing could be more simple, and everything was now entirely explained. No, she said, irritation beginning to rise in her voice, she did not know what kind of doctor Wallace was. Psychiatrist, psychologist, licensed social worker, they were all the same. No, she had not taken one of the doctor's business cards. "What difference does it make, Joe?" she said, as though he could ask the most preposterous questions on earth when he wanted to.

Still, for the first time in fifteen years of a turbulent marriage, she had attended a counseling session, as promised, and was committed to going back, and he would one day get to go with her. They had turned a corner. They were on a different trajectory now, and in time he would begin to see a longed-for glow on the horizon. He was so relieved he could almost see it now. Had he not stopped himself, he could have daydreamed foolishly, imagining scenes of intimacy and honesty with Kate and conversations, respect, shared confidences, and a bright rekindling of those qualities with which he believed their marriage had begun. But that was all premature, for the future, awaiting its own time, he told himself. For now, what was happening was good, and he was grateful for the progress. His anxieties over family life had been soothed for months since the intervention with the Gallaghers and Kate's acknowledgment of drinking and her promise to them and to him to follow through. It was a blessing. He had waited and prayed for it, for all three of them, his sweet wife, his son, himself too. He could almost think that he did not deserve such relief.

It was better with Catherine too. Kate had finally looked at all the brochures and made a couple of reasonable decisions, culling out those they could not possibly afford and borrowing one of Joe's county road maps. She had spent a week traveling around, even taking a "personal day" from St. John's, and had visited all the places that looked like possibilities. One of them had appealed to her. The costs appeared manageable, and she was impressed by the aid who showed her around, the manager, and the decor. In what in Joe's eyes amounted to nothing less than a miracle, a room was available immediately. It was small, but Catherine could have a television and some furniture. There were activities. The visiting physician was someone Joe knew, a connection that interested Kate not at all but that Joe supposed might be helpful. Lookout Manor was a new building resembling a motel, perched on a hilltop near a small town almost an hour's drive away. The distance was troubling, but it couldn't be helped. It would be expensive, but there was no way around that either. With help from Ray and Fawn, Catherine's small income, and their own salaries and savings, it could be managed.

Joe felt that applying for the room was a matter of some urgency. Fortunately, everyone else on the waiting list was seeking a slightly larger room, and the manager thought the potential resident who was ahead of Catherine for this particular room was going to decide on a larger one too. He was encouraged when Kate telephoned Ray without an argument, although she insisted on talking privately with him, with Joe out of the room. He left the room and went to another floor when she called Ray on their home phone. He would have gladly gone to the West Coast, anywhere, anything necessary to encourage conversation between Kate and her brother. Kate must have telephoned Ray from other places as well, or Ray had called her at St. John's, because she announced one night when the three of them had sat down for dinner that Ray generously had consented to pay one half of what Catherine's income would not cover.

After Ted had gone to bed, Kate admitted to Joe that Ray was noncommittal at first and then objected to the cost. He was not convinced that Catherine was ready for nursing home care. It seems they had discussed it for a half hour or so on three separate occasions, an amazingly long time for the two of them to talk together. Kate had been graphic, apparently, in describing their mother's special needs and how hard Kate was finding it to meet them all with everything else she had to do. Ray was certain he could find a place for Catherine in Georgia for much, much less. For a while the talk had turned in that direction, Kate very willing to have Catherine move to Georgia and Ray evaluating his wife's reaction to such a plan. Fawn would be the one who would have to look for a place for Catherine because Ray was particularly busy at work this time of year, and Ray didn't know if Fawn really had the time to look right now or not. Joe knew that Fawn would end up doing a great deal more than that if Catherine moved to Georgia, but he was certain this point had not been part of the conversation. Kate emphasized that Catherine needed a change immediately, and eventually Ray evidently agreed that the fastest change was to go ahead and take the room Kate had found. They would just have to apply Catherine's income to the cost, and he would agree to split the balance with Kate.

While you're on the phone with him, ask him why he never called me back about you, Joe said to himself. But that was another matter, and Ray was cooperating in this case. It was necessary to move on.

"How can he be so...so...I mean, we're doing all the work. You'd think he would just jump at the chance to get Mom settled somewhere. I told him, I said, 'Give me a break. You come up here and take care of her and see how long you last!' And you know what he said? He said I was being 'overdramatic.' That's the word he used. Me, 'overdramatic,' and her laying in there right now waiting for me to fix her dinner."

Anyone watching would have seen Joe wince very, very slightly. It was after eight o'clock. "Do you mean she hasn't eaten tonight?" he said quietly, calmly.

"How could she, Joe? I've been on the phone with Ray ever since I got home from work."

"When did you get home?"

"When I usually do. Five thirty."

He got up immediately and took a can of soup from the pantry and pressed it into the electric opener. It whirred like a dentist's drill, and then, with his back to Kate, he dropped the sticky disk into the garbage. He shook the contents into a saucepan and added a half can of milk as Kate, still talking, got out bread and some sliced roast beef and began to make a sandwich. Joe took a plastic dish of chicken salad from the refrigerator and pushed it toward her on the counter. It was softer than roast beef. Catherine could chew it easier with her dentures.

"Let's drive Catherine down there and let her see the place this Saturday. Can you arrange with the director for a short tour?"

"I don't know about Saturday. I have to work, remember? It's spring cleanup day, and everybody is supposed to help clean up the place and plant flowers. It's a lot of work, and I have to supervise the kids planting stuff around the circle in front of—"

"How about Sunday afternoon?" He dreaded going anywhere when he finally arrived home on Sundays, physically and emotionally exhausted.

"Sunday afternoon is when I'd planned to rearrange stuff in my lab closet. You should see the mess the kids made in there this spring. I can hardly—"

"When, then, Kate? We have to move on this thing. Call right now and leave word with the night receptionist for the manager that we'll definitely take the room."

Kate wheeled around, shocked. "We can't just tell them that without her seeing it first. Mom ought to have a say too."

"Then tell them we want it but we want her to have a chance to see it too, and pencil in her name. Something. We have to move on this, Kate. A thousand people are always out looking for nursing home care."

"I beg your pardon! I'm the one who had to spend days driving around, and *I* didn't see anybody else looking. *I'm* the one who talked to the director. And I have to work, Joe. Relax. I'll take her to see it this coming week. Nobody's going to steal it out from under us! There was nobody else looking at it but me. She can see it next week, when I have time!"

He despaired of any more progress than this and settled down to wait. Kate must have called the director the following morning, anyway, because she announced the following night that they would hold the room until Catherine could see it on Wednesday. She would take her down after work. Joe would have to come too to carry her out to the car and help get her into a wheelchair at the nursing home. How he wished Kate had called him that morning too. He and Milly had finally managed to arrange a telephone conference with the diocesan finance committee and the bishop. It had taken Milly most of the afternoon to coordinate a date and time with the other four members and three additional people and the bishop's clerk, all of whom would have to be part of the conference call or any attempt to change the date. Joe had answered the incoming calls and typed a half-dozen letters and dealt with a walk-in who needed food and a place to sleep, while Milly arranged the conference call. Wednesday afternoon at five o'clock had finally suited everybody. Nobody would be happy about having to change the conference call now. Especially Milly.

Milly. He looked at his watch and went back into the bookstore to call her. From the other side of the store, he heard the fat woman yelling at the young child. The child's voice rose in a thin wail, and he could barely hear it over hers. "You don't ever listen, do you?" she was saying.

* * *

In early February, two families in the parish had invited Joe and Ted to join them in a day of offshore fishing during the second week of June. The families vacationed together every summer in a popular place on the coast about fifty miles south of Wicomico. They had chartered the same boat for many seasons, and their annual day offshore was one of the highlights of their year. The prospect of going offshore had excited Joe. He had been that far out only once before, years ago while he was still teaching. The rest of his saltwater fishing had been in the surf and on the coastal piers. The yearning to catch anything had long ago become secondary for him. He enjoyed pulling in a big fish like everyone else, an accomplishment his friends were quick to remind him he managed to do much less often than they did. But he had been releasing the big ones for years. Being outdoors was enough, in old clothes, in the wind and water and sun, feeling the powerful tug on his rig and enjoying a respite from his workaday routine. Fishing and other outdoor adventures cleared his head. Still, if he wasn't careful, he could soon find himself meditating on the problems at home.

The thought of going out to the Gulf Stream was exciting in itself, but having Ted along made it all very special. He had looked forward to the trip all spring. Ted and Kate were already in Wicomico each summer by early June. Joe would drive down and spend the night, and he and Ted would set out the following day to join his friends at their cottage farther down the coast. Milly would help him plan ahead and clear his calendar.

Leaving home even for a few days required some preparation, and especially in the summer. Kate had never understood it, another of the domestic issues to which she was blind or pretended to be. Joe had long ago reasoned that the issue was largely his alone, an excess of caution arising from his years in law enforcement. Kate rolled her eyes and shook her head and wondered what all the fuss was about. Leaving home was merely a matter of locking the door and driving away. Joe saw it differently and couldn't help himself. He approached it the way his father had done when he was a child, except that his father could share all the tasks with Joe's mother and his siblings.

Two acres of lawn had to be mowed before leaving, because it would need cutting again as soon as he returned. Cutting the grass with his old mower was almost impossible if the grass was too tall; when it got that way, he had to mow it twice. He made arrangements with one of the neighborhood children to feed Cory and give him clean water every day. He knew most of the children in the neighborhood and had learned that a few of the teenagers were responsible and would remember Cory and keep quiet about the house being unattended. It was a real concern to him in their corner lot, surrounded by a belt of trees on three sides with open fields beyond. The house was the most vulnerable in the neighborhood, sitting in trees far from the public street. Someone had tried to break in twice over the years when he and Kate were at work and Ted was at school. Far more protected houses nearby had suffered intruders. Some of the lights must be put on timers. He had to go to the newspaper office and the Post Office and sign forms to have delivery held until his return. He called the Sheriff's Office and arranged for a deputy to drive by a few times. These and another dozen matters required attention and seemed to make no difference to anyone but him.

Other clergy in his denomination had to be contacted to be available for emergencies at Redeemer. Although the regional clergy did their best to cover for one another, the few neighboring priests were not always available. He would not be away on Sunday this time, so the difficult chore of finding a supply priest—often he and Milly had to search for someone in other states—would not be a problem. He had to proof bulletins for the coming two Sundays and prepare two sermons and the adult educations classes he would teach between services. He would leave phone numbers with Milly, the Wardens, and his neighbors next door so he could be reached in emergencies. Always before leaving, for even a few days, he talked with Harry Campos, alerting him to anything likely to arise in his absence. No priest could have had the sensitive pastoral regard for Redeemer and her people as Harry. His long and faithful ministry had blessed a thousand lives. In leaving for any length of time, Joe was comforted knowing that this good man was standing watch.

With the peace of mind that comes of responsibilities fulfilled, Joe drove south on the busy interstate highway. A rare mild euphoria began to fill his heart and mind. The thought of seeing Kate and Ted was enough in itself. The excitement of a break from the routine and leaving everything arranged and in good order, anticipating the two days outdoors and fishing out of sight of land, seeing old friends, and especially doing something fun and with Ted, elated him like a child on Christmas morning.

He drove south in dazzling morning sunshine. The massive tractor-trailer trucks roared and thundered about him, crowding the road ahead as far as he could see like a prehistoric herd migrating southward. In the same way all his journeys began, a reflexive prayer began to ramble within him. It began instinctively like a smoker lighting a cigarette at the touch of a coffee cup and underway before his mind knew what he was doing. The inventory of his blessings and cares, like a compass needle seeking north, sought the direction of God as he began this small detour within his larger journey forward. It was a function of duty and awe, a natural consignment of all important things into hands he trusted without quite knowing why, as normal a thing to do in leaving home as saying goodbye to his parents when he was a child. His wife and son were in their summer home, where they longed all year to be. Ted had finished the school year with a B average. His parents were in good health for now and looking forward to their own vacation later in the summer with Kate, whom they dearly loved. For the time being, his brothers' and sisters' lives were stable, his nephews were working at summer jobs, and everybody was well. The parish was in decent order and most of the people in good health, a blessing as important to his peace of mind as the welfare of his family. Many of them were away enjoying their own vacations. Several of the children and teenagers had received special honors at the end of the school year, and their names had appeared in the newspaper. The early summer parish picnic had been a great success. Several of the men in the parish had formed their own prayer group, a very healthy sign. Attendance continued to go up. He was grateful.

A few days earlier, he had given Cory his first home haircut, a minor domestic triumph. Shocked by the bill from the last visit to the clip shop, Joe had purchased an electric clipper and sharp scissors, determined to do it himself next time. The night he came home from the store and emerged from the car with his purchases, Cory took one look at the unopened brown bag and, alerted by what canine telepathy Joe could scarcely imagine, scuttled off like a crab to the other side of the house and hid under some big rhododendrons. A month later he unwrapped the clippers at the kitchen table, snapped on what looked like the proper cutting head, freed the scissors from their plastic wrapper, and went out into the yard. On any other day of his life, Cory would have been waiting at the back door with a smile on his face and his tail drumming on the walk. On this one occasion, he was nowhere in sight. It took Joe twenty minutes to track him down, cowering beneath the forsythia on the northeast corner of the property. Commanded to sit in the wheelbarrow in front of Joe, who positioned himself in a lawn chair with his tools on the grass nearby, Cory whimpered and fidgeted like a child about to get a flu shot. It had taken a little while and some soothing words, and although it did not have quite the style of a professional cut, Joe concluded that it wasn't bad for the first time. While he brushed the fluffy clippings into a grocery bag, the ecstatic dog raced around the lawn in circles as though just released from the pound. Although he would never have foreseen it at the time, the memory of all this came back to Joe inexplicitly as he counted his blessings.

At a recent regional clergy meeting, the bishop had taken him aside and thanked him personally for his work with the executive and finance committees and for his service at Redeemer. To Joe's amazement, he had gone on to ask his opinion on a legal matter concerning some land the diocese was attempting to buy. This evidence of confidence in him had come as a pleasant surprise, and he found himself warming to the bishop. The years of embarrassment and disdain at his hands had been deeply troubling, especially as it had been impossible to determine the reason. He wondered if their relationship was changing, and he counted the possibility as a blessing.

The vestry was supportive and appreciative for his ministry. Lollie Bascomb and her sneaky coconspirators had been less active all spring, although he had learned that with them he should expect surprises. He was grateful there were so few of them, and he thought of his colleagues whose detractors in some cases numbered in the dozens. He was content with himself, for the time being, for managing his own enemies with patience and good humor. He was grateful for the strength to maintain his own standards, and whatever past pain had so molded the lives of this angry group, he prayed they would be moved to change.

For the past three months, he had been able to make a few good deposits into Ted's college account. With the end of classes and the start of her summer vacation, Kate had become more relaxed and reasonable. The few days between the end of school and her departure for the coast had been hectic with shopping and packing and she had left her customary disorder for him to clean up when she finally drove away. Compared to the spring and early summer, however, the last few days had been rather relaxed at home. Catherine's health had improved since entering the nursing home. She was even moving about in a wheelchair and, to Kate's and Joe's immense delight, had become friends with another patient, a shriveled elderly gentleman called Aubrey. After meeting Aubrey, Joe suspected he and Catherine had in common the mutual cessation of their drinking days. He wondered if they ever discussed it. On his last visit, he had found them side by side in their wheelchairs sound asleep in the dayroom in front of a blaring television. Two small figures finding company at the end, Joe wished all people could be so fortunate. Catherine had confided to Joe that in his younger days, Aubrey had worked for the CIA "as a spy, most likely. I can tell just being around him." Aubrey's doctor had forbidden him to eat sweets, a rule the staff sought to enforce rigorously. A great-nephew visited him weekly, however, and left him with a cache of Junior Mints and bite-size Almond Joys, which he secreted in a number of places and routinely shared with Catherine. For her part, Catherine divided the candy Joe brought her, surreptitiously concealing it in newspapers and magazines passed casually to Aubrey, clandestine trafficking that infused their nursing home lives with an adventurous camaraderie. Joe went all the way to a candy store in Carterstown to buy sugar-free chocolates for Catherine, carefully tearing off the label before presenting them to her. Both she and Audrey claimed they could tell the difference with sugar-free candy and refused to eat it. Their confiding in him about their smuggling was a sign of confidence, and Joe recognized it. He was certain he was the only visitor who told them the latest jokes, a few of which he felt he could share with them without crossing a certain line. Despite her behavior toward him for so many years, it was clear Catherine enjoyed Joe's visits. He thought of all that now as he lazily reviewed the gifts in his life.

And in addition to all these blessings, he was free for a few days. He was happy.

The happiness was genuine and comforting, but in every instance came with a shadow side. As always in counting his blessings, he grew exponentially aware of his own sinfulness, failures, things done and left undone. He regretted not spending more time with Ted. Because of diocesan responsibilities, he had missed half his soccer games. When his team traveled to distant places for Saturday afternoon tournaments and stayed overnight, Joe could not go. Kate usually went, irked at having to do so, resentment she made clear enough to Joe although she was careful to hide it from Ted. Joe suspected she did not mind going as she had always preferred driving around to spending time at home. She got on well with two of the other team parents and enjoyed herself when they went too. It worried Joe that he could not go also or go with Ted alone and give Kate some time to do whatever she wanted to do.

Schedules were easier to modify or rearrange with his parish work; diocesan duties came with a mandate, and a soccer game was no excuse. It grieved him to think of the nights Ted went to sleep, and Kate too, before he had gotten home to kiss them and say good night. He was ashamed of himself for trying to manage family finances so meticulously and wondered if it was a sign of the weakness of his faith. Perhaps it was the same too with other family responsibilities. Was the loneliness he felt a sign of it, evidence of his growing self-reliance in a self-centered world? If he stood by and let Kate spend every dime or neglect their social life because he knew God would care for them, would it demonstrate the depth of his reliance upon God alone? Were his ideas of family responsibility and stewardship mere excuses, proof of his ultimate mistrust of divine guidance? Could reason degenerate into a disguise for doubt? However reasonable and careful he sought to be with all things touching upon his family, Kate's inflexible, persistent cunning in having her own way with things eventually prevailed in almost every case, destroying any semblance of mutuality and trust. Was the dilemma in her iron will or in his frustration in having to oppose it? Did he trust God enough to let his guard down? Perhaps God had brought him together with Kate for a purpose. He did not believe that everything in life was orchestrated by God. But suppose their marriage *had* been God's specific intention. In addition to the love he and Kate had shared in the beginning, and to Ted being in the world, what purpose could their marriage satisfy in the great plan? Would their great-great-grandchild create a cure for cancer or save the oceans? Or was it as immediate as Kate's survival? Was he meant to take care of her, keep her sober, prevent her from hurting herself? And was he meant to care for Catherine as well? Someone had to. Who, if not him? The role of caretaker with a spouse was real enough in every marriage at times, but a relationship based on caretaking was unbalanced by its very nature and eventually inadequate and dysfunctional. He did not want to raise a wayward daughter. He wanted to live as husband and wife, with intimacy and integrity.

He regretted his harshness in pushing Kate to act in Catherine's situation. What he actually regretted was having to force her to take the necessary, reasonable steps in her own mother's interests. Why did his forcing her to be reasonable always leave him feeling discouraged and exhausted, as though he was the one causing the difficulty? True to form, Kate had waited until a half hour before setting off for Wicomico to announce that she needed an additional five hundred dollars for repairs to the water pump and the floor of the downstairs bathroom. She had never mentioned it before. She was annoyed when he tried to make her understand how a five-hundred-dollar surprise was not fair, not like seventy or a hundred dollars, and he could see her start to close him off as she always did when he tried to discuss family finances. In questioning her, it became clear that she had known all spring about the water pump and the floor. She had never brought it up, preferring to sweep it under the rug with everything else in her denial. It seemed to him that she had waited to raise the issue until just before driving away for the summer so that she could depart in irritation at his surprise, and he could be left to his own guilt for having caused this troubled parting. They had been married for fifteen years.

The repairs to the big, rattling lawn mower would have to wait until July, and he hoped it would last that long. He had an aversion to withdrawing money from Ted's college account, which was what Kate would have done in an instant. Supporting Catherine had reduced their savings to less than a thousand dollars, most of which Kate was taking with her to Wicomico until summer rentals could bring in some income. The disagreement over hiding the repairs meant her departure had been marred by an argument. In addition, it had been very quickly discerned by Ted, who would have the benefit of hearing all the way to Wicomico how unreasonable his father was, how cruel to send his mother away with her feelings hurt. Sometimes it seemed she planned things this way, but he knew that could not be true. It was completely unreasonable. She loved Ted and would not turn him against his own father.

Thus he headed south on the interstate highway in the summer sun with his mind now agitating like an old washing machine, stirring up a rambling prayer for patience in his marriage and for a deeper understanding of himself.

These domestic and professional preoccupations shamed him. In a strange way, he disappointed himself in bringing such trivialities before God, taking up divine time with these manageable issues he should have been able to resolve on his own. God had blessed him with a thousand gifts, and the least he could do was serve with dignity and a minimum of complaint in his small corner of the broken world. There were people who lived without food and clean water, children who had never seen a doctor, whole regions devastated by earthquake, forest fires, floods, drought. The oppression and unfairness of life in most of the world were terrifying. His mind reeled at the iniquities of Africa, Burma, North Korea, Colombia. Hands and arms chopped off by warlords. Rampant AIDS. Rape as a political practice. Kidnapped children forced into militias. Muslim fanatics blowing up families, occupied buses, and markets while the Islamic world looked on without interest or action. And Joe Stephenson was angry over a five-hundred-dollar toilet bill. He was ashamed of himself. He prayed for forgiveness.

He had set forth in giddy happiness a half hour earlier and, now, not fifty miles from home, found himself in these depressing considerations. This too, ruining his own time of rest, made him ashamed of himself. He shook his head as though fending off a wasp and for ten minutes recited the list of names, more in his heart than his mind, that represented the relationships of his existence: Kate and Ted, his parents and every family member, old friends who filled his past with joy, parishioners, his students of years ago, people he had known in the law, neighbors, victims he had represented, defendants he had sent to prison, homeless people who had come to his office in the past month. With each name, the inevitable face emerged and aroused its own momentary mingling of thanksgiving, hope, and anxiety.

He drove south, watching the road. His preoccupations would not have surprised his friends, but they would have concluded once again that he was insane. Perhaps they were correct. After a while, he ended his time with God and allowed himself to become aware again of the champagne light flooding the valley about him.

In a distant field, someone was busy with late plowing, and Joe looked in hopes of seeing seagulls. On the far side of the fields, some billboards stood rudely against the gentle forested hills, interrupting some of the loveliest vistas in eastern North America with reminders of fast food and inexpensive lodgings. The swelling summer fields ran out to the blue mountains far to the east and west of the road. In the clear bright air, individual trees could be distinguished on distant ridges. Here and there in the cooler air against the slopes, wild cherries still held a few colored blossoms, scattering a fading glory on the breeze. He passed a cluster of barns and sheds quite close to the road, and for a moment, the car was filled with a blended scent of honeysuckle and horse manure, a wondrous rich fragrance wholly unappreciated by city people. He was happy, but he knew it would take a hundred miles or more to cleanly outrun his cares. It had been worse in the law. For years following every trip away from home, the inevitable four- or five-day jury trial awaited him, lowering like a storm ready to break on the following day and buffet him back into reality.

The relentless tractor-trailers roared by menacingly on his left side like battleships plowing through Hampton Roads, heavy and fierce, emitting clouds of smoke and trailing gusts of sand and dust. A vast cargo of chickens thundered by, their crates stacked a dozen high, scattering pitiful feathers behind them like limp snow. Already the vans and SUVs were barreling toward the coastal resorts, boogie boards and bicycles strapped aloft and immobilized children visible through the smoked glass listening to Walkmans and playing video games. He thought about his own rare vacations as a child when he and his rapt siblings, faces pressed to the windows of his parents' ancient Woody, watched the road and scanned the countryside, fascinated by the foreign panorama. No more. Children today rejected engagement and demanded distractions from the passing world.

When they could, their parents saw that they got it. Curiosity of the land was going the way of dinner table conversation and proper manners.

He felt around on the passenger seat and found his cassette of Chopin's First Piano Concerto and shoved it into the player on the dashboard. Ahead of him, the sapphire light of a police cruiser winked on the right shoulder. Within a few hundred yards, traffic began to slow, and he started watching for a chance to move into the passing lane. He eased in between an approaching black Mercedes and the rear of a big dilapidated flatbed truck. The truck lumbered on ahead of him with a load of something protruding over its high tailgate like a pile of bouncing jousting lances. The traffic slowed almost to a stop and then alternately crept and cantered forward as the drivers ahead assumed the unpredictable rhythm of rubbernecks. There was some confusion on the roadside, a few flares sputtered whitely in the sunshine, and a state trooper in big dark glasses stood at the end of a line of three parked cars, talking with some anxious-looking people. Joe observed all this with a glance. The erratic movement of traffic around him brought uncomfortably to mind, as it always did, the many accident cases he had tried over the years. A number of them had involved fatalities.

Just past the accident, every driver began to speed up quickly to recover lost time, and as they were all gaining speed, the big truck in front of him inexplicably and suddenly stopped. Joe applied his breaks immediately and instinctively turned the wheel toward the left shoulder. The Mercedes behind him had vanished, and the big beer truck that had taken its place smashed into the rear of Joe's small Honda, slamming it forward into the high flatbed truck ahead of him on a slight angle. The truck's crazy dangling load, hundreds of rigid iron reinforcing rods, shifted backward from the bed like spaghetti shaken loose from a box and crashed through the windshield of Joe's car, penetrating all the way through, knocking out the rear window and spilling over into a pile on the road behind him. In a burst of crackling glass, the stiff rods raced past him in seconds. The nearest two clipped his forehead and right ear, their trajectory mercifully deflected by his last-second attempt to turn the wheel to the left.

With the long savage rods protruding from both ends of his car and some of them jangling over the road, his small compact came to rest between the two heavy trucks, all three vehicles settled at crazy angles in the rising dust. Windshield glass glittered down around him as Eugene Ormandy and the Philadelphia Orchestra proceeded dutifully with the first movement of Chopin's sublime masterpiece.

Ted, he thought. *I was going fishing with Ted. Of all times for...* A second thought, deeply disturbing, prompted by something glimpsed or sensed in the preceding seconds, followed immediately. He wrenched open the door with difficulty and stepped out and got unsteadily to his feet beside the car. He started around the front of his Honda, balancing himself with his right hand on the hood. He tried to squeeze under the gruesome jam of reinforcing rods that connected his car and the heavy truck like a primitive parasitic growth, but he could not get through. He shook his head and turned and went round the rear of his car. The trunk tailgate had popped open but the fan of rods prevented it opening all the way. He heard the beer truck idling a few feet behind his car. Someone stood in his way, saying, "Sir? Are you all right?" Someone came up behind him and said something. He kept moving around his car toward the truck ahead of him, searching for movement somewhere. The passenger door of the flatbed was already hanging open, and he saw what he dreaded most: a child scramble out, about ten, twelve, boy or girl he didn't notice, but he clearly saw the child bend over and vomit. At the sight of it, he felt like vomiting too.

"Is anyone hurt?" he called. "That child. That little girl..." There were several people in the way now, holding out their hands toward him. He moved sideways, looking between them, his every nerve straining toward the small figure just now straightening up. He distinctly heard the child say, "Fuck!"

That's good, he thought.

"Sir? Here! Let's wipe that off," said someone kindly.

"Is that child hurt?" said Joe calmly. Someone behind pressed a roll of toilet tissue into his hand, and he grinned as he thanked him. He unwound a spool onto his hand and began dabbing at the blood on his face and neck. "Thank you, but let me through, please. I want to know if that child is hurt," he said calmly.

"He's okay. Just shook up. We ain't hurt," said a big woman in a Redskins jersey, getting down from the cab of the big flatbed. "We was going down to Gum Springs to deliver this load. You got blood on your face! You hurt?"

"Yeah, buddy. You ought to sit down here. You bleeding," said someone else.

He could see now the child was a boy with longish hair who looked like a small leftover from the sixties. Throwing up had restored the child to reason and he waved at Joe and managed to smile.

"I'm all right," said the boy. "Just puked is all."

The big woman borrowed a wad of Joe's toilet paper and blew her nose with vigor. A man with a tremendous gut whom Joe took to be her husband waddled around the front of the old flatbed, scratching his rear and crotch and shaking his head. "Goddamn," he said.

"Man! I hope ain't nobody hurt or nothing. Anybody hurt? Anybody hurt? Tell me you all ain't hurt," said a frenzied young black man from the door of a soft drink truck.

Joe appeared to be the only one bleeding, and he assured everybody that he had only scratches, all superficial.

"I do need my glasses, though," he said. They had been knocked off in the collision. Against the advice of everyone standing round, he went back around to his open door and searched on the floor, or as much of it as he could reach, for his lost eyeglasses. As he was bent over into the car, a new voice boomed forth.

"Mister? You bleeding?"

He turned to face a concerned state trooper. He appeared to be a little miffed at having two accidents to oversee. He was polite and organized. Joe glanced at his name tag.

"Trooper Orndorff, my name is Joe Stephenson. Catoctin Springs. Is anyone hurt that you know of?"

"Don't think so, Mr. Stephens. Gentlemen," he said to everyone in general. "May I please see your operator's license and registration?

We got an ambulance and a wrecker on the way. Lady back yonder is a nurse, case anybody needs one."

* * *

He wouldn't ride in the ambulance to the hospital, preferring to sit in the cab of the wrecker and go with his car, or what was left of it, to the body shop. An additional worry was mercifully resolved just before the wrecker pulled away when someone handed him his glasses, discovered somewhere in the long patch of wildflowers planted in the median. He could see again. Once his car was checked in at the locked compound of the body shop in Catoctin Springs, he let the shop manager, whom he knew from Rotary, drive him to the emergency room to have his injuries examined. What he had assumed were a couple of scratches turned out to require four stitches and several hours of lounging around on a gurney. He listened, now and then with amusement, to nurses and patients in bays around him contending with all manner of situations. Someone had been bitten by a snake at an office picnic, and the whole crowd had come in, bringing the snake with them in a jar to see if it was poisonous and causing consternation among the nurses. A child in the next bay cried incessantly until wheeled away to have her appendix removed. Summoned by an emergency room doctor who knew them both, Harry Campos appeared, alarmed and reassuring, and waited with Joe until he was discharged. Harry helped him remove his luggage and fishing gear from his shattered car and drove him home. Joe was supposed to lie down for the rest of the day, but after he had cleaned up a bit and changed clothes, Harry drove him to a car rental agency.

* * *

Missing the day's fishing with Ted troubled him more than smashing up the car or having almost twenty stitches in his forehead. Of all times for it to happen. All those five- and six-hour drives to diocesan committee meetings in the morning and evening darkness, fighting off fatigue, worried about what might be happening at home. No, it has to happen in bright daylight on his way to go fishing with his son, on the first precious day of a rare vacation. *Of course... Yes, I know, dammit! It could have been worse. Nobody was hurt, and I came within a quarter inch of a face full of iron construction rods. I could have been decapitated, blinded, or...* At the thought of living the rest of his life with a brain injury, he felt like vomiting like the child from the truck, and he said "Thank you, Lord" about a thousand times over the next week. *God is good. I've been rescued once again. God is good. Thank you, Lord.*

He sat at the kitchen table and dialed Kate's number in Wicomico. A guest answered.

"Mrs. Stephenson is out shopping. Looking for a new bathing suit and going by the bookstore. Probably won't be back till late this afternoon," said a pleasant young female voice. "Can I tell her who called?"

"May I speak to Ted?" said Joe.

"Can you hold on while I go get him? It'll take a few minutes. He and his friends are out on their boards."

Joe told her not to call Ted in and thanked her anyway. He said he would call back later in the afternoon. "If Kate comes in before I call again, ask her to call Joe at home."

He sat at the kitchen table where he had spent so much time in deep thought over the years. Each fiber of his being glowed with the conviction that he was a blessed man. God had been good to him. His wife, son, parents, sisters, brothers, friends, education—all blessings in his life before he knew them to be. The more he contemplated his own brokenness, the more conscious he grew of God's favor and goodness toward him, wholly unearned and absolutely undeserved. Each time he thought about the world and the debacle of human history, his appreciation for his own blessings grew clearer and more astonishing. His countless blessings. Merciful gifts to a sinner.

Even in his self-indulgent appetites and egocentric ways he was conscious of being a responsible person. His free will was genuine. God would let him make his choices. He could choose to live as he desired and satisfy his every base yearning, and God would let him do it and love him anyway. He knew there was good in him, and it had nothing to do with any effort on his part. It was God acting in him, most of the time in spite of himself. He knew it as he knew left from right. And in the craziness of life he felt most complete, most human and free, when he was conscious of this wondrous movement within him and in the world. He knew he had done nothing to make it be this way, but choosing to live his life in harmony with it created a bit of rightness in the great brokenness.

The difference a human being could make was in being aware and grateful. Gifts. His faith and his very awareness of it were gifts. His ability to depend on them increased in proportion to the selfishness he could cast off, like a snake shedding its skin. In the unsearchable process, he was conscious that the indefinable movement in his life was distinctly in harmony with something elementally right and unspeakably powerful.

The stitches in his scalp itched and tingled as the numbness wore off. He resisted the urge to scratch them. *They should never have been separated,* he said to himself, staring at the kitchen wall. *Law and theology. Justice. Made in God's image, the means through which divine will is made manifest. Bringing order out of chaos... The world was made to be inhabited.*

The phone rang. The friendly voice of Harry Campos, wanting to know how he was doing, soothed his injured ear, reminding him of home and friends, making him feel valued, furthering again his understanding of grace. They talked for a few minutes and hung up, and the mellow comfort of old friends filled him with wonder, lingering in the air like a homey aroma. He looked at the clock and thought how good it would feel to talk to Kate.

Chapter Twenty-Seven

They had moved Catherine into a small sunny room at the nursing home on a cold day in the early spring. They had made her bed and placed her things carefully in the closet and bureau drawers, cheerfully discussing the activities and orderly appearance of this new place and speculating about the interesting people she would meet here. Ted placed her television on the fern stand they had brought from home, making sure it was visible from both the bed and the easy chair and setting the remote control on the nightstand in between. Joe hung some pictures and a curtain rod. Kate arranged clothing in bureau drawers and the closet, announcing each item's place and advising Joe on how the pictures should be arranged on the wall. The subject of all this commotion surveyed it all from her chair with a curiosity and quiet enthusiasm that Joe found impressive. Still, he kept glancing at his diminutive mother-in-law like a man waiting for a pot to boil over. Age and poor health had put behind her Catherine's days of acting out her anger, but the combustible temperament still smoldered. Years of conditioning had left in Joe a nervous caution, an attitude from which he supposed he would never recover. If this move troubled Catherine, she gave no sign of it.

Weeks earlier, while Kate attended an evening faculty meeting and Ted worked on a history assignment, Joe had talked with Catherine. It had become clear to him that Kate had told her nothing about their search for a nursing home. He had spoken quietly and reasonably about the whole matter, emphasizing the dangers and unfairness of her being alone all day and explaining in the kindest way he knew how that they needed to make a change for her own health and welfare. She had listened quietly, interrupting now and then with very reasonable comments and questions. She had already guessed from what she had overheard that Kate was looking for a place for her but told him they had never talked about it. She asked if her income would cover the costs, and Joe said that it would so she would not worry. He told her they would visit her throughout each week and that when she had recovered her strength, they would take her out to dinner and shopping. She would, of course, return to their home for holidays and weekend visits as soon as she was well enough. He said several times that it was important that she no longer be alone all day, and she had agreed. Catherine suggested they say nothing to Kate about their talk so that Kate could bring the matter up when she was ready. Joe was perfectly willing to tell Kate about their talk and that he had initiated it but agreed to do as Catherine wished. At the end of their conversation, in one of the few signs of what might have been affection that he had ever known from her, she tapped the back of his hand once, lightly, with her fingers as he got up to leave her room. He accepted it as a sign of approval, or at least that they understood each other.

Once the selection of a nursing home was made and the financial arrangements agreed to by Ray and his wife, Kate's anger toward Joe and irritation at her mother's situation had cooled. He told himself that it had been her way of managing the stress of her only parent approaching the end of life. On a deeper level, he knew it was her natural way of dealing with any change. He knew that giving her the benefit of the doubt in the whole matter had been the loving thing to do, but he was weary and relieved that it was no longer necessary to do so. It was one less complication in living with the mystery that was his wife. Today Kate was laughing and animated as she went about arranging Catherine's closet and bureau drawers, chatting in her charming way with the staff who kept coming in to meet the new resident. Kate had made yellow curtains trimmed in white for the window and long matching dusters for Catherine's bureau and bedside table. She was a marvelous seamstress, a true artist with needle and thread, another of her many admirable skills. He admired her work and told her so although he knew she found it very hard to accept compliments, even from him. So gifted at sewing and cooking, her avoidance of domestic life and its responsibilities mystified him.

Joe put these thoughts out of his mind and focused on the pleasant experience of doing simple chores together with Kate and her mother and Ted. It was especially nice to have Kate and Catherine in pleasant moods together at the same time. Ted came in from the van with the last box of whatnots, as Catherine called them, and Kate took it from him happily and began to place them carefully on the top shelf of the closet. As he watched her, he knew that no one looking on would ever imagine how difficult and stubborn and exasperating she had been in finally getting to this day.

Residents took meals together in a bright dining room. Organized activities took place daily. Joe was encouraged by the sight of residents propelled along the halls in wheelchairs toward these gatherings. The thought of Catherine interacting with others was a relief to him, and he suspected that Kate must surely feel the same.

A few days after moving Catherine in, Kate began making the hour-long drive to visit her after work three times each week, and occasionally on weekends, staying about twenty minutes at each visit. Her contract required her to eat her evening meal at St. John's each Tuesday and Thursday, so with the start of these visits, she was away from home during the dinner hour every weekday night. She drove the long, winding hypotenuse that snaked through the countryside, taking her time and listening to the radio. This was the long way, through farmland and vast orchards and small stores squatting at intersections and battered vehicles every mile bearing hand-lettered FARM USE signs. Joe agreed it was more interesting than traveling the two straight main highways that formed the other, shorter way.

He was glad she was visiting her mother, but it worried him to have her time at home cut down even further. Now that Catherine was some distance away, Kate was spending more time with her than when she lived in their home. Before the move, several days would pass with Kate going in to check on her mother for a minute or two a few times daily. Now she was devoting some six or seven hours each week to seeing her, although most of the time was spent in travel.

Meals together as a family had become a rare interlude in their convoluted routines of commuting and work. Joe craved their infrequent family dinners together, usually in restaurants, despite the monopolizing conversations between Kate and Ted that quickly drifted into school gossip. And he could not blame their scant time together on Kate alone. His work too required many evenings out, and often it was more reasonable to pick up a quick hot dog at a convenience store than drive home for dinner and return immediately for an evening meeting. The whole combination of schedules and impediments frustrated him and made him increasingly sad because he knew the precious time they had together as a family was slipping by. Still, other households seemed to manage. Many of their neighbors contended with long commutes that meant that one or both parents did not return home until seven or eight at night.

Kate was now spending most of her time at St. John's. Joe could not determine how much of it was avoidance of home and how much was work truly required of her. He had hoped that Catherine's move might mean that Kate would be home more. Although teachers' contracts were modified each year to meet the changing demands of life at St. John's, life in the Stephenson household seemed to shift continually to accommodate Kate's need to be at the school. Joe did not know how to interpret it. Kate was ready with a reasonable explanation for any question he might raise, and he could not bring himself to suggest that she was being untruthful. The amount of time she spent there would have led anyone to suppose she was the headmaster. He remembered asking her, a year or so after their marriage, about the time she spent at the high school, pointing out that other teachers had three and four children at home and surely could not be raising families while spending the time at work that she spent. She had become defensive and replied that he was not a teacher and had no idea what he was talking about. Short of going to the high school and spying on her, there seemed no way to determine why she had to remain at the place until dinnertime and then spend the whole evening grading papers and making out tests in front of the television. It never occurred to him that she was merely continuing in the pattern her life had taken on since the first grade.

It was rare now that Kate accompanied Joe to parties or dinner with friends. She went with him when an invitation did not fall on the night of an athletic event, school play, dance, or some other school event. There were always occasions for students, and she seemed to have to chaperone them all. She did not socialize with members of the faculty. The few events planned for faculty seldom included spouses. When they were first married, he had attended her school "functions" (as she liked to say) with her, but as much as he loved her, his craving for adult companionship had become compelling too. He was used to making excuses for Kate, saying that she had to work for this event or that and assuring everyone of her disappointment in not being able to attend. In time, people gradually came to accept that he would show up alone. They asked about Kate less frequently.

When Kate did accompany him somewhere, Joe watched others stand around smiling as she presented her monologue of academic responsibilities, scheduling minutia, and momentous decisions in faculty meetings and how valiantly she was struggling to keep up with it all. She said all this with complete confidence that her listeners were interested in every detail. Joe knew it was the only subject she could talk about and that it would never cross her mind that after a few minutes, others might find it tedious. People were polite, but anyone but Kate could perceive their boredom. They soon drifted away and were quickly laughing and talking with others. Joe observed all this as he had watched for years the activities and expressions of people in court while he listened to someone next to him talking into his ear. He saw with resignation and disappointment how a choice of seating, always hers, sometimes others, often left her isolated. On the rare evening out together, as he relaxed and enjoyed the company, he was sooner or later confronted with a choice: continue in the company of friends or get up and look for Kate. He would find her seated alone in the farthest room from the center of things and listen himself to her talk about her job. When guests began to sit down for dinner, he tried to maneuver Kate into groups with him. If he was successful, she assumed immediately the role of observer, chipper and smiling in a way her grade school teachers would remember, like a child being polite while the grown-ups talked and talked. He felt sorry for her because he understood that she felt threatened and apprehensive. She did not read newspapers or watch the news, knew nothing of local affairs, and knew few people outside the St. John's faculty. She knew some people at Redeemer but seldom spoke with them outside of church. Alcohol might have relaxed her, but she did not drink, she said to anyone who asked. Joe had known lawyers who had the same problem: they could talk about their work or they had nothing to say at all. Years passed, and people changed, but not Kate. He felt sorry for her and protective, but he felt something else too.

Throughout any social gathering, he anticipated the unpleasant lecture that would occupy their drive home. She would criticize everyone for something said, the way they looked, opinions expressed, jokes told. Any woman who had been especially gregarious or visible came in for special scrutiny. As almost everyone present was better known to him than to Kate, her criticism was accompanied by an implication that he was somehow responsible for them and that they were just like everybody else he knew. If he raised any objection to this critique of his or her friends or tried to tell her she was being unfair, she would declare that "everybody is so fake" and stare out the window in silence the rest of the way home.

On a few occasions, she talked with him briefly in the spring before signing her contract for the following year. Duties that would later proliferate and surprise him seemed never to be written out, or perhaps she described them in a code he did not recognize. When he expressed surprise when new contractual responsibilities arose all year long, she told him about them with the exasperated impatience of somebody having to explain the obvious to a child. In negotiating their time and responsibilities, with no third party participating as referee to enforce some basic rules, conversation with Kate was like a game in which the rules were always changing. It was impossible to know what the next play would bring. To argue with her seemed to stiffen her determination to gain her point. He could keep up if he chose to.

One evening he asked her why she was now driving hours each week to visit Catherine when for months she would not even enter her room at home unless he insisted. She had startled him with her candor by saying it was because she felt guilty and was trying to make up for ignoring Catherine while she was with them. He understood and went out of his way to accommodate her new schedule. At first, he left work early and drove to St. John's to pick up Ted and bring him home and prepare supper and then often drove back to Catoctin Springs for evening meetings. He did not like to leave Ted at home alone at night and began changing meetings and appointments to stay with him. In later years, he would revile himself for not doing more of that anyway, regardless of Kate's personal schedule. Ted was old enough to be at home on his own, but Joe still didn't want to leave him.

It caused some difficulty with his ministry. Parishioners who worked found it hard to meet during the day. Lollie Bascomb or one of her handful of cohorts who carefully avoided him spoke to the bishop about his "chronic unavailability," resulting in an admonishing letter. He tried to discuss it with the bishop by telephone, but the bishop refused to tell him who had complained or even what the complaint was about. "A priest has to be available to people in the evenings," the bishop had said, "and you can take an hour or so off in the morning to balance it out." But his family came first. In his efforts to accommodate Kate's schedule, he did not understand that he was making matters worse.

He understood by then—Ted was fifteen—that Kate was determined to have her own way in life and that marriage and a husband were either aids or impediments to that end. She slept at home but spent every possible waking moment, and all her social time, on the grounds of St. John's. Embedded in its small, rarified community, she could escape the responsibilities of the adult world and avoid social encounters with people whose lives seemed invariably more privileged and fortunate than her own. The clear rules and constraints that prevailed at the little school, her well-defined place in its pecking order, and the reliable academic routine that structured every hour of each day all eliminated life's threatening uncertainties. Knowing each member of the limited cast and understanding the roles they performed dispelled the worry of dealing with strangers, being exposed to one's husband's acquaintances, neighbors, or domestic distractions. St. John's reduced the frictions and demands of the adult world to a predictable routine of manageable proportions. As much as she complained about them, the constraints of school life comforted Kate. As long as she obeyed the simple rules, crafted primarily for teenagers, she felt secure. As soon as school ended in May, her same all-inclusive focus shifted to her house at Wicomico.

She had shocked Joe painfully about a year before, the autumn before the spring intervention with the Gallaghers. Late one afternoon, she and Joe had driven Ted into town to shop at a sporting goods outlet. They had dinner in a restaurant. He had enjoyed being together as a family. He had grown to accept by then the exclusive talk of St. John's and knew that it would have been different had it just been him and Ted. But when Kate was with them, Joe was soon invisible. He sat by and made the best of it, enjoying their presence and the food.

During the drive home, Kate stared away from him for a while through the passenger window into the darkness. Then, as though it was a minor thing she, just that minute, remembered, she said, "Oh, by the way. Ted and I are going to start living over at the school during the week, and we'll be home on weekends."

He had nearly run off the road. He slowed down and asked her what she was talking about.

Looking straight ahead, she replied calmly, "Father says it would be better for my job. We can live there in my apartment over the infirmary during the week and come home on weekends. That way, I can be there more, and we can cut down the fifteen-minute drive two times a day. Save some gas money." As though what could be more reasonable?

"The hell you are!" boomed Joe, loudly enough to be heard across the fields on both sides of the car. His every marital and parental instinct suddenly hummed like a plucked bowstring. "We are a family, and we are going to live together! You are not going to live at the goddamn school. Hervey has some damn nerve telling you that! Tell me what he said!"

"Don't yell at m—"

"Tell me *exactly* what he said, damn it!" His every instinct was on alert, and realizing already that she was shifting the burden to Hervey, he shouted, "And what you said too!" Understanding that she had pushed him too far, she became suddenly alarmed. In the back seat, Ted was completely silent.

"He said it would be better for my job if I just made the change."

"Do you mean he told you that you had to move there?"

"He said it would be better for my job," she said again, with a hint of irritation at having to repeat herself.

He knew he would get no more out of her until he could sit opposite her and watch her face as she talked. He drove the rest of way home burning with anger. Kate's feelings were hurt at having been shouted at, and she sat in stony silence, refusing to make the slightest sound. Part of him, seriously conscious of Ted hearing everything inches behind them, did not want her saying anything else, fearing what she might concoct to defend herself. The nerve of Hervey, the gall of the bastard to intrude upon their family life. When they entered the house, Ted went straight to the dining room table and began his homework without prompting, without even pausing to unwrap his new shin guards and socks. Kate went upstairs. Joe sat down at the kitchen table and dialed Hervey at home. When he finally answered, Joe demanded to know what he had told Kate about moving to the school.

"I never told her she had to," said Hervey, moving with provocative haste to a charge Joe had not yet made. "It was just an option." He would say no more, implying that the talk had been a professional discussion between him and an employee. Joe told him plainly that his wife and son would live at home and scheduled an appointment with him to discuss it all in person and hung up. There was still enough lawyer in him not to add any suggestion of action if his wife were somehow penalized for not moving to St. John's. Even in his anger, he could imagine Hervey's excited call to the school's attorney—"And he threatened to sue us, to sue *St. John's*! Just because

I was trying to help Mrs. Stephenson, his own wife, with her career. I nearly fainted. And he's a clergyman, for goodness sake!" How the subject of where his wife and son would live had come up in the first place, Joe did not know, and he had been unable to get Hervey to say.

When he went upstairs, Kate was reading comfortably in bed, as though nothing had happened. She knew they had spoken. Still, she asked not a single question. When he confronted her with Hervey's claim that he had presented her moving to the school as "an option," she looked back at her book and continued to read. When he asked her how the whole idea had come up in the first place, she looked at him with momentary, puzzled circumspection and replied innocently, "Well, let's see. I don't know. I think it just, like, came up. Maybe when we were talking about scheduling?" as though asking Joe a question. Any statement could become an interrogative in the teenage vernacular of her world. He could get nothing more from her; when he began to question her again, she became hostile.

They had moved into their house years ago so that Ted could enroll in what they were assured was the best public school district in the county. They had chosen it too in anticipation of Catherine's declining health, because it had a first-floor room that could become a bedroom. Both purposes had been served. It was a good house in a rural, leafy neighborhood. Keeping it up took a great deal of time: mowing over two acres of grass and trimming around the many bushes and trees, clipping the hedges, spraying and removing bagworms, trimming limbs in the big trees, keeping up with the aging heat pump, clearing snow in winter, fending off the marauding groundhogs, which, in spite of Cory, would tunnel beneath the porches in minutes if left to themselves. And inside (he had some help with that), Tina came every two weeks to vacuum, dust, and clean the bathrooms and kitchen.

But neither Ted nor Kate took any interest. Joe had planted roses, butterfly bushes, iris, daffodils, clematis. He had grown vegetables, zinnias, and other flowers for cutting, planted a flowering cherry for contrast against the Japanese maples put in by a previous owner. Even with the destruction wrought by moles (it was only after moving in that he learned the neighbors referred to the place as Mole

Hill), it was a beautiful place. Parishioners and neighbors came, as they had in Jeffersonville and Dorchester, to admire the plantings and talk with Joe about horticulture. Ted's friends came around, and until he entered St. John's, the house had been filled with their chatter and the noise of their video games.

But it was clear that Kate had no affection for the house, no interest or investment. He recalled spending a weekend at St. John's with her a year after they moved in, refurbishing and putting back into use a small greenhouse built long ago as an extension of the school's science classroom. He had cleared out years of packed dirt and refuse, washed the many small windowpanes, and replaced the crumbling hoses, while Kate carefully rearranged the contents of her supply room. Then had come a rainy May with cool nights, followed by a glorious warm June. The grass at home had grown quickly. He was mowing with a small secondhand riding mower with a narrow cutting deck. It was all they could afford at the time. After each cutting, the grass lay across the big lawn in windrows like mowed hay. It had to be raked into mounds of grass clippings and moved to a growing compost pile at the edge of the lawn. Failing to keep up with it meant the grass died in long patches under the mowed clippings, leaving the lawn streaked with dead zones. It was too much for him to manage alone, and several times he asked Kate and Ted to help him rake the grass and move it by wheelbarrow to the compost pile at the edge of the woods. They did so unenthusiastically, silently, resenting having to spend time on such rustic endeavors. During one of those intervals, Kate had broken her silence and paused with her rake long enough to say, "See, you help me with my work at the school, and I help you with your work here." In her view, it was as simple as that: her work at St. John's and his care of the house and yard at home. She could see nothing more logical than such a division of labor. The vast inequities and selfishness in her perception were beyond her; she was oblivious. He should have spoken up and tried to set her straight on some basics, in this seventeen year of their marriage, of making a home together. He could have reminded her that he was parish priest of the fourth-largest church in the diocese with hundreds of people, and that *that* was his work. He knew she would have heard it with no more understanding than she had brought years ago to his law practice. Neither his profession nor his vocation figured in her narrow personal experience of the world and were therefore beyond her comprehension. It was not intelligence she lacked. It was mere interest.

She turned from him and continued pawing with her rake at the clumps of dried grass, and years of frustration told him that nothing he might say would make any difference. The way she turned, the finality of the back of her head and set of her shoulders were familiar signs, like closing doors, that she had dismissed him from her consideration. Others might get a hearing and a bit of understanding, but not him. He was the contender, the competition, the one who made unreasonable demands. It would be dark soon, and he anticipated an unusually heavy day tomorrow, and the thought of her angrily storming into the house and leaving the endless grass to him and Ted made him weary and kept him quiet. Small skirmishes on the domestic battlefront, he said to himself; others managed them so much better. Would he ever learn? And the future, the reason for going forward, the bright unfolding energizing hope of his latter days called to him from beyond a holly hedge and said, "Dad! What time is it? Let's go in and watch *Braveheart*."

* * *

At the end of Ted's sophomore year, Father Hervey offered Ted a chance to become a boarder at the school without additional charge. He confided to Kate that he would like to eliminate day students altogether. Joe was mystified by Hervey's continuing to share with Kate confidential professional matters. If this was truly happening, if Kate was relating these conversations accurately, it meant that Hervey was unaware of the way she talked about him. This surprised Joe, who suspected that word traveled quickly in the small closed community of rural St. John's. In his own way, Hervey lived in denial as stubborn as Kate's, seeing only what was in his own interests and routinely discounting those whom he perceived as inferior. Joe had long understood that a special place was reserved in this category for him. Hervey saw Kate, however, as naive, amusing, and culturally limited but completely harmless and genuinely loyal to him and the school. He confided in her now and then.

The problem with day students was that they were more under the control of their parents than their headmaster, and this presented an awkward personal challenge on his own territory. As Joe had once analyzed issues from a legal standpoint, he was now attentive to the theological point in situations. In Hervey's desire to eliminate non-boarding students, Joe recognized the theological issue of control.

Kate had wisely told Ted that first they would have to discuss boarding at the school with Dad. Ted had brought it up that evening when Joe returned from Redeemer and was changing clothes in the bedroom. Joe had shouted down the stairs to Kate, grading tests and watching television, asking if she would come up and talk with them. She came in and sat in silence while Ted explained his case, although Joe guessed she had found plenty to say about it when she told Ted what Father Hervey had offered. After listening to everything Ted had to say, Joe had said no.

"I just couldn't stand it, Ted. In another two years, you'll be on your way to college. You'll be away from home most of the time from then on. It probably seems far off to you, but I'm already dreading not seeing you. I know you would like to board at St. John's. I understand that. But I wouldn't be able to see you all week long. You spend almost every weekend there. There's always something, a game, a dance, a field trip, a party. And even when you are at home, you're out with your friends around here. I miss seeing you."

"I know," said Ted reasonably, calmly, maintaining eye contact.

"Before we know it, you'll be going away. Between now and then, I'd go crazy if I couldn't see you...if we all weren't here together at night. It's what I live for. This is home. If you aren't here, it's not the same."

"Aw, Dad," he said, grinning and bouncing a bit on the bed.

"I just couldn't stand it. I have to say no. Next year is your senior year. If you get the same offer, and if you really want to go, I'll probably say yes, then. It would be a good transition into being away at college, I guess. But for right now, I just couldn't stand it. And please, don't be angry."

"I'm not mad, Dad. I understand." And it seemed to Joe that he *did* understand. He understood as much of it as a teenage son can endure in a father's bumbling attempts to say "I love you, and the thought of missing you tears me up inside." Neither then nor in the coming days did Ted give him any reason to think he was sad or frustrated and not even visibly disappointed. He had never been the sort to sulk, and there was certainly no brooding now. In fact, in the following days, Ted seemed even more genial and easygoing than usual.

Joe knew the conversation had been one of those that should have rightfully taken place in a family discussion. But Kate had simply laid out for Joe Ted's "option," as Father Hervey had probably said, and then withdrawn to watch from the sidelines as father and son worked it out. This meant she wanted Ted to become a boarder. Joe knew that if she had felt strongly about him remaining at home, she would have joined the discussion to press her point. But knowing what Joe's feeling would be in the matter, she chose to avoid taking part.

One of the many comfortable faculty residences on the St. John's campus, a pleasant two-story brick house with a narrow flagstone terrace across its front, had been offered to Kate when she applied for a job as her faculty residence. Whether it was unclear to Father Hervey at her initial interview that her husband was parish priest in a nearby county, or whether Hervey, who had never served a parish and was unlikely ever to do so, did not understand that priests for a thousand good reasons lived in their parishes, Joe did not know. But Hervey had pointed out this house to Kate as the faculty home she could occupy. Since that interview, she had referred to it over the years as "my house" and, in spells of depression, had brought it up as though she had been cheated out of something precious that was rightfully hers. The other faculty members were satisfied with their assigned dwellings over the years, and the house had continued empty. Whenever someone occupied it for a semester or two, Kate announced it wistfully to Joe with a clear implication that interlopers had invaded *her* space.

A reference to it—"I passed the social studies teacher in his new car, right there on the road beside my house"—had set Joe thinking one day. It was clear to him that their home meant little or nothing to her. She spent as little time in it as she could manage, knew few of their neighbors, and was critical of those she did know. She did not use their community pool, took no pleasure in the lawn, the plantings. It was a beautiful place, but she drove in and out, walking from her car to the door without looking around. When the hundreds of daffodils and lily-of-the-valley (her favorite flower, Joe had planted dozens of them) bloomed in the spring, she went out a few times to behold them and picked big bunches to carry to work, where they brightened her classroom. She watched the birds at the winter feeders Joe kept going but only if she happened to be standing at the kitchen window anyway.

They never entertained unless Joe initiated the idea and made all the arrangements. He would propose dates for dinner parties and invite the guests. He coordinated the Friday or Saturday evenings with Tina's schedule, whenever possible, so the house would be clean. He did all the shopping, buying whatever Kate jotted on her cryptic lists after going over them with her, making sure he understood them. He would spend Thursday night and Friday, his day off, straightening the house, extending the dining room table, bringing up dishes from the basement cabinets and bringing in flowers and placing them around. He would set the table, set up a small bar, and get out serving dishes and glasses for drinks and wine and water. He wrote out place cards. He trimmed the lawn close to the house if it appeared ragged and swept the walks.

Kate would prepare the food, silently and without enthusiasm. In the early years of their marriage, she insisted on beginning to cook once the guests had arrived, ducking out of the party to labor in the kitchen, while Joe chatted with their guests. When he convinced her to shift her preparation as much as possible to the night before, offering to do all he could to help, she obliged after a few years and sat with him and their guests, wrapped in an apron and observing everyone and talking about her work.

The guests were always friends and acquaintances of Joe's. She never wanted to invite anybody from St. John's or from any other school where she had taught. Joe knew some of the St. John's faculty. He liked them, enjoyed their senses of humor, and thought it would be fun to have them and their husbands or wives. But Kate would not invite them, not even Hervey, although Joe pleaded with her to do so each time they entertained.

When Ted began his second year at St. John's, Joe had talked with Kate and Ted about moving into a smaller place closer to St. John's. There would be less to care for, he told them, especially with less mowing. He wondered as he talked with them, speculation kept entirely to himself, whether a move would make any difference with Kate, but he was convinced that a change was possible with Ted. He wanted his son to go into life with a love of his home and a willingness to accept responsibility for it, convictions he would one day impart to his own children. The equity from the sale of their house and the savings with a smaller mortgage payment could go into Ted's college fund, and they could make repairs to the Wicomico house. Travel time would be less. They could all be home more, have a little flexibility. They listened without comment, Kate watching the floor and Ted looking at Joe and the two of them occasionally glancing at each other. They were silent when he stopped talking.

Ted was the first to speak, saying he liked their house and did not want to leave it. After a long silence, Kate said that she thought they should stay too. Moving was just too complicated. She paused and glanced at Ted, who continued to look at Joe. Yes, she was sure of it; they should stay where they were.

Joe accepted what they said. He wondered if the thought of moving made them value what they had. Would Kate take some interest, help with cleaning, the yard? Months went by, and everything remained the same.

The family counselor he saw twice each month talked with him at length about setting chores for Ted and holding him to account. Joe explained the many times over the years he had done exactly that and how Ted had followed through well at first. His years of teaching had taught Joe the value of setting clear, uncomplicated, achievable goals. Ted was an intelligent child. Joe had not had to reduce his simple expectations to writing or create charts after Ted was nine or so. Ted knew what was expected of him and followed through fairly well. He had been a good sport about emptying the trash, feeding Cory and his gerbils and hamsters, and picking up after himself. He needed occasional reminders like any other child. But once the expectations had been made clear and agreed upon, and a week or so went by, unless Joe was there to provide the reminders, Ted began to follow through less and less. Joe would return from a few days' travel for the diocese and find that Ted had not completed his chores. Ted always apologized and said he forgot. Kate always had an immediate excuse for him, sometimes providing a story about why Ted had not followed through that contradicted Ted's own excuses. She seemed to believe that he was not responsible for missing his chores so long as she had failed to remind him to do them. In some ways, Joe believed it would have been easier teaching Ted responsibility if Kate had not been part of the picture. In the early years of their marriage, he would have been thoroughly ashamed of himself for such a thought. As Ted became a teenager, however, it became more and more difficult trying to maneuver around her. He had always thought they could have reasoned with each other if she had only been willing to seek counseling with him. But she would not consider it, not even when he urged it upon her for Ted's personal well-being. She was inflexible, impenetrable, closed. He began to wonder if even a professional counselor could get through to her.

Ted had a lot of friends. He was warm-hearted, affable, and polite in a normal boyish way. People liked him, especially girls. Joe was proud of him and told him so. Yet a conviction had grown in him since childhood and been strengthened progressively by teaching, practicing law, and his years in the church that there must be an essential integrity at the core of a thing, and that without it, even the finest outward appearance could crumble in time. A glossy apple with a rotten core, a fatal omission waiting to surface in a contract, the businessman who failed to pay taxes a decade ago, a friendly neighbor with a mean streak, it all became obvious in time, despite the best of appearances. Foundations must be sure. If a dark underside exists, the sunny surface will show its sinkholes eventually. The heart must shine out in action and attitude.

Many of the personal qualities Joe was able to raise up in Ted—planning ahead and saving, respect for all teachers, the realities of delayed gratification, being helpful at home in general, kindness to the poor and needy, an abhorrence of bullies—all but disappeared during the easy summers in Wicomico, where domestic rules and standards were largely left behind with all the other troublesome impediments of life back home. Since Ted had been very young, throughout the early fall each year, Joe had to reintroduce him to his table manners, chores, and picking up after himself. In his good-natured way, Ted did not object to these reminders and soon recovered his better habits. Kate loved Ted as much as Joe did, but in having to choose between enforcing the rules and letting him have his childish way, the choice for her was clear. Joe had learned that such an inclination did not extend to rules she was professionally required to enforce on school property. In this she acted with an iron will. He suspected that her resistance to enforcing home rules was because she saw them as primarily his creations. She never initiated anything more than insisting that Ted complete his homework. The simple rules were not unreasonable to her in the abstract, but neither did she see them important enough to enforce them in day-to-day family living. It remained a source of discouragement for Joe that she would neither initiate nor follow through with these routine lessons of conduct and self-control in the son they loved. Joe saw them as wholly for Ted's benefit and a way of teaching him responsibility for his own nest. However much Kate might agree in theory, Joe was alone.

In raising his child, as in all else in life, Joe regarded the broken world with a wry cynicism that evoked smiles in him rather than outrage or pity. In his heart, human history notwithstanding, he believed God had it all under control. The murderous chaos was a symptom that said little about the core of reality, where beat a heart of love that surpassed human understanding. Somehow in the cosmic plan, God had permitted Kate and him to meet and join in marriage. God had blessed them with a child, and God would nurture them as they sought to raise him. Suffering in families all around him did not discourage Joe unduly. Suffering and distress were unacceptable but inevitable growing pains, symptoms of becoming, signs of an eventual wholeness, evolutionary evidence of a coming maturity. He knew his view was limited; only God could see it all. If a human being could draw cosmic conclusions from the evidence of a lifetime, he knew he must conclude that the battle was being lost. Chaos and evil were advancing to victory in individual lives, families, and all of history. Twenty million dead under Stalin, forty million under Mao. The mind could not conceive of it. But this was the world in which he lived. It was into this world that he would see his son go one day, and he was determined that Ted would go with a core of integrity.

He always examined the posters of missing children inside the entrances of Walmart stores. For years he had stared at them as his every spiritual instinct vibrated inside him as though his chest was filled with hummingbirds. What greater horror was there than losing a child? Each face, each description of wretched circumstances, radiated pain like heat from invisible coals. He could not pass them by without threading each name into a silent petition for miracles. Juanita. Kamisha. Edward, may call himself Maddog. Carlos. Rayshon. Thomas, may be traveling with noncustodial father. Ben. Charlene, last seen wearing green tank top, baggy denim shorts, and pink-and-white athletic shoes. She has a mole below her left eye and may have dyed her hair. The anguish in the heart of a searcher somewhere, it would take the psalmist to forge it into language.

But Joe knew the battle had already been won. He knew humankind could never have won it anyway on its own, that from the beginning we needed a savior. Victory was already assured, regardless of how the world appeared in the limited view of a human life. And as he waited and looked around, he was convinced that his own sorrows were blessings compared with the suffering of others. His were mercifully few, mere elusory froth on the surface of worldly sin and anxiety. His troubles were nothing compared to what others endured. God was good. His family counselors had always offered excellent advice. The people he knew in his parishes and elsewhere were decent and courageous. His Al-Anon group, old friends, and countless others were supportive and encouraging. If Kate would not communicate, cooperate, and if she did not love him, she and Ted and he were still way ahead on the course and running well in the open. He knew he would be given what he needed to cope.

Joe thought about the house at St. John's, the one Kate called "my house." He had served at Redeemer long enough by then to have gained the trust and liking of the congregation. He knew they would understand, or at least acquiesce, if he moved into faculty quarters at St. John's. It would put his home outside the parish and across the river in another diocese, but it would be no further from the church in miles or driving time than their present home. He believed the parish and the bishop would be supportive.

When he talked with Kate about the idea, she was visibly pleased and promised to take it up with Father the following day. He knew better than to inquire when she studiously avoided the subject over the next few days. When he finally gave in and questioned her, she told him that yes, it would be possible to move there and that "Father and some others" were planning now for the new faculty housing assignments, and she would have an answer the following week.

Several weeks passed, again without mention of what was occurring. Joe questioned her again. It seemed suddenly that "my house" might be reserved for the new English teacher and her husband, a man of delicate health who had been drawn to the place and its inviting terrace at first sight. More questioning elicited that another place had been promised to her, however. This was a comfortable old two-story farmhouse in a shaded yard on what Kate called, with a hint of irritation, the rear of the school property, meaning that one reached it by driving a mile along a narrow country road. This distance made it a less desirable faculty residence than those nestled around the campus and its big buildings. With a wistful sigh, Kate conceded that she would probably get used to the drive. For his part, Joe was pleased at the prospect of merciful privacy the distance from the campus would ensure, but he was careful not to say so. Still, it would take several months for all this to be finalized. If they were to sell their home, the sooner it was put on the market, the better, said Joe. But Kate said they would have to wait a while to be sure, although she did not foresee any problems. As the weeks passed, she was visibly excited about moving closer to St. John's and appeared even less interested in their home than she had ever been. She had not swept a walk or done any ironing for years. Joe wondered if she would notice if all the trees blew over in a storm.

Chapter Twenty-Eight

J oe remembered the moment the pain began in his side the way house fires or traffic accidents were burned into the memory of others. It was in law school, in the stacks of the library, one evening near closing time. He was standing up after two hours of sitting cross-legged on the floor surrounded by books on intellectual property. Why it had not happened in reading agency or secured transactions or even contracts rather than in something in which he would develop great interest was something never understood. Perhaps it was the return that day of his real property essay on which the professor had scribbled B- with an observation that the references to Hannah Arendt and Jacob van Ruisdael were "lax and fuzzy."

"Lax *and* fuzzy," Joe had exclaimed. "It sounds like a child's cartoon show. How can a paper be lax and fuzzy at the same time?"

"Trust me," said the professor.

Joe's argument that ownership of real property was one factor in the careless, neglectful ebb and flow of American public values was obviously, even in the 1970s, too marginal for young real property professors. How could anyone claim membership in Western civilization without an appreciation of Dutch landscape painting?

Or perhaps he had been worried more than usual about things at home or his perennial proximity to academic probation or the inevitable distracting need of money. Getting by on little or nothing increased his admiration for his honest, hardworking parents who were still raising children at home and struggling to get them through school. His proposal that he drop out of law school for a year or two and find a job and help with family expenses had been ruled out and was *res judicata*. His parents would not hear of it. ("Stay right where you are, goddammit! It's the best thing you can do for your future," said his father with agitation.) Joe still hesitated.

Or perhaps it was as uncomplicated as not having sex in months. He missed his former girlfriend and the community he had said goodbye to more than anyone could imagine. He longed for the safety of old relationships and communities and pined away in wonder at what might have been had he done this or that, taken one road rather than another, behaved better, studied more, worked harder. It all churned in the windstorm forever on the horizon of his mind, gusts of consideration and worry that seemed to him to disturb the lives of few other people, evidence of how much he still had to learn about the world.

As he stood up in the narrow aisle between the library bookshelves, pain had suddenly spread through his innards like a flush of boiling water. He had never experienced anything like it. He braced himself against the bookshelves on either side and closed his eyes and waited. A hot, throbbing ache began in his head. As if in response, the librarians, several floors below, switched the lights on and off a few times, signaling the building was about to close. After a minute, believing it to be a cramp that would surely pass, he bent down and slowly began returning reference volumes to their shelves until he thought of the little signs all around reminding students that only librarians should reshelf books. He pulled them all out again and was suddenly alarmed by a resurgence of hot pain in his abdomen. It did not go away. He went out of the library and slowly across the parking lot to his car, every painful step advancing him further into a personal crisis that would remain invisible to the world.

After a few days of sleeplessness, unable to eat, he went to a doctor who diagnosed diverticulitis and inquired about his eating habits. He took the doctor's medicine, the pain subsided, and Joe began to follow a new regimen. In time, the new diet made a difference. So did an occasional evening off, having dinner with friends, and sitting quietly, doing nothing.

His education in painting and sculpture had done little to prepare him for law school. He worked day and night to keep up with his classmates, most of whom were prelaw or economics majors with good understandings of commerce and government and all fresh from the finest undergraduate schools in the east. Joe was six or seven years older than most of them, although he looked generally younger. Many of them had begun planning their law careers while still in the womb. Joe had conceived the idea a mere two days before the final registration date for the LSAT. The other students lived and breathed the law, and Joe followed their example, an easy enough discipline while immersed in the closed confines of law school. Still, during discussions of the Rule Against Perpetuities or a circuity of liens issue, he found it easy enough to drift into van Ruisdael's astounding views of Bentheim Castle or recall passages from *Gatsby* or Yeats, or daydream about fly-fishing.

The painful condition continued, subsiding for days or weeks but always returning, often at the most inconvenient times. Sometimes he could look back over days or weeks and connect its onset to his schedule, feelings, or fatigue. The doctors said it had nothing to do with stress, that it was all about diet and adequate sleep. Joe was sure they were right. He followed their directions and didn't bother thinking about it until a flare-up happened again.

His law school colleagues remembered him as a quiet, affable, skinny young man and were very surprised when he began trying cases soon after graduation. He opened a general practice but spent much of his time in court, where his client usually prevailed. Litigation came with great tension, and he knew he would have to learn to manage it gracefully or shift his focus to work behind a desk. Trial work, adventurous and cerebral, was active, educational, and challenging. It appealed to his strong curiosity about people and why they behaved as they did. In defendants, victims, judges, police officers, jurors, other lawyers, witnesses of all kinds, and all the rest who came together in the legal system, he always found something to admire, portraits he longed to paint, stories he thought he could write. The rules of criminal and civil evidence and procedure enclosed the search for truth in structures that ensured a basic fairness to everyone, good or bad, unknown outside the system. The ethical standards and moral values moved him and appealed to his natural sense of order and progress. He encountered a high standard of conduct in his local bar, and he was impressed. One could rely upon the word of others and upon their doing their duty. The system was overburdened and had its faults, but it worked well most of the time, and justice was done.

He felt good about being part of his profession. He had come in just before the close of the era of trust in professional people. In each community, the lawyer, doctor, banker, pharmacist, and cop on the beat had all been trusted and trustworthy. Children respected teachers. Obeying the rules was associated with good character. People knew their neighbors and were polite even when they did not get on well together. In the communities where he grew up, attended college, taught school, and set up his law practice, a sense of right and wrong and an appreciation for truth had marked society with a boring but nourishing sameness. All this was changing as he began to build his practice.

He was determined not to allow the pain in his gut to become a limitation. He didn't talk about it. During an acute spell of it, he went about his routine, saw to his responsibilities, and except for taking medicine and drinking clear liquids, carried on as usual. If anything, he was quieter and moved about a bit slower. This and his pills controlled the symptoms more or less, but over the years, the condition worsened. An onset meant days of distracting pain and fatigue. His doctors told him there was no cure, and he had accepted it. No one knew about it except his family and a few friends. Even to them he did not complain. They would not know an episode was in progress until noticing that he ate almost nothing and drank water for lunch. He shared the aversion most people have to complainers. If he had been burdened by that tiresome fault, his complaining would have had to reflect his ailment's progressive nature. He knew people who never shut up about their suffering, and he was determined not to be like them.

Kate's response to his condition was perplexing at first. He remembered talking with her about it before their marriage, seated in rocking chairs on the porch of Catherine's house in Wicomico. Kate had asked a few questions ("Does it hurt right now?" and "Could it just be really bad indigestion?") and then gone on to tell him about her own ailments. He was relieved to hear they were confined to occasional sinus headaches and delicate skin that bruised annoyingly at the slightest thump. This last tendency was especially irritating because bruises showed up at the worst possible times, causing her considerable embarrassment. He recalled they had then talked for a while about the excuses she could use to explain her latest bruise: from opening so many champagne bottles and caviar tins, for instance, or from signing so many autographs or having to wave so often to her fans. They decided that the Queen of England must bruise easily also because of her restrained waving, just the slightest elegant turn of a wrist.

After their marriage, when an episode began, Kate was silent about it once he told her it was happening. He told himself it was her way of helping, not making it worse by calling undue attention to it. A couple of times she had driven him to hospital emergency rooms. She sat by and observed as a doctor had prescribed some additional medication and recommended that he see a specialist when he felt better. The emergency room physician thought it probably was diverticulitis, but she recommended that Joe see a gastrointestinal specialist quite soon. Every six weeks or so the pain became so acute that for a few days at a time, he could neither eat nor sleep, and the spells were always accompanied by headaches that grew worse and worse. Ted was about nine when Joe began having to lie down for a day when he felt his worse. Being immobilized in a dark room helped in some ways, but he could not sleep, and his preoccupied mind hurtled forward like a runaway train through matters of home, issues at work, Ted and his future, and always, always his relationship with Kate.

Where others found peace and refuge at home, over the years Joe had become used to uncertainty and frustration. It would have been comforting to go home at night to a confidant, but he had learned the hard way that Kate would say anything to anybody and repeat the most careful confidences after a glass of wine or a bourbon and ginger ale. Any misconception she gained in what he told her would invariably return to plague him the next time she became angry. His capacity for intimacy with her suffered, and he could do nothing about it. If they could have only talked.

When Kate refused to refer to it at all, even when it was active, Joe told himself it was her way of helping. That Ted was adopting this and some of her other attitudes never occurred to him. He would explain to his son that he was having a flare-up, but not being a complainer himself, and with Ted's sunny disposition, Joe attached little significance to his son's seeming indifference. In his heart, Joe believed that Kate loved him as she did Ted and that she was being the best companion she knew how to be.

Joe knew that untold millions had struggled through the world with far graver troubles than his and had managed their lives with more grace than he would ever know. When he assessed his life, he felt only gratitude, and dwelling on that gratitude was healing in itself. The act of giving thanks eased his mind as his medicine soothed his intestines, and it was his conviction that both remedies came of the same divine source. He knew God would give him what he needed to cope. Everyone had something. Even St. Paul had suffered from his "thorn in the flesh," whatever it was. Joe knew he could have been born deformed or blind.

As a child, he had been a daydreamer, at first, to the amusement of the adults around him. Later many of them would become annoyed and caution him to wake up and pay attention. His parents were exceptions, accepting him for who he was and loving him and the rest of their children unconditionally. His art teachers and a few English teachers were exceptions. In his love of drawing, comic books, and reading, he escaped routinely into a world of excitement that school and home seldom provided. For a nickel, he and his friends rode the city bus downtown and explored mysterious parts of the city. They roamed the warrens of shuttered tobacco warehouses on the riverfront and imagined the wicked inhabitants of the big crumbling mansions of vanished tobacco heirs. Neither ancient Athens nor the Forbidden City could have roused their imaginations more. Against everybody's permission, they explored the grimy railroad tunnels and massive trestles, big as Roman aqueducts, that formed a maze beneath the town and spanned the bottoms between her hills. A few days camping on the Appalachian Trail or spelunking in the great Valley caves would sustain him for weeks as he daydreamed through the routine of school, homework, and church.

He had never understood the connection of all this to sadness. He sensed that a link existed, a perception that in time he came to feel more than understand. The want of excitement he had craved as a boy and the action that nourished him as a young man intensified as he grew older. Life's routines and responsibilities, fulfilling in many ways, lusterless drudgery in others, created satisfaction, contentment, and gratification in proportion to whatever amiable courage one could bring to them. A certain sense of hope and humor in perceiving the world was indispensable to good mental health. Whether conscious or unconscious, resignation led to submissiveness, passivity, and apathy even in truly good people—better people, he knew, than he would ever be. In many of them, fatalism often was mistaken for patience or other virtues. Achieving the precious balance in life between hope and despair was part gift and part personal accomplishment. Joe was keenly aware that part of it was up to him.

He knew himself well enough to take his own advice. He considered himself a trusting man—perhaps impatient, but unsuspicious and credulous—who believed in putting others first, and he tried to live up to these beliefs. For years as a counselor in the law and ministry, he had urged others to seek help for depression and anxiety. He had counseled others that medicine and the healing professions were channels of God's grace in the world. He felt goodness and value flowing into him through them, and he was grateful. At the same time, he was increasingly sad.

If a man had to rely on what he could perceive in eighty or a hundred years, the whole business of life would appear hopeless. But one with eyes to see and ears to hear could gain a minute perception, no bigger than the glimpse of a seed pearl through a needle's eye, of the reality of the whole. He was beginning to comprehend that there is no peace, strife is constant, the innocent will suffer until the end, but that the eschaton will fulfill all the gifts and promises. So his eyes were sad, but not entirely so.

* * *

"So is God still dead or what?" said Dr. Colin O'Connor, Joe's general practitioner, another lapsed Roman Catholic, now that the medical issues had been thoroughly discussed. He grinned as he wrote out three prescriptions for anti-depressants and an anti-anxiety drug and handed the white slips of paper to Joe one at a time. Joe received them at that moment in his life with a mixture of relief and disappointment. He regarded them in silence for a moment, fanned out like playing cards in his right hand, wondering if they would win him some better days. He glanced up and met O'Connor's reassuring smile.

"Doctor, do I detect wonder in you that fashionable disbelief is on the wane?"

Joe was drained by the discussion just ended about his marriage. Even a good physician like O'Connor, who had handled their discussion with tact and empathy, could do little to soothe the stress of such a subject. Like so many counterparts in his own critical conversations, Joe welcomed the moment when talk could turn naturally in a new direction.

"Not wonder, Father, but nostalgia." The doctor leaned back in his big desk chair and looked at the ceiling. "The sixties and early seventies... The mood was rational, autonomous, intrusive."

"Rational?"

"Of course. We knew we would discover the deepest truths of the universe. And we talked about it all the time." He paused and thought a moment and added, "With passion. *Young* passion, but it was still passion."

"But not with God," said Joe.

"God was an embarrassment. Resurrection, eternal life...it was all part of what had made the twentieth century so goddam horrible."

"In the way you saw existence, was there any sense of the mysterious?" asked Joe.

"Yes. We were mystified that people could be so gullible." He laughed.

"And Marx, Freud, Marcuse, Nietzsche, they were all totally rational? I can't quite imagine that at—where was it?—MCV? Your own medical Manhattan Project, the hostility of faith to science..."

"No. Science to faith," said O'Connor.

"I suppose you could never imagine then the number of scientists who would believe in God now."

"No. Actually, I wasn't one of the most ardent ones. I preferred to listen to jazz," said the grinning doctor. "And it was Johns Hopkins, by the way."

Joe had liked O'Connor from their first meeting for his irreverent humor. He was intelligent, not merely trained, but possessed of an old-style liberal arts education that gave him a certain compassionate insight to existence. Enlightenment hope glowed bright in him, fueled by a religious upbringing in spite of all his early efforts to disassociate the two. Joe would have enjoyed hearing him as a young man, holding forth with his Jesuit teachers, teetering on the border between faith and philosophy. He could imagine him sparring with the existentialists, challenging their conclusion of life's bleakness, and intrigued by the young Marxists, who were about to recreate the future with their messianic fervor. The doctor appeared to be a contented man now, but behind the smile and irreverence was a perpetual cautious alarm as though he understood the world thoroughly.

"Colly," said Joe, "how in the hell did you happen to come *here?*"

"It was Mary. My wife, not the virgin. She's from—I'm glad you're sitting down—Crooked Creek."

Joe raised his eyebrows at the mention of the scene of half the crime in the county.

"We got in a hell of a fight halfway through medical school, and I promised her that if she would just stick it out with the kids and me, I'd move to anywhere she wanted to live. After that, she had me by the balls. Catoctin Springs was the biggest town near Crooked Creek still in the state. Now that we're here, she drives out to the old farm once every six months and walks around for twenty minutes in a nostalgic fog then comes home all full of shit about how wonderful it is living here. Twenty-four hours later, she's back to bitching about moving to Wilmington or Florida or somewhere. Christ!"

"And since coming here, you've had seven children. And I thought you were a lapsed Catholic."

O'Connor laughed heartily, like a good-natured man hearing a good joke, and said, "I am lapsed, and proud of it. Mary was raised Baptist, and now she's more Catholic than I ever was. She's more Catholic than my grandmother who refused to learn English after being here eighty years. What am I going to do?" he said, slapping his knees and standing up.

Joe got up to go. It always happened when he came here for an office visit; O'Connor insisted on sitting and talking, and Joe always ended up staying longer than he had anticipated. The nurses knew Joe and liked him, and when he entered the waiting room, they made him promise to get the doctor back to them as soon as he could. One of them would soon be tapping on the door, inquiring diplomatically what they should tell Mrs. somebody or other in room 4. The doctor would get up reluctantly and sigh, ending their conversation with obvious regret. Each visit spawned a discussion of some new book they both wanted to read, a development in one of the world's many trouble spots, saltwater fishing, what to do about crime, capital punishment, and always, every time, some reference to the faith. It was not Joe's collar so much as the doctor's self-awareness. He would invariably raise issues that Joe would consider for days. Each time they met, they promised each other to get together with their wives for dinner, but they never did.

"It'll take those prescriptions a week or so to kick in, except for the Buspar. You should feel a difference with that one right away. Call me here or at home in about a week and let's see where we stand." He shook hands with Joe and ducked immediately into an examination room, followed by a flustered nurse. Before the door closed behind them, the whole suite filled with the raucous wail of a terrified child, anticipating a shot or worse.

"What did you guys talk about this time?" asked the young nurse who filed the insurance forms.

"I can't remember," said Joe. "But it must have been interesting because it took a while."

"That the truth," said several nurses and a physician's assistant, in unison.

He drove to the pharmacy. When she saw Joe, the genial pharmacist herself came out from behind her glass partition, waving photographs of the deer her husband and son had shot the weekend before. Joe marveled at the fine rack, ten sturdy points, which as they spoke was being mounted by somebody way over in Manassas. The pharmacist figured that with luck, their teenage son would get the mount back before he died of old age, and Joe laughed and agreed.

He handed over his prescriptions, a little embarrassed but determined to do as he had so often advised others. He reminded himself again that medicine was one of God's ways of healing and that our reason was God's gift so we could concoct medications from the earth's bounty. He did not need to remind himself of this; it was part of his faith. It made him feel good to do so anyway. Anything that helped him to feel good right now was, he believed, another blessing.

Part two of this novel, titled *Lovers in a Small Café,* will appear soon.

About the Author

Edmund Burwell is the author of two novels and a collection of short stories. His work has been recognized by the Academy of American Poets and he attended the Bread Loaf Writer's Conference.

CPSIA information can be obtained
at www.ICGtesting.com
Printed in the USA
BVHW031947030619
550025BV00001B/3/P